Carrie Elks
The Shakespeare Sisters

Absent in the Spring

piatkus

PIATKUS

First published in Great Britain in 2018 by Piatkus

1 3 5 7 9 10 8 6 4 2

A CIP catalogue record for this book
is available from the British Library.

ISBN 978-0-349-41554-3

Typeset in Caslon by M Rules
Printed and bound in Great Britain by
Clays Ltd, St Ives plc

Papers used by Piatkus are from well-managed forests
and other responsible sources.

MIX
Paper from
responsible sources
FSC® C104740

Piatkus
An imprint of
Little, Brown Book Group
Carmelite House
50 Victoria Embankment
London EC4Y 0DZ

An Hachette UK Company
www.hachette.co.uk

www.littlebrown.co.uk

*To my mum, who taught me that
to open a book is to dive into a new world.*

1

Lucy Shakespeare shook the rain off her Burberry umbrella – plain black, with the traditional beige check patterned inside – and placed it in the stand, reaching up to make sure the Edinburgh rain hadn't dampened her blonde hair. She'd taken a cab from the Sheriff Court to the offices of Robinson and Balfour, but even the short distance between the kerb and the smart sandstone entrance hadn't been enough to save her from the spring shower. Shrugging her raincoat from her shoulders, she slid it onto a hanger before placing it on the coat stand, making sure to smooth out the wrinkles. Then she turned and walked into the main office area.

'The conquering hero returns.' Lynn, her assistant, stood up, a smile lighting up her face. 'Congratulations, you must be delighted.'

'Not as delighted as the clients,' Lucy said. 'The last I saw of them they were headed for the pub, talking about ordering champagne all round.'

'They didn't ask you to join them?' Lynn asked, taking Lucy's brown calfskin briefcase from her grasp.

'They offered, but I declined. I wanted to finish up the paperwork.' And maybe come into the office to gloat a bit. But who could blame her? Today's court session was the result of months of diligent work. Of combing through old documents, taking untold numbers of depositions, not to mention coaching her clients to keep things as cordial as they could. Estate law was just as emotional as family law, even though it meant dealing with wills and property. It was amazing how quickly relationships fell apart as soon as money was involved.

Lucy glanced over at the frosted-glass offices where the senior partners worked. 'Has Malcolm heard the verdict?' Her eyes lingered on the plaque affixed to the metal frame: *Malcolm Dunvale, Head of Family & Estate Law*.

'He's the one who told me. Had a big smile on his face, too.' Lynn's own grin widened at the memory. 'He'd like to see you when you get a chance. I'll let him know you're back.'

'Just give me a couple of minutes to freshen up,' Lucy said, walking over to the thick oak door that led to the toilets.

'Would you like a coffee?' Lynn called to her retreating back.

Lucy turned and smiled. 'Yes please, that would be lovely. I haven't had anything to drink since I went into court.'

Five minutes later, with her hair restyled and her face touched up, Lucy walked into Malcolm Dunvale's office. Like all the senior partners' offices, it had huge glass windows that overlooked the city, revealing Edinburgh's old town in all its rain-soaked glory. In the distance she could see the castle rising majestically from Castle Rock, the building looking almost organic as it emerged from the grassy hill, as though it had grown from a seed rather than been built by man.

Little boxes of aspiration was what Lynn called these offices.

Malcolm looked up from his laptop. 'Ah Lucy, there you are. Take a seat,' he said, gesturing at the black leather chair nearest her. He ran a hand over his grey cropped hair, then took off his reading glasses, folding them carefully and placing them beside his keyboard.

Lucy sat down, smoothing down her skirt as she crossed her legs at the ankles and straightened her spine. 'Hello, Malcolm.'

'I was pleased to hear about the verdict,' he said, leaning back as he took a sip of his coffee. 'You must have been too.'

She nodded, letting a hint of a smile curl at her lips. 'It could have gone either way, but the right side won in the end.' It didn't always work that way – she'd had her fair share of losses, after all. But when everything came together, there was no feeling like it.

'Robert Douglas called me while you were on your way back here. He's so happy with the result he wants to transfer all his dealings to Robinson and Balfour, and as you know, that's a lot of business.'

'That's wonderful news.' She kept her expression neutral, though her fist curled up. 'I'm always glad to help the team.'

'Ah, I like your English understatement,' Malcolm said. 'But in all seriousness, I'll be singing your praises at the next partners' meeting. You deserve recognition for this.'

She let the warmth of his flattery wash over her. 'Thank you, I appreciate your support.'

'And now I've a favour to ask you,' Malcolm said, placing his coffee cup down and reaching for a buff folder on the far side of his desk. 'Do you have space for an extra case?'

'I think so.'

'An interesting one has landed on our desk, from an American friend of mine. They're looking for someone with expertise in Scottish estate law, and naturally you're the person that sprung to mind. It involves some travel – that's okay, right?'

'Of course it is. I'm always free to travel when it's needed.' It was one of the best things about her job. She loved seeing new places.

'And we appreciate it. It's amazing how many of the team aren't.' He passed the folder across the desk to Lucy.

'You can rely on me.' She opened the front page, her eyes scanning the file notes. She licked her lips as she took in the details of the case, feeling the familiar rush of adrenaline through her veins.

'That's why you're one of the best. And I think you'll like this one. A family dispute over some property in the Highlands, except both members of the family live in the US. That's where we come in. The other party's already engaged a local solicitor, so you'll be playing catch-up.'

From what she could see catch-up was an understatement. She looked at the first page again, her eyes sliding from left to right, before she brought her attention back to Malcolm. 'That's not a problem. I can get up to speed very quickly.'

'That's what I hoped you'd say. The client wants to meet with you as soon as possible.'

'At his estate?' She ran her finger down the paper, stopping at the details of the property. 'Glencarraig Lodge?' The name had a beauty to it, making her think of Landseer's *Monarch of the Glen*. A majestic deer rising from the craggy highlands, violet hills in the background.

4

'No, he's too busy to come over here right now. He wants you to fly to Miami, that's where he has one of his offices.' Malcolm grimaced. 'I know it's short notice, but he wants to meet you early next week. I get the impression he wants to make sure you're as good as I said you were.' He cleared his throat. 'He'll foot the bill, of course.'

'Of course.' Lucy nodded. The first rule of being a solicitor – the client always foots the bill. She'd learned that as soon as she'd entered the firm as a trainee, and was shown the billing system before she even learned where the toilets were. 'I can catch up over the weekend.'

Malcolm picked his glasses up, sliding them back up his nose. 'I knew we could rely on you. The client's booked your hotel, and Lynn's already booked the tickets and taxis. If you go and see her now, she should have the itinerary all printed out for you. Your flight leaves first thing on Monday.'

'Okay.' She flashed another smile, even though her mind was already halfway out the door, making lists, locating her passport, and working out how many American dollars she had in her foreign currency wallet at home.

Of course she'd have everything she needed. Ever since she was a child organisation had been her middle name. And that was exactly how she liked it.

'This one's yours.' The bellhop slid the plastic card into the dull steel mechanism, making the door whirr as it unlocked. 'It's the Biscayne Suite, one of our best.' He wheeled her suitcase into the middle of the marble floor, stopping next to a white leather sofa that was facing a wall of glass. 'The suite was refurbished last year, along with the rest of the hotel. I hope you like it.' Grabbing a folding luggage rack from the closet on

5

the far side of the room, he deftly lifted her case and put it on, before turning back to her with a smile.

Lucy slid a ten-dollar bill into his hand. 'It's lovely. Thank you.'

'Is there anything else you need, ma'am?' he asked, folding the money into his pocket.

'No, I'm fine, thank you.' A wave of fatigue washed over her, as she spotted the coffee machine in the corner. 'I'll just make myself a drink and unpack.'

'Well, if you need anything at all, just dial zero on the phone. We're here to please.' He left, closing the door gently behind him. She stood on the spot for a moment, appreciating the view. The floor-to-ceiling glass doors opened out onto a balcony. Far below, a row of deep green palm trees led down to a pale, sandy beach and a cerulean ocean. Waves gently lapped onto the beach, sliding up the sand, until they almost met the row of red sunbeds that peppered the yellow. The sun was bright and warm – a contrast to the grey misery she'd left behind in Edinburgh, where winter was still clinging on to the city with every bit of strength it had.

She'd been travelling for over twenty hours, stopping over in Heathrow to catch a connecting flight, and her body was dog tired. She looked over at the bed – the pillows plump, the sheets crisp – and for a moment considered skipping the coffee and just lying down to catch her breath. The other part of her wanted to run out of the hotel and grab a cab, making sure she saw all the sights before she left the next morning. There wasn't much chance of that, though – not when there was work to be done.

Rolling her shoulders to soothe her muscles, she unzipped her case and lifted the lid. Her clothes were still perfectly ordered – each piece wrapped in tissue paper to keep it smooth – and she took them out and hung them in the closet. Slipping her black Saint Laurent pumps from their cotton bag, she placed them carefully on a shelf, brushing a piece of lint from them.

She was about to take her L'Occitane toiletry bag into the bathroom when the telephone rang. Kicking her grey leather travelling shoes off, she walked across the room in her bare feet, and picked up the cream receiver.

'Hello?'

'Miss Shakespeare?'

'Yes?'

'This is Maria, I'm your concierge. I just wanted to check if you needed anything.'

Lucy looked around the suite, at the stocked wet bar and the top-of-the-range television and speakers, and that view that drew the eye every time. 'No, I have everything I need.'

'Mr MacLeish has asked if you'd join him for dinner. I've made a reservation for eight o'clock if that works for you.'

Lachlan MacLeish – her new client. The one who was apparently footing the bill for this gorgeous suite. Lucy checked her watch; it was just gone six p.m. local time, which made it the middle of the night back in Edinburgh. Way, way past her bedtime.

'Eight o'clock is fine.'

'I'll let Mr MacLeish know.'

Taking a deep breath, she rolled her shoulders again, ignoring the way they protested at the movement. So much for a power nap. Who needed sleep anyway?

7

2

Give them great meals of beef and iron and steel,
they will eat like wolves and fight like devils

– Henry V

'Good evening, Mr MacLeish,' the hotel valet said, opening the car door as Lachlan unbuckled his seatbelt. He left the engine running – no point turning it off – and stepped out of the gunmetal-grey Porsche Panama, grabbing his phone from the console just as it started to ring.

Again.

He looked up at the white art deco façade of the Greyson Hotel, towering over them both, and then back at the valet, sliding the phone in his pocket and ignoring the call.

'How's the family, Paul?' he asked, shaking the valet's hand, sliding a note into his palm.

'They're great.' Paul looked past Lachlan and at the car, whistling with appreciation. 'This one's a beauty,' he said, taking Lachlan's keys. 'I'll take good care of her for you.'

As Paul climbed into the car, Lachlan rolled his shoulders, trying to ease the kinks out of the muscles there. The smell of the ocean surrounded him, the salty aroma clinging to the warm evening air. Unlike New York, it was temperate enough to wear only suit pants and a jacket – his tie had been taken off and rolled up in his pocket hours ago.

His phone buzzed again, that familiar vibration pushing into his hip bone. He'd spent most of his day in meetings, trying to stave off a crisis in New York. The three hours of videoconferencing, followed by two more in tense talks with his investors, hadn't added to his good humour at all.

'How are you this evening, Mr MacLeish?' the concierge asked him as he walked into the hotel. 'Your guest has made it to the restaurant. We let her know you'd be a few minutes late.'

'Thanks, Maria.' Lachlan nodded at the young woman. It had seemed a good idea at the time – to arrange a dinner with his prospective Scottish attorney – to see if she'd be suitable to take on his case. But right now he'd much rather collapse into bed.

'And reception have a few messages for you. I asked them to forward them to your room.'

A group of tourists – ones with deep pockets and expensive clothes – walked into the hotel lobby, their suitcase wheels squeaking across the marble floor. Almost immediately the triple-storeyed space was filled with loud voices that echoed across the indoor pond.

'I'll leave you to deal with these guys,' Lachlan said, inclining his head at the crowd. 'Have a good evening.'

'Thank you, sir. And you, too.'

As he crossed the lobby – weaving his way through the giant silver abstract sculptures and the huge potted trees – Lachlan felt a shot of pride blast through his veins. When he'd first invested in this hotel it had been run down and losing money in spite of its grand location. It had taken a few years of finding the best people, investing in the facilities, and attracting the kind of guests who would be willing to pay the prices they charged – but finally the place was back in profit.

Like everything he touched, he'd made it succeed.

As he turned the corner into the restaurant, the maître d' smiled warmly, reaching his hand out to shake Lachlan's firmly. 'Your guest is seated at your usual table, Mr MacLeish.'

Lachlan checked his watch. Twenty minutes late. He felt a little guilty for keeping her waiting after she'd flown all this way.

The Palm Room was a half-indoor, half-outdoor restaurant, with a wall of folding glass doors that led out to a palm-tree-lined terrace. Though the interior was painted an off-white, everything else in the room was filled with colour, from the purple velvet chairs to the hand-picked Jackson Pollock paintings.

Like the rest of the hotel, since it had been renovated the Palm Room had become a fashionable haunt for the rich and famous. In the corner he could see an old shipping magnate friend of his father's, dining with a girl who was young enough to be his daughter. On the other side was a semi-famous actress, scanning the room to see if anybody was looking at her, and totally ignoring her dining companion – a notorious ex-criminal, who had enough money to buy whatever company he wanted to dine with. Lachlan nodded at them, then continued to the doors, and stepped outside.

The terrace was his favourite place to eat, even in early spring. Though the temperature was just below seventy, the heaters were lit, making the outside feel as warm as the interior.

His usual table was on the far side, set back from the others to provide some privacy, as it overlooked the Atlantic Ocean. As the sun slid into her watery bed, the sky was darkening, the palm trees that divided the hotel from the beach becoming black silhouettes against the blue-grey water.

But it wasn't the view that drew his eye. It was the woman sitting at the table, her face turned as she looked out at the bay.

He almost stopped dead in his tracks. There was something about her that made him want to stand and stare for a moment. It wasn't just the way she looked – though that would have been enough – but the way she held herself that intrigued him. As she stared out at the ocean, her blonde hair pulled back into a perfect bun, her expression perfectly serene, he imagined her to be like some kind of female Canute. But in her case, if the Atlantic Ocean had dared to move any further up the sand, she'd only have to hold up her hand for it to scurry away again.

Christ, it really had been a long day. He was seeing things that weren't there.

Shaking his head at himself, he walked over to the table, and relaxed his face into a friendly expression. Business was business, no matter how tired he was.

'Miss Shakespeare?'

Almost immediately she turned to look at him, her lips curling into a smile. It lifted her cheeks, making the skin at the corner of her eyes crinkle. 'Mr MacLeish?' she asked. When he nodded, she stood, offering her hand.

'I'm sorry I'm late. I was held up in meetings,' he said, shaking her hand. Her palm was warm and soft in his. He looked down at her fingers – and her perfect manicure. When he brought his eyes back to her face, they met hers, deep and blue. There was a softness to her gaze that contrasted with her steely exterior. He could see himself reflected in the darkness of her pupils.

'It's not a problem,' she said, pulling her hand back to her side. 'I've been admiring the beautiful view.' Her voice was smooth yet clipped – the kind of accent he heard whenever he visited London. Strange that she was from Scotland, then, where the accent was more lyrical and deep.

The way his father's had been.

'How was your journey?' he asked, pointing at her chair and gesturing for her to sit down.

'It was long, but I managed to get lots of work done.' She smoothed her skirt out as she sat, and he followed suit, leaning back on his chair and crossing his legs beneath the table. 'It gave me a chance to reread your case notes. I wanted to be up to speed.'

'I apologise for the rush,' he said, picking up the water bottle and pouring it into his glass. 'Would you like a top-up?' he asked her. She nodded and he refilled it, then screwed the lid back on. 'This inheritance is very important to me, and I want to make sure I have the right kind of advice. You came highly recommended.'

She smiled again, and it was impossible to drag his eyes away. It was almost a relief when the waiter arrived at their table, asking if they were ready to order.

'A glass of the Bryant Cabernet, please,' Lachlan said to the waiter. He hadn't intended to drink, but a glass might take away his edginess. 'How about you, Miss Shakespeare?'

'It's Lucy.' She shook her head when the waiter offered her the wine list. 'And I'm fine with the water, thank you.'

The waiter left, and there was silence for a moment, save for the sound of the ocean behind her, and the low level of chatter in the restaurant surrounding them. 'This is a beautiful restaurant,' Lucy said, looking over his shoulder at their surroundings. 'Were those Pollocks I saw hanging up in the main room?'

'Yes they are.' He was relieved they weren't launching straight into business, no matter how tired he was. 'We worked hard to get the restaurant just right. And the food is even better than the interior design. The chef and his staff are excellent.'

The waiter brought his wine over, then melted away. Lachlan lifted it up, letting the bouquet fill his senses for a moment before he took a drink. It tasted as good as he remembered.

'I went to a Pollock exhibition at the National Gallery in Edinburgh a couple of years ago,' she told him. 'It was fascinating. There's something hypnotic about his paintings that make you just want to stare at them for hours.'

'Have you always lived in Edinburgh?' he asked, still wondering about her voice.

'No, I was born in London. I moved to Edinburgh when I was eighteen, to study law at the university. I guess I fell in love with the city and never looked back.'

'That explains the accent,' he said. 'I couldn't quite place it.'

'I've lived there for ten years,' she said, that smile playing at her lips again. 'But I still can't shake off the English tones. Luckily my clients don't seem to mind it, even if most of them are Scottish born and bred.'

There was a loud cheer from the table a few yards down from them, as a waiter brought out a huge chocolate dessert covered in candles. Lachlan glanced over his shoulder to see what the noise was about, then turned back to her. 'What made you decide to become an attorney?' he asked. It felt strange asking her the question, even if this was the point of their dinner. He was supposed to be interviewing her, making sure she was the right person for the job. That was the reason she'd flown over two thousand miles to meet with him, after all.

13

He'd still rather know what she thought about the hotel, though.

'It's something I've always been interested in,' she said, looking up and catching his eye. He lifted his wine glass and sipped at it, holding her gaze.

'What interests you about it?'

She tipped her head to the side, considering his question. 'Without laws, society as we know it couldn't exist. They provide a framework for us all to live in. For the most part, they stop people from behaving badly, and even if they do, they ensure that the wrongdoers are punished.'

'Sounds like you should have gone into criminal law,' Lachlan murmured.

'I always thought I'd end up as a criminal lawyer, but then I did my traineeship and I quickly discovered I disliked it.'

'Why's that?' He looked genuinely interested, leaning forward to hear her reply.

'Because way too many of my clients were criminals.'

He laughed, and she did, too. Her laugh was throatier than he'd expected, and it jolted him momentarily. 'You only like being on the side of the good and the right?'

'Something like that.'

'I guess I should take that as a compliment.'

'Well, from your case notes, I'd say you're on the right side,' she said, her tone light. 'But I can't comment on anything else.'

A wave crashed onto the beach behind her, the silhouetted palms swaying in the breeze. But before he could say anything else, the waiter came to take their orders, and he had to drag his gaze away from her.

*

Lucy slid her knife through the tender lamb cutlet on the plate in front of her, looking up through her eyelashes at Lachlan, stealing a glance as he speared a piece of his steak. From the minute he'd walked into the restaurant she'd noticed him, her heart flipping in her chest as she'd watched him talking to the maître d'. Annoyed at herself – and her reactions – she'd turned away, staring out at the ocean until her pulse had reached an equilibrium, though it had sped up again as soon as he'd said her name.

And for a moment, as they'd both stood, his hand folded around hers, she'd felt as though she was being sucked up into the ocean, pushed and pulled by the waves. But then she'd taken a deep breath and pulled herself together.

Yes, he was gorgeous, with eyes that seemed to see right through her, but he was also her client. And Lucy Shakespeare was always professional.

'Do you spend a lot of time in Miami?' she asked him now, determined to get herself back on track, to ignore the way he looked in his perfectly tailored jacket. That kind of cut didn't come off-the-peg, it had been made to order. 'From the case notes I understand you're based in New York, is that right?'

'Yeah.' Lachlan nodded, placing his cutlery back on his plate. When he looked at her there was a magnetism that drew her eyes right back to his. He was intensely masculine, but not in an obvious way. It was in his confidence, the way he held himself. 'Most of my business interests are in New York, but I have this hotel and a few other investments here in Miami. Plus my family are here, of course.'

Of course. She knew from his notes that his father had lived in Miami. That's where his will had been signed. 'I'm sorry to hear about your father,' she said, her voice soft. 'My condolences.'

He blinked a couple of times, like something had got into his eye. Then he nodded, accepting her offer. 'Thank you. Though as you'll find out, we didn't always have the easiest of relationships.'

She knew something about difficult families. Who didn't? 'I specialise in estate law,' she said, wanting to reassure him. 'Believe me when I tell you that's my bread and butter.' She'd only managed to eat half her dinner, but her stomach already felt over-full. She put her knife and fork down on the plate, then covered it with her napkin. Once full, she hated looking at leftover food. 'Actually, I have a few questions about your case. Is it okay if I ask them?' Talking about the case made her feel like she was back on an even keel. The law grounded her, made her feel safe. She knew where she was when it came to being a professional.

'Of course.'

'Do you mind if I take notes?' she added, looking down at her briefcase. 'I wouldn't usually do this over dinner, but since we have such a short time, I want to make the most of it.'

'I'm sorry about that,' Lachlan said, offering her an apologetic smile. 'It's just that my father's death and his funeral took me away from work for too long. I've got a hundred people trying to get an hour of my time. Tonight was all that was left.'

'You don't need to apologise to me,' Lucy reassured him. 'You're the client.' Or at least her potential client. 'You make the rules.'

His eyes flickered at her words. 'In that case, ask away.'

'Maybe I can start by telling you what I know.' She always found this the best way to begin a case meeting. Restate the facts and make sure they were right. It was amazing how often they weren't. 'I've read through your father's will, of course, and it seems pretty clear. He's left you one bequest, a lodge in the Highlands of Scotland. Though as with so many things in Scotland, lodge is a bit of an understatement.' She raised her perfectly groomed eyebrows. 'It's more of a castle than a lodge. The Glencarraig estate consists of three thousand acres of land, a loch, plus a salmon farm and a herd of deer. It also comes with ownership of a number of workers' cottages in the nearby village, and currently employs around thirty staff, some of them seasonal.'

'Yes, that's right,' Lachlan agreed, nodding. 'A castle in the middle of nowhere, with a title that means nothing. Thanks, Dad.'

She swallowed down a laugh at his sarcasm. 'Did your father ever use his title?' she asked.

'Only if he wanted to impress people. I don't remember him going around calling himself a laird all the time.' Lachlan shrugged. 'Though I didn't see him that often.'

'How about you?' she asked him. 'Will you be calling your-self Laird of Glencarraig?' It seemed an impertinent question to ask, but she was trying to work him out. To see what part of his inheritance was important to him.

Lachlan laughed, his chuckle deep and low. 'I don't think so, no.'

'But you understand it comes with another role, don't you? That by inheriting the lodge and the title you'll also become head of the MacLeish clan?'

'I assume that means about as much as the title does,' Lachlan said, taking another sip of water. 'As in not very much at all.'

'You'd be surprised,' Lucy replied, scanning the notes she'd made during her flight. 'Though the feudal system in Scotland ended centuries ago, the clans are still a big thing to some people. And not just to Scottish MacLeishes either. There are clan members all over the world, and they'll look at you as their leader. Occasionally clan chiefs have been asked to intervene in disputes.'

'You can't be serious.'

'Surely your father must have had some experience of that. Do you remember him ever getting involved in clan issues?'

'No. But that doesn't mean anything. As I told you, we had a very fractious relationship. I didn't see a whole lot of him growing up.' He shook his head, still looking incredulous. 'Is that really a thing? It sounds like something from a movie.'

'It really is. The internet has changed everything. Some clans have Facebook groups or Twitter accounts. It might sound like an anachronism but a lot of Scots, particularly ex-pats, like it.'

She made a note to herself to find more out about the MacLeish clan. Anything that could lend credence to Lachlan's claim on the estate would be a help.

'So what do I need to do to shut this all down?'

Lucy put down her pen and looked up at him. 'The main problem is another party has asserted their right to the land and the title. Duncan MacLeish Jr. – that's your brother, right?'

'Half-brother.'

'And he's five months younger than you?' Her voice was matter-of-fact.

'That's correct.'

She lifted up the letter at the front of his file, scanning it quickly. 'Your half-brother – Duncan – is asserting himself to be the rightful heir. His solicitor has written to you, asking for you to settle the claim. Otherwise he's threatening court action.' She looked up from the paper. 'Were you expecting that?'

'It doesn't surprise me that he'd do something like this.'

'The two of you don't get on?' she asked. Her eyes had softened, but her tone was still businesslike.

'Duncan isn't my biggest fan,' he told her. 'He'd contest anything our father left me, even if it was worthless.'

'He would? Why?' She tipped her head to the side.

'Because I'm his illegitimate half-brother. Does that make a difference?'

'No, it shouldn't.' She kept her gaze firmly on his. 'Scottish history is full of illegitimate children becoming heirs. It would depend on the terms of the will and if there are any caveats on the lairdship. And so far I've found nothing. As far as I'm concerned the terms of the will are clear, and Scottish law supports it.'

'So will Duncan's claim stand up in court?'

Lucy shook her head slowly. 'No, I don't believe so. But I should warn you, the wheels of our judicial system are slow. The claim could be caught up in court for a while, and this could end up very expensive for you.'

'I don't care how much it costs,' he said, leaning forward with a serious expression. 'I'll pay whatever it takes. I want to win.'

3

There is a tide in the affairs of men, which,
taken on the flood, leads on to fortune

– Julius Caesar

The waiter cleared away their plates, leaving the table empty save for their glasses and Lucy's notepad. Lachlan watched as she moved her pen across the blank page, black ink staining white, her handwriting as perfectly formed as the rest of her. If he'd thought she was attractive when he first saw her, right now she was so much more, with her eyes narrowed and her lips pursed in concentration.

She finished writing and looked up, popping the lid back on her pen. Two lines appearing above her nose as she gave him a questioning look. 'Why do you think your father left you the estate?' she asked him.

He'd been thinking about that himself, ever since he'd sat in the attorney's office and heard his father's bequest. It was hard not to wince at that memory, as he recalled his half-brother's angry surprise. Duncan had thought he was going to inherit everything – and Lachlan had thought the same. Why would an illegitimate, unwanted son be left a single thing, let alone a castle in the Highlands of Scotland? He closed his eyes, thinking about that sandstone building in the middle of another country, about the mirror-like loch and the green forest that led up to the craggy mountains. How long was it since he'd visited? It had to be more than twenty years. And yet the thought of it made his heart beat a little faster, bringing back memories he'd long since buried.

'I don't know,' he said truthfully. The waiter slid their coffee cups in front of them, both Lachlan and Lucy having declined a dessert. 'The only thing I can think of was that the times I visited I was happy there. He must have seen that.'

'Did he ever talk about leaving it to you before he died?' she asked.

'No. I didn't speak with my father very much, not after I came of age. He wasn't that interested in me.'

It didn't hurt to say it – not the way it used to. And he was pleased at the way she didn't flinch at all – the last thing he wanted was sympathy. He'd come to terms with his relationship with his father. What was done was done.

'And what about the rest of your family?' she asked. 'Was there an assumption among them that Duncan would inherit?'

'We always knew he'd inherit my father's business,' Lachlan said. 'He was groomed to take over the cruise line from the earliest age. But I don't remember the estate in Scotland ever being mentioned. Compared to the business, it was small fry.'

In money, perhaps, but not so much in meaning. His father had grown up on the estate, after all. It was their heritage – his and Duncan's – and only one of them could have it.

The thought of losing to Duncan felt like a knife in the heart.

'Okay, that's about all the questions I have for now,' Lucy said, offering him a smile. 'If you decide you want me to act

21

for you, I'll draw up a plan of action, and then we can talk next steps.' Her voice had become hoarse from talking so much. She took a sip of water. 'Do you have any questions for me?' she asked him.

About a thousand.

'What are my chances of success?'

She smiled at his question. 'Honestly? I can't give you a firm answer. But as you're the one named in the will, it's up to your brother to prove his case. And unless he can show coercion, or bring up case law that supports him, then he's going to lose.'

They'd both finished their coffee – and the waiter appeared almost immediately, stealing their cups away with a flourish. Lachlan asked for the check – not that he needed to pay, but at least he needed to sign. Everything in his businesses was done above board.

When the waiter took away the check, and Lucy had put her notes back into her briefcase, they both stood up. Lachlan felt reluctant to say goodbye, knowing that tomorrow she'd be on a flight to London and he'd be speeding his way back to New York. All those questions he had were still swirling around his mind, fighting for supremacy. And that exhaustion he'd felt earlier had disappeared, replaced by an edginess, and a need to find out more about the woman next to him.

'Thank you for a lovely meal,' she said. 'Please feel free to email me if you think of anything else. And let me know if you want me to take on your case.'

Lachlan frowned at her question. 'Why wouldn't I?' he asked her.

Standing up, their height difference was so much more obvious. He towered above her, in spite of her heels. She had to lift her head up to look at him. 'It's clear this inheritance is important to you. You wouldn't have flown me all the way here if it wasn't. Choosing the right representation isn't just about getting the best, but about finding somebody you can trust.'

Her eyes flashed as she spoke, and he took a step forward until there was only a couple of feet between them. He scanned her face, studying her, though her expression gave nothing away. There was the merest hint of a scar that disappeared beneath her hair, and he found himself wondering what had caused it. 'You want me to trust you?' His voice was low.

Her eyes never left his. 'Yes,' she said, nodding slowly. 'Or this won't work at all.'

'Then I trust you,' he said. 'And I'd like you to represent me on this case.'

As they walked towards the exit, he felt the strongest urge to put his hand in the small of her back, but he clenched his fist tightly, keeping his arm by his side. She was his attorney, not his date, for God's sake.

They made it to the lobby. They were both staying in the hotel, in different rooms, on different floors. And it felt awkward lingering in the marble-clad hall, neither one of them quite willing to say goodbye.

'It's late,' he said, glancing at the clock above the reception desk. 'You must be tired, with all the travelling.'

She glanced at the bank of elevators to her left, nodding. 'It's been a long day,' she agreed. 'I should get back to my room, and call my boyfriend before I go to bed.' She offered him the smallest of smiles. 'I haven't had a chance yet, and he'll want to know I arrived safely.'

'And I've got some work to do before bedtime.' He reached his hand out, shaking hers before stepping backward and giving her a final smile. 'Thank you again for taking the time to meet with me.'

'It was a pleasure, Lachlan.'

He liked the way his name sounded on her tongue, the first part sounding more like 'loch' than 'lach'. It reminded him of his childhood, of a life when things didn't seem so complicated, and everybody wasn't constantly vying for his attention.

'Good night, Lucy,' he said, giving her one final glance. She was looking straight at him, and their gazes locked. For a moment he could hear the blood rushing through his ears, blocking out the sounds of the hotel. He smiled, and her lips slowly curled up, making her look more enticing than ever.

'Sleep tight, Lachlan.'

As soon as the elevator doors closed behind her, Lucy leaned her head on the mirrored wall, holding on to the handrail as it began to ascend. Though he was in the lobby, she could still smell his cologne, still see that dimpled smile. She'd never met somebody with so much presence, with such an easy ability to take her breath away. He was danger, dressed in a designer suit.

And her response to him scared her to death.

Was that why she'd lied to him about having a boyfriend? To provide her with a barrier, something to stop her from being caught up in an attraction that was almost impossible to ignore? She shook her head, catching a glimpse of her reflection in the mirrored wall. This was so unlike her it wasn't funny. She was always calm, in control, and she never crossed boundaries. Lachlan MacLeish was a client, no matter how attractive he was. She needed to remember that.

Lifting her hand up, she smoothed her hair back, squaring her shoulders as the elevator approached her floor. She could do this – could be the professional she always had been. He might have been the most handsome man she'd laid eyes on, but she was better than that. And so was her professional reputation.

The elevator pinged, and she walked out onto her floor, pulling her room card out of her case and sliding it into the lock. And as she stepped inside, pulling off her shoes and carefully placing them into the closet, she felt a sense of relief wash over her.

A good night's sleep would do her the world of good. Then she'd fly back home, and get back to her work, leaving Lachlan MacLeish thousands of miles away.

Life would go on, just the way she liked it, and that would be the end of that.

4

As they say, 'When the age is in, the wit is out'

– Much Ado About Nothing

'You missed a few calls. The list is on your desk,' Lachlan's assistant, Grant, said, following Lachlan into his office. He leaned down, pulling open the small refrigerator beside the bookcase, and took out a bottle of water. Unscrewing the cap, he filled up a long glass and put it on Lachlan's desk. 'How was your workout?'

Lachlan grabbed a fresh towel from the cupboard hidden in the far wall of the room. His office had a small bathroom attached, perfect for cleaning up after his lunchtime training. 'Hard. That's what happens when you miss a few weeks.'

Grant Tanaka was a year younger than Lachlan, but had been by his side since the day he'd set up in business, the same way they'd been for most of their lives. They'd grown up in next-door apartments – Grant was the child of Japanese-American parents who had practically adopted Lachlan as one of their own. With Lachlan's mom working all the hours God sent, the Tanakas had made sure he was fed, did his homework, and didn't get into trouble.

Well, not too much trouble, anyway.

'I forgot to ask you, how was Miami?' Grant asked him.

'Warmer than this place, that's for sure.' Through the plate-glass window of his office, Lachlan could see the New York skyline. Grey, overcast, barely acknowledging the fact that spring was supposed to have arrived. 'It was worth it just to meet the Scottish attorney. Hopefully we managed to strategise the Glencarraig case.'

Grant cocked an eyebrow. 'You're still stuck on this Connor MacLeod of the Clan MacLeod thing?'

'Hey, don't knock it. According to this attorney, I get to intervene in clan disputes.'

'There can be only one.'

'Are you going to quote *Highlander* to me all day, or can I go grab a shower before my next meeting?'

'Yeah, you really should do that.' Grant screwed his nose up. 'You stink. Go.'

'Thanks, man.'

'Oh, and Jenn wants to know if you can make dinner a week on Friday. She's making sushi.'

Lachlan looked back over his shoulder at Grant. 'In that case, it's a date. A gorgeous woman and gorgeous food are too good to turn down.'

Grant lifted his hands up. 'Hey, that's my wife you're talking about. I'll be there too.'

Lachlan winked. 'I know, I know. But when she makes sushi, I don't have eyes for anybody else.'

'Yeah, well keep your eyes to yourself,' Grant warned, still grinning. 'That girl is mine.' He glanced at his watch then back at Lachlan. 'Best hurry, your next meeting's in ten minutes.' Suddenly, they were back to being boss and assistant.

'I'm on it.'

'You want me to bring you in a coffee?' Grant asked, turning to leave the room.

'Sure thing.'

Lachlan watched as Grant walked out of his office, pulling the door softly closed behind him. Not for the first time he felt a strange combination of envy and confusion when it came to his friend. In the years since they'd been working together he'd tried to promote him countless times, knowing Grant would make an excellent director. But Grant refused, telling Lachlan he preferred to have a work–life balance that allowed him to spend time with his wife.

He was a great assistant, and Lachlan's oldest friend. Some would say his only friend. Either way, Lachlan was glad to keep him around, even if it meant being constantly nagged.

The lights in the outer office were dimmed, Grant having long since gone home. The rest of the floor was silent too, save for the occasional ring of a phone that wasn't answered, and the stealthy footsteps of the cleaning crew as they gave the desks the once-over, emptying trash cans and filling up the water coolers before they wheeled their trollies away.

Behind him, through the floor-to-ceiling glass, darkness had descended over Manhattan. The hum of the traffic had quietened, and Lachlan didn't need to look out to see that every second car was a cab. Full of people leaving work and heading out for dinner, and tourists exploring the city while the cab drivers fleeced them.

Not Lachlan, though. It was one of the rare evenings when he didn't have a late-night meeting or a business dinner.

He picked up his phone, intending to scroll through his contacts, then put it down again. The thought of an evening on the town didn't light him up with enthusiasm – the opposite, if anything. It must be the jet lag, the heightened emotions of his father's funeral and the surprise of his bequest. Maybe an early night would do him better, instead.

He reached forward to give his emails one final check before he switched off his laptop for the night. Clicking on his mouse, he scrolled through the updates, the circulars, the invitations – each one personally scrutinised by Grant before he'd passed them on.

Halfway down, he saw a message from Lucy Shakespeare. Raising an eyebrow, he clicked on it, his eyes scanning the content.

Dear Lachlan,

Many thanks for dinner on Monday, and for taking the time to meet with me. Attached to this email is a client care letter, outlining the terms of our agreement and the fees you'll be charged. Please read through it carefully, and return one signed copy to me. A scanned version will be fine.

As agreed, I'll send you a strategy document by the end of the week, and perhaps we can then arrange a videoconference to discuss next steps.

Kind regards,

Lucy Shakespeare

It was a simple business message, brief and concise, yet he could hear every word in her elegant English accent.

He glanced at his watch, twisting his arm until it appeared above the line of his shirt cuffs. It was seven thirty in New

York, which made it past midnight in Edinburgh. He let his mind wander for a moment, remembering the way she'd looked when he stepped into the restaurant. The way she held herself, her chin pointed up, revealing the perfect lines of her profile against the backdrop of the inky sky. She was as intriguing as hell, and beautiful with it.

Yeah, and she's also your attorney.

Shaking his head, he reached forward to switch off his laptop, then rolled his chair back and got up to grab his jacket. He was in a funk after his father's death, that was all. Nothing more than that. He grabbed his phone from his pocket, clicking on the contacts and placing a call. When the woman on the other end picked up, he was walking out of his office and heading over to the bank of elevators on the other side.

'Hey, Julia,' he said, his voice echoing down the line. 'It's Lachlan. I was just heading off to my club and I thought of you. Would you like to join me for a drink?'

5

I am as vigilant as a cat to steal cream
– Henry IV, Part I

Lucy turned her key in the lock, opening the black-painted door to her smart Edinburgh apartment. It smelled of polish and cleaning cream – Elena must have given the flat the once-over that morning. She'd left Lucy's mail in a pile on the table by the entrance way, plus a fresh vase of spring flowers. One of the perks of having a cleaning service.

With the door wide open, she turned to grab her suitcase, as a flash of orange and white dashed across the tiled hallway. A small, tabby cat slid past Lucy's legs, her fur soft against Lucy's calves. She lingered for a moment then made a dash for the warmth of the apartment.

'Come here, cheeky,' Lucy crooned, grabbing hold of the pint-sized feline. 'There's nothing for you in here. Where did you come from anyway?'

As she gently placed her back in the hall, the cat purred, her body vibrating against Lucy's hands. Standing back up, Lucy went to grab her case and walk inside, and of course the cat ran back in before she could stop her.

Even with an intruder inside, stepping into her apartment

made Lucy smile. She loved this place – had done ever since she'd bought it five years ago. A converted Georgian townhouse, in the heart of Edinburgh's New Town, her home was an elegantly decorated two-bedroom, two-bathroom apartment, with a huge, modern kitchen that she hardly ever used. Though she liked the pale painted walls and the polished wooden floors, the thing that sold it to her when she first saw it had been the garden. A small, walled escape, filled with greenery, it was her favourite place to spend the afternoon in the summer.

Unpacking her clothes and throwing most of them in the laundry basket – Elena would sort them out – Lucy walked into her rainfall shower, letting the steamy droplets soothe her skin. When she stepped out, twisting a towel around her hair in a turban, and wrapping the rest of her body with a stark, white robe, she walked back into the kitchen, grabbing the kettle and filling it with fresh water.

Elena had restocked the fridge, too. There were some Waitrose ready meals and a couple of bags of salad, plus the usual milk, cheese and bread. Lucy grabbed the milk and a small bowl, filling it up and putting it on the floor. The tabby sashayed her way over and took a lick.

'This is just me being polite,' Lucy pointed out to the cat. 'Don't think you can take advantage, because when that milk's gone, so are you.'

As if the cat could understand, she looked up, glancing at Lucy over the china bowl, before lowering her head and licking at the milk.

Lucy was about to make a coffee when her telephone started to buzz. She looked at the display, frowning when the number flashed up. She didn't recognise it.

'Hello?'

'Is that Miss Shakespeare? Lucy Shakespeare?'

'Yes, that's right.'

'My name's Martha Crawford. I don't know if you remember me, but I live two doors down from your father.'

Lucy clicked the kettle off, frowning. 'Hello, Mrs Crawford, I remember you. Is everything okay?'

'There's nothing to worry about, not really. I mean, he's okay; well, as okay as he ever is. He's not really one for saying much, is he?'

'Has something happened to my father?' Lucy asked.

'I didn't even know if I should call. He told me not to, but you never know, do you? And then I spoke with Deidre, she's the lady who lives on the other side of your dad, and she said it was for the best.'

'Could you tell me what's happened?' Lucy tried – and failed – not to sound impatient.

'My husband found him wandering around in his pyjamas this morning. Well, he spotted him out of the kitchen window when he was making our tea. We both love an Earl Grey first thing. I know a lot of people like breakfast tea, but as far as I'm concerned it's a waste of a tea leaf.'

'Dad was in his pyjamas?' Lucy asked, sitting down on a stool. She leaned her elbows on the breakfast bar. 'Where did he go?'

'He was walking up towards the shops. So Bernard – that's my husband – followed him up there. Luckily he wasn't in his pyjamas. Bernard, that is.' Martha gave a little laugh. 'When Bernard caught up with your dad, he was a bit confused. Didn't seem to know where he was. Luckily that girl, his carer – what's-her-name with the short hair – she was just arriving and helped get your dad back into the house.'

'So he's okay?'

'He was a bit shaken up. Bernard said he didn't recognise him, and you know the two of them used to spend a lot of time talking roses back in the day.'

'Do you know if his carer called the doctor?' Lucy asked.

'No idea, love. I just thought you should know, that's all. Luckily Deidre had your number from the last time you were down here. I hope you didn't mind me calling you.'

'No, no, I'm glad you did. Thank you.' Lucy gave a quick smile, even though Martha was four hundred miles away. 'I should go now,' she said, already making a mental list of people to call: the care company, her father's doctor, and of course her sisters. 'But thank you so much for letting me know. I appreciate it.'

'Any time.' Martha lowered her voice. The woman was as hard to brush off as an ardent suitor. 'Though between you and me, I think it's all getting a bit much for him. Have you thought of putting him in a home?'

'Well, thanks again, Mrs Crawford, and please pass on my thanks to your husband,' Lucy said with a loud voice, quickly ending the call before Martha could start talking again. She grabbed the notepad and pen she always left next to the microwave, and started to write on the lined paper.

If in doubt, make a list. It worked every time.

'So how was Miami?' her sister Juliet asked, her voice echoing down the line. Lucy had almost managed to catch up on the work she'd missed while travelling to Miami. That's when she wasn't on the telephone to London, talking to doctors and her father's carer, trying to agree a plan of action. It hadn't exactly been the peaceful return to Edinburgh she'd hoped for.

She wedged her phone between her ear and her shoulder as she tapped a few amendments to the document she was working on. It was late afternoon in Edinburgh, and another rainstorm had whipped itself into a fury, lashing water against her windows. The cat had found her way into the flat again, and was curled up on Lucy's lap as she typed. She'd discovered it belonged to the downstairs neighbours, but liked to roam around the building as though it owned the place. And maybe Lucy liked it a little bit, too. 'It was brief. I flew in, had a couple of meetings then flew out again.'

'Sounds exhausting,' Juliet replied. 'You should be in bed now, not calling me.'

'I'm fine. I'll have a lie-in at the weekend.' Lucy highlighted some words and inserted a comment. 'I think only being there for a day was good for me. Not enough time for the jet lag to take hold.'

'I don't doubt it,' Juliet said, a grin in her voice. 'If anybody can beat jet lag, you can.'

Juliet was younger than Lucy by two years. Growing up, she'd been the lieutenant to Lucy's general, the two of them ruling the roost, and lording it over their younger sisters, Cesca and Kitty. Then, when Lucy was fifteen, their mother died, and the play-roles they'd taken on somehow became real. Maybe that's why her father had been so insistent that she moved to Edinburgh to study law when she was eighteen. To make her start living her life again.

'I wish I could beat old age,' Lucy said softly. 'Dad's not been himself again. One of his neighbours found him wandering around the village in his pyjamas.'

'Oh no.' Juliet sounded alarmed. 'Is he okay? Did he catch a cold? What does the doctor say?'

Lucy spent the next few minutes filling her sister in. 'It's all under control,' she reassured Juliet. 'I just wanted to let you know what's happened.'

'He's getting worse, isn't he?'

'It's to be expected.' She kept her voice gentle. Even though she was the second oldest, everybody was always gentle with Juliet. 'I spoke to the doctor, and he's sent me up some details of care homes near Dad. He thinks it's time we look into them.'

Juliet was silent for a moment. Lucy could picture her in her big American living room, with the huge sofa and the plump easy chairs.

'It will all be fine,' Lucy promised her. 'I'll speak to a few of the homes and report back. You don't need to worry.'

'But I do worry . . . '

'So tell me,' Lucy said, choosing to change the subject, 'how's Poppy getting on?'

Juliet sounded as grateful as Lucy was for the distraction. 'She's doing great, really enjoying school. Did I tell you what she said to my mother-in-law the other day?'

As Juliet regaled her older sister with stories of her fearless daughter's escapades, Lucy found herself smiling, her whole body relaxing at Poppy's antics. That little six-year-old really was a chip off the old Shakespeare block, and it was a relief to finally talk about something else.

'You in a rush to be somewhere?'

'Nowhere – in – particular.' Each word came out with a gasp of air. It felt as though every muscle in Lachlan's body was burning. But he wasn't going to stop, not until Grant did. It was a question of honour.

Central Park was teeming with people. The benches were

36

full, the green lawns peppered with blankets, children weaving in and out between the chequered wool, and swarming over the grass like ants attracted to a morsel of food. The aroma of hot dogs and popcorn floated with the breeze, the carts surrounded by tourists and locals, jostling to make the front of the line. It was as though nobody had seen the sun before. The first warm day of spring had brought them all out to enjoy the greenery.

'You're running faster than normal. I thought maybe you had a girl waiting for you.'

Lachlan shook his head, grinning in spite of the pain in his legs. 'If I had a girl waiting for me, I wouldn't be wasting time with you, my friend.' Sometimes bantering with Grant beat the need for air. This was one of those times.

'Hey, if you had a girl waiting for you at home, I'd be beating the hell out of you for leaving her.'

'You think you could beat me?' Lachlan laughed, as the two of them came to a stop next to the duck pond. He leaned against the nearest tree, the rough bark pressing into his palm. His breaths were short, more gasps than anything else. His heartbeat pounded in his ears.

He felt good. Damn good. Like he could rule the world, if only the world would let him.

'Ah, the last time I beat you was in fifth grade. And that was because you sprained an ankle.' Grant leaned over, resting his hands on his thighs. 'Jesus, we're getting too old for this shit.'

'We're not even mid-thirties,' Lachlan pointed out. He'd got his breath back, and was leaning against the tree. One good thing about training daily – it meant his recovery time was practically pushed to nothing. 'We're in the prime of our lives.'

'Speak for yourself, man. I'm an old married guy.' Grant didn't look too miserable about it, though. He lifted his hand up, watching as the sun glinted off the metal of his wedding band. 'I need to slow things down.'

'You slow down any more, you'll be walking backwards,' Lachlan said. 'Anyway, if you let yourself go, you won't be married for much longer.'

Grant laughed. 'Yeah, Jenn's not into beer bellies. Or at least I don't think she is.' Finally he stood up, blowing out a mouthful of air as he did. 'Speaking of Jenn, I'd better get back. We've got a lunch date with her folks. I can't be late.'

'Pussy.'

'Nah, just married. And loving it.'

The two of them walked past the duck pond, heading west towards the subway. That's where Grant would catch his train downtown, while Lachlan continued walking to his apartment on the Upper East Side.

Blood brothers, divided by wealth and geography.

'You still on for Friday?' Grant asked, as they reached the entrance to 103rd Street Station. He lingered at the top of the steps, holding on to the balustrade.

'Sure. What time do you want me?'

'Eight okay?'

'Works for me.'

'Don't forget your passport. You'll need it to get to the poorer part of town,' Grant teased. There was no real animosity to his words. Why would there be? He had chosen his life, and clearly loved it. Even if Lachlan couldn't understand why he wasn't driven to achieve more.

'I'll get my shots done too,' Lachlan replied. 'Wouldn't want to pick anything up.'

'Are you sure?' Grant winked. He put his hand to his ear. 'You hear that? A thousand girls just threw themselves into the Hudson.'

'Hey, stop trying to live your life vicariously through me. You're the one who decided to tie yourself to one woman for the rest of your life.' Lachlan bumped his shoulder against Grant's. 'And I don't pick women up, they pick me.'

'Whatever you say, Casanova.' Grant stepped back, punching him lightly in the arm. 'I'll see you at the office tomorrow, man.'

'See you tomorrow.' Lachlan raised his hand in goodbye as Grant turned and ran down the steps to the subway, his footsteps echoing through the stairwell.

6

There's a skirmish of wit between them

– Much Ado About Nothing

'Do you have everything you need?' Lynn asked, hovering in Lucy's doorway as she wound her cotton scarf around her neck. 'I need to leave on time tonight, Marnie has a school concert going on.'

It was nearly six o'clock, and the office had already thinned out. Laptops had been closed and locked away, coffee cups placed in the dishwasher which was whirring in the kitchen. Half of the partners' offices were dark and the fast gunfire of emails arriving in her inbox had already thinned to the occasional ping.

Lucy glanced up from the letter she'd been reading. 'I'm all good here, thanks, Lynn. And best of luck with the concert.' She gave her assistant a quick smile.

'I'll need it. And thanks, I'll see you in the morning. I'll be the one who can't hear anything because she's been deafened by a thousand squeaky recorders.' Lynn waved a goodbye, closing the door behind her and leaving Lucy alone in her office. She checked the time on the clock. She had time to draft a quick reply before her videoconference was due to begin.

But then her laptop lit up, a green camera icon showing her

incoming call. She grabbed her mouse with one hand, patting the back of her hair with the other. A brief click on the screen and the call began.

'Good evening, Lucy.' Lachlan's deep voice echoed through her laptop speakers. It was the first time she'd seen him since their meeting in Miami, but the time and distance had done nothing to dampen his attractiveness. He was sitting in what she assumed was his New York office, his tie loose but still knotted, his shirtsleeves rolled up to reveal tanned forearms. Behind him she could see the blue sky, dotted here and there with wispy clouds.

'Good afternoon,' she said, inclining her head at him. The noon sun was shining through the window behind him, illuminating the Manhattan skyline. It looked glorious compared to rainy Edinburgh.

'Thanks for making time to see me. I just wanted to go through your proposed next steps and make sure we're on the same page.' He smiled, and that dimple flashed in and out of his cheek, giving him a hint of youthfulness that he didn't usually display. She dragged her eyes away, taking in the rest of his office. There was a painting on the far wall – almost out of shot. She could just see the edge, pale paint splatters arranged in a hypnotic spiral. Was that another Pollock? She opened her mouth to ask him, then shut it again. They were supposed to be talking about his case.

She grabbed the folder next to her laptop, opening it to the front page. 'Did you get the draft letter I sent over earlier today?' she asked, pulling her own copy out and taking the lid from her red pen. 'It's the reply I propose we send to your brother's solicitor. I'd like to get it in writing that we completely refute his claims.'

'I managed to take a look at it a minute ago,' Lachlan said, glancing at his screen. 'It all looked fine. But do we really need to send a letter? Aren't we giving his claim credence if we reply to it?'

'It's all part of the legal process. They write to stake a claim, we refute it, they then file in court. I know it sounds long-winded, but if they miss any steps they could have their claim thrown out, and if we miss any we could forfeit. The real action won't happen until we're up before a judge. That's if it gets that far.'

'You think it won't?' he asked her.

'That depends. There are a lot more steps to take before anything gets to court. Once their claim is lodged we'd have two weeks to respond. Then the judge would consider whether the case has any merit before allowing it to go further. It would be my job to convince him it doesn't.'

There was a hint of a smile on his lips when she finished speaking. His eyes were softer than she remembered, but they still did something to her. She felt her stomach flip flop when their gaze met.

Dear God, she needed to get a hold of herself. She was twenty-nine, not nineteen.

Somebody walked into Lachlan's office and placed a coffee cup and some papers on his desk. Lucy couldn't see their face – only their hand as it came on screen. Lachlan murmured to them, and whoever it was said something just as unintelligible back.

'Is it raining there?' Lachlan asked, his eyes narrowing as he stared closer at the screen. Lucy automatically turned to look at the window behind her, the glass spattered with raindrops.

'When isn't it?' she asked, turning back to her screen.

'I spend half my life either scurrying under an umbrella or wringing out my hair. It's one of the downsides of living in Edinburgh.'

'But there are upsides, too, aren't there?'

She smiled. 'Yes, there are. It's a beautiful city, full of culture and interesting people. It's as vibrant as London, but it doesn't feel anywhere near as vast and busy. It still has a small-town feel to it that I love.' She could have spoken about the place all day.

'I went there once as a child, I think,' Lachlan said, narrowing his eyes as though he was trying to remember. 'We visited the castle, and I remember being forced to eat some disgusting food in an old pub somewhere, but apart from that I know nothing about the place.'

'Well, if you come over here to visit Glencarraig, you should definitely stop in Edinburgh. It's a couple of hours' drive from the Highlands, which feels like forever to us, but I imagine it's a tiny distance to an American.'

He nodded slowly, looking straight at her. 'Maybe I'll do that.'

A tiny bit of panic pulsed through her. It was easy to talk to him when there was a distance between them, but the thought of having him here, in her home town, was a different matter. 'But in the meantime, let's finish this letter up and get it off,' Lucy said, back to business. She lifted her arm, deliberately twisting her wrist so he could see her checking her watch. 'It's getting late here and I'm going out tonight. And I'm sure you're very busy too.'

'Are you doing anything nice?'

She swallowed, her mouth dry. 'Just dinner with some friends.' She caught a glimpse of the Pollock again, a shaft of

43

sunlight suddenly illuminating that corner of his office. In her mind's eye she could picture him trawling art galleries, admiring the displays, pulling his black Amex out of his wallet . . .

It was just a flight of fancy. He had people to do that for him. Interior designers, decorators, assistants. He probably didn't even know what the painting was worth.

'Okay then,' she said, picking the paper up again. 'Let's go through this line by line, and I can get it sent off tomorrow. Who knows, maybe it will be enough to make your brother rescind his claim.'

For the next couple of minutes she was all business, her voice firm, her eyes carefully trained on the paper in front of her, and not the man on her laptop screen. And when the meeting finished and they said goodbye, she felt her body relax for the first time since she'd accepted that damn call.

When it came to client relationships, there were lines you didn't cross. But with Lachlan MacLeish it felt as if they were everywhere, and when she opened her mouth she was stepping far too close to the edge.

She needed to be more careful. Otherwise it was only a matter of time before she fell right into the abyss.

7

Things sweet to taste prove in digestion sour

– Richard II

'Hey, you made it.' Jenn opened the door with a beaming smile.

Lachlan leaned forward and pressed a kiss to her cheek, before passing her the bottle of Caymus Special Selection. 'I wasn't sure what to bring, I hope this is okay.'

'A cheap bottle of Cabernet would have been fine,' she told him, raising her eyes at the expensive bottle of red. 'Anyway, would you like a glass?' She inclined her head and Lachlan followed her into the small apartment she shared with Grant. The two of them had moved there shortly before their wedding. Part of a block in the East Village, it felt warm and homely, stuffed with photographs and books, plump cushions and soft throws.

'That would be great. Thank you.'

'How's the exciting world of research?' Lachlan asked as she grabbed a glass from the kitchen shelf.

'As exciting as the world of finance, I expect.'

'I didn't hear the door,' Grant said, walking out of the bedroom. His hair was wet, as though he'd recently showered.

'Thanks for making it, man. I know things were crazy at the office.'

'Grant said you were still in meetings when he left. Who schedules meetings for seven on Fridays?' Jenn asked.

'I do.' Lachlan had the good grace to look embarrassed. 'But it was an emergency.'

'All sorted now, I hope,' Jenn said, passing him a glass of the red wine he'd brought. 'I want you to kick back and relax, not be talking shop all night.'

'We don't always talk shop,' Grant protested, taking the glass his wife offered. 'Sometimes we talk about football.'

'And baseball, hockey, not to mention basketball,' Jenn teased, kissing her husband tenderly on the cheek. 'I'd just like us to have a nice meal without talking about Lachlan's plans for world domination.'

'Don't worry, Pinky,' Grant whispered to Lachlan, a grin splitting his face. 'We'll take over the world tomorrow. Tonight we'll just eat cheese.'

'Or sushi,' Jenn said, raising her eyebrows. 'I've been slaving over a hot stove ever since I got home.'

'I thought sushi was raw,' Lachlan said, confused.

'It is. I was speaking figuratively. Now stop bothering me and go and sit at the table.'

'Whatever you say, sweetness.'

Since he'd first met Jenn, almost seven years earlier, Lachlan had liked her no-nonsense attitude, and the way she didn't take any shit from Grant – or from Lachlan, for that matter. But tonight she seemed a little more edgy than usual.

He smiled as he remembered the first time Grant had mentioned her. He'd been running late at work, bitching about

46

some blind date a friend had set him up on. Back then, like Lachlan, he'd been a confirmed bachelor, claiming no woman was going to tie him down.

But then, he'd never reckoned on Jenn, had he?

'So, Grant tells me you're going to be some kind of duke or something,' Jenn said, sliding a tray of sushi rolls onto the table. Small and round, their dining set was nestled in the corner of their living room, next to a window overlooking the city. 'Lord Lachlan, it has a good ring to it.'

Lachlan laughed, shaking his head. 'It's Laird of Glencarraig, actually.'

'Oh, get you! Do I need to curtsey when I see you?'

He picked up his chopsticks, expertly sliding them between his thumb and fingers. Growing up next door to Grant, he'd had years of practice. As a kid he'd practically lived at his friend's house. 'It's a courtesy title. It means nothing.' He slid the sticks around a piece of nori-covered fish, lifting it to his plate. 'Anyway, it's not even mine yet.'

'Why not?' Jenn took a sip of her water.

'I thought we weren't supposed to be talking about business?' Grant said, frowning. 'This sounds distinctly like business, right?'

'Hush up. This is interesting.' Jenn tapped him good-humouredly. 'So come on, why haven't you been crowned, or whatever it is?'

'Only kings get crowned,' Grant pointed out.

'Shush.'

Lachlan grinned. There was something so comforting about the two of them and their bickering. 'Because my half-brother also wants the title.'

'Duncan?' Jenn looked surprised. 'I hadn't put him down

as being the Lord of the Manor type. He seems too interested in his cruise business for that.'

'I don't think it's the title he's after,' Lachlan said. 'It's the principle. And a big F.U. to me.'

'And you want to F. him right back. Am I right?' Jenn's face lit up. 'You're not going to give in, are you?'

He slid another sushi roll into his mouth, swallowing it down before replying. 'These are really good. And no, I wasn't planning on it.'

'I'm pleased to hear it. I'd hate to see him win.'

'You've never even met Duncan,' Lachlan pointed out. The last time he'd seen his half-brother was at the reading of the will. A glance between them was all that had happened.

'Yeah, but I already know I don't like him.'

'Ah, I knew you'd be on my side.'

She wrinkled her nose. 'It's just going to make you more arrogant, isn't it?' she said. 'All those girls already falling at your feet are going to be vying for your attention now you're a lord.'

Lachlan moved his head from left to right, scanning the floor. 'There are girls at my feet? Where?'

'Oh shut up.' It was his turn to be hit. She wasn't so gentle, either. 'You know what I mean.'

He winked at her. 'I don't need a title to get a girl.'

'Do I need to separate you two,' Grant asked, 'or are you going to behave?' He poured Lachlan another glass of wine. 'And anyway, it looks like more than a courtesy title to me. Have you checked out the MacLeish website?'

Lachlan frowned. 'What website?'

'Remember the attorney told you a lot of clans have websites and social media presence?' Grant reminded him. 'So I had a little Google and came up with this.' He grabbed his

48

phone and pressed on it, passing it to Lachlan with a flourish. 'There's a forum and everything. Not that it's used much any more, but back in the day it looked busy. From what I can tell, most of the MacLeish clan prefer to tweet and post in the Facebook group now.'

Lachlan pulled his eyes away from the phone screen. 'There's a Facebook group, too? Seriously?' His thoughts turned to Lucy Shakespeare, and her whole explanation of the clan system. He couldn't help but smile at the fact she'd been proved right. Again.

'Hey, what have I told you guys about having your phones out at the dinner table,' Jenn chided, grabbing the phone from Lachlan's grasp. She really was strong. 'Oh my goodness, is that the MacLeish plaid?'

'They call it tartan,' Grant told her.

The website's header was a blue and green plaid, with thin lines of red criss-crossing through the squares. 'Do you have to wear that?' Jenn asked him. 'I can't imagine you in a kilt.'

'I've worn one before,' Lachlan said mildly.

Jenn grinned. 'When? And why haven't I seen any pictures?'

'I was a kid. And all the evidence is destroyed.' Lachlan smiled back at her. 'Sorry to rain on your parade.'

'You're not raining on anything. You're making my day. Lachlan MacLeish in a skirt. It's too good.'

'I'm glad it amuses you.'

Jenn didn't reply, she was too busy scrolling through the phone. 'Oh boy, there's so much information here. Babe,' she said, turning to Grant, 'did you know that Lachlan comes from a long line of MacLeishes, stretching back to at least 1638?'

Grant gently took the phone from her. 'No phones at the table, remember?' He slid the phone back in his pocket, then looked at her from the corner of his eye, as though he was expecting reprisals.

Lachlan smirked. 'The hunter hunted.'

'And just for that,' Jenn told him, folding her arms across her chest, 'you can both clear the table. And I don't care if you're the king of Scotland, make sure you put everything away.'

'Is Jenn okay?' Lachlan frowned. She'd finished clearing up the kitchen, shooing away any offers of help, and then told them she needed an early night. Grant had grabbed the two of them a beer, suggesting they climb up to the rooftop garden, the one overlooking the city. 'She didn't eat much. Didn't say much either, after dinner. Did we make her mad with the phone thing?'

Grant shrugged, leaning back on his wooden chair. He had his feet up on the table, ankles crossed, a beer bottle resting in his hands. 'She's just exhausted. She's been in bed by seven most evenings.'

Lachlan frowned. 'Is she sick? Can I help? You know you're both fully covered, right? And I'll pay any deductibles.'

Grant grinned. 'We might have to take you up on that. But not for a few months. Did you notice Jenn was only touching the veggie sushi? She can't have raw fish.'

Lachlan twisted on his chair, the frown still playing around his lips. 'Why not?'

'She can't drink alcohol, either, for that matter.'

A slow sense of unease tugged at Lachlan's stomach. It combined with the realisation dawning in his mind, making him feel off-kilter, like a ship lurching in the sea. 'She's pregnant?'

'As a metrosexual, supportive husband, I guess the right way to say it is "we're pregnant".'

50

'Well, that would be a minor fucking miracle.' Lachlan rolled his lip between his teeth, staring out into the inky black night, his eyes caught by the dots of lights peppering the tower blocks across the city. 'Congratulations, man.'

'Say it like you mean it.' Grant laughed.

Lachlan took another mouthful of beer, the cool liquid snaking down his throat. 'I do mean it. That's great, you're gonna be a dad. Jeez, that sounds so grown up.'

'We are grown-ups. Have been for a while,' Grant pointed out. 'We do our own laundry, cook our own meals. Well, I do at least. You pay someone to do that for you, but that's grown up, too, right?'

Lachlan said nothing for a moment, staring out into the distance. Is this what Peter Pan felt like, watching all his friends grow up around him? 'Being a father takes it to a whole new level, though,' he finally said. 'You're responsible for somebody else, for the rest of your life. Things will never be the same again.'

'You're making it sound like a life sentence.'

Lachlan sighed, mentally kicking himself. 'I didn't mean to make it sound bad. It's just . . . different, you know? Yeah, I run a business, and I have an apartment. But those things don't feel like a burden. I could walk out and leave it all behind at any time. You can't do that to a kid.'

Except you could. He knew that from personal experience.

'You couldn't walk away from the business even if you wanted to,' Grant pointed out. 'You have employees to take care of. They have homes, bills, medical issues. You're just as tied up as anybody else, even if you choose not to believe it. And anyway, having a kid isn't a burden, not to me. Not with the right woman.'

Lachlan sat up, turning to face Grant. 'Hey, you're right. You and Jenn are going to be fantastic parents. Every kid must be jostling to be the one ending up here. Hell, we can even set a nursery up at the office if you like. That's assuming Jenn's planning on going back to work.'

'Yeah, about that ...' Grant trailed off. The smile disappeared, as he failed to meet Lachlan's stare. 'I, ah, don't know what we'll be doing for childcare.'

Lachlan shrugged. 'You've got plenty of time to think about that.'

'She's due in five months.'

'But she gets maternity leave, right?'

'She's leaving her job.' Grant was suddenly cagey.

'She wants to be a stay-at-home mom?' Lachlan asked, his eyes wide. 'I thought she loved her job.'

'She's been offered another position. A better one. They've agreed she can take it up after the baby arrives.'

A genuine smile split Lachlan's face. 'That's amazing. I'll call her tomorrow to give her a double congratulations. She must be buzzed.'

'There's something else,' Grant added quickly.

'What?'

'It's at the University of Florida,' he said, his voice low. 'We're planning to move back south.'

Lachlan opened his mouth to reply, but nothing came out. Just a soft whoosh of air that dispersed into the night. He took another sip of beer, to moisten his dry mouth more than anything else, trying to work out why his chest felt like it was being squeezed by a constrictor.

'Florida?' he repeated.

'Yeah.' Grant lifted his bottle up. 'Go Gators.'

A shrill siren cut through the silence of the rooftop garden, and Lachlan followed the van's progress, his eyes tracing the blue lights as it criss-crossed the city streets. He felt as though he'd just been punched in the stomach, a Grant-sized fist leaving a hole in his gut.

'We really want to bring this kid up away from the big city,' Grant told him. 'Plus we'll be closer to family, and only hours away from Miami. It makes sense to make the move when the baby comes.'

'Yeah, sure.' Lachlan nodded.

'It won't be for a few months. Six at least.' Grant was almost stumbling over his words. 'I'll help you source a replacement, you won't be left hanging, I promise.'

'A replacement?'

'A new assistant. We have enough time to train somebody new. And who knows, they may even be better than me.'

'Never.' Lachlan wanted to ask if Grant would source him a replacement friend, too, but pushed the thought down as soon as it flashed through his mind. 'You're irreplaceable.'

Grant laughed. 'That's what they say.'

'Florida, though, that's a hell of a long way to move.' Lachlan finished his beer, putting the empty bottle on the table. 'You can still work for me down there. I've got the hotel, and I'm looking at some other places to expand into. What do you think?'

Grant rubbed his chin. 'Yeah, maybe. I don't know what we're planning to do with the baby yet. But if the offer still stands when we make the move, I'll seriously consider it.'

'If you want a job, it's yours. You know that.'

'You don't need to do me any favours,' Grant said. 'Not that I'm not grateful for everything you've done. Because I really am.'

'It wouldn't be a favour. You're too good a worker to lose. If you want to work part time, full time, from home or whatever. Just say the word.'

'I appreciate that. Thank you.' Grant sounded choked. 'It's going to be a big change, being a dad, moving away from here. It's nice to know there are options.'

'You're a good friend,' Lachlan told him. 'My best friend.' His only friend, but that didn't need to be mentioned. 'I'll always be here for you.'

'And I'll be there for you, too,' Grant promised. 'Man, we're getting all goddamned emo, aren't we? Shall I grab us another beer?'

Lachlan checked his watch. It was almost midnight. 'Nah, it's late, I should be getting home. And you should be getting to bed with your wife.' He stood, offering his hand to his friend. 'Thanks for a good night. And congratulations, on all counts.' This time he meant it.

He really did.

The car crossed Manhattan in less than fifteen minutes, not bad for a Friday night. Lachlan nodded at the guard as he walked into the lobby and headed straight for the elevator and to his thirtieth-floor apartment. As soon as he slipped his key into the door and pushed it open he could smell the soft floral scent of the cleaning supplies his housekeeper used. Everything was neat, his breakfast dishes long since cleared away, his clothes laundered and folded, and placed back in his wardrobe.

There was nothing to do except shower, clean his teeth and climb beneath the thousand-count sheets on his bed.

Maybe he should have called an old girlfriend. Or stopped at a bar. Anything to get rid of the echo of his footsteps as he walked through his empty apartment. Anything to soothe the ache that hadn't left his chest since he'd said goodbye to Grant.

It had to be the sushi. Maybe it hadn't gone down well. Or it could be the beer. He grabbed a couple of indigestion tablets from the mirrored medicine cabinet in his bathroom, leaving a thumbprint on the glass as he pushed it closed.

An almost perfect oval, with a swirl and loop design. At least it would give his housekeeper something to clean on Monday.

After climbing into bed, he checked his phone one final time before turning off the light. A dozen emails from different business contacts, five meeting requests for the following week. But not a single message from a friend.

He flicked it off, throwing it carelessly onto the table next to him, where it landed with a thump. Closing his eyes, he turned over, ignoring the dull ache in his chest. He was wealthy, he was powerful, he was successful. He had things he'd dreamed of growing up as a child.

What wasn't to like about his life?

8

Good counsellors lack no clients

– Measure for Measure

Lucy stepped out into the spring air. The sun was battling its way through the wispy clouds, the yellow hues lighting up the puddles from the earlier rain. She blinked twice, letting her eyes become accustomed to the light. The temperatures were warming up, enough for her to wear only a lightweight coat, ditching the gloves and scarf that had become like a second skin for her.

It was only a short walk to the office – a ten-minute brisk pace through Princes Street Gardens and across the railway line. The footpaths were lined with flowerbeds, the green shoots of daffodils and tulips forcing their way through the brown earth. Tiny buds were unfurling on the once-barren trees, the pink candyfloss blossom heralding the brand-new season. In only a few weeks it would fall and coat the grass and footpaths, and the leaves would begin to grow. After a long, cold winter, it felt as though everything was finally coming back to life.

She clambered up the steep stone stairs that seemed to be everywhere in Edinburgh, her lungs protesting at the sudden exertion. By the time she made it to the top she was out of breath, though there was no telltale sign of vapour as she panted. The air was too warm for that. Thank goodness for small mercies.

'Coffee?' Lynn asked, as soon as Lucy walked into the office. 'I was making one for Malcolm anyway.'

'Yes please. And when you're ready can you come in and find me,' Lucy said, hanging her jacket on the stand in the corner of her office. 'I need to move a few meetings around.'

As Lynn wandered off to make the coffees, Lucy pulled her laptop out and plugged it into her workstation, lifting up her office phone to check for any voicemails. She didn't get that many these days – most people either emailed or called her mobile. But she still had a few traditional clients – mostly older ladies with more assets than they knew what to do with – and occasionally they'd leave a tremulous message, asking her to call them back.

Not today, though.

After coffee she made some phone calls, then sorted through the piles of letters Lynn had left, filing them into importance. That's when she saw the one from Dewey and Clarke, the solicitors Duncan MacLeish had appointed. She picked it up, scanning through the words. They proposed a meeting to discuss a compromise, to avoid filing in court.

She licked her lips, reading the words again. Then she scanned the letter and sent an email straight to Lachlan. It was still the middle of the night in New York, or Miami, or wherever the hell he was today, but he'd get it when he got to work in the morning.

It was less than five minutes before her phone lit up, and his name flashed across the screen. She felt a pulse of excitement – or maybe it was adrenalin. Every time she spoke to Lachlan MacLeish it felt like she was going in to battle with a side of herself she didn't recognise.

'Good morning. You're up early,' she remarked. 'Or is it late?'

'It's almost five in the morning,' he told her. 'I need to fit in a run before I get to work.'

For a moment she pictured him in his running gear. Strong, muscled legs, iron-like arms. He had the kind of body that could shelter you from a storm, if only you would let him.

Oh, for goodness' sake. Get a hold of yourself, Lucy.

'Well, don't let me stop you,' she said. 'Good health comes first. You can always email me later if you have any questions.'

'I would,' he said, sounding amused. 'But your email didn't have any attachments, so I can't read the letter.'

Oh bugger. She pulled up her emails on her screen, and he was right, there was no paperclip icon to show the scan was attached. How the hell had she managed to mess up something so simple?

'I'm so sorry, I'll resen—' Her apology was interrupted by a loud blast of a horn reverberating down the phone line. Then there was some shouting, the words muffled so she couldn't hear them. 'Lachlan, is everything okay?'

'It's fine. Some taxi driver thinks the lights don't apply to him.' Lachlan sounded a little breathless. 'It was something and nothing.'

'Are you running right now?' she asked.

'Yep. Just reached Central Park.'

'And you can still carry on a conversation?'

'I'm just warming up. Once I'm going a bit faster it'll be

harder, but it's all about the breath. As long as the conversation matches the rhythm of my run, I could talk for the whole time.'

She tried to imagine Central Park at this time of year. She'd visited New York when she'd graduated, using the golden handcuff payment she'd received from Robinson and Balfour to fund her travels. 'What part of the park are you running in?' she asked him.

'I'm just doing a circle of the reservoir and then I'll head back downtown. I've got a meeting at seven.' She could hear the rhythm of his breathing now. 'In fact, I've got meetings at seven, nine, eleven and one. Plus a site visit this afternoon. So I won't be able to take a proper look at the email until tonight. Will that be a problem?'

Her heart was beating in time to his exhalations. 'It'll be fine. I'll check my emails later, in case you reply before I go to bed. And if you need to call me, then do. I don't want the different time zones to cause us any problems.'

'I appreciate that,' he said, his voice still as clear as day. 'But don't stay up on my account. I'm going to be stuck in the office until late, so it could be the middle of the night before I get to read it. I'm not going to wake you up over this.'

She waited for the relief to wash over her, but it didn't. Instead, she felt a sense of disappointment so sharp it made her wince. Did she want him to call her in the middle of the night?

'Sounds like you're burning the candle at both ends,' she said. And yet wasn't that what she did too? You didn't get to the top of your game by working nine to five. You pushed yourself to the limits, then pushed a little more.

With his good looks and his natural charm, it would have

been easy for him to glide through life. But instead he had this determination to always come out on top. She couldn't help but be impressed by it.

'Yeah, well, it's a dog-eat-dog world. I worked hard for what I've got. I don't intend to lose it now.'

She could tell from the cadence of his words that he'd sped up. 'I should let you go,' she said, feeling reluctant to end the call. 'You need to finish your run, and I need to send you this email, this time with the letter attached.'

He laughed. 'Okay, Lucy, I'll speak to you later.'

She ended the call, placing her phone down on the desk beside her laptop, and tried to ignore the way his words made her feel. *I'll speak to you later.* She wasn't sure whether that felt more like a threat or a promise.

The way he was making her feel – as though her perfectly ordered world was being tipped on its edge – it was almost certainly both.

Lachlan leaned back on his chair, running his fingers through his hair as he closed his eyes for a moment, blowing out the mouthful of air he'd been holding. It had been a long, damned day, and it wasn't looking like ending any time soon. His inbox was loaded with emails that Grant had marked urgent, and his cellphone voicemail had been flashing full all day. At sometime around seven that evening, a delivery guy had brought him a bag full of Chinese takeout, but the cartons remained on his tables – their contents cold and congealed.

He shrugged off his jacket and unbuttoned his shirt, loosening the collar that had been rubbing at his neck all day. Scanning the contents of his inbox, his eyes immediately stopped on a familiar name, one that made the corner of his lips curl up. *Lucy Shakespeare*. She was like a cool balm on his overworked soul.

He looked around his office, at the sleek interior, the marble floor, the expensive paintings mounted on the wall. He was in no position to complain – not when he'd achieved more than he'd ever dreamed of as a kid, kicking around the streets of Miami, trouble following him like a bad smell. And for years he'd been satisfied with what he had – with the magazine articles that lauded him as the next big thing, with the invitations to exclusive galas and premieres – all the things that accompanied success. And yet now, alone in the office, it didn't feel as fulfilling as before.

It was hard to put his finger on the reason why. He thought of his father, the man who'd gone to his grave hardly knowing his first-born son. Had Duncan MacLeish Snr. been content with his life? Lachlan thought he probably had. He'd built an empire, after all, one that had turned him from impoverished Scotsman into Miami magnate. What wasn't to like about that?

Moving the cursor to Lucy's message, he clicked it open, quickly reading through her words before downloading the attachment. Her emails were so similar to the way she talked that he could almost hear her voice as he skimmed her concise note. Could almost picture her typing it, her eyes slightly narrowed, her lips pursed in concentration.

In the weeks since they'd first met at his hotel in Miami, she'd proved to be exactly the attorney he needed. It was crazy the way he looked forward to their discussions, so much that he'd called her that morning when the sun had hardly risen in the New York skyline, the desire to hear her voice outweighing any good sense he had left. Even crazier that his morning run, accompanied by their conversation, had been the best part of his day.

He'd never had a crush before, if that was what this was. Grant hadn't been wrong when he'd said women came to Lachlan. He liked their company, enjoyed their conversation, and yes, sometimes they went to bed together. But that was as far as it went. He certainly didn't spend his free time thinking about them.

Until *she* came along.

He shook his head at his own thoughts, a half-smile lifting the corner of his lip. She was good at what she did, and that's what he liked about her. She was key to him getting the inheritance he wanted so much, and that was what mattered.

Not her beauty, not her poise, nor the way she pulled him in every time they spoke. She might have been unlike any other woman he'd ever met, but that was all irrelevant. She was his attorney and she lived two thousand miles away. His life was complicated enough – he didn't need to add to it.

A glance at the clock on the far side of his wall told him it was almost eleven p.m. He rubbed his dry eyes and sent a message to his car service, asking the driver to pick him up in half an hour. That left him enough time to reply to Lucy's message and then read through his other emails, before getting home and heading straight for bed.

All work and no play was definitely making Lachlan an exhausted man.

'So it's all agreed, then?' Cesca asked. 'Thank goodness the home can take him, it's going to be so much better for everybody.'

'I still hate the idea of him being in a care home.' Juliet screwed up her nose. 'I just feel so ... guilty, you know? Like

62

I'm neglecting him. I haven't seen him for more than two years.'

'You've got nothing to feel guilty about,' Lucy said. 'None of you have. He wouldn't want you to give everything up to take care of him. If anybody should be taking care of him it's me. I'm the one who lives closest.'

A barrage of 'No's came through the laptop microphones. Lucy's screen showed her three sisters all sitting in different parts of the world. Cesca was still in Budapest, where Sam was filming on location. If you looked close enough you could see the telltale signs of her hotel room – generic paintings on the walls, plain yet elegant bedding, not to mention the three suitcases in the corner of the screen.

Juliet, on the other hand, was sitting in her kitchen in Maryland, USA. Expensively modern and beautiful, and yet somehow soulless. Poppy was in the corner, colouring in her usual way – full of gusto. Thomas, Juliet's husband, was nowhere to be seen.

Then there was Kitty. The baby of the family. She was sitting outside a coffee shop in LA, the morning sun illuminating her long, blonde curls. In her hand was a supersized insulated cup, and she was sipping on it as they spoke. She looked beautiful – and no wonder. Falling in love had been good for her.

'So what about the house?' Cesca asked. 'Will the insurance let us keep it empty? We can't rent it out while it's got all that stuff in.' They all knew their father was a hoarder.

'I've spoken to a couple of companies that specialise in house clearance,' Lucy told them. 'I don't think we should do anything until he's settled, but after that we'll have to look at selling it – we'll need the money to pay for his care.'

'It feels horrible, selling the family house,' Kitty said. 'Dad loves that place. So did Mum.'

Lucy glanced over to the side table, covered with a collection of family photographs in silver and black frames. On the left-hand side was a small black-and-white print of a tall, handsome man and a beautiful woman, laughing as they ran down the steps of the register office. Her mother was resplendent in a short, cream dress; their father wearing a smart suit and perfectly knotted tie. It looked more like a vintage advert than a family snap.

'We don't have much choice,' Juliet said quietly. 'We want Dad to have the best care, and the house will pay for it.' She swallowed, her voice lower still. 'Anyway, it's not as if he's ever going to be able to live in it again, is it? He's only going to get worse.'

That silenced them all for a minute. When Lucy glanced at the screen her sisters were all looking down.

'We're doing the best we can for him,' Lucy finally said. 'And that's all we can do. I know it's horrible, but at least this time we get to do it right.'

'Of course we are,' Cesca agreed.

'Anyway, tell us about Budapest. Is the Danube as pretty as they say it is?' Lucy asked. The change of subject was like a weight lifting from all their shoulders, and suddenly they were chatting again, their expressions softening as they exchanged news, talking about husbands and boyfriends, jobs and houses.

Lucy leaned back in her chair, surveying them all with a warm smile. She loved her sisters fiercely. Since she was fifteen years old, it had been her job to take care of them, to make sure they were happy.

To all intents and purposes, it still was.

9

My mother came into mine eyes
and gave me up to tears
– Henry V

There should be a car waiting for you in Miami. I've
rescheduled tomorrow's meetings, and cancelled your
appointments. Give my best wishes to your mom. Grant

Lachlan skimmed the text then shoved his phone into his
pocket, pulling his small, expensive case behind him as he
walked into the airport arrivals lounge. Cabin-sized, it con-
tained everything he'd had time to throw inside it, before
racing to JFK Airport for the first flight he could get on.

It was eleven p.m. local time. Darkness had descended,
lending Miami International a quieter atmosphere, suiting
Lachlan's mood completely. He strode across the tiled floor to
the man holding the sign with his name on, nodding and allowing the driver to take his case as they walked out to the car.

A few minutes later they were pulling onto the freeway.
The driver made a couple of half-hearted attempts to begin a
conversation, but Lachlan's replies were terse, almost taciturn.

He preferred to stare out of the window, or check his messages to see if there were any updates from his mother's nurse.

'It's the university hospital, right?' the driver asked, pulling into the fast lane.

'That's right.'

'I'm guessing it's not a regular appointment at this hour.'

'My mother's been taken sick. I've flown down from New York to see her.'

'I'm sorry to hear that,' the driver said.

'Thank you.'

'My father was in Mercy last year,' the driver continued. 'Heart attack. They gave him a week at best. Within two months he was dancing at my sister's wedding. They said it was a minor miracle.'

Lachlan half-smiled. He wasn't expecting any miracles – minor or not – for his mom.

It was less than fifteen minutes before the car pulled up outside the hospital. The driver flicked his hazard lights on and climbed out to grab Lachlan's case from the trunk. Lachlan stood and looked up at the cream stuccoed building. If it wasn't for the green-and-orange *University of Miami Hospital* signs, you could mistake it for a high-end hotel. Hell, some of the top-level rooms had fantastic views of the beach and city.

Slipping the driver a twenty-dollar tip, Lachlan grabbed his case and walked through the glass sliding doors and into the entrance, immediately heading for the information desk. It was quiet inside – regular visiting hours were over, and the general public were safely at home for the evening. Even the staff spoke softly as he asked for directions to his mom's room.

When he made it to the Pulmonary and Critical Care ward, the nurse quietly directed him down the hallway. 'The pulmonologist has gone home for the evening,' she told him, her voice low. 'He'll be back in at eight for ward rounds. You'll be able to speak with him then. But in the meantime if you have any questions, I should be able to help.'

'How is she?'

'Critical but stable,' the nurse told him. 'She had a chest infection which developed into pneumonia. She's being treated with an antibiotic drip, and she's on oxygen, but her heart is weak. We should know more tomorrow.'

'Will she make it?'

The nurse's face softened. 'It's hard to tell. There's a fine line between treating her and exacerbating her pain. As you know, COPD is progressive, we can only treat the complications. But we're doing all we can to help her fight.' She stopped outside the room, pushing the door open. Lachlan stepped past her, his eyes immediately drawn to the pale woman resting on the hospital bed. She was hooked up to a machine, lines leading from her wrist up to a drip. An oxygen mask covered her nose and mouth, and every time she inhaled he could hear a rattling from her chest.

'That's a venturi mask,' the nurse explained. 'It delivers high levels of oxygen to her lungs. It's more effective than a nasal cannula.'

Lachlan nodded, though he was barely listening.

'She's also had two steroid injections to improve her lung function. I expect they'll send her down for another chest X-ray tomorrow.'

Tomorrow. Seeing his mother lying on her bed, he wondered if she'd even see it. Leaving his case by the door, he walked over, pulling the chair close to the bed. Picking her hand up, he clasped it between his own.

'She feels hot,' he said.

'She's had a fever. It's coming down. We'll be taking her vitals again in half an hour, hopefully she'll be a bit cooler by then.' The nurse checked her watch. 'I'll leave you in here for a while. If you'd like some refreshments, the café is open all night, it's just down the hall. And if you need one of us, you can either press that button,' she said, pointing to the red button on the wall, 'or come find us at the nurses' station.'

'Thank you,' he replied, still staring at his mother.

'You're welcome.'

He spent the next hour sitting with his mom, listening to the regular beeps from the heart monitor, and her irregular breathing as she struggled still for air. The wheezing rattle from her chest made him wince, it sounded as though with every breath she took she was going in to battle. A couple of times her eyes fluttered open, and she stared at him glassily, not recognising who he was, or if she did, unable to find the energy to acknowledge him.

By midnight he'd fallen asleep on the padded leather chair, his head lolling to the side as his long legs stretched out in front of him. But his slumber didn't last for long. Every hour the nurse came in to check the machine and the IV, making notes on her tablet to record his mom's hourly stats.

The second time the nurse woke him up, his neck was stiff, his back muscles complaining at the awkward position. He circled his head a couple of times, feeling the knots clicking against each other. 'Where did you say the café was?' he asked. Right then, the lure of a caffeine injection was too strong to ignore. It was a shame they didn't serve anything stronger.

'Down the corridor and to the left,' she told him, adjusting the machine. 'If you're lucky the terrace might still be open. It has a nice view of the city.'

There was no queue at the counter. The barista served him quickly, using the same low tones everybody else seemed to have in the hospital. Did they put them on some kind of training course? Lachlan handed over a note then carried his coffee over to a corner table. The doors to the terrace were locked but the sounds of the city still found their way through the gaps. His phone screen told him it was half past one in the morning, and it felt like it, too. Sitting there in the corner of the deserted café, Lachlan felt a pang of loneliness sting his stomach.

Do you have anybody you'd like us to call? Wasn't that what they said when a patient was close to death? If the nurse asked him there and then if there was somebody she could call, who the hell would he say?

Grant probably cared, but only because he was Lachlan's friend. And he'd be fast asleep at this time. He couldn't imagine Jenn would be very impressed if Lachlan woke them up just to talk.

Did he even have any other friends? Maybe, but not the kind you'd call in the middle of the night, looking for sympathy. He spent his life surrounded by work colleagues, employees, friends who liked to have a good time, but would a single one of them be there for him if he sent them a message right then?

He didn't think so, no.

Taking a sip of his coffee, he let the bitter taste swill around his tongue, and then swiped his phone, checking the time once again. One thirty-three a.m. – only a few minutes since he last checked. It was as though time moved at a slower pace in the night, the same way the nurses lowered their tones once the midnight hour had passed. He checked his emails, his messages, his diary. Took another sip of his drink. Two nurses walked into the café and headed straight for the counter, then left as soon as their to-go drinks were made.

He glanced at the news, the weather forecast and the closing share prices across the globe. His coffee was half-drunk now, the liquid cooling fast in the air-conditioned café, and he pushed the cup away with one hand, still holding the phone with his other.

Sighing, he pressed on the search box in his web browser. What could he look up next? He wasn't interested in gossip, didn't follow any TV shows, and couldn't remember the last time he'd read a book. The keyboard popped up on the screen, and he slid his fingers across the boxes, making letters appear in the search.

The MacLeish clan.

As soon as he pressed the little magnifying glass icon, a list of results appeared. An online shop selling Scottish tartan, a Wikipedia page, and then the website that Grant had told him about. Lachlan pushed on the third result, and it immediately took him to the same page he'd seen before, the one with a tartan background, and a photograph of Glencarraig Lodge in the banner.

The menu held a number of options, and he clicked on the history one first. He glanced through it, reading about the clearances in the eighteenth century, and how they resulted in so many poorer Scottish families being evicted by their aristocratic landlords, leading to a mass emigration to the New World. He read about Bonnie Prince Charlie, and how the head of the MacLeish clan had supported him in his quest to defeat the English occupation, leading to the clan chief being forced into exile, a hunted man.

There was so much information in there, Lachlan could barely take it all in. Who had written this? He couldn't believe his father had either the interest or the technical expertise to run a website. There was no information about the author – just links to the forum, which as Grant had said was pretty deserted – as well as details of the accommodation that Glencarraig Lodge offered to paying guests, and an annual gathering.

Interested, Lachlan clicked on the gathering page. A photograph of Glencarraig castle came up again, but this time there was a host of people standing in front of it. Men wearing kilts in the traditional MacLeish tartan, ladies in longer skirts wearing tartan blankets wrapped across their shoulders. There were even children, boys in kilts and flat tam-o'-shanter hats, girls in shorter skirts and long socks. At the bottom of the photograph was a caption: *MacLeish Clan Gathering 2017.*

He blew up the photograph, scanning the people to see if he recognised anyone. But none of them looked familiar. Neither his father nor his brother were there, and that gave Lachlan some satisfaction.

The café door opened again, and this time there was a bigger influx of people. He glanced at the time and was shocked to see that over an hour had passed. He stood quickly and headed back to see his mom in her private room.

Learning more about the MacLeish clan would have to wait.

10

Scotland has enough treasures to satisfy
you out of your own royal coffers

– Macbeth

'Mr MacLeish?' Dr Farnish walked out of the hospital room, pulling the door closed behind him. 'I've had the results of the X-rays back. Your mother's chest is looking clearer than yesterday. The antibiotics seem to be working.'

Lachlan nodded quickly. The relief made his muscles feel loose. 'She's more lucid than yesterday, too. We managed to exchange a few words.'

'Yes, that's a good sign. If her recovery continues we should be able to discharge her before the weekend. The fact she has twenty-four-hour care at her home should make things easier.'

'Will there be any lasting damage?' Lachlan asked. 'Do we need to review her care?'

Dr Farnish shook his head. 'As you know, each episode of exacerbation causes some damage to her lungs, which will make breathing harder for her. But she already has a ventilator at the care home, and that should be sufficient for now. I'll want to review her in a week, and then monthly from then. But if she's well enough to discharge, then she'll be well enough to go back to her care home.' He lowered his voice, enough for Lachlan to have to lean a little closer. 'At some point you'll need to have a discussion with her about her wishes. Maybe think about a living will. Her COPD will have an effect on her quality of life, and eventually the pain is going to outweigh any positives.'

Lachlan leaned back on the painted wall. A nurse walked past them, pushing a trolley of equipment, the rubber wheels squeaking against the tiled floor. The doctor was right – he knew that. They'd consulted enough experts to know there was no way but down for his mother.

'I'll speak to her when she's back at the home,' he agreed, though he was already working out when he'd have a chance to do it. Now she was on the mend he had to get back to work – he'd already cancelled four days' worth of meetings, he couldn't cancel much more.

'I know it's not easy, but it would be the kindest thing to do.'

Lachlan nodded again, then walked back into the hospital room, where his mom was still sleeping, her breathing audible against the backdrop of the bleeping monitors. There were pillows propped around her, and the tubes were still attached to her wrist, but the mask had been removed, replaced by a nasal cannula that allowed her to speak, for the few minutes she had enough energy to stay awake. He sat next to her, in the chair that had already moulded to his body, the cushions sinking beneath him as though they were tired of staying plump.

It was hard to look at her like this, even knowing she was getting better. She looked so different to the mother he remembered growing up. The young, vibrant woman – too

73

young, probably – who would kiss him like crazy then disappear for hours, leaving him to fend for himself. From the earliest age he'd learned to be independent – to find his own food, his own entertainment, his own comfort. He'd quickly learned that if he didn't take care of himself, nobody else would.

Looking back, he could have gone either way. For a few years there as a kid, he'd skirted the lines of the law, hanging out with the wrong crowd, looking for a fight – any fight – just to prove he existed.

Strangely, it had been his father – the man who hadn't seemed to care much for him – who'd made the difference. Or rather, it had been the times Lachlan had stayed with him and his family. They'd shown him an alternative to the lifestyle that had been all around him. Even Glencarraig had played its part. It was hard to be angry when you were surrounded by the beauty of nature, and almost impossible not to want more from this world than a lifetime of thuggery.

So he'd worked hard, harder than he'd ever knew he could, first at school and then in business, pushing himself out of his old life and his neighbourhood, bringing Grant right along with him. He hadn't stopped fighting – he probably never would – but the things he was fighting for had changed.

His mother's eyes flickered open for a moment, her watery blues meeting his, before they closed again and she took a deep, rattled breath.

In her own way, she was a fighter, too. She'd done the best she could as a mother – with the scant resources she had available – and he didn't hold his upbringing against her for that.

He let his head fall back in the chair, until it met the cushioned back, and took in a deep breath of cleansing air. Everything he had was hard fought for – and won – and

Glencarraig wouldn't be any different. He could sit here in Miami or New York and wait for things to happen, or he could take the fight to the place it mattered most.

Maybe it was time to go to Scotland.

'Marcus took over the meetings,' Grant told him. 'And I've couriered over a whole set of documents for you to sign. They need to be back with our attorneys this week. How's your mom doing?'

'A lot better. She's being discharged tomorrow.'

'That's wonderful.' Grant sounded genuinely pleased. 'Her recovery is continuing then?'

'Yes. They're moving her onto oral antibiotics. And the care home is ready for her.'

'That must be a weight off your mind.'

'You could say that.' Lachlan smiled.

'When do you think you'll be back in New York?' Grant asked. 'Do you want me to book your flights?'

Lachlan took a sip of his coffee. In the days since he'd arrived in Miami, he'd made this corner of the hospital café his own. He'd found it surprisingly easy to run his business from there – with Grant's help. 'I'm not coming back to New York,' he said, placing his cup down on the Formica. 'I want to meet with my brother's attorney,' he said. 'And I want to do it in Scotland.'

'Are you sure?' Grant asked, sounding confused. 'You've already been out of the office a while.'

Lachlan smiled. Grant wasn't used to him being so impulsive. But really, flying to Scotland made sense. It wasn't just about taking the fight to his brother, but also about seeing that land in the Highlands. Reminding himself exactly what it was he was fighting for.

And if he had to see Lucy Shakespeare again ... well he could handle that, too, couldn't he? She was his attorney and she had a boyfriend. That was all he needed to know.

'Yes, I'm sure. Find me a flight to Edinburgh,' he said, the smile still curling his lips. 'And let Miss Shakespeare's assistant know I'll be arriving next week.'

There it was. The game was on, in more ways than one.

11

Pray, do not mock me. I am a very
foolish fond old man
– King Lear

'Are you okay? You keep checking your watch.' Cesca was sitting in the chair opposite Lucy's, with their father between them. It was lunchtime in the Wickstead Care Home – a well-regimented affair that allowed the patients – or guests, as they insisted on calling them – to have some familiarity around them. The same menu every week, the same seat every day. Even the music, piped in through the speakers in the dining room, was repetitive.

'Do you need help with that, Dad?' Lucy asked, watching their father push his chicken around the plate. 'Would you like me to cut it up?'

'I'm not a child.'

Lucy swallowed, painting a smile on her face. 'I know.' She turned her attention on Cesca. 'I'm fine. I was just wondering if my client had arrived at Heathrow yet. He's flying in from New York.'

'Surely you get the day off on Sundays,' Cesca remarked. 'You don't have to meet him or anything do you?'

'Oh no. He'll be catching a connecting flight to Edinburgh.'

Cesca looked confused. 'So why does it matter what time he arrives in Heathrow?'

'It doesn't.' Lucy frowned. 'I was just wondering, that's all.' She shook her head at herself. Even Cesca was noticing how weirdly she was behaving. It was all Lachlan MacLeish's fault, with his deep blue eyes and dimpled smile, not to mention that voice that made her skin tingle every time they spoke.

Oh God, she needed to get a hold of herself. She didn't have time to spend all weekend thinking about *him*. And now he was going to be in the same city as her – the same office as her, come to that – she needed to take control. It was just for a few days, after all.

She could handle that. She'd handled much worse.

Cesca narrowed her eyes. 'Okay.'

'I've finished. I think I'll go back to my room.' Their father pushed his plate away, the cutlery rattling against the china.

Lucy looked up from her own plate of food, only half-eaten in front of her. 'Do you want me to come with you? Show you where to go?'

'I know where to go.' He was in one of those moods. 'I'd like some peace and quiet, if it's all the same to you.' He stood and left before she could protest. What was the worst that could happen anyway? The whole home was built around people who chronically lost their way. The worst he could do was end up in somebody else's bedroom. And as the nurse had reassured them, that happened a lot.

'Moody old bastard,' Cesca muttered.

'Cess,' Lucy said. 'It's not his fault.'

'I know, but you'd think that the times he's lucid he'd actually try to be nice, wouldn't you? He's done nothing but moan and criticise you all day. He even started being rude about Mum—'

'What did he say?' Lucy's voice was terse.

'Nothing. Just the usual rambles.' Cesca shrugged. 'You know what he's like.'

'He says a lot of stupid things,' Lucy agreed, her chest feeling tight. 'You should ignore them.'

'I do. But when he has a go at you, I want to shake him. Doesn't he know how much you've done for him? Bloody hell, you practically took over when Mum died. He just disappeared into his room all the time. It's like he forgot he had four daughters to look after.'

Lucy pressed her fingers to her temple, rubbing the skin there. 'Yeah, but we managed, didn't we? And I know he's annoying sometimes, but remember, there'll come a time when he can't talk any more. We'll long for him to bitch at us then.'

Cesca's eyes were glassy. She blinked them a couple of times. 'You're right,' she said, her voice a whisper. 'It's so horrible, isn't it? I don't know how you've coped with it all this time. We owe you a lot, Luce.'

'I'm your big sister. It's what I do.'

'You're so much more. I just wish you'd let us look after you sometimes. You look worn out.'

'I'm fine. I've just been working hard, that's all. I've got this client flying in, and a big meeting on Tuesday afternoon, so I had to work late all last week.' She didn't mention that the client had been on her mind all weekend, too. Ever since her sister had fallen in love with Sam, she'd become a born-again romantic. And the last thing Lucy needed right now was a sermon.

'And then you came down and helped Dad move into this place,' Cesca gestured at the home. 'You even gave up your weekend. Without a thank-you from him.'

'I don't do it for thanks.'

Cesca leaned forward. 'Then why do you do it?'

'Because we're family. And we may be scattered all over the world, but we have blood tying us together. I do it because I love you. We were torn apart once before, and I won't let it happen again. Not on my watch.'

'You can't control life.' Cesca shook her head. 'Look at me. I've ended up with the one man I hated. You think I planned for it? Life is messy, Luce. You just have to go with it.'

'How is Sam, anyway?' Lucy asked, diverting the conversation. 'How's the shooting going in Budapest?'

'He's tired, grumpy, overworked. But once this is wrapped we get a lovely long break,' Cesca said.

'And what are your plans after that?' Lucy had long since given up hope that her sister would move back to the UK. Sam was riding way too high for that. Not to mention the fact that Cesca's star was on the rise, too. Her play had had a successful run in the West End, and there were rumours of a Broadway production. Still, Cesca did her best to visit whenever she had a chance.

Cesca bit down a smile. 'I can't really talk about that yet.'

Lucy raised her eyebrows. 'Why not? Don't tell me Sam's going to be the next James Bond.'

Cesca laughed. 'Not likely. He's only just got over being stereotyped as a lifeguard, I don't think he's planning on doing any other movie franchises soon.' She looked down at her nails, that smile still playing on her lips. 'It's me that has to keep schtum. I'm in negotiations about a script.'

'A playscript?' Lucy asked her.

'No, it's a series. I'm in negotiations with a popular streaming service, but I can't say much more.'

'You signed an NDA?' Lucy knew all about non-disclosure agreements. They seemed pretty common in LA – Kitty had asked for her advice about one, too.

'Yeah.' Cesca raised her eyebrows. 'But hopefully I'll be able to tell you more soon. Just as soon as we sign on the line.'

'Wow.' Lucy couldn't hide her happiness for her sister. 'That's two of you taking Hollywood by storm, now. You and Kitty should team up. The Shakespeare Sisters Productions has a good ring to it.'

'Sam said the same thing. Reckons we should make it a big family business. Though I suspect he just wants to get all the best roles.'

'Maybe I should move over there,' Lucy teased, 'I could become an entertainment lawyer.'

'I wish you would.' The smile slipped off Cesca's face. 'I miss you when I'm over there. We all do. I hate thinking of you being left here with all the responsibility while the three of us live it up in the States.'

'You're not exactly living it up,' Lucy pointed out. She opened her mouth to point out that Juliet and Kitty weren't either, but a crash from the kitchen drowned out her words. Somebody had pushed over the trolley of trays and dirty dishes, causing cutlery and crockery to fly out across the linoleum floor. A second later an army of nurses and orderlies came rushing in, some of them heading straight to the residents to make sure the calamity hadn't caused them any anxiety, the others to clean up the mess.

'I guess that's our cue to leave,' Cesca said, when the noise started to die down. 'I'll just head up and say goodbye to Dad, and then I'd best grab a cab to Heathrow. My flight leaves in a couple of hours.'

Lucy checked her watch. For a moment she imagined Cesca and Lachlan being in the same place at once. They could pass by each other and not even know they were connected through her.

She shook her head, trying to get rid of that silly thought. Of course they weren't connected. He was only a client, after all.

The two of them walked out of the dining room and into the large, whitewashed corridor, heading to the heavy door that led to the residents' bedrooms. The sound of their shoes hitting the tiled floor echoed through the hallway.

'It feels weird, doesn't it? Having no idea how long it's going to take for Dad to get worse? Not really knowing what worse even means. It's so scary.'

'And if it's frightening for us, imagine how he must feel,' Lucy said, nodding. 'That's what I keep telling myself whenever he's having a day like today. He must be so scared, not really understanding what's going on, not knowing what day it is. Imagine looking at somebody you don't know and being told you're related to them. It's impossible to put myself in his shoes.'

This time the tears forming in Cesca's eyes rolled down her cheeks. 'Poor Dad.'

'And poor us. This whole thing sucks.'

'It does,' Cesca agreed. 'But it would suck ten times more if it wasn't for you.' She squeezed Lucy's hand. 'Thank God we all have you to rely on. Our lighthouse in a crazy storm.'

A flame of warmth flickered in Lucy's chest. She was doing okay. Life kept throwing curveballs, but somehow she was keeping them all under control. The same way she'd keep Lachlan MacLeish under control, too, or at least her stupid reactions to him. She'd be cool, calm Lucy, and that was just the way she liked it.

Lucy reached the office steps at just after seven on Monday morning. She'd taken the late flight from London the previous evening, and then spent a couple of hours finishing her preparations for Tuesday's meeting, aware that Lachlan MacLeish would be arriving at the office around nine. They'd spoken briefly about the big meeting with Lachlan's half-brother and his solicitors, but Lucy knew they had a lot more work to do on it yet.

She walked into the reception. It was empty at this time of the morning – even the daytime receptionist hadn't arrived yet. Instead, there was the night guard, his uniform wrinkled thanks to hours of sitting in the same position, his black peaked cap perched securely on his head.

'Good morning, Miss Shakespeare.'

'Hi, Mark.' She came to a stop in front of the desk. 'I have a visitor coming today. Can you make sure he's booked in on the system?'

'Sure, what's his name?'

'Lachlan MacLeish,' a deep voice said from behind her. She felt a shiver snake down her spine, slithering its way from her neck to her tailbone. Why was it that every time she heard his voice he had this effect on her? Well, she wasn't having it. As far as she was concerned those shivers could slither the hell out of town.

Taking a deep breath, she arranged her mouth into a smile, before she turned to look at him.

'Hello, Lachlan, I wasn't expecting you so early.'

He was wearing a navy single-breasted suit and a white shirt. A thin dark grey tie was perfectly knotted at his neck. He reached out for her hand, his jacket sleeves sliding up to reveal two simple gold cufflinks shining against his wrists.

'I couldn't sleep,' he said, smiling at her. 'Plus we might need a little bit more time. I want to talk about our strategy.'

Lucy's smile didn't waver, even though she was thinking of all that work she'd done last night. 'Oh?'

'Don't look so worried. I just had a few thoughts while I was on the plane. We can talk about them later.'

'I wasn't worried.' She met his gaze. 'You're the client, if you want to make some changes, then that's what we'll do.' You see? She could be professional. Cool, calm, Lucy.

She stood and watched as Mark checked Lachlan in, taking his details and printing him out a visitor's pass. Then the two of them headed for the doors that led into Robinson and Balfour's offices, and Lucy slid her card into the reader to release the lock.

'Why don't I get you settled into an office?' she suggested. 'The visitors' ones are over there.' She pointed at the bank of glass doors that led to three small, yet perfectly outfitted rooms. 'You can join our visitors' network – the wifi code is on the back of your pass.'

'Sounds good.' Unlike most clients, he didn't let her lead. Instead, he walked ahead, choosing the office on the right. 'Is there anywhere I can get a coffee?' he asked her. 'Just in case the jet lag hits.'

She'd be willing to bet a thousand pounds that Lachlan MacLeish never suffered from jet lag. He looked way too fresh and composed for that. 'I'll have one brought in. Americano with room, right?' Damn, was that too obvious? Or was it a simple courtesy to remember her clients' drink preferences? She tried to remember how Mrs Dalgliesh – one of her favourite clients – took her tea, but she couldn't for the life of her recall.

His gaze softened. 'Yeah, that's right.'

'Okay then.' She glanced at her watch, as much to drag her eyes away from his as anything else. 'I have a few messages to respond to and some phone calls to make, so why don't we meet in my office in half an hour?'

'Can we make it an hour? I've got some emails to respond to myself.'

'Of course. If you need anything in the meantime, let me know. I'm on extension three-four-two. And Lynn, my assistant, will be in soon.'

'I'm sure I'll be fine.' He nodded. 'But if I need you, I'll definitely call.'

She'd been rereading this email for the last ten minutes, and it still hadn't sunk in. Maybe it was something to do with the way she kept looking up through the glass of her office wall, and over to the visitors' rooms. She could just about see him typing away, and making the occasional phone call. A couple of times he'd stood and paced as he talked, and his eyes had met hers from across the office.

Yes, she'd felt her heart gallop in her chest. And no, it didn't mean a thing.

Sighing at herself, she closed her laptop up and headed to the toilets for a quick freshen-up. Lynn was already in there, standing at the wall of mirrors beside the sinks, touching up her matt pink lipstick.

'How did your weekend go?' she asked, dabbing the corner of her lip with a piece of tissue. 'Is your dad okay?'

Lucy glanced at the stalls, but all the doors were open. Lynn was the only one in the office that knew about her father, and she preferred to keep it that way. 'It wasn't too bad. I think he kind of likes the company really, though he'd never admit it. Now there's just the house to sort out, and we're almost there.'

Lynn smiled sympathetically. 'You did the right thing. But you must be exhausted. Mark said you were here with the larks this morning. Along with your client.' Lynn raised an eyebrow. 'Who is gorgeous, by the way. Why didn't you tell me? I would have worn a nicer dress.'

'Is he?' Lucy said, running her hands under the cold tap and then putting them under the automatic soap dispenser. 'I hadn't really noticed.'

In the mirror she could see Lynn's smile. 'Then you're blind. Every single woman has been craning their heads around his office to get a glimpse. And Anneka has taken him in at least three coffees.'

Lucy stifled a groan. 'Doesn't she have anything better to do?' Anneka was one of the interns, though she didn't work in family or estate law. She'd obviously made a special trip across the building. 'The poor guy will end up with caffeine poisoning.'

'I'm pretty sure Anneka wants him to end up with something,' Lynn said pointedly. 'Though it's not poisoning.'

'Well, I hope she doesn't make a fool of herself. It reflects badly on the firm.'

'Ach, she's a good intern,' Lynn said. 'And he'll be gone tomorrow. Let her enjoy him while she can.'

Lucy sighed, sliding her hands under the dryer. 'This is why I hate having visitors come in. It disrupts everything.'

When she walked over to Lachlan's office to collect him, Anneka was leaning on the frame of his door, talking quietly as he looked up at her. As soon as Lucy appeared behind her, Lachlan's eyes slid over to hers, and he smiled. 'Hello, Lucy.'

Anneka turned to look at her. 'Hi, Miss Shakespeare.'

'I hear you've been looking after Lachlan for me,' Lucy said, nodding at the intern. 'Thank you.'

'She makes a good cup of coffee,' Lachlan said, standing and unplugging his laptop. 'Thanks, Monica.'

'It's Anneka,' the girl corrected him.

'Of course it is.' He grimaced. 'Thanks again.' He nodded as Anneka walked out of the room, clearly miffed at the way he'd forgotten her name.

Lucy couldn't help biting down a smile.

Lachlan followed Lucy over to her office – much bigger than the visitors' cubicles, with a small table in the middle where they would be able to work a little easier. 'I'm sorry about Anneka,' she said, as he laid his laptop bag on the table. 'She's young but very keen. I hope you managed to get some work done, too.'

He glanced around her room, taking in the view of Edinburgh, the old sandstone city a contrast to the sleek lines of her office, with its modern glass-and-steel furniture. There were photographs everywhere – framed ones on her desk, snapshots pinned to her board, and some affixed to the walls that separated her office from the ones beside her. He looked more closely at them. Some showed Lucy standing with some other girls and an older man – her family, maybe – while others had her grinning in cities and tourist sites across the world. Some he recognised – Machu Picchu, the Taj Mahal, Sydney Harbour Bridge – while others he couldn't place at all.

'Do you travel a lot?' he asked, still taking the photographs in. She looked so different in them – out of her sharp suits, with her hair flowing in the breeze. There was a easiness to her that he hadn't seen whenever they'd met. She was relaxed and clearly enjoying herself.

'Sometimes,' she said, pulling a water bottle and two glasses from the table on the side. 'Not as much as I'd like any more. It was easier when I was training – I had more time and I could get student discounts too. Nowadays getting away takes a bit more planning.'

He picked up a photograph of her standing at the top of a tall building, Manhattan laid out in a chequerboard pattern behind her. 'The Top of the Rock,' he murmured, still looking at it.

'That's right. I preferred it to the Empire State Building. It felt less touristy, which I know sounds stupid since it's a tourist attraction and all. But it had this buzz to it that I liked.'

'I prefer it too,' he agreed, smiling at her. A thousand questions came into his mind – about what she'd seen, where she'd eaten. It was strange to imagine her in his city, maybe haunting the same locations he did. They could have passed each other in the street and he wouldn't have known. 'What's your favourite place to visit?' he asked her, wanting to know more.

'I loved New York, of course,' she said. 'But Sydney was great, too. And then there's all the European cities – full of history and culture. Lisbon's gorgeous, and Barcelona is full of life.'

'How about Paris?' he asked her. 'Do you like it there?'

Her cheeks flushed. 'Would you believe I've never been? I always mean to, but it hasn't happened. It's so close that I always think I'll go there next time, but then something else crops up.' She gave a little laugh. 'You're going to tell me you've been there, aren't you, and put me to shame?' She passed him a glass of water, their fingers touching as he took it. A tiny pulse of electricity – static from the floor – passed between them.

She looked as shocked as he felt.

'It's one of my favourite places,' he admitted, smiling at the red on her cheeks. 'I can't believe you haven't been. Has your boyfriend never taken you?'

'What boyfriend?'

As soon as the last syllable escaped her lips a look of horror came over her face. She glanced at him for a moment, then looked away almost immediately. But it was long enough for him to see the truth in her eyes.

She'd been lying about having a boyfriend.

There was silence in the room, apart from her soft breathing and the thrum of his pulse in his ears. He lifted the glass to his lips, moistening them, as he tried to find the right thing to say. But there was nothing that he could think of to end the awkward moment, to take that look from her face.

Nothing apart from changing the subject completely, that was.

'Shall we talk about tomorrow's meeting?' he asked her. 'I know we don't have much time, and I wanted to make sure we're on the same page.'

Her shoulders relaxed, the faintest of smiles crossing her lips. 'Yes, let's do that,' she said, gesturing for him to sit down at the table. 'I'll just get the files out and we can make a start.'

*

Lucy rarely drank on a week night, and almost never more than one glass, and yet that evening she found herself pouring out a second, filling the generous goblet two-thirds of the way. She twisted the lid back on and put the bottle back in the fridge – which was where it would stay for another day – and then sat down on the sofa, lifting the glass to her lips.

As she swallowed the cool Sauvignon, she closed her eyes, savouring the crisp bouquet. Even though it was chilled, the alcohol immediately warmed her stomach, relaxing her in a way she hadn't felt for days.

What a bloody mess, and it was all of her own making. Though Lachlan hadn't mentioned her boyfriend – or lack of one – at all for the rest of the day, a couple of times she'd caught him looking at her, a question in his eyes. He didn't have to verbalise it either, she knew exactly what he was thinking. Why the hell had she lied about something so stupid?

It was a question she kept asking herself, too. She'd just made herself look completely foolish in front of a client, and though he'd been kind enough to change the subject, he couldn't help but think less of her for that.

That hurt, because his opinion of her mattered.

It was only eight o'clock, although it seemed much later, maybe it was the exhaustion kicking in. She'd be on better form tomorrow. She'd put this awful day behind her, along with her imaginary boyfriend and any stupid attraction she felt towards him whenever he walked into the room.

She had another chance to prove how good a professional she was. And this time, she wouldn't ruin it.

Taking another mouthful of wine, she pulled her laptop towards her. The screen automatically flickered to life.

She moved the cursor until it was flickering over her inbox, but then diverted it to her internet explorer, bringing up the search box. Her fingers hovered above the keys, hesitating at what she was planning to do. Because it was wrong and it was unprofessional and it proved she was losing the battle.

She drained her wine glass. What the hell, she'd be professional tomorrow.

Before she could think about it twice, she typed Lachlan's name into the little grey box, then pressed enter with her finger. Almost immediately the screen filled with results, and a line of little square images appeared, depicting Lachlan in different poses. In some he was alone, in others with a partner. She ignored them, clicking on the first article instead. It immediately took her to *Business Buzz*, a financial news website with an irreverent edge.

A photograph of Lachlan loaded up. He was wearing a dark business suit, a striped tie cutting through his white shirt. He was leaning on his desk – well, she assumed it was his desk – looking as relaxed as ever. Did nothing faze him? She scrolled down to the article, her eyes quickly scanning the words, looking for something – anything – that gave her some insight.

Thirty-four-year-old Lachlan MacLeish may come from good stock – his father owned the Fiesta Cruise Line, after all – but this up-and-coming entrepreneur is fast becoming a businessman to be reckoned with, and all in his own right. His company, MacLeish Holdings, was set up in 2007, possibly the worst time to start a business in recent economic history. But rather than let the subprime collapse slow him down, MacLeish saw an opportunity, and threw himself right in.

'I learned from my father that the best time to start anything is right now. If you wait for the stars to align, and for everything to be just perfect, you'll be waiting for ever.'

A self-confessed workaholic, MacLeish has built his business up from nothing to a company employing over 2000 people in the space of ten years. But it's not the size of his staff that's impressive, it's his portfolio that covers everything from hotels in Miami to steel mines in the Midwest. If it's profitable, MacLeish wants in on it.

Growing up in a poorer part of Miami was, says MacLeish, the best sort of education he could have hoped for. 'It was on the streets that I learned how to fight for what I wanted. I also learned that winning isn't the same as not losing. You have to keep going until there's no contender left.'

A small quote aside, MacLeish is less forthcoming about his relationship with his father. Duncan MacLeish Snr. was a notorious figure in the Miami business scene. Known locally as the Scottish Onassis, he built his own business up from scratch, creating a fleet of cruise ships from one broken-down boat.

His son was remarkably quiet on the subject of his relationship with this side of the family. 'It's a private matter,' was all he said when asked about whether he attended his father's funeral, and if they were on good terms when he died. Nevertheless, this is one businessman you should look out for. With fingers in a whole lot of American – and international – pies, Lachlan MacLeish isn't going anywhere, apart from right on up our highest earner list.

She moved the mouse, fully intending to click on the next article, but then stopped herself.

Enough was enough.

She closed the browser, and pushed on the lid to close down her laptop. She felt dirty, as though she'd been browsing through porn rather than reading what turned out to be a fairly innocuous article.

She was better than this. She was a professional through and through. She might have made an idiot of herself this morning, but she would make damn sure she didn't do it again.

She was Lucy Millicent Shakespeare. She ate American businessmen for breakfast.

12

The first thing we do, let's kill all the lawyers

– Henry VI part II

It was as if her admission yesterday morning hadn't happened at all. As though she hadn't shown him a tiny chink in her armour, revealing her soft skin beneath. He looked at her from the corner of his eye as they were waiting in the reception area, taking in the black fitted skirt and jacket, the high-necked blouse, and those shoes that should have looked sensible, yet made her legs look amazing. Not that he was looking.

She looked calm, collected and completely unaffected. Not to mention as attractive as hell. Even more attractive now he knew she didn't have a boyfriend after all.

She was still his attorney, though. He should remember that.

'Mr MacLeish, Miss Shakespeare? They're ready for you now. Please take the lift to the top floor, and you'll be escorted to the meeting room.' The receptionist smiled up at them.

Without waiting for him, Lucy walked over to the lifts and pushed the button. By the time Lachlan arrived the doors were opening.

'Are you all right?' he asked her.

'I'm fine, why wouldn't I be?' She looked serene. 'I'm used to meetings like this. They're nothing to be afraid of.'

The lift started moving, and Lucy reached out for the handrail that circled the inside of the cabin. Automatically he reached out to steady her, his hand brushing against her waist. She looked up, surprised.

And he immediately pulled it back again.

'Are you ready for this?' she asked him. 'It's a lot more personal to you than it is to me.'

'I'm fine, Lucy. In fact, I'm great.'

'So I'll do most of the talking, as we agreed,' she said, as the floor numbers ticked over. 'Feel free to add detail when you need to, but I want you to remain in the background as much as you can.'

'I'm good with that.'

'Let's not leave them in any doubt we're going to fight this. Show no weakness.' This time she smiled.

'That's what I like to hear.' He grinned back.

They came to a halt and the metal doors slid open, revealing a man standing on the other side. Almost immediately Lucy walked out, and offered her hand. 'Sinclair, it's good to see you again.'

As soon as Lachlan stepped out, she introduced them. 'Sinclair, this is my client, Lachlan MacLeish. Lachlan, this is Sinclair Dewey, representing your brother.'

'Half-brother,' Lachlan murmured.

That earned him an eyebrow raise from Lucy.

'Can I offer either of you a drink?' Sinclair asked them, as he led Lucy and Lachlan through a pair of double doors embossed with *Dewey and Clarke, Solicitors* on them. They followed him down the corridor into a large, wood-panelled boardroom at the far end.

'I'm fine, thank you,' Lucy replied. Lachlan shook his head in response, too.

On one side of the room were two large screens. One of them displayed Duncan MacLeish Jr., and on the other was the boardroom they were standing in, showing all three of them in their shining glory. He'd sent his apologies for not being there in person, but Lachlan couldn't pretend to be sorry. Having his brother thousands of miles away, his image on a flat screen put Lachlan immediately at an advantage. And that was exactly the way he liked it.

'Please sit down,' Sinclair said, pointing at the chairs opposite him. A man in his late fifties, he was well known in Edinburgh circles for only representing the richest people in the city. He turned to the screen. 'Duncan, can you hear us?'

'Yes, I can hear you.'

Lachlan stared at his brother for a moment, but Duncan was too busy looking at his phone to notice him.

'Well, let's start by saying that this meeting is without prejudice, as we agreed. And on behalf of your brother, I'd like to thank you for coming today, Mr MacLeish.'

Lachlan nodded, but said nothing. He glanced at Lucy from the corner of his eye. Her face betrayed nothing.

'As you know, we're here to discuss the claim you both have over Glencarraig Lodge.'

'And the title,' Duncan added, his voice loud through the speakers.

'It was my impression I'm the only one who has a claim,' Lachlan said mildly. 'I'm the one named in my father's will, after all. And I'm his eldest son.'

96

'Not a legitimate one, though,' Sinclair pointed out. 'And my client believes he has a fair claim on the land and the title.'

Lucy shuffled her papers, and all attention moved to her. Lachlan hid a smile. Point well made, he'd shut up now.

'Perhaps you can start by explaining why your client wishes to claim ownership of the land and title,' Lucy said, looking first at Sinclair and then at Duncan. 'As far as we know, he's shown no interest in it for years.'

'Because it's mine,' Duncan said. 'I'm the eldest legitimate son, I was brought up to be heir. Ask anybody, they'd tell you it's true.'

Lucy looked at the man on the screen. 'When did you last visit the estate, Mr MacLeish?'

'What?' Duncan frowned. 'What's that got to do with anything?'

'Miss Shakespeare, my client's claim on the estate has nothing to do with when he last visited,' Sinclair pointed out.

'I'm simply trying to work out his connection to it, and why he wants it so much,' Lucy replied, her face completely relaxed. 'Because if he has no connection then he really has no reason to stake a claim.' She gave a little laugh, though Lachlan could tell it was fake. 'I think we can all agree that there's no way my client coerced his estranged father to leave it to him, and I'd be extremely surprised if your client believes their father wasn't of sound mind when he made his will. So that means you need to demonstrate a strong and continued link to the Glencarraig estate and title in order to make a case.'

Duncan leaned forward, until his face was only inches from the screen. 'I went there all the time when I was a kid.'

Lucy nodded. 'So the last time you went there was at least

sixteen years ago?' she asked. 'Can you tell me why you haven't been there since?'

'No he can't.' Sinclair put his hand up. 'This isn't a court of law, Lucy,' he reminded her. 'We're simply trying to avoid litigation, because it's not in anybody's best interests.' He nodded at Lachlan.

Lucy looked down at the papers Lachlan had given her. 'Maybe I can ask another question instead?' she suggested. 'Mr MacLeish – Duncan – have you ever attended a MacLeish clan gathering?'

'What the hell is a gathering?' he asked.

'Duncan, don't answer that one either. This is all way off the beaten track. We're simply here to remind your client,' he said to Lucy, 'that as an illegitimate son of the previous Laird of Glencarraig, his claim to the title is tenuous at best.'

'I don't agree,' Lucy countered. 'He was named in the will and there are no caveats on the property or title stating the inheritor has to be legitimate.'

'Because nobody ever thought that an illegitimate heir would inherit.' Sinclair leaned back on his chair. 'If their father had left the land and title to a goat, we would contest that too, even though there's no caveat covering that either.'

Lachlan sat straighter in his chair. He wanted to remind them that he was actually a living, breathing person and not a goddamned goat. But Lucy reached for his hand beneath the table, and patted it, making sure neither Duncan nor Sinclair saw her movement. Lachlan didn't need to be an expert in body language to know she was telling him to keep quiet. He clasped his hands together, moving them away, making sure to keep his mouth shut.

'If that's your only argument, I think this might be the

shortest case the session court has ever seen,' she replied, her voice light.

'When was the last time you visited the damned place?' Duncan asked Lachlan. 'It's not as if you've got a link to it either.'

'I'm going tomorrow.' Lachlan smiled at his brother's anger. 'It's the first time I've been allowed to visit since I was a child. I'm looking forward to learning more about my heritage. The history of our family is fascinating, don't you think?'

Duncan stared at him, saying nothing.

'As you can see, my client feels a very great connection to Glencarraig,' Lucy said to Sinclair. 'It's not about the money for him, it's about the history, the tradition, the beauty of the land.'

Sinclair let out an inadvertent sigh. 'Let's cut to the issue, shall we? My client is very interested in making an offer of a settlement, in order to avoid court proceedings. He'd prefer not to put the family name through a long and drawn-out trial.'

'Then don't do it.' Lachlan said the words without thinking. And almost immediately Lucy's hand went under the table again, but this time his own hand wasn't there. Instead, her palm landed on his thigh, the warmth of her skin apparent through the thin barrier of his suit pants. He felt her jump in her seat next to him, pulling her hand away as fast as she could, her eyes widening as she realised what she'd touched. He had to bite on his bottom lip to stop from laughing at her horrified reaction.

'What's it going to take to pay you off?' Duncan asked. 'We both know you don't want the place.'

Lucy paused a moment longer, as though collecting herself, before she finally addressed Sinclair. 'Mr MacLeish isn't willing to settle. And as far as we're concerned any claim lodged in court will be seen as frivolous. I think we all know we'll win, and on top of that we'll counterclaim for costs.' She looked over at Sinclair, whose face remained impassive. 'This could be an expensive mistake for your client.'

'So there's nothing we can do to persuade you to compromise?' Sinclair asked them.

'Nothing at all.'

On the screen, Duncan was shaking his head.

'Then this meeting has come to an end,' Sinclair said, glancing back up at his client. 'We have no choice but to file a claim against you.'

'There's always a choice,' Lucy pointed out. 'You could drop the whole idea completely.'

Slowly, Sinclair shook his head. 'This is about more than just an inheritance. This is about family and my client's right to be seen as the Laird of Glencarraig. I'm certain we can persuade the court of the veracity of his claim, against a man who isn't even entitled to bear the MacLeish name.'

'Then we'll see you in court.'

'I think that went rather well.' As soon as they made it out of the office building and down the steps, Lucy allowed a smile to break out on her face. 'They were on the back foot from the start.'

'You were cool as a cucumber in there.' Once they reached the bottom of the steps he stopped and looked at her. 'Thank you.' He didn't mention her touching his thigh by accident, and for that she was grateful. After yesterday's faux pas, she really didn't need to be embarrassed any further.

She shrugged. 'It was a pleasure. You wanted to take the fight to them and it worked. Now you need to go up to the

Highlands and stake your claim. Make sure you meet all the locals and tell them how delighted you are to be laird.'

A car pulled up at the edge of the pavement, and Lachlan waved at the driver but didn't make a move. 'I'd like you to come with me,' he said, turning to look at her. 'You know this country and the people. I need your advice while I'm there.'

Her own taxi pulled up behind his car. She nodded at it, and the driver waved back.

'You do?' Her mouth felt suddenly dry. 'Are you sure?'

Of course it made sense for her to go up to Glencarraig with him. She'd be able to talk to the staff, to find out more about the estate, and make sure the interview he'd arranged with a journalist went according to plan.

But the thought of spending two days with this man in the middle of nowhere scared her to death. She'd already stumbled twice, who knew how many lives she had left?

'Yes I'm sure.' He nodded, still looking straight at her. 'I don't want to come across as an idiot. This visit is important to me, and I'll need your help.'

The smile he gave her was thoroughly disarming. Enough for her to mentally check through her diary, and to think about how much petrol she had left in her car. Enough for her to think about her overnight bag, and how she'd already re-packed it after her trip to Miami.

'I'll need to move around a couple of things. There's a meeting first thing tomorrow morning I can't miss.' She couldn't believe she was agreeing to this. 'But I could drive up and meet you there before lunch.'

'That works for me. I'm heading up after breakfast, so it'll give me a chance to scout things out. I'll call the estate manager and let him know you'll be coming.' He reached out and touched her fingers, giving them a half-shake half-squeeze. 'I'll see you tomorrow.'

And as he walked to his car, the driver jumping out to open the back door, she found herself staring at him, and wondering how on earth she'd got herself into this situation. Calm, confident and professional, wasn't that what she was supposed to be?

Then why did she feel so flustered every time he was around?

13

Oh Scotland, Scotland
– Macbeth

The drive to the Highlands had taken just over three hours. Lucy had left Edinburgh in a mist of drizzle, the grey clouds casting a pall across the sandstone buildings of the city. But after she passed Perth and joined the A9, the rain turned to sleet, obscuring the views of the beautiful green hills that she knew were there. So much for springtime.

The entrance to the Glencarraig estate was through two huge wrought-iron gates, attached to brown walls that must have circled the land. She turned her car onto the sweeping gravel driveway, bordered on each side with majestic alder trees, which led to the rambling lodge. The large, castle-like building was surrounded by heather, the purple flowers almost coming into first bloom, reflected in the glass-like water. It felt like stepping back in time, to a Scotland she'd only learned about at university, a place where the clans ruled the land, and real men wore kilts.

The photographs she'd seen really didn't do the place justice. And for the first time, she had a glimpse of exactly what Lachlan was fighting for.

By the time she'd parked up, next to a large Bentley and a smaller, sportier car, Lachlan had opened the main door and was walking down the steps. As she climbed out she could hear his feet crunching against the gravel.

A solitary snowflake drifted down from the heavy grey sky, landing on her cheek. She looked up, feeling it melt against her skin, leaving a cold wet kiss before it disappeared.

She shivered, in spite of the thick coat she was wearing.

'Welcome to Glencarraig,' Lachlan said, reaching out for her bag. 'You made good time.'

He looked as relaxed as ever, wearing a pair of dark jeans and a light grey cashmere sweater that somehow matched their surroundings. She took in a deep breath of Highland air, feeling the rush of oxygen relax her. She'd been looking forward to seeing him again, and yet dreading it at the same time. But now she was here, everything felt right.

'I'm disappointed,' she said, glancing down at his legs. 'I was expecting a kilt.'

He grinned, leading her over to the steps that led up to the lodge. 'I thought I'd save that for later. Didn't want to send you into a frenzy as soon as you arrived.'

She stifled a laugh. 'I'll look forward to that.'

'I bet you will.'

A man was standing in the entranceway, where the black lacquered doors had been opened wide. He was older – maybe fifty or so – and wearing a pair of brown woollen trousers and a tweed jacket, patched at the elbows.

'How long have you been here?' she asked Lachlan, as they made their way up the stairs.

'I got here about an hour ago. Alistair let me in.' He nodded at the man who was watching them. 'He's the estate manager.'

Alistair walked forward to meet them as they reached the top of the steps. 'Miss Shakespeare, it's a pleasure to meet you.' He had a low Scottish brogue – it sounded almost lyrical. 'There's coffee brewing in the kitchen, and the cook has made some biscuits for you.'

She shook his hand, enjoying its warmth against her cold skin. 'It's a pleasure to meet you, too. And please call me Lucy.'

'Lucy it is.'

They made their way into the hall, a huge double-storeyed room with a sweeping staircase that flanked both sides. Lachlan placed her bag on the floor, and they followed the older man, who Lucy assumed was leading them to the kitchen.

'Alistair's worked here for over thirty years,' Lachlan said as they made their way down the corridor. The floor was laid with huge grey flagstones – beautiful to look at but no doubt freezing on the feet. 'He started off looking after the livestock and worked his way up.'

'You must have seen it all.' They finally reached the kitchen. Lucy could feel the warmth hit her as soon as they stepped inside. It smelled of vanilla and sugar, a delicious combination. Her stomach rumbled at the onslaught.

'Things have changed quite a lot over the years,' Alistair said. 'We've renovated the lodge, built up the salmon stock, and then of course had broadband put in, which wasn't easy with us being so remote.' He looked pleased at being asked. 'There's a lot more to do, of course. This heating system needs a total overhaul, and we've been in constant talks with the phone networks about trying to improve the signal.' He smiled. 'For our visitors, it's a blessing and a curse being so remote and cut off.'

'If you've been here thirty years, you must have been here

when Lachlan visited,' she said. She felt Lachlan stop next to her. 'Do you remember him?'

'Of course. I remember taking him and his brother out on a hunt one day. And I was always shooing them away from the loch, they were fascinated by it.'

She turned to look at Lachlan. Two tiny lines formed between his brows as he frowned. 'Do you remember that?' she asked him.

'Not at all.' He gave her a small smile. 'I remember the house and the land, spending time walking out by the loch. But I don't ever remember spending time with Duncan.'

There was a wistfulness to his tone she'd never heard before. Outside of his office – and those suits that always made him look so in charge – there was a softer edge to him, and it only made him more intriguing.

'Do you have any records of when he visited?' she asked Alistair. 'Guest books or photographs or something? It would be good to have some solid evidence.'

Alistair leaned on the kitchen counter, rubbing his chin with his thumb. 'We must have somewhere. I'll ask my staff to look through the old records. Everything's up at the estate office, in the old gatehouse now.'

'There's no rush,' Lucy said. 'It would just be good to see.'

Lachlan shifted next to her again. Maybe he wasn't quite as relaxed as she'd thought.

'Have you had a chance to look around yet?' she asked him.

'No. We thought we'd wait for you. We have a few hours before the journalist is due to arrive, so we can fit it in.'

Marina Simpson, a journalist from the *Scottish Times*, had agreed to run a piece on Lachlan in their Sunday supplement.

It had seemed like a good idea to stake his claim on the public record.

'That sounds lovely.' She smiled at him. 'And have you arranged to meet all the staff?'

Lachlan looked amused at her question. 'Yes, Lucy, I have. And Alistair's booked us in for lunch in the village pub tomorrow, so we can meet the locals.'

'Here's your coffee.' Alistair passed her a mug. Steam rose from the rim, as she lifted it to her lips. 'And help yourself to biscuits.'

Lachlan took two and passed one to her, his fingertips brushing against hers as she took it. She felt that tiny buzz again, as though she'd touched a low-volt electric fence.

'Thank you,' she murmured, then took another sip of her coffee, ignoring the smile that had broken out on Lachlan's face. Either he'd felt the buzz too or he'd seen her reaction to it, and either scenario felt dangerous.

It was going to be a long twenty-four hours.

'So tell me, Lachlan, when did you discover you were going to be the Laird of Glencarraig?' Marina Simpson asked. The three of them were sitting in the wood-panelled drawing room, Lachlan and Marina on the easy chairs while Lucy perched on the window seat behind them, trying to keep out of the conversation. Since the journalist's arrival an hour ago, the skies had darkened further, and Alistair had built a roaring fire in the brick-built hearth to head off the early April chill.

'When my father's will was read,' Lachlan replied smoothly. 'It was mentioned in that.'

'Ah yes, your father, he was an interesting man. Tell me a bit about him.'

Lucy leaned forward, away from the window. Her breath had misted up the glass. She listened carefully, tipping her head to the side. Her thoughts immediately went back to that article she'd read. Lachlan had been very vague about his father in that.

'What do you want to know?'

'What kind of man was he? From all accounts I hear he was a bit of a recluse. Is that right?'

'He was a self-made man,' Lachlan replied. 'He built up a business from nothing. In his later years he preferred to spend time enjoying the fruits of his labour rather than stay in the spotlight.'

'Not quite self-made,' Marina pointed out. 'He was a laird before he moved to America, wasn't he?'

'A very poor one, yes. He worked his way up until he had enough money to buy his first ship. After that he built up his business until it became the premier cruise liner company in the world. That's a pretty big achievement for a Scottish boy who left the country with practically nothing.'

'You sound very proud of him,' Marina said. 'And understandably so. But I also hear that all wasn't well with the two of you when he died. Tell me a little about the family rift.'

Lachlan shifted on the sofa. An imperceptible move to most people, but Lucy could see his back straightening. 'There wasn't a rift.'

Lucy held her breath. The next moment he was looking over at her, his blue eyes meeting hers. Exhaling softly, she gave him a reassuring smile.

He didn't return it.

'Your parents weren't married, is that correct?' Marina went on.

'That's correct.' Lachlan nodded.

He shifted in his seat, crossing one leg over the other. His left jaw twitched as he stared back at the journalist.

'That must have been hard for you, growing up with the stigma of illegitimacy hanging over you. Especially as your father was already married when you were conceived.'

Outside the window, a flurry of snowflakes fell, dancing as the breeze lifted them before letting them reach the ground. But Lucy was far more interested in what was happening inside the lodge. The frosty atmosphere in the drawing room could rival the biting temperatures outside.

On the sofa, Lachlan leaned his head to the side, keeping his gaze on Marina. 'Many children suffer hardships,' he said. 'It's how we learn and grow.'

'But you appear to have suffered more than most,' she pointed out. She seemed unperturbed by Lachlan's intense stare. 'According to your bio, you grew up in relative poverty, in spite of your father's wealth. Why was that?'

'You'd have to ask my parents,' Lachlan said. 'And compared to some kids I was lucky. I always had a roof over my head, food on the table. I wasn't exactly living in a shack.'

'Well, I can't ask your father.' The journalist gave a little laugh. 'But maybe I could speak to your mother some time.'

'That won't be possible,' Lachlan replied. His tone left no room for questions.

Lucy swallowed, though her mouth felt dry. Lachlan was as stiff as a board. She shifted in her own seat, trying to get comfortable.

'Maybe you could tell me some more about your mother then,' Marina said, rifling through her papers. 'I managed to find out a little bit about her from a few sources.'

'You did?' Was it possible for his voice to sound even shorter? 'Why?'

Marina brushed her dark hair from her face. 'It's my job, Lachlan. If I turned up here without doing my research what sort of journalist would I be?'

Lachlan swallowed, but said nothing.

Marina tapped her pen against her teeth, then put it back down on her pad. 'Well, if I can't speak to her, maybe I can ask you. How did she and your father meet? Is it correct that she was an escort?'

Lucy's mouth dropped open. She sat very still and looked between Marina and Lachlan again. She could see the tightness of his jaw, the narrowness of his eyes.

'No. She was a nightclub hostess,' he replied. 'But I'm not sure what that has to do with anything.'

'Is that how they met?' Marina asked again. 'Did your father pay her for ... ah ... favours?'

'I've never asked how they met.'

Marina scribbled something on her pad. 'And what does your mother do now?'

Though Lachlan's face was impassive, his hands were clasped together so tightly Lucy could see the white of his knuckles. And then he glanced at her, and he looked almost like a child. Vulnerable, hurt, in need of protection.

So completely unlike him it brought Lucy to her feet. 'Is that the time?' she said, walking over to where Lachlan and Marina were sitting. 'It will be dark soon, and we'd love you to take a walk around the estate before you leave, Marina. And I know your photographer was hoping to get some photographs of Lachlan while the light is good.'

'But I have some more questions—'

110

'No problem at all. Just send them over and I'll get Lachlan to answer them.' Lucy wasn't taking no for an answer. 'Why don't I get somebody to bring you and the photographer a cup of tea, and then we'll get on with the pictures?'

The old estate office smelled musty – as though the rain that had soaked through the stone walls for centuries could never quite be chased away. It was located in the gatehouse – a small, turreted cottage built with the same stone as the main lodge – where once upon a time the estate manager would have lived, his whole life squeezed into these tiny rooms. Nowadays Alistair lived in his own cottage in the nearby village, leaving the gatehouse to be the main administrative offices, though of course there was a much more luxurious library in the main house that Lachlan's father had used whenever he visited.

Lachlan looked up from the spreadsheets he'd been surveying, and across the ancient wooden desk to where Alistair was sitting. 'You've kept good records.'

'For what they're worth. We keep the place ticking over, but it really needs investment. To attract the kind of paying guests the lodge needs to keep it going, we should be offering luxury. The Americans expect it.' Alistair offered Lachlan a small smile.

'What kind of investment?' Lachlan was interested. He leaned forward, scanning the sheets again.

'I don't know. A lot, I guess?' Alistair shrugged. 'We've done the basics, the wifi and the roof, and that was far more than your father wanted to pay. But the kind of clients we want to attract would be executives. Investing in an upgrade would help a lot.'

Lachlan nodded, his hand still hovering on the keypad.

Talking about business made him feel steadier, as though he was on firmer ground. 'I'll need to get my finance guys to run the figures. Do you have any estimates of the type of income we could attract?'

'At the moment we run a few hunting weekends a year,' he said. 'But some of the other estates are fully booked, and host weddings as well. I don't know how much you know about the MacLeish diaspora, but we have a lot of clansmen all over the world who'd jump at the chance to learn about their heritage, surrounded by luxury.'

'The diaspora?' Lachlan questioned.

'Scottish people who emigrated abroad. Did you know there are more MacLeishes in Canada and America than there are here in Scotland?'

Lachlan tipped his head to the side. 'No. I had no idea.'

'There are also thousands of MacLeishes in Australia, New Zealand, Brazil ... Honestly, they're all over the world. And because they're in a new world, they want to know about their past, their heritage. That's where we come in. A lot of them already visit us during the MacLeish Gathering, though the majority stay in the village. I'd like to build on that.'

Lachlan tapped his fingers on the old oak desk. 'I read about the gathering on the website.'

'Oh, you've seen that?'

'Yeah, that was one of the things I wanted to talk to you about. Who runs it? One of us?'

Alistair looked pleased. 'I do. I set it up and maintain it; it's pretty easy really, based on a WordPress site. And we have social networks too. I even set up a Twitter page last year.'

'There's a lot of information there,' Lachlan observed. 'Your knowledge of MacLeish history is impressive.'

The smile on Alistair's face widened. He leaned forward, resting his leather-patched elbows on the table. 'I've worked on this estate for more than half my life. My wife tells me I'm obsessed.' He gave a little laugh. 'But seriously, it was only when I set up the website that I realised how interested people were. After that we started having gatherings every year. People fly in from all the corners of the earth for the weekend. We have a church service, a tour of the estate, and then the highlight of the weekend is the garden party.' He lowered his voice again, as though somebody was listening. 'And I mean it as no disrespect to you at all, Mr MacLeish, but the Americans especially really lap it up.'

Lachlan smiled widely. 'I bet they do.'

Glancing down once again at the figures, Lachlan turned the possibilities over in his mind. The kind of investment Alistair was proposing was huge, and it would take a massive jump in income to compensate for it. If he was looking at it from a pure investor's eye he'd turn it down.

But this wasn't just an investment, was it? It was a legacy, given to him by a man he'd hardly known, in a country he'd hardly visited. He had a lot to think about.

Turning his head, he stared out of the small window that overlooked the lodge itself. The flurry of snowflakes that had accompanied their walk up here earlier had stopped, and a shaft of sunlight had broken through the clouds, shining down on the loch behind the building, the surface reflecting the mountains beyond. It was strange how little he could remember of this place – or of the people who worked here, come to that.

Pushing down on his feet, Lachlan stood, his muscles complaining about being confined to the old office chair for too long. His mind wasn't feeling much better, either. After yesterday's confrontation with his brother, and today's interview with the journalist – not to mention Alistair's single-handed push to save the MacLeish name – he needed to do something to clear it.

'I think I'll take a walk,' he told Alistair. 'Just up to the loch.'

Alistair looked up. 'Of course. You should wrap up warm, though. The sun might be trying to come out, but those rays do nothing to warm the air up until summer gets here. That beautiful view can be deceiving.'

Lachlan nodded and grabbed his coat, looping his scarf around his neck. Lifting his hand in a goodbye, he left the gatehouse and found himself walking back along the gravelled driveway, and then taking a left around the east wing of the lodge.

'You seem to be working hard.'

Lucy looked up to see Alistair standing in the doorway of the library.

'I just had a few emails to send,' she told him, stretching out her arms. 'Have you finished your meeting with Lachlan?'

'Yes, we're all done for now.' Alistair nodded. 'I'm going to head back to my cottage for the evening. Is there anything else you need?'

'Where's Lachlan?' she asked. 'Is he around somewhere?'

'He headed out for a walk,' Alistair told her. 'He said something about seeing the loch.'

'In this weather?' She glanced at the half-frosted window, overlooking the grounds. The snow had stopped as soon as it started, but the frosty air remained. Even inside there was a chill she couldn't quite shake off.

'He wrapped up warm, don't you worry.' Alistair gave her a smile. 'And from what I can tell, fairer weather is on its way, finally. You might miss it, though, which is a shame. Maybe you can come back in the summer.'

'Maybe.' She smiled back at him. 'It's certainly very charming.'

'Well, good evening, Miss Shakespeare. I believe the cook has dinner in the oven for you. I hope you have a restful night.'

After Alistair left, she stared at her laptop for a while longer, scrolling through her emails and answering the urgent ones. But her heart wasn't in it. She kept thinking of Lachlan, of him walking out in the cold, frosty air. Was he still thinking about the interview? They hadn't had much chance to talk since Marina left, but she couldn't help but think about the expression on his face when the journalist had asked her intrusive questions.

Lucy felt a pull, like a boat being tugged into the shore. It was inevitable that she would find her coat and scarf, and slide her legs into her polished brown leather boots, shaking her hair to free it as she walked out of the front door and down the steps. Before she knew it her feet were crunching against the blades of grass, as she walked in the direction of the valley.

After a few minutes she found herself approaching the loch, marvelling at the blue water as it reached the frozen shore. In the distance she could see snow-topped mountains, their white peaks reflected in the mirror-like surface. On the other side were a series of rocks, brown crags – or carraigs – that gave the estate its name.

From the corner of her eye she noticed a movement. A flash of brown against the green background. Slowly she turned her head to see a proud stag standing in the distance, his antlers still, yet menacing. She couldn't help but think of that Landseer painting again.

'Don't move.' Lachlan's voice came from her left. 'I saw some does earlier, but I didn't expect to see the stag, too.'

Lachlan was standing as straight and tall as the stag. His vulnerability from earlier had gone, replaced by a ruggedness that mirrored his surroundings. A gust of wind lifted up his dark hair, revealing his smooth brow, unfurrowed by lines.

'He's beautiful,' she whispered, afraid to disturb the scene ahead of them. 'So elegant and grand.'

'If my father were here, he'd shoot him.'

'Then it's a good job your father isn't here,' she said, smiling.

The stag slowly turned to look at them, his disdain for all things human clear on his face. Then he shook his head, leaning onto his back legs before he pushed himself into a run, cantering around the side of the lake and into the woods beyond.

There was something so beautiful about the scene before them, that it took her breath away. There was no sign of civilisation, no sign of humans at all, just nature at her wildest, rising up in craggy mountains and dipping down into wooded glades. They could have been in any moment in history, and the view would have been the same.

'I'm not sure I've ever seen anything so lovely,' she whispered.

'This is the view I remember,' Lachlan said, his voice as quiet as hers. 'When I was a kid I'd come out here and pretend I was just an animal like the deer and the fish. That I didn't have any worries, that I didn't have to fight and scramble my way through life. I haven't thought about it for years, but now I'm here, it's all coming back.'

116

She looked at him out of the corner of her eye. He was staring right at her, his eyes gentle. And just like that he took her breath away again, more than the stag, more than the view. When Lachlan MacLeish was around, everything else faded into insignificance.

'It's views like this that make me think that one day I'll give up the rat race and spend my time travelling,' she said. 'I spend so much of my time looking at the same four walls, it's easy to forget how beautiful the world can be.'

'I hear you,' Lachlan agreed. 'Grant once did an analysis of how I spent my year. Apparently I was fifty-one per cent in the office, twenty-four per cent on airplanes and twenty-one per cent at home. That only left four per cent of the time that I was actually out in the open air. And most of that was spent running.'

'Do you run every day?' she asked him, remembering their conversation while he was in Central Park. The way he'd barely had to catch his breath while they spoke.

'Whenever I can,' he said, smiling at the thought.

'Do you like it?' she asked him. 'Or is it just one of those things you do to stay healthy, like drinking water and eating your five a day?'

'It's not so much that I like it, more that I'd go crazy without it. Sometimes I can only jump on the treadmill in my office for half an hour, but even that's better than nothing. It's the one time I can clear my mind, and just be present in the moment.'

'Except when you're talking to me.'

He laughed, and it lit up his face. 'Touché.' He turned until he was looking right at her, only a few feet between them. 'How about you?' he asked, that soft look back in his eyes. 'Do you run?'

'Only if my house is on fire.' She shrugged. 'I have a gym membership that's not been used for the last eighteen months. Apparently you have to actually go for it to make a difference.'

'Who knew?'

'Seriously, though, I should go more often. I'm just always so busy. If I'm not at the office, I'm catching up with work at home. There's not a lot of time to get on the treadmill.'

Lachlan frowned at her answer, as though it made him sad. 'What do you do to relax?'

'Go out with friends, talk with my sisters. Oh, and I have timeshare on a cat. That's a good way to be mindful.'

'You have a cat?' he asked.

'Don't look so surprised.' She smiled at his expression. 'And no, I don't really own her. She's just this little tabby that belongs to my downstairs neighbours. She seems to have become attached to me – every time I come home she's waiting, and slinks into my apartment with me. Then she curls up next to me while I finish my work.'

'Lucky cat.'

Their eyes met and her heart thudded against her chest. 'She stops me from being a boring old workaholic, I guess.'

He raised an eyebrow. 'I might have a thing for boring old workaholics.'

'What kind of thing?'

He grinned. 'Are you really asking me about my thing? I thought we were professionals. Now here you are, interrogating me about—'

'Stop it.' She was grinning too.

He reached out, his arm closing the distance between them, running his gloved finger across her cheek. It was the smallest

118

of touches, yet it felt so intimate, so sensual, that it set her whole body on fire.

'There's never a dull moment with you,' he murmured.

Right back at you, Mr MacLeish.

Though a barrier of leather separated her skin from his, Lachlan could practically feel the chill on her face as he stroked his finger along her jaw. Her cheeks were bright pink, her eyes shining, her lips a deep red from the cold. It had been a mistake to get so close. With only a few inches between them, his whole body was begging him to close the gap. He wanted to taste the cold on her lips, to heat them with his own. He wanted to slide his tongue inside that soft, velvety mouth, to feel her breath battling with his.

He'd thought of her as a cool blonde before. But out here in the wild, she was so much more than that. It was as though she'd thawed along with the dusting of snow on the ground, exposing her real self. Not the perfectly groomed, perfectly professional Lucy she projected in meetings, but a softer, gentler side that was only for him.

After the few days he'd had, she was like a crackling log fire after a cold spell, and he wanted to bask in her.

'Am I crazy for wanting to keep this place?' he asked her.

Was it his imagination, or was she leaning closer into his hand? 'Almost certainly,' she said, closing her eyes for a moment. 'But why would that stop you?'

'It would take a massive investment.' He ran his thumb across her cheek. It took everything he had not to pull his glove off, to remove the final barrier between them. It was crazy the way she pulled him in every time, he couldn't escape, even if he wanted to. 'Renovating this place would be a fool's errand.'

She turned her head to look at the space where the stag had stood. All that remained were his footprints now. 'But it isn't always about money, is it?' she asked him.

His hand hovered in the air as she moved her head away. Reluctantly he pulled it back, resting it at his side. How was it that he already missed their connection? There was something so addictive about it. Like a drug, he wanted her, but knew she was going to kill him in the end.

'No,' he agreed. 'It was never about the money. But I don't want to lose money on it, either.'

'I guess it depends how you look at it,' she said, staring at the trees where the stag disappeared. 'People pay money to go on holiday all the time. They come back with nothing but memories. The same goes for hobbies – what one person calls a waste of money, another one thinks of as money well spent.'

'Are you saying I should keep this place as a hobby?' Lachlan asked, amused. 'Do you know how much it costs to run?'

A ray of sun had fought its way through the grey layer of cloud, and she squinted where it hit her face. 'All I know is that if I owned this place I could never let it go. No matter how much I was going to lose.'

The first time he'd seen her, in that Miami restaurant, he'd thought she was attractive. But standing there in the middle of the Scottish Highlands, surrounded by rocks and water untouched by time, he could see she was so much more than that. Beautiful, captivating, untouchable.

She was temptation, made into a woman. And he wasn't sure how much longer he could hold out.

14

I that did never weep now melt with woe. That
winter did cut off our springtime so

– Henry VI, Part III

'So tell me again, you're in some castle in the middle of nowhere, with Mr Hotty McLaird in the bedroom down the hallway, and you decided you wanted to talk to me. What the hell are you thinking?' Kitty sounded amused. They were chatting on Skype, so much better than trying to use the non-existent mobile connection. Lucy made a mental note to thank Alistair for the powerful wifi.

'He's not a hotty,' she told her sister. 'He's my client.' She didn't sound too convincing.

'Luce, I just Googled him. If he's not hot, then Adam's not the best documentary maker in the whole wide world. Which he is, by the way.'

'How is Adam? Has he started that new project yet?' Lucy asked.

'Oh no, don't you go trying to change the subject; I know you too well.' Kitty laughed, sounding delighted to finally turn the tables and interrogate her older sister. 'So come on, spill. Is he as gorgeous in real life as he looks on the computer screen?'

Lucy shivered, pulling the covers up to her chin. Glencarraig may have been the most beautiful place she'd ever seen, but the lodge was absolutely freezing. There was an old iron radiator in the corner of the room, but it had long since given up with its battle against the cold. Every time she exhaled, her breath lingered in front of her in a smoky curtain. Even her goosebumps had goosebumps.

'Have you been talking to Cesca?' Lucy asked. 'Because you sound exactly like her.'

'Maybe.'

Lucy sighed. 'He's easy on the eye,' she said. 'If you like that kind of thing.'

'And he's rich,' Kitty said. 'Not to mention he looks amazing in a tux. Did you see the picture of him at the Met Gala last year?'

'Kitty, please stop ogling my client,' Lucy said, letting her head fall back on the headrest. 'It's unprofessional.'

'So what?' Kitty asked, a smile still in her voice. 'Professionalism means nothing when it comes to attraction. Look at me and Adam, I was supposed to be working for his brother but I ended up falling for him anyway.'

'That's different.'

'How?' She sounded genuinely interested.

'Because you were just nannying for a few weeks. If something happened between me and a client it could put my whole career on the line. I've worked really hard to get where I am, and I'm not going to jeopardise it over some guy I've just met.'

'But you *are* attracted to him, right?'

Lucy pursed her lips together, blowing out a mouthful of air. She watched as it turned to vapour again. 'I don't know,' she admitted. 'Maybe a bit. But it doesn't make any difference.'

'Oh Luce.'

'Don't Luce me.'

'I'll Luce you all I want. And if anybody deserves a good Lucing it's you.'

Lucy laughed. 'What the heck are you talking about?'

'Look, this guy, Lachlan. He's easy on the eye, he's sexy, and from what you've told me you're wildly attracted to him.'

'I didn't say anything about wild.'

'And he likes you too. Right?' Kitty prompted.

'I don't know—'

'He flew into Edinburgh and demanded you drop everything to spend the next twenty-four hours with him, when we both know a guy like him doesn't need to be babysat by you. He's practically perfect. So why are you sitting alone in your room and talking to me, when you could be ravishing the crusty old laird?'

'He's not crusty.'

'I know.'

'Or old.'

'Mm hmm.'

'And he's not a laird. Not yet.'

'But you still want to ravish him, right?'

'It's not funny.' Lucy squeezed her eyes shut for a moment, wanting to block everything out. 'I'm doing everything I can to be a professional here. Can't you give me a bit of support?'

'You can resist all you want,' Kitty said, 'but you can't fight against nature. When the attraction is there, it's impossible to ignore. Believe me, I know.'

Funny how Kitty had emerged from her shell since she'd met Adam last winter. And now she seemed to think she was the fount of all knowledge when it came to relationships.

123

'We're not savages,' Lucy pointed out. 'I'm a grown woman, I'm pretty sure I can control myself.'

'You keep believing that,' Kitty said. 'And next week you can tell me how Santa Claus truly exists, and that the Tooth Fairy is building a palace with all of our molars.'

'Goodbye, Kitty.' Lucy pulled the phone away from her ear, and stuck her tongue out at the screen.

Kitty was too busy laughing to reply.

Her room was silent apart from a gurgle every now and then from the all-but-redundant radiator in the corner. Out in the hallway she could hear every creak and groan that an old building had to give, plus a few extra screeches and scratches added in for good measure. She shivered in her bed – more from the cold than from fear – her fleecy button-up pyjamas and sleep socks no match for the cold Highland breeze.

A deep peel of bells from the grandfather clock in the entrance hall echoed through the corridors, telling her with twelve rings that midnight had finally arrived. She turned on her side, curling her body into a ball, willing herself to go to sleep.

Another noise. This time from her phone, charging beside her on the table. She picked it up, scanning the message.

Are you asleep?

So Lachlan was messaging her in the middle of the night. Somehow that felt more dangerous than being close to him.

She decided to cut him off quickly, tapping out a reply.

Yes

124

His reply was almost immediate.

Liar

In spite of the frigid temperature, she could feel a fire start to
burn inside her. The corner of her lip turned up.

Is there something I can help you with,
Mr MacLeish, or do you message all your
attorneys in the middle of the night

You type amazingly well for a sleeping person.

The smile finally burst out on her face. Kitty was right, he was
hard to ignore.

If I could be asleep, I would. It's almost impossible
to sleep in sub-zero temperatures. Somebody needs
to tell Glencarraig spring is supposed to be here.

It's cold in there? It's like a goddamn furnace in here.

What?

The next minute her phone was ringing. She didn't need to
glance at the screen to know who it was. 'Lachlan.'

'You're cold?' he asked, his voice deep and low.

'Freezing,' she told him. 'Even the radiator's put its coat on.'

He laughed. 'What about your fire? Is that not keeping you
warm?'

'What fire?'

His laugh got louder.

'No, I'm serious, what bloody fire?' She was indignant. 'I haven't got a fire. Have you got a fire?'

'Yes, I have. A big orange one. It's as hot as Hades in here.'

'That's not fair.' She wanted to pout. 'Where's my fire?'

'I could build you one up,' he offered. 'Are there logs in your room?'

'There's not even a fireplace.' She shook her head, even though he couldn't see her. 'How come you get the hot room?'

'I'm practically the laird. I get all the good stuff.' His tone was enough to tell her he was teasing. Didn't stop her from wanting to hit him. And kiss him.

Stop that right now.

She huffed. 'I'm sending a complaint in tomorrow. Right to the top.'

'They'll be quaking in their boots, I bet,' Lachlan said. 'Pretty much like you are now.'

'Shut up.'

'Ah, you're full of the one-liners tonight.'

'It's hard to think of one-liners when your whole body is succumbing to frostbite. Seriously, what kind of place is this? Why would they put me in this room when you have the fire?'

'You want to swap?' His offer sounded genuine. For a moment she imagined climbing into his bed. Would it still smell of him? Would she be able to feel where he'd been lying? Would it still hold his warmth?

'No,' she managed. 'I'm fine.'

'You're not fine. You should come in here.'

'But then you'll freeze,' she pointed out. 'It's fine, I can take it for one night. And after that all bets are off.'

'Lucy, just get your butt in here. I'm your client, and that's an order.'

She hesitated, not sure if she was turned on or appalled by his offer. In the end, good sense won out. 'Good night, Lachlan. Sleep tight.' Not waiting for his reply, she ended the call, and for good measure turned her ringer to silent. There was temptation, and then there was *temptation*. The only way to avoid it was to pretend it didn't exist.

Banging her phone on the bedside table with a satisfying thump, she lay back in her bed, folding her arms across her chest. She closed her eyes, scrunching them tightly, but it was no good. She was too on edge to sleep. Her mind was too full of him, thoughts punching at her skull like a middleweight determined to win the title.

She huffed, turning on her side, curling her legs up to try to conserve the warmth. But it was only getting colder, the night air stealing into her room through the gaps in the window.

It was like the Arctic in here.

She sat straight up, pulling her fleece pyjama top a little closer around her. Without letting herself think, she swung her feet onto the wooden boards and padded across the room, her footsteps almost inaudible. Within moments she was standing in front of a large oak door, all too aware that on the other side was the man she couldn't get out of her mind, no matter how hard she tried.

She lifted her hand, curling her fingers into her palm to form a fist. But just as she moved it forward, about to knock on his door, good sense got the better of her.

What the hell was she doing?

She was his attorney, not his lover. She had no place to be standing outside his bedroom, no matter how cold she was.

The layer of professionalism she'd worked so hard to cultivate was stretched so thin it was almost broken.

She walked backwards, pulling her fist tightly to her side, then turned and all but ran back to her room, not caring if he heard the footsteps. Her heart was pounding when she climbed back into bed, though it had done nothing to warm her body. The only place that had any heat was the redness on her cheeks.

Her door creaked, and she looked up to see it opening. Lachlan stepped inside, wearing pyjama pants and nothing else. She could see every ridge of muscle in his torso, exposed in the pale glow of her bedside lamp. Dear God, if she'd thought him attractive before, it was nothing compared to this overwhelming desire she was feeling now.

He didn't say a word. Instead, he walked towards her and lifted the blankets away, scooping her up as if she weighed next to nothing. He cradled her against his bare chest, and she reflexively grasped onto the tops of his arms, afraid she might fall.

He was all hard muscle and supple skin. Not an ounce of fat nestled among the ridges of his deltoids. And he was warm, so so warm. She couldn't help but press her face against his chest, closing her eyes to inhale him. He turned, carrying her out of the bedroom, his footsteps getting louder as he reached the wooden floor in the hallway. Then he was carrying her into his bedroom, across the carpet and to the four-poster bed on the far side.

He laid her on the mattress, pulling the covers back over her, before climbing in beside her. The bed was tiny for a double. There was no escaping him if she tried.

Her whole body was shivering, as though it had finally

realised just what it was missing out on. The fire in the hearth crackled and spat, the orange light glowing on the whitewashed walls. Then he was reaching out for her, pulling her body against his. His arms wrapped around her waist, holding her tightly.

The thin layer of professionalism she'd worked so hard to conserve melted into the warm air. She curled into him, closing her eyes. 'God, I'm so cold,' she whispered, pressing her face against his chest, her ice-cold flesh meeting his heat.

'I'm trying to get you warm,' he told her. 'The quickest way is body heat. Like in those survival shows on TV.' He slid his hands beneath her pyjama top, and a series of shivers snaked up and down her spine.

Neither of them spoke as he held her tightly, her skin slowly thawing as his warm flesh pressed against her. Every time she inhaled she could smell him – woody, earthy, unbearably sexy.

Then he started to rub her back in slow, sensuous circles, his palms hot and smooth. She couldn't help but arch into his touch, her whole body coming alive with each movement, like a frozen landscape melting into spring.

Was it wrong that her hips started to circle in time, pressing against him with each rotation? Was it wrong that her whole body was tingling, her nipples hard and peaked against his skin? If that was wrong, then the heat forming between her thighs was so sinful it didn't bear thinking about.

She lifted her head to look at him. He was staring down at her with an intensity that shot straight through her. Her lips parted, enough for her to force out the air that wanted to stay captured in her throat. Everything about him was consuming.

He moved his hands down her back, his fingers leaving a

129

trail of fire and ice along her spine. His palms pressed into the dip just above her bottom, sending her nerve endings into a frenzy of activity. His cloth-covered thigh was between hers, causing a delightful friction that made her whole body tingle. She couldn't concentrate on anything else.

'Lucy.' His voice was soft but urgent.

'Huh?' Actual words were impossible right then.

'If you keep moving your ass like that I won't be responsible for what happens. You're driving me crazy.'

She couldn't help the smile that broke out on her face. Couldn't help the fact her hips moved again, just to test his will-power. He squeezed his eyes shut, the torture written all over his face. They were both playing with fire now.

'You want to see me lose control?' His voice was like gravel. 'Just keep doing what you're doing.'

He caught her eye, as though he was searching for permission. She held his gaze, her expression telling him she wanted this as much as he did. He reached for her buttons, deftly unfastening them one by one. His eyes lowered, taking in her half-exposed breasts, his lids turning heavy as he unbuttoned the final one.

She was silent as he slid his warm hands up to her shoulders, pushing the fleecy material down her arms. Then he pulled until it slid from her back, dropping to the mattress. Wrapping his arms around her, he hugged her against him, until her breasts were pressed against his hard chest. She could feel her breath hitch as she tried to inhale, his proximity driving her crazy.

His hands moved lower, and in spite of the fleece pyjamas bottoms, she could feel every finger pushing against her flesh.

She angled her head until her lips were against his ear, her breath soft against his cheek. He let out a strangled moan, one that caught in his throat, the sound echoing against her. 'Lucy ...'

'Lachlan ...'

'Just ... Christ, what are we doing?'

'You're warming me up.'

'Yeah, that.' He slid his hands beneath the elasticated waist of her pyjamas, his heated palms sliding down her bottom. The sensation of flesh against flesh sent another jolt of pleasure through her. Who was controlling who here?

There was only an inch between her lips and his cheek. She could practically feel his night-time beard brushing against her mouth. Exhaling, she closed the gap, pressing her lips to his jaw.

'I should have let you freeze,' he muttered. 'You're a fucking temptress.'

A small rumble of laughter escaped her mouth. She couldn't remember the last time she felt this good. The last time she was so in the moment. 'I should have let you burn.'

'You're the one burning me.' He turned his head until her lips grazed the corner of his mouth. 'Jesus, woman, what do you want me to do?'

'Nothing,' she whispered against the corner of his lips. 'Nothing at all.'

It was strange how she hesitated now, just before she kissed him. As if it were more intimate than the way their bodies were entwined, more meaningful than his hands pressed against her flesh. A kiss laid you bare, made you vulnerable. It was a leap from a cliff edge with your eyes closed.

Lachlan pulled his hand from her back, reaching up to cup her cheek. His thumb stroked the line from her ear to her lips.

Her chest felt strange, as though the air was slowly squeezing out of her.

Closing her eyes, she moved closer to the cliff edge, hesitant as she took a step into thin air. But before she could take that final leap, Lachlan moved his mouth onto hers. His lips were hot and demanding, kissing her as though she held his final breath. And she was kissing him back, her hand still cupping his jaw, the other reaching up to curl around the back of his neck. Their legs were still entwined, and they ground against each other in a subconscious rhythm, gyrating to a silent tune only the two of them knew.

It wasn't heaven, it wasn't hell, it was somewhere far, far away from there. Somewhere only the two of them existed. And she never wanted to leave.

This had to be the most sensual night of his life. The most painful one, too. He held her in his arms, her body soft and pliant against his, moving his lips against her with an urgency he didn't quite understand.

How long was it since he'd had a woman? A month, two? No wonder his body was so responsive.

Lucy was responsive, too. Her mouth was warm, her lips welcoming him in when he slid his tongue against hers. And when they broke the kiss her breath was short, hot against his skin, her chest rising and falling in an effort to catch some air.

He circled his finger lower, until he could feel the tight flesh of her areola, his touch gentle and teasing. She arched her back against him, encouraging his movements until his hand was brushing against her nipple. She gasped, and he kissed her again to taste her excitement.

And now the temptation was excruciating. His whole body

pulsed with the need to have her, to be inside her. His spine was tense, his muscles contracted, and the throbbing between his legs was impossible to ignore.

Rolling her nipple between his thumb and forefinger, he kissed her again, their tongues tangling together as they tasted and licked. Her moan sent a rush of pleasure through him, his body vibrating in response. But it was too much, way too much. He wasn't sure he could resist much longer.

'Lucy ...' he murmured, against her soft lips. 'Is this okay?'

'Yes,' she breathed against him.

'Do you want more?'

Her legs parted beneath him as if in answer to his question. He slid his hand beneath her waistband, feeling the softness of her stomach against his palm. He moved lower, his fingers making slow sensual circles until he could feel her slickness, her heat, and she let out a little moan against his mouth.

'Do you want this, Lucy?'

'Yes.' Her voice was firmer this time, though her lips were still soft against his. 'But I don't have any protection.'

'I do.' He looked deep into her eyes, at the way they were staring at him, as though he had all the answers. And damn if it didn't turn him on more than ever. He tugged at her pyjama pants, and she arched from the mattress as he pulled them off, quickly taking off his own, too, and throwing them to the floor. Reaching for his wallet on the bedside table, he pulled out a foil packet, deftly opening it and sliding on the condom. Then he was over her, caging her in with his arms, their bodies inches from each other.

He stroked her chin with his hand, his thumb trailing across her lip. His body throbbed insistently, reminding him how he ached for her, how he needed to be inside her. He felt himself brush against her wetness, felt the give of her flesh as she welcomed him, and the shock of pleasure that ripped through his spine as he slowly moved inside her. She gasped, her legs wrapping around his hips, her body demanding a rhythm he was all too willing to give.

He rocked, thrusting inside her, wringing another moan from her mouth. Kissing her, he swallowed the sound, feeling the vibrations rack down his spine. She felt good. Too good. Enough to make his body tighten with the pleasure spiking through every sinew. He slid his hands beneath her, angling her until she gasped every time he thrust.

If he was going to hell, she was coming with him.

'Where's this from?' he murmured. They were lying there in a post-coital haze, the air around them thick and heavy with the scent of sex. Her eyes were still glassy – the way he imagined they'd look after a mouthful or two of wine. She blinked, staring at him questioningly, her chest still heaving from their exertions.

Her naked chest.

Get a handle on it, MacLeish.

'Your scar,' he whispered, running his finger over the raised white line. 'How did you get it?' His breathing was almost back under control.

Lucy reached her hand to her forehead, following his finger as he traced it. 'I was in an accident when I was younger.' Her frown deepened.

'Did it hurt?' he asked.

'I . . . ah . . . it needed stitches,' she said, still breathless. She looked as confused as he felt. 'But I can't really remember the pain. Everything was so messed up.'

'Messed up?' He lifted the sheets to cover her chest. That was better.

'My mum was driving the car. She didn't make it.'

He didn't like the way her voice wavered. 'She died in the car crash?'

Lucy nodded.

'I'm sorry to hear that.'

'It was a long time ago.'

Lachlan racked his brain for something to say, but there was nothing there. Just a blank space where his good sense used to live. He pulled her closer, until her head was nestled against his arm, her body curled into his. He hadn't expected her to be so light when he'd lifted her out of her bed. Her strong personality somehow made her seem bigger than she was, weightier, too. But in reality she was petite, small-framed with gentle curves, and the contrast between her body and her soul was enticing.

She placed her hand on the centre of his chest, where he imagined his heart must be. Her fingers splayed out, as though she were bracing herself against something. It felt different from her earlier touch, more gentle, more comforting. He swallowed hard, trying to ignore the cocktail of emotions rushing through him. He wasn't sure what any of them meant.

They lay there silently, Lachlan on his back, Lucy curled into him on her side, their breath slowing as the excitement of earlier ebbed away. In its wake it left him with questions, and an overwhelming sense of apprehension.

15

Flesh and blood, you, brother mine

– The Tempest

'Good morning.' Alistair looked up from his newspaper when Lachlan walked into the kitchen. There was a fresh pot of coffee on the table, along with a jug of orange juice and a rack full of toast. 'Help yourself to breakfast,' he said, gesturing at the food.

'Has Lucy come down yet?' Lachlan asked, pulling out a chair. She hadn't been in his bed when he woke up – he assumed she'd gone back to her bedroom at some time before dawn. He should have been relieved – it wasn't as though either of them had meant to cross the line, maybe it was best to pretend it never happened. And yet he couldn't shake off the edgy sensation that had been gripping him all night. Ever since he'd let his desire overtake his good sense.

'She left about an hour ago. Said something about an emergency at work.' Alistair raised an eyebrow. 'I'm surprised she didn't tell you.'

Lachlan blinked for a moment. A glance at the clock above the old range-style cooker told him it was only eight thirty. 'Is she coming back?'

Alistair's expression softened. Lachlan didn't like the way the man tipped his head in sympathy. 'I don't think so, Mr MacLeish. She took her suitcase with her, and thanked me profusely for the hospitality. She's a lovely young lady, isn't she?'

'Yeah, she is. Lovely.' Lachlan tried to ignore the spark of frustration that heated up his veins. He reached for the coffee and poured some into a mug. 'Are we still on for lunch?'

'Of course. I'm looking forward to it. Even if Lucy can't join us.'

Lachlan rubbed his chin with his thumb. The skin around his neck felt tender. A memory flashed through his mind, of Lucy scraping his throat with her teeth as he thrust harder into her.

Christ, he needed to stop that.

They'd had sex, she'd left, and there were no regrets. If anything, he was glad he'd gotten her out of his system. He didn't need any more complications.

'Oh, and I found something last evening, in our files. I thought you might be interested.' Alistair grabbed an envelope from his bag and slid some papers out. 'We have so many old photographs. One day I'd like to have them all catalogued. Even better if we could scan them all in to the server. They're such a great part of your heritage.'

He handed over a small rectangular photograph to Lachlan, who looked down at the image – surprisingly colourful and unfaded in spite of its age – and frowned.

There were two boys standing by the lake, both holding fishing rods. They were dressed identically – in MacLeish tartan kilts, grey jackets and long blue socks. Lachlan stared at it for a moment, recognising himself immediately. He remembered the kilt, too. Try as he might, though, he couldn't remember smiling with his brother.

'Is that me and Duncan?' he asked, the frown still pulling down at his lips.

'That's right. I think I must have taken it, though I don't rightly remember. I was in charge of the salmon back then, and you boys were royal terrors.' Alistair laughed. 'In the end, I taught you to fish so you could give me some peace.'

'I don't remember playing with my brother.' Lachlan shook his head. 'If this wasn't so old I'd swear it was Photoshopped.'

'You two looked so similar back then, I couldn't tell you apart. You both loved running around the estate, too. Like two peas in a pod.'

'I've never heard us described like that before,' Lachlan said quietly. He couldn't stop looking at the photo, at the way he was smiling, next to Duncan grinning from ear to ear. It was so different from the memories he had of his childhood, of the way he was treated every time he visited his father. Of the anger he always saw on Duncan's mother's face.

'Can I keep this?' he asked. For some reason it felt important to have it. 'I'll be sure to scan it in and send you a copy.'

'Of course. I have another very similar, anyway. I must have been snap happy that day.' Alistair smiled.

And for a moment, just a moment, it felt as though Lachlan's world was tilting on an angle. Not too acute, just enough to make him feel as though he was listing to one side.

Then he took another mouthful of coffee, and let the bitter liquid warm his throat, and the caffeine soothe his mind.

Memories were strange and unsettling things. He'd much prefer to focus on the present.

*

The Glencarraig Inn was an old-fashioned family-run pub, perched on the edge of the village, next to the main road out to Inverness. Lachlan and Alistair had walked there – a fifteen-minute stride from the lodge gates – and though the air around them was cold and blustery, the snow seemed to have disappeared for now.

The pub itself was as old as the village, and for more than three centuries it had been refreshing both the locals and the drovers who would lead their sheep down the banks of the glen, stopping at the pub for food and drink before making their way south to the livestock markets.

As they walked inside, a wall of warmth hit Lachlan's face. The interior was dark, the ceiling low, the burgundy-painted walls decorated with stags' heads and old paintings. It was like stepping into the past.

'Would you like a pint?' Alistair asked, raising his voice above the drone of conversation. It was surprisingly busy for a week day, with most tables occupied by diners.

'Let me buy you one,' Lachlan said, reaching in his pocket for his wallet.

'Not at all, this one's on me. Put your money away.'

It took them ten minutes to get to their table. As they walked through the pub, everybody stopped them, talking to Alistair, slapping him on the back. They all looked pleased to see him. And when he introduced Lachlan, the locals' smiles widened, as they asked him about his plans, whether he would be moving here, and offered condolences for his father. It was all a little overwhelming.

He couldn't help thinking that if Lucy was here, he'd have felt more relaxed.

When they made it to the table – still laid for three – Lachlan took a long, deep sip of his beer. It was cool and refreshing, and he closed his eyes for a moment, feeling it slip down his throat and into his belly.

'They're all delighted to finally meet you, you know,' Alistair said quietly. 'The village gossip has reached boiling point. Everybody wants to know what's going to happen to the estate.'

'Hopefully we can get this all sorted soon,' Lachlan said, 'and things will settle down.'

'That would be nice.' Alistair's smile was tight. 'I even had an email from a MacLeish in Australia last night, asking if it was true you were fighting with your brother over ownership. Of course, I told them it was all stuff and nonsense.' He lowered his voice further still. 'We don't want that sort of speculation around these parts.'

Lachlan bit down a smile. There was something about Alistair that he really liked. The man was honest and forthright, and clearly loved being in charge of the estate. 'Of course we don't.'

'What can I get you to eat?' the waiter asked, stopping at their table. 'Or do you need a few minutes?'

Lachlan glanced at the menu and then back up at Alistair. 'What do you recommend?'

'The pie is always good, and of course there's haggis if you want to be really traditional. But my favourite is the venison casserole and tatties,' Alistair said, closing the menu. 'That's what I always go for.'

'Then we'll have two of those.'

After the waiter left, Lachlan looked around again, noticing how more than a few of the locals were looking at him. He caught the eye of one woman, who turned away immediately, and started giggling with her friends.

'Did I come here as a child?' he asked Alistair.

'Not that I know of. Your father never was very keen on coming to the village. He preferred to stay on the estate whenever he visited.'

'From what I remember, he wasn't keen on much of anything,' Lachlan said, keeping his voice light.

'Ach, he wasn't so bad. A little taciturn, maybe, and hard to pin down. But he always sent the staff gifts at Christmas, and contributed to the village fair every year.' Alistair lifted up his pint glass. 'At least he didn't parcel the whole place up and sell it off in lots. You'd be surprised how many Highland estates have been lost that way.'

Lachlan gave a wry smile. 'A bit like buying companies and breaking them up before selling them on, you mean?'

'Exactly like that.'

'Yeah, well, my dad was all about building things. Me, not so much.'

'What makes you say that?' Alistair asked. He leaned forward, resting his chin on his hands.

Lachlan shrugged. 'I tend to invest in other people's dreams. It's my job to make as much profit as I can out of them.'

'And you enjoy your job?' Alistair asked. It didn't sound as though there was an agenda to his question – he seemed generally interested.

'Yeah, I love my job.'

Alistair nodded slowly, pursing his lips together. 'Well, maybe you're more like your father than you think.'

16

Thou hast her, France; let her be thine

– King Lear

It had been more than twenty-four hours since Lucy left Glencarraig Lodge, and yet she still couldn't think about anything else. Every time she closed her eyes she could see Lachlan, every time she touched her lips she could feel his mouth against hers. They'd crossed the line so far it wasn't funny. She should forget everything that had happened.

But some things were easier said than done.

Lifting her hand up, she ran her fingertips along the scar that zigzagged from her temple, remembering how gentle Lachlan had been as he traced it.

Where's this from?

His question had been so casual, and yet it had stirred up a maelstrom of emotions inside her. Reminded her what happened when you took your attention from the road. What happened when you were reckless, when you didn't bother clipping in your seatbelt.

What happened when you lost control.

'Here's your coffee, and the mail arrived.' Lynn placed the mug carefully on Lucy's desk, then passed her the pile of envelopes, varying in size and colour. 'Oh, and your sister made the gossip rags, again. Did you know she and Sam are expecting twins?'

Lucy smiled, for the first time that day. 'Cesca called me last night. She said she was shocked, especially since they broke up last week according to *Entertainment Weekly*. Apparently next month they'll have a secret wedding.' The lies the tabloids wrote were a source of amusement at the Robinson and Balfour office. Lucy had long since stopped believing any of them were true.

'Well, make sure I'm invited.' Lynn winked.

After she left, Lucy covered her face with the palms of her hands, sighing. What a bloody mess. Every time she thought about Lachlan her stomach tightened, as though it was being tied in a thousand knots. What the hell had she been thinking?

She hadn't been thinking, that was the problem. She'd thrown herself into the moment, hadn't thought it through. Had been completely unprofessional.

Taking a deep breath, she took a quick scan of her emails. The one at the top grabbed her attention. Not from *him*, but about him at least. A last-ditch offer from his brother to relinquish his rights to the land and title at Glencarraig. At least some things in life were predictable.

Her cursor hovered over the forward button. She should send this to Lachlan straight away. Licking her lips, she hesitated, afraid of what opening their communication might unleash.

Why couldn't everything be normal?

This was why she should never have gone to Glencarraig with him. It made things murky, made her question herself when she should be on top of her game. She'd played with fire and it had burned her, and she should learn a lesson from it.

Sighing, she clicked on the forward button, quickly tapping out a note asking Lachlan for his orders. Dammit, she meant instructions. She highlighted the word, replacing it, feeling the relief washing through her as she clicked the send button.

Just the thought of him giving her orders was enough to set her whole body on fire. She dropped her head into her hands, squeezing her eyes shut. If she was this affected by the thought of him, what would she be like when they were face to face again? He only had to look at her and she'd go weak at the knees.

Lifting her head up, she looked through the glass wall of her office, and across to the partners' rooms on the other side. The thought of Malcolm finding out what she'd done in Glencarraig made her feel sick. Everything she'd worked for would be ruined.

And yet she still couldn't get Lachlan out of her mind.

The rest of the afternoon was a write-off. Letters that would usually take her minutes to deal with lay unread on her desk. She asked Lynn to hold her phone calls – half afraid he'd try to circumvent her mobile phone and call the office instead. She left her coffee undrunk in her mug, a thin film covering the top of the liquid as it cooled.

Thank God it was almost the weekend. Her father was safely settled in to his home, her sisters were fine in their lives across the world. She could afford to hole up in her apartment, to actually get the work done that she should have finished this week, and by Monday everything would be back to normal.

It would be calm, quiet and completely under control.

Just the way she liked it.

*

When Lucy's email flashed up on his screen on Friday afternoon, Lachlan was sitting in the library at Glencarraig, his laptop resting on the polished oak table as he took part in a videoconference with his directors in New York. It was early morning in Manhattan, and spring sunshine shone through the window behind Marcus, his finance director, making the laptop screen work overtime to adjust to the light.

'Cash flow is good. We have a few overdue items, but nothing to get twisted about,' Marcus was saying. Lachlan leaned back on his leather chair, flicking at the report in front of him as Marcus continued to speak. His eyes were drawn to his phone, his fingers twitched as he reached for it.

'When are you coming back to the office?' Marcus asked. 'There are a couple of things I need to take you through in person.'

Lachlan put the phone down and concentrated on the screen. 'I'll be back on Monday afternoon. Ask Grant to slot you in for an hour, I should be at the office by one.'

The meeting was winding down. He could hear Sean, his marketing director, murmuring about leaving at lunchtime to head to the Hamptons. From what Lachlan could see it was a fine spring day in New York, with temperatures almost in the seventies, according to his weather app. A contrast to the cold front that had followed him up to Glencarraig, and the biting wind that was howling around the windows of the lodge.

'How about you, are you staying in Scotland until Monday?' Marcus asked.

'No.' That was one thing Lachlan was certain of. He wanted a distraction, a way to quell his thoughts. His body still thrummed with the memory of her touch, giving him an ache that he couldn't quite shake off.

He'd tried, God knows he had. And yet he still felt this discomfort, this unbearable itch that he couldn't quite reach. It was aggravating.

'But you're not back in town until Monday?' Sean said. 'Are you heading somewhere else for the weekend?'

'I might head to the mainland,' Lachlan said quietly. Surely somewhere in Europe could provide him with a distraction.

The videoconference had barely ended before he grabbed his phone, impatiently unlocking it and pulling up his emails. There was her name, right at the top of the list. He stared at it for a moment, trying to work out if he was angry or relieved.

Maybe a little of both.

We've had another offer in from your brother's
solicitors (see below). Nothing unexpected.
Please let me know how you'd like me to proceed.
Kind regards, Lucy

That was it. No friendly note, no hint of flirting, just pure professionalism. It was as though their trip to Glencarraig had never even happened. His lip curled down as he read her words again, then closed the email as quickly as he'd opened it.

He needed to go somewhere that didn't hold memories of her smile. Somewhere that he wouldn't spend the whole time thinking about how she felt as he moved inside her.

Paris. He'd go to Paris.

Anywhere was better than here.

It was eight o'clock on Friday evening. Lucy was curled up on her sofa, mindlessly flicking through the television channels, finding nothing worth stopping to watch. The rain was pattering on her window, a not-so-welcome change from the snow she'd seen in Glencarraig earlier that week, and she'd cranked the heating up even though it was April, and it really shouldn't be needed.

An hour ago she'd called Juliet, wanting to check on her sister, but she'd been diverted to voicemail. Then she'd called Kitty, and got her voicemail too. She hadn't bothered calling Cesca – not wanting to hear a recorded voice for the third time. Even her furry house-invader had better things to do – she hadn't seen the neighbours' cat since she got back from Glencarraig. It was as though she was the only one without plans, and Lucy couldn't help but feel lonely.

After another half-hour of reality shows that managed to kill off more than a few of her brain cells, she turned the television off, and carried her half-eaten meal for one over to the kitchen, scraping the remnants into the bin and sliding the plate into her dishwasher. She'd just closed it when her phone started to ring – the loud beeps making Lucy almost run to answer the call. A chat with one of her sisters was just what she needed to get herself back on track, to remind herself who she was.

And then she saw the name on the display and everything turned upside down.

She hesitated for a moment, her finger hovering over the call button the same way her fist had hovered near his door that night. Watching, waiting, debating.

She hadn't spoken to him since she'd left him in Glencarraig on Thursday morning. He hadn't responded to the email she'd sent, either. Was he angry at her, or was he as regretful as she was? Lucy wasn't sure which she'd prefer.

Her phone rang for the seventh time and she knew it was now or never. One more beep and it would go to her voicemail, and any courage she had might disappear for ever. Taking a deep breath, she finally pressed accept and slowly lifted the phone to her ear.

'Hello?'

'Hello?'

He hadn't expected to feel the relief he did when she answered the phone. His whole body relaxed into his chair, the tightness in his shoulders dissolving into the quilted fabric. Crazy how just one word made all the tension disappear.

He'd been in Paris for three hours. In spite of his best intentions, the city had done nothing to stop him thinking about her, and nothing to stop him wanting her. Instead, it had just made him obsess about her even more. As the taxi had weaved its way through the pretty Parisian streets, he'd found himself wanting to point things out to her. Wanting to show her the way the Eiffel Tower lit up at twilight, the way the bars in the side streets had spindly metallic tables that people spilled out onto. The way everybody smoked here like it was still 1989, the blue plumes twisting up into the cool night air.

'Lucy, it's Lachlan.'

She didn't answer. He leaned forward, picking up the whisky he'd ordered half an hour ago. The ice had melted, but the drink was still strong as it hit the back of his throat.

'What are you doing right now?' he asked her.

Another pause. Jesus, this was such a bad idea. But then she answered and he immediately felt better.

'I'm thinking about going to bed.'

'And what are you doing tomorrow?'

'Working. I've got lots of emails to catch up on, plus one of my clients is in court next week. I need to make sure everything's ready.'

He took another mouthful of whisky, letting it warm his tongue the same way her voice warmed his soul. 'Come to Paris.'

'What?' The shock in her voice reverberated down the phone line.

'You've never been here, right? So come over and join me, come and see some sights. Tick another thing off your bucket list.'

'You're in Paris?' She sounded confused. 'I thought you were in Glencarraig?'

'I had some air miles to use up.' He smiled. Edinburgh to Paris would barely make a dent in his air miles.

'What are you doing there?'

'Right now? I'm sitting in a bar on the Rive Gauche, watching the world go by. And I'm thinking how much better it would be if you were with me.'

He could hear her take in a deep breath of air. 'I'm your solicitor, Lachlan. What we did at Glencarraig ... it should never have happened. We should pretend it never did. Just go back to being client and attorney.' She sounded as unconvinced as he felt.

'I know we should. But it's Friday night. You're not an attorney right now, and I'm not a client. We're just a man and a woman without anything better to do. So why not throw caution to the wind and get on a plane? Spend the weekend with me, and then we'll pretend that none of this ever happened.' He hadn't realised how much he needed this until he heard her voice. Now his whole body was tense again, as he bit down on his jaw, waiting for her response.

'It's nine o'clock at night,' she said. He could almost picture her shaking her head. 'I wouldn't be able to get a flight until tomorrow, and that wouldn't leave us any time.'

'There's a flight leaving Edinburgh in an hour and a half,' he told her. 'And if you look outside your window, you'll see a car there. I've told him to wait for twenty minutes, long enough for you to pack a bag and get in. He'll drive you to the airport.'

He heard the pad of footsteps as she was walking across the room, then the swish of curtain as she pulled it back. He was on tenterhooks, waiting for her response, desperate for her to say yes.

'Oh my God, there is a bloody car there.' She laughed, and it made him smile. 'You really are crazy, do you know that?'

Yes, he did. But she was the one driving him crazy. 'I'll have another car pick you up as soon as you land. You can be here in a couple of hours.'

'You've got it all worked out, haven't you?' In spite of her words, she didn't sound annoyed. More intrigued than anything else. 'So I fly out, we spend the weekend together, and then we go back to being professional?'

'I just want to show a beautiful girl a beautiful city. So what do you say?'

Another swish as she closed the curtains, then the knock of her feet as she walked somewhere in her apartment. Lachlan found himself holding his breath, waiting for her answer, desperate for it to be the right one.

'Okay,' she finally said, her voice soft. 'I'll get on a plane and I'll meet you. But you'd better have a big glass of French wine waiting for me.'

'It's a deal,' he said, ending the call, a huge grin breaking out on his face. As far as he was concerned he'd buy her every damned bottle in France if she wanted it.

17

*Teach not thy lip such scorn, for it were
made for kissing, lady*

– Richard III

Lucy looked up at the hotel in front of her, the white brick façade looming high above the street, illuminated by the bright Paris moon. Before she could even walk towards the entrance a doorman had appeared, taking her suitcase from her and ushering her into the entrance hall. 'Mademoiselle Shakespeare?' he asked, rolling the 'r' of her name. 'Monsieur MacLeish is waiting for you in the lounge.'

Lucy followed the direction of the doorman's arm, past the elegant chairs in the lobby, and towards the old paintings that adorned the walls. Past them was a door, the word 'Salon' painted in gold above it.

'I'll have the bellhop take your case to your room,' the doorman told her.

Lucy nodded, thanking him in her terrible French, and then breathed in sharply. It wasn't just this beautiful entranceway that felt foreign to her, it was everything she was doing right then. She wasn't the sort of woman who flew to Paris at a whim, and she definitely wasn't the type who agreed to spend the weekend with a man she hardly knew. And yet here she was, her heart cantering in her chest like a thoroughbred, her feet propelling her towards the room where he was waiting for her.

The salon was as eye-catching as the entranceway had been, its tall windows framed by expensive draped curtains, the walls dominated by dark tapestries that spanned from floor to ceiling. But it wasn't the décor that she was staring at, it was the man sitting in a chair on the far side of the room, his white shirt open at the neck, his sleeves rolled up. He was lifting a glass of amber fluid to his lips. But then their gazes met and they both froze.

Just one look and it felt as if her whole body was catching fire. She tried to take a breath, but her throat was too tight. Then he was standing, putting his glass down and walking towards her.

'You came.'

'I said I would.' It had only been two days since she'd last seen him, but she'd already forgotten how beautiful he was. And there was that horse again, running around inside her chest like it was a racecourse.

His lips slowly curled into an easy smile, one that did nothing to calm her heart. And then she was smiling too, laughter tickling the back of her throat, because this really was so crazy.

A waiter walked into the room, carrying a tray with two glasses on it. '*Du vin, mademoiselle?*'

One of the glasses had white wine, the other red. 'I didn't know what to order you,' Lachlan said, inclining his head at the tray. 'So I asked them to bring both.'

'I'll have white,' she said, reaching out as the waiter passed her the glass. '*Merci.*'

'*De rien.*' The waiter disappeared as quickly as he'd arrived, and it was the two of them again, standing in the empty salon, smiling at each other until their cheeks started to ache.

'You should drink it before it warms up,' Lachlan said. 'Come and sit down.' He took her hand and led her to the table he'd been sitting at, holding her fingers until she sat on the easy chair. As soon as he let go she missed his touch.

'I'm sorry I didn't meet you at the airport,' he said, sitting in the chair opposite hers. 'I had a telecom I couldn't miss.'

'It's fine, I enjoyed the drive through the city.' She didn't tell him that she'd stared out of the window like the tourist she was, her mouth wide open as she took in the sights she'd only seen in photographs before. Why had it taken her so long to visit?

She took a sip of her wine – cool, crisp and expensive. Idly she wondered if he'd be charged for both glasses.

'I always enjoy it too.' He was smiling at her, as though pleased they had that in common. 'This place never gets old. I could visit a hundred times and there'd still be more to see.'

'How often have you been here?'

'I don't know.' He frowned. 'Ten, fifteen times, maybe? I used to have some investments here, but I sold them.'

'Did you own this hotel?' she asked. She wouldn't put it past him.

He laughed. 'No, not this one. I'm not sure even I could afford this.' He put his glass down – empty. Hers was still half full. 'Do you want to look around?' he asked. 'I can take you on a quick tour if you like. There are some amazing paintings here, worth taking a look at.'

She wasn't sure if she should feel disappointed that he wasn't jumping on her as soon as she walked through the door.

Not that he seemed the type to do that. He was too sophisticated, too urbane. The man knew how to seduce slowly and with intent.

She glanced at her watch. It was almost one a.m. in the UK, which meant it was already two a.m. here in France. No wonder she felt tired. A few hours ago she was contemplating an early night, and now she was in a different country.

'Can we do the tour tomorrow?' she asked him. 'I'd really like to freshen up if I can.' And then go to bed. But she wasn't brave enough to say it.

There was a flicker in his eyes that matched the beating of her heart. He watched as she finished her wine, then placed the glass on the polished wooden table between them.

'Yeah, that sounds perfect to me.'

Lachlan glanced at the bathroom door, watching the steam curl its way through the gap. He could hear a tap running, and the buzz of what sounded like an electric toothbrush. She'd only been in there for ten minutes, and he was already getting antsy.

He caught a glance of himself in the mirror, and stared at it, bemused. A few hours ago he'd been certain that he could keep the layer of professionalism between them; now she was almost certainly naked in his bathroom.

The thought sent a shot of desire through his body.

Lucy opened the door and a wall of steam escaped into the living area. She stopped short as soon as she saw him standing there, pulling her white fluffy bathrobe tightly around herself, her wet hair brushed off her face.

There was that scar again. It reminded him of that night he held her. Below it her skin was pink and clean, the aroma of flowers clinging to her. It drew him in, making him walk towards her, his eyes never leaving hers.

He watched her neck bob as she swallowed, then followed her line of flesh down to her collarbone. God, her whole body was delicate. Like a perfectly crafted work of art. He took another step, reaching his hand out to touch her skin, exposed by the 'V' of her robe. His finger traced a line down from the dip at her throat to the top of her cleavage, his touch making her chest lift as she inhaled sharply.

'You're afraid,' he said. 'You don't need to be afraid.' He found it enticing, the way she reacted to him.

'I'm not afraid,' she whispered. 'I'm just trying to work out if this is a good idea. I don't do this sort of thing.'

'We can stop if you want.'

'No.' She placed her hand over his, pressing his palm to her warm, damp skin. When their eyes met, there was a resoluteness in her gaze he hadn't seen before. 'Don't stop.'

He angled his head until their mouths were barely touching. Her breath was fast, hot, her heart barrelling against her chest where he touched her. God, her responsiveness was a turn-on. Her apprehension was, too. And the sensation of her body beneath his hand was almost too much to bear. Pulling his lips away from their almost-kiss, he said, 'We don't have to do anything you don't want to.'

'Okay.'

He could feel her relax beneath her touch. 'You're in control,' he said, looking down at her. 'In fact, let's take it a step further. Tonight is all about you. You tell me what you want, you tell me what to do, you're in charge of everything.'

Her tense muscles loosened. Interesting.

'What's in it for you?' she asked.

His eyes were heated when he looked at her. 'You are.'

She laughed in spite of herself. 'You haven't lost your charm along the way, then?'

'I haven't lost anything,' he told her. 'I play to win, remember?'

She looked like she remembered, her eyes turning glassy as she stared at him.

'Speaking of which,' he continued, 'I have an ulterior motive.'

'Which is?'

He cupped the side of her face, his palm covering her skin. 'If you're in control tonight, then tomorrow night I get to be in charge.'

Her mouth dropped open again. Without thinking, he pressed his thumb against her lips.

'What do you think?' he whispered.

Her lips closed around him, her tongue grazing the pad of his thumb, before she slowly slid her mouth back, releasing him. 'It's a deal.'

It was the second time she'd crawled into bed with Lachlan MacLeish, but it felt like the first. As though everything was new. As though Glencarraig had been the appetiser, and this was the main course, a chateaubriand for two.

'Just lie there for a minute,' she told him, sliding in beside him. 'Don't take your boxers off, okay?'

'Okay.' He looked amused.

Slowly, she pulled at the sheet until his torso was exposed. Her brain exploded with the memory of how it had felt when he'd held her that night in Glencarraig, the strength in his muscle, the taut, smooth skin.

'Don't move,' she whispered, reaching out. With her index

finger, she followed the line of his collarbone, lingering in the dip beneath his throat. Then she continued, until she'd traced her way to his shoulder, and down his arm, along the swell of his bicep. The skin beneath her finger flexed, and when she looked down she could see his hand clenched into a fist, the tendons of his wrist tight and prominent. She traced the inside of his elbow, making him shudder, and a soft chuckle escaping from his lips.

She smiled at the sound. 'Are you ticklish?' she asked him. 'No.'

Licking her bottom lip, she moved her finger back up his arm, feathering it across the crease between his chest and bicep. This time his laugh was higher pitched, and he moved away from her. She couldn't help but laugh too.

'You are. You're ticklish.' The grin split her face. 'The implacable Lachlan MacLeish has a weak spot.'

'Don't go there,' he said through clenched teeth.

'You told me tonight was all about me. I can do what I like, remember?' She clambered over him until her legs were straddling his waist. Hmm, there was that other sensitive part of him, too, pressing in a way that made her feel very, very good. 'Now put your hands above your head and don't move.'

He shook his head. 'That's not happening.'

'Are you reneging on our deal?' she asked. 'Because I distinctly heard you say I could tell you what to do tonight.'

'You didn't say anything about torturing me.'

She grabbed his hands, folding her fingers around them. They were big, strong, just like the rest of him. 'I don't remember you placing any caveats on this.'

'Some things go without saying,' he told her. 'Tickling is definitely out of bounds.' She loved the way he was looking at her, desire and apprehension all mixed into one. As though she was the only thing that mattered in the world right then.

With her eyes on him, she lifted up his hands, so that his arms were pointing to the ceiling. 'I disagree,' she said, pushing them further still, until his knuckles were brushing against the headboard, leaving him exposed. So many tender points were in front of her. The sides of his torso, the soft skin beneath his arms. Where to start?

He curled his hands around her wrists. 'Remember,' he said, his jaw tight, 'I'm in charge tomorrow night.'

'Tomorrow schmorrow,' she said, tugging to get her hands free. 'Now let me go.'

'Lucy ...'

She gave him a mischievous grin, shuffling back until she grazed against his erection. She rotated her hips, and he gave a groan, his head dropping back.

'Jesus, you're going to kill me.'

'Well, then I wouldn't have to worry about tomorrow,' she said, her voice light. 'Now let go of my hands, Lachlan.' She moved again, grinding herself against him. Jesus, he felt hard.

Slowly, he unfurled his fingers, releasing his hold on her. He swallowed, his Adam's apple bobbing. 'I guess it's a good way to go.'

'Being tickled to death?' she asked, wiggling her fingers just to see his reaction. 'Yeah, I can think of worse ways.'

He bit his lip as she moved her hands to his chest, splaying her fingers until they grazed his nipples. He inhaled sharply at her touch, his hips moving in an attempt to gain friction against her. She lifted herself up enough to foil his plan.

'I could get used to this power,' she said, slowly inching her hands to the side of his body. 'I could get used to touching you, too.'

'If you're going to tickle me, get on with it.' He groaned. 'I can't deal with this.'

She leaned forward until her face was only a few inches from his. 'I'm not letting you off that easily,' she breathed. 'The best part of tickling is taking somebody by surprise.' Closing the gap between their mouths, she pressed her lips to his. 'Don't kiss me back,' she murmured. His lips were soft, warm, and still as she moved hers against them. It felt strange to kiss him when he wasn't responding, but delicious, too.

Emboldened, she ran the tip of her tongue along the seam of his mouth, feeling as much as hearing the moan escaping from him. Still kissing him, she stroked his nipples with her thumbs, circling her hips again until she felt his hard ridge against her.

'You're slaying me,' he mumbled.

'Ssh,' she whispered, 'I didn't say you could talk.'

Was it wrong that she was completely turned on by the man beneath her? There was something intoxicating about being able to touch him the way she wanted. About teasing him until he was barely able to keep control. She knew he was letting her do it, that in a second he could flip her over, show his strength. And yet he was resisting, letting her take the lead. It only made her want him more.

Dragging her lips along his jawline, she could feel his scruff scraping her tender skin. Then she moved further, down his throat to his chest, feeling his strangled breaths vibrating against her mouth.

This was turning her on like crazy. Her whole body was

tingling every time she touched him. And every time she rolled her hips, pleasure shot through her like a pulse of electricity.

She paused when she reached his pectorals, breathing warm air onto his skin. Glancing up, she could see his hands still above his head, his tight fists gripping the pillow. He was staring at her, his eyes heated and dark, as he watched her slowly move her lips around his nipple. Curious to see what he'd do, she reached the tip of her tongue out, barely grazing the raised skin. He hitched his hips in a reflex response.

'Goddamn it.' His head dropped back.

'You're swearing a lot tonight.'

'You're making me swear.'

She slowly sucked his nipple into her mouth, circling it with her tongue. He moaned, his whole body tensing beneath her. God, it felt good to bring him to the edge. She sucked again, harder this time, wanting to give him a taste of what was to come. She could taste him, clean and yet somehow masculine. It was intoxicating.

She slid her mouth down to his stomach, kissing each ridge of muscle as she went. Her fingers feathered down the sides of his abdomen, and for a moment he tensed again, waiting for her to attack him.

But she was too far gone for that. Any thought of making him laugh had vanished. She wanted to make him sigh, moan, call out her name. She wanted to drive him crazy in a way nobody ever had before.

She wanted him to remember this night for a long, long time.

Shuffling down, she kissed the skin just above the waistband of his boxer shorts. His erection was tenting the material, and as she hovered over him, his tip grazed the valley between her satin-clad breasts.

Sliding a finger beneath his waistband, she moved her head until her lips were hovering over his tented shorts. Then she kissed the tip, her eyes immediately seeking his to see his response.

His chest hitched. 'Jesus, I think you already killed me.'

She licked the fabric – and him – turning it dark grey. 'In that case, welcome to heaven.'

'Let me touch you,' he said, still gripping the pillow over his head.

'Not yet.' She didn't doubt for a minute he'd disobey her. He'd done everything he could to make her feel comfortable, powerful. And she was revelling in it.

Hooking her thumbs beneath the elastic, she pulled his pants down. He sprang up, thick and veined. She licked her lips, seeing liquid bead at his tip. Reaching her tongue out, she scooped it from her skin.

'Are you trying to make me beg?'

'Oh, you can beg,' she said, smiling. 'You can definitely beg.'

'Put your lips on me.' The rough tone of his voice made her feel even hotter. Was this what tomorrow night was going to feel like? Was she going to be the one lying with her arms above the head, hearing his harsh commands as he dominated her body? Even the thought of it made her shiver.

'Please?' she prompted.

'Put your lips on me ... please.'

In her peripheral vision she could see his hands releasing the pillow by his head. 'Keep your hands up,' she told him.

'I want to touch you.'

'No. Leave them there.'

'Or what?'

'Or I'll stop.'

Lachlan sighed, but he kept his arms where they were. 'You win.'

She grinned up at him, her lips less than an inch away from where he so clearly needed her. 'No, Lachlan, I think you'll find you do.'

18

Virtue is beauty

– Twelfth Night

A hand sliding softly down her back woke her up. Lucy blinked, her eyes slowly becoming accustomed to the light that was shining through the small gaps in the linen curtains. Her lips were dry, her whole body stiff where she'd been lying. A glance at the clock on the table next to her told her it was almost nine a.m.

And those insistent fingers, still caressing her skin, told her she wasn't alone.

'Good morning.'

She turned her head to see Lachlan lying beside her on the king-sized mattress. His hair was a little mussed, and the white sheet was gathered around his waist, revealing the toned ridges of his abdomen and chest, his skin tanned in the half-light. 'Hi.'

'You didn't run this time,' he said, moving his hand around from her back to cup her stomach, pulling her back against him. He was warm, so warm, reminding her of another night when they'd gone so much further than she intended.

'Give me time.'

He laughed. 'Maybe I should impound your passport. That way there's no escape.'

'I'd like to see you try.' She bit down a smile. 'Anyway, you promised me a weekend in Paris, why would I want to leave?'

'I promised you a weekend in bed,' he corrected her.

She turned to look at him, an eyebrow raised. *'I just want to show a beautiful girl a beautiful city.'* She did a passable imitation of his accent. 'Remember?'

'You saw the city last night.' He was drawing circles on her stomach with his fingers, dipping lower and lower.

'I was in a cab and it was dark. I barely got to see any of it.'

He pressed his lips against her shoulder. 'We got to see each other. That's what matters.'

She closed her eyes for a moment as he brushed his lips across her neck, kissing his way to the other side. Her whole body tingled at his touch. 'Lachlan ...'

'Mmm?' His voice was muffled by her skin.

'I can't come to Paris and not see anything.' Though right then she was sorely tempted. 'What about the Eiffel Tower, the Arc de Triomphe? The Louvre?'

'They're lovely. But not as lovely as you.' He reached for her chin, turning her head so he could kiss her. 'They can wait.' His kisses became more insistent, lighting her on fire until she almost forgot about her need to sightsee. She could feel his excitement as he turned her around until their bodies were pressing together, his hands running down her back to the base of her spine, where every single nerve seemed to tingle at his touch.

'Lachlan,' she whispered against his lips.

'Yeah?' His voice was thick with desire.

'We're definitely going sightseeing this afternoon.'

*

As soon as they walked out of the lift, the wind whipped at her hair. Though the sun was still shining down from a clear blue sky, the air on the top floor of the Eiffel Tower was considerably cooler, and she pulled her jacket a little tighter against the breeze.

They walked towards the edge, Lachlan taking his hand in hers. She looked up at him, as if surprised at the intimate gesture. He suppressed a grin. If she thought holding hands was intimate, then what the hell had they been doing all night?

Below them, Paris stretched out like a contented cat, only slightly obscured by the criss-crossing of wires that encircled the viewing platform. She reached out for the handrail, and he slid in behind her, his arms encircling her as they stared out at the city.

It had been strange, seeing a city he knew so well through her eyes. He'd been caught up in her excitement as they wandered the banks of the Seine, and had bitten down a grin at her disappointment when she saw just how small the *Mona Lisa* was. By the time they'd climbed the Arc de Triomphe, Lachlan had spent more time looking at her than he had at the beautiful city before them. And now they were at the Eiffel Tower – the last place on her list – she seemed more radiant than ever.

'It's beautiful,' she whispered. They took in the Tuileries Garden as it stretched from the Louvre to the Place de la Concorde, the rectangle of green intersected with pale yellow walkways, and two ponds – one circular, one octagonal – that topped and tailed the terraces.

He leaned closer into her, his body caging her in. 'It all looks so small from here,' he said, his mouth close to her ear. 'It makes everything seem so insignificant.'

165

She half-turned her head to look at him. 'That's because we *are* insignificant.' A smile was playing at her lips, and he couldn't work out if she was teasing him or being serious.

A shaft of sunlight hit her face, illuminating her skin, and he couldn't help but stare at her, absorbing her beauty the way she was absorbing the rays. Her lips parted, but her words were stolen by the wind. She repeated herself – louder this time.

'I can't believe this is the first time I've been here.' She shook her head. 'All the travelling I've done, and this place was always on my doorstep.'

Lachlan swept the hair away from her face with his hand, exposing her neck. Leaning forward, he pressed his lips against her throat, gently kissing his way up to her chin. 'Remind me why we aren't in bed right now,' he murmured, feeling her laughter through her skin.

But instead of talking, she turned her head until her lips met his, their kisses becoming heated within seconds. He wrapped his arms around her waist, pulling her against him, leaving her in no doubt that he'd rather be in their hotel room right then.

'Because the anticipation is almost as good as the real thing,' she whispered into his lips. 'And we have all night, remember?'

But that was all they had, and he wanted to make it last as long as he could. Because when morning came, all bets would be off. She'd be heading back to Edinburgh, and he'd be on a plane to New York, and it would be like this weekend never happened.

He ran his hand through her hair, feeling the silken strands curling around his fingers. The way she was staring up at him, eyes soft, lips open, made him want to push her against the railing and kiss her until neither of them could breathe. But they weren't alone – they were surrounded by tourists, brushing past them, grumbling, sending them strange looks.

He leaned his head forward, until his brow was pressed against hers. When she blinked he felt her eyelashes touch his. Her chest hitched, her breath stuttered against his skin, and all he could think of was how much he needed her right then.

'Let's go back to our room,' he whispered, his voice hoarse. He brushed his lips against hers again, feeling a flash of desire shooting through his veins.

'One more stop,' she said, her lips moving against his. 'Let's just see one more thing and then we'll go back.' She closed her eyes as he moved his mouth to her neck, softly kissing his way to her throat. 'You can choose where we go.'

He breathed in her warm skin, smelling the fragrance of her perfume, mixed in with the floral notes of her shampoo. 'Okay,' he agreed, 'we'll see one more thing, and then for the next fourteen hours the only sight I want to look at is you.'

He knew exactly what he wanted to show her as soon as she'd said the words. And it wasn't a huge in-your-face monument like the Eiffel Tower, or a tourist mecca like the Louvre. It was smaller, more intimate, and yet he still found himself hesitating for a moment, before leaning forward to tell the cab driver where to take them next. It wasn't that he didn't want to share this with her, more that he was afraid she wouldn't see it the same way he did.

'We're going to another gallery?' she asked, looking at him quizzically. 'I didn't think you liked the paintings at the Louvre that much.'

'I liked some of them,' he said, still feeling that strange edge. 'But this place is different. It doesn't have paintings.'

Within minutes they were pulling up outside a tall glass building, the light inside flooding out into the Paris streets. Lachlan leaned forward to pay the driver, then climbed out first, offering his hand to Lucy as she left the taxi.

'Always the gentleman,' she said, sliding her palm into his.

'Almost always.' If she could read his mind, she'd probably change hers. Every time he looked at her there was a need he was finding it harder to ignore. As though their weekend together was only bringing him to a boiling point.

Still holding her hand, he led her inside the gallery, nodding at the dark-haired lady standing behind the desk. There were only a few people inside, wandering around the exhibits, their voices little more than low murmurs in the resounding silence. But it wasn't the people inside he was looking at, it was *her* and her reaction. Would she see the beauty that he did, or would it simply be another sight for her to add to her collection? A photograph that would disappear among all the others on her desk.

He hated the thought of that, as much as he hated the thought of her leaving on Sunday.

'What *is* this?' Lucy asked, staring around the room. It was filled with ceramics – old ones, by the looks of them. From their designs and colours she recognised them as oriental – Japanese or Chinese, maybe. But it wasn't their ethnicity that drew the eye. It was the jagged lines on each piece, filled with gold resin, making new patterns across the old glaze.

'It's called Kintsugi,' Lachlan told her, as they walked into the centre of the room. His voice was strangely hesitant. 'The Ancient Japanese art of ceramic repair.' He pulled her towards a large plate. 'This one is a few hundred years old. See the way each piece is glued together? That lacquer is mixed with powdered gold.'

She leaned forward, her eyes tracing the criss-cross pattern of glue. 'But why?' she asked. 'Do they do it on purpose?'

He shook his head, smiling. 'Not originally, though I'm sure some do now. It's more than an art, it's a philosophy. The belief that things can be more beautiful if they're broken. That an object's history only adds to its appeal. That we should enhance our imperfections, not hide them.'

His expression was intense as he stared at her, and she could feel her body responding to his gaze. He looked as excited as he had that day out by the loch, surrounded by nature's beauty. As though he was springing to life. 'How do you know so much about it?' she asked.

'I lived next door to a Japanese family when I grew up,' he said, as they moved to the next piece. 'They found me crying one day when I'd broken my mom's vase. It was only a cheap thing from Walmart or somewhere, but I knew she was going to be crazy upset by it. The grandma showed me how to repair it and make it look more beautiful. She told me the gold lacquer was like a scar, that we should wear our scars with pride, because they proved to everybody we were survivors.'

Almost immediately her thought was drawn to her own scar. With her free hand – the one not holding on to Lachlan – she reached beneath her hair and touched it.

'When I first saw that scar, I thought of Kintsugi,' Lachlan murmured, watching her. 'You hide it away as though it's something to be ashamed of. But scars aren't disfigurements, they're medals. They show you survived.'

He'd done it again: said something that brought tears to her eyes. She rolled her lip between her teeth, biting on it to stem her emotions. Some things were too horrible to be proud of.

He stopped walking, and reached out to her, tracing the scar with his finger. She held her breath, the touch of his hand like fire against her skin. For a moment it felt as though they were the only people in the gallery, just the two of them, surrounded by ancient Japanese works of art. And the way he was looking at her, as though she was the most beautiful of all of them, was sending her soaring.

'Why do you try to hide your scar?' He traced it again, his touch as soft as cotton. 'It's part of you, and that makes it beautiful.'

A single tear escaped the barrier she'd tried to create, rolling down her cheek. She tried to swallow, but the congestion in her throat prevented her.

'It's an imperfection,' she finally whispered, her skin on fire beneath his touch. 'By its very nature, it makes me less than perfect.'

'What the hell is perfect?' he asked, sliding his hand until he was cupping the back of her neck. Gently, he kissed away the teardrop that was lingering by her mouth. 'It's pretty damned overrated if you ask me. All those women with Botoxed faces, not able to smile or frown? It's horrible. And these ceramics – before they were broken and mended, they were nothing. Unremarkable. And now they're exquisite, enough to be displayed in one of the most beautiful galleries in the world.' His thumb rubbed circles into her neck.

She looked up at him. 'Is that why you like them?' she asked. 'Because of their imperfections?'

'I like them because they represent a second chance. A second life. They show that no matter how broken things get, they can be mended. And they can become even better than

170

they were to start with.' He leaned towards her, rubbing his nose against hers. His lips ghosted the corner of her mouth. 'One man's imperfection is another man's work of art,' he whispered, his breath tickling her skin. She held her own breath as he pressed his mouth to hers, kissing her hard enough to send shivers pulsing through her spine.

Christ, the man knew how to kiss. She was like potter's clay in his hands, moulding to him, aching for him to form her into something new. Every time he touched her, every time he said something to her, she was sinking deeper. Into a need she didn't know she had, and a desperation she had no idea how to control.

'What are you doing?' she asked, watching him pull the white terry-cloth belts from both their bathrobes, laying the cords on the bed in two parallel lines. 'What are they for?'

'Insurance,' he said, trying to hide a smile. She was so fucking cute.

'Against what?'

'Against your better judgement.'

Her mouth dropped open. She was sitting on their bed, her bare legs curled beneath her. When they'd got back from their day of sightseeing he'd run her a bath, pouring her a large glass of white wine to relax her. Her skin was still pink from the heat, her eyes a little glassy from the wine. An intoxicating combination.

'Stop trying to frighten me,' she said, sending him an icy stare, though her smile spoiled the effect. 'I've seen a bluff before, remember? It's my job to work out the truth.'

He'd spent the time she'd been in the bath trying to work out what he was going to do with her. When he'd made the bargain last night, it had been more of a joke than anything else. A way to get her to relax. And it had been pretty fucking hot, too.

But now a whole world of opportunity lay in front of him. Or rather sat in front of him, wearing one of his old, grey T-shirts, her hair wet and brushed back from her face. There was her scar again, a little pinker than the rest of her, a jagged line from her brow to the top of her ear. For some reason he was drawn to it, his curiosity eating at him like a hungry wolf.

'As soon as I take my shirt off, it's on,' he said, pulling it from his waistband. 'After that you don't talk back, you don't question, you just do what I ask. Okay?' Deftly, he unfastened his buttons, his white cotton shirt gaping to reveal his chest.

Her mouth was slightly open, her eyes wide, her gaze following his hands as he unfastened his cuffs. He could see her swallow, the emotion in her face making her so goddamn expressive. He wanted to kiss the worry lines from her brow.

'What if I want you to stop?' she asked him.

'You won't want me to,' he said, grinning. God, this side of her was so different to the Lucy he saw in the office. 'But if you do, then just say it. "Lachlan, please stop."'

'And you'll stop?'

'Yes, I will.'

'Do you do this often?' she asked.

'What?'

'Dominate women?'

He couldn't help but laugh. 'I'm not a dominant, Lucy. I'm not going to do any more to you than you did to me last night. I'm going to be in charge, tell you what to do, but believe me, we're both going to enjoy it.'

'The way you did last night?'

'The way we both did.'

'What about those?' She inclined her head to the belts, still laid out beside her.

'I meant them as a joke,' he admitted. 'Unless you want to try them.'

'Okay.'

Her answer shocked the hell out of him. He shook his head as though to send some sense back into it. 'Seriously?' She never failed to surprise him. It was one of the things he liked about her the most, he could never quite guess what she was going to do next.

'Seriously.' She nodded.

His cuffs released, he shrugged out of his shirt, watching it fall to the floor in a pool of white cotton. 'You have one last chance to back out,' he warned her, more for effect than anything else. This kind of thing had never floated his boat before. Sex had never been about being on top, or planning intricate ways to dominate another human. It had been a way of getting off and that was it.

But now, seeing her sitting in front of him in his over-worn T-shirt, he couldn't think of anything he'd rather do. It wasn't about controlling, it was about pleasing her, about giving her the things she didn't know she wanted.

Until she had them.

'Take the T-shirt off,' he told her, deliberately making his tone sharp.

Her eyes flashed as she hesitated, before pulling it over her head. She was wearing only a small pair of pale pink panties, the rest of her was bare.

Naked, blonde, curled on his bed. Jesus, did it get any better than this?

'Put your arms above your head.'

This time she did it straight away. Her arms stretched above her, lifting her breasts, her nipples visibly hardening. Wearing only his pants, Lachlan closed the gap between him and the bed, kneeling on the mattress. Grabbing the belts, he tied them around her wrists, fastening her to the intricate iron headboard behind her.

'You okay?'

She nodded.

'Trust me?'

She tugged at the belts tied around her wrists. He'd left them loose enough not to cause her any discomfort. Enough force and she'd have them undone in no time – he was no Boy Scout. Still, something about the way she was staring up at him sent a jolt of pleasure through him. Sure, he'd never done anything like this before but with her, it felt goddamned amazing.

'Do you trust me?' he asked again, somehow needing to hear her say it. He knelt over her, straddling her hips with his thighs, just as she'd straddled him last night. He looked down at her, drinking her in. It was taking everything he had not to pull her panties off right then.

'I trust you,' she whispered.

Relief coursed through his veins. Unbuckling his belt, he let the leather hang loose, unbuttoning his pants and sliding them off. Then he was just in his shorts, the ridge of his excitement prominent against the black fabric.

She trusted him. Hearing it was as much an aphrodisiac as seeing her almost-naked body splayed beneath him. He could feel his dick pulsing hard as he lowered himself to her, desperate to feel her skin against his.

She trusted him.

It was everything he needed to hear.

19

The good I stand on is my truth and honesty

– Henry VIII

Lucy could barely keep her breathing under control. Every time he touched her she could feel her heartbeat speed, her skin singing to the tune of his fingers. He brushed his lips against her inner thigh, soft and teasing, and she arched her back to show him her need.

'Remember last night?' he asked her. 'The way you teased me until I begged?'

She nodded, lifting her head from the soft pillow. She tried to arch into him, but her tied-up hands prevented her getting purchase.

'I want to hear you beg now.' He kissed her thigh again, and she could feel him smile against her skin. 'I want you to beg like you've never begged before.'

'Lachlan ...' She sighed, the breath rushing out of her in its haste to be free. 'Please don't.'

Another smile, this one as wicked as the last. His eyes were twinkling as he stared at her. 'I'm not sure how I like you best,' he said softly. 'Kneeling over me, or supplicant beneath me. Both ways you're gorgeous.'

Her hands curled into fists, making the towelling cords dig

into her wrists. She could taste the anticipation, a metallic tang that coated her tongue. She inhaled a fresh lungful of air to take the flavour away. Slowly, she unfurled her fingers, relaxing her hands as they remained above her head.

He was still looking at her, still waiting, and there was something about his reticence that touched her. And at that minute she knew that whatever she said, he'd abide by. He wouldn't push her any further than she was willing to go.

'I want you,' she told him. 'I need you inside me.' She pulled at her hand, intending to stroke his soft hair. She couldn't help but feel frustrated at the cord holding her back. He reached for his wallet, grabbing a foil packet and opening it. She watched silently as he unrolled the condom down himself.

'Never change,' he said, placing his hands either side of her, taking the weight of his body. She could feel his skin brushing against hers. Chest against chest, thighs against thighs.

God, it felt good.

He hesitated for a moment, looking down at her, before brushing her lips with a sweet, half-there sort of kiss. One that left her wanting more.

Then he was pushing inside her, a rush of breath escaping his mouth. He stilled himself for a moment, as though he was already reaching the edge. She wasn't far behind, the pleasure already pooling in her stomach, and she inclined her hips, encouraging him to move, needing to feel him grinding against her.

'Still killing me,' he whispered, his lips grazing against hers. 'But it's a damn good way to die.'

'Are you okay?' Pulling out of her, he cupped her face with his hands, his body heavy on hers as they both tried to catch their breath. Her arms were laid by her side – he'd unfastened the belts almost as soon as he'd pushed inside her, begging her to touch him, to hold him, to run her finger through his hair.

'I'm more than okay,' she whispered, her voice thin from a lack of breath.

He grinned, leaning back on his elbow, running his fingers down her arm. 'You look so beautiful.'

That was another thing about him, he knew how to say all the right things. But more than that, the way he looked at her only underscored his words, making her feel as though she was the most important person in his life. An illusion, of course, but a pleasurable one anyway.

'You don't look bad yourself,' she said.

'You want anything? Water? A shower?'

'Maybe in a while,' she said, her body leaden from all their exertion. 'I just want to lie here for a bit.'

He put his arm around her, pulling her close until she was nestled into his side. Her legs were curled beneath her, her head resting on his shoulder. He stroked the hair from her face, kissing her exposed skin. She could feel his lips trace the line from her brow to her ear – the same line her scar intersected.

'It's still my night, isn't it?' he whispered.

'You want to go again already?'

He laughed. 'No, but you have to do whatever I say, right?'

Her eyes flickered to his. 'Yeah ...' Her tone was suspicious. She didn't think he was suddenly going to get a flogger out, but still, the way he asked put her on edge.

'Tell me about the scar,' he said softly. 'Tell me why you got so upset at the gallery.'

Immediately she felt her stomach contract. 'That's not fair.'

'You didn't put any caveats on it,' he pointed out. 'I'm still in charge. And I want you to tell me about this.'

She frowned, trying to read his expression. 'Why do you want to know?'

'Because I want to know you.'

His words were enough to send her heart racing. 'Maybe you don't want to know this part.'

'It doesn't work like that,' he said softly. He ran his fingers through her hair, his thumb trailing along her neck.

She closed her eyes, a scene playing behind them. The rain pouring down, the screech of tyres on an already slick road. A sickening crunch as reality shrank to the size of a pinhead, the darkness eating it up. She started to shake with the memory, and he pulled her closer, murmuring softly in her hair.

'How old were you when you got this?' he asked, brushing his lips against her brow.

'I was fifteen.'

'That's young.'

'I didn't think so at the time. I thought the world revolved around me. It was all so black and white back then.' She'd always segmented her life into two – before the accident and after. 'Everything changed, everything, and it was all my fault.'

'How was it your fault?' Lachlan frowned. 'You weren't driving, were you?'

She shook her head, feeling the familiar ache forming in her chest. 'No, but it was my fault anyway.'

'Of course it wasn't, how could it be? Your mom was driving, right?'

'Yeah.' Her voice was low.

'So how was it your fault?'

'We had an argument, I was screaming at her. Telling her she was the worst mum in the world. She turned to look at me and jumped the lights, and the next thing I knew she was trying to swerve away from a van coming head-on towards us. She clipped the kerb and we span back into the road, smashing into a van parked on the side.' Lucy reached up to wipe her eyes. 'I don't remember much else, not until I was in the ambulance. They told me she wasn't wearing a seatbelt. That wasn't unusual for her. She always had her head in the clouds, she didn't think about things like safety. She thought she was invincible.'

'It wasn't your fault she didn't wear a seatbelt,' he said, his voice low. 'And you didn't make her look at you. She should have known better than to take her eyes off the road.'

'You're wrong,' she whispered. 'It was all my fault. It was me who started the argument. Me who wouldn't shut up even when she told me to. Me who threatened to tell my dad everything...' She trailed off, shaking her head. 'It doesn't matter anyway.'

'Threatened to tell your dad what?'

Nervously, she twisted the sheet between her fingers, rubbing the pads against the soft fabric. 'It doesn't matter. It's old history.'

'You're shaking,' he said, his hands gentle as he held her. 'It's okay, babe. It's okay.'

She knew it was. She'd made it all okay – by sheer force of will. She was still making it okay, as much as she could.

And yet this need to tell somebody – to confide the secret nobody else knew – was almost overwhelming. More than that, the need to tell *him*, the man who thought imperfection meant beauty, the man who thought scars were like cracks filled with gold, was nagging at her core.

'I found out she was involved with another man,' she told him. Her voice didn't waver, not a bit. 'I was screaming at her in the car, telling her she was a terrible mother, a terrible wife. I shouted some horrible things at her.'

Lachlan blinked, lifting his head up to look at her. 'What? How serious was it?'

'I don't know how long it had been going on, I guess I'll never know now. I've never told anybody about it.'

'That must have been a shock.'

'I was so angry at her. And then she died, and it felt as though my whole life was crumbling away. I only had minor injuries, a cut-up face and a broken wrist where I slammed into the dashboard. They released me the next day, and then when I got home it was as though everything had fallen apart.' She closed her eyes, remembering that house in Hampstead, more mausoleum than family home. 'My dad just couldn't cope with the grief, he pulled away from us all. And my sisters were inconsolable. Seeing everybody so broken, and knowing I'd caused it . . . ' She shook her head. 'I had to fix it.'

'But your sisters know now, don't they?' Lachlan asked. 'You told them about it?'

'I didn't . . . I couldn't.' She screwed her face up. 'They idolised her, especially after she died. And when I tried to talk to dad about it, to tell him about her affair and our argument, he looked straight through me and refused to talk about it. By the time we were older, we were all doing so much better, there was no way I wanted to blow their worlds apart again.'

'They'd understand.' He frowned. 'It's not your responsibility to hide the facts from them. It's not your responsibility to carry everything on your shoulders.' He brushed a lock of hair from her brow. 'You really should tell them the truth.'

'It doesn't matter any more,' she said softly, her words muffled by his skin. Warm and soft against her lips. 'It was years ago. What matters is now. We're doing okay, all four of us.'

Lachlan looked down at her for a moment, brushing her

cheek with a kiss. She could feel his lips against the dampness of her skin. 'You're amazing, you know that?'

Part of her wanted to sing at his words. The other part of her – the girl who screamed at her mother, the one who had to watch her family disintegrate in front of her – knew so much better than that.

He twisted in the bed, a smile on his lips. 'You want to stop talking about this?'

'Yes please.' She gave him a watery grin.

'Wanna tickle me instead?'

His offer was so out of left field, yet so perfectly right for the moment. 'That's a big sacrifice,' she said. 'But yeah, I'd love to tickle the hell out of you right now.'

Sighing in mock-resignation, Lachlan rolled on to his back, lifting his arms above his head. 'I don't do this for all the women, you know.'

'Glad to hear it.'

'Just for the ones that are as messed up as me.'

'That's rude.' She clambered over him, the smile still playing around her lips. 'True, but still rude.'

'I can be ruder.' He thrust his hips beneath her. 'And it's still my night, remember?'

She could get used to waking up with aching limbs. The soft white sheets surrounded her, soothing her skin. The morning sun was shining in through the gauzy curtains, the light diffused as it hit the cream hotel-room carpet.

Her eyes blinking in protest at her sudden wakefulness, Lucy looked around. The other side of the bed was empty, the sheets carefully rearranged so as not to disturb her. The only evidence that Lachlan had ever been sleeping beside her was a dent in the white self-striped pillow.

And that aroma, sugary and sweet. What was it? She sniffed, her eyes drawn to the table on the other side of the room. There was a tray there, filled with fruit and pastries, plus a large flask of what could only be coffee. A jug of orange juice was beside it – simply seeing it there was enough to make her dry mouth call out.

Climbing out of the bed, she grabbed her robe, wrapping it around herself. No belt. Ah. She blushed, remembering exactly why that was.

Next to the breakfast tray was a brief note.

Good morning, sleeping beauty. Didn't want to disturb you with my brash American voice so I'm making some calls in the business lounge. Let me know when you're awake. Lachlan x

His handwriting was as masculine as he was. Slanted and strong. She'd seen it before, of course, but only in business. She found herself folding the notepaper carefully, and sliding it into her pocket.

Pouring a juice, she lifted the glass to her lips and tasted the sweet nectar, letting the liquid linger on her tongue. This weekend was full of firsts, and being brought breakfast in bed – or at least in her bedroom – by a man was another.

Yes, she could definitely get used to this.

But she shouldn't.

Her flight left this afternoon, and by tonight she'd be back in Edinburgh. Back to her old apartment, to her old life. To predictability and comfort. And that's what she wanted, wasn't it? To be in control. Not living at the whim of some rich American guy, no matter how luxurious the surroundings.

She caught sight of herself in the window, at her messy hair and her flushed cheeks. She didn't quite recognise the girl reflected back at her. And maybe that was a good thing, maybe she could leave that girl behind in Paris, along with any feelings she might have for Lachlan, because they'd both agreed this weekend was a one-off.

Even if the thought of it made her heart ache.

Her stomach growled, as she looked at the pastries. Croissants and pains au chocolat, along with raisin brioches. Sweet and flaky, their crumbs already covering the tray, they looked almost too good to eat. Unsure she could last much longer, she flicked her phone on, sending Lachlan a quick text, letting him know she was awake.

Within a minute he replied.

Get back into bed and don't eat a thing.
I'll be up in ten.

Part of her bristled at his orders. A bigger part felt hot at his words. She smiled, tapping out a reply.

You're not in charge any more, remember?

His next reply came almost as soon as she pressed send.

Please?

Grinning, she put her phone on the table, shrugging off her robe and letting it fall to the floor. Her stomach rolled again, making its need for food vocal. Reaching out, she picked up a crumb with the tip of her finger, lifting it to her lips and licking it with her tongue.

God, it was delicious, so buttery and sweet. Disobeying the rules had never tasted so good.

Their cab pulled up beside the pavement at Charles De Gaulle airport's departure zone. Lucy grabbed her bag, turning to Lachlan. 'I guess this is it.' She glanced at her watch. 'I'd better go, before I miss my flight.'

Lachlan's own flight didn't leave for another four hours. She'd be back in Edinburgh before he even took off.

He reached for her bag and opened his door, climbing out and offering her a hand. She placed her palm in his and he closed his fingers around hers as she followed him onto the pavement.

The driver walked around the back of the cab and opened the trunk, pulling Lachlan's cases out and laying them upright on the concrete. She tried not to smile at the fact he had so many more cases than she did.

'I'll wait with you,' Lachlan said. 'I don't need to check in for a couple of hours.'

'No, it's fine.' She shook her head, painting a smile on her lips. 'I'm sure you've got lots to do.' She tried to swallow down the taste of regret on her tongue.

He carried on as if she hadn't said anything. 'It's the least I can do.'

'Please don't. It would be weird.' She needed to be alone, to think about everything that had happened. Every time he was next to her she couldn't get her mind straight.

'Thirty euros, please,' the taxi driver said.

Lucy went to grab her purse, but her hand froze in the air. She felt her face flush as Lachlan paid for the fare.

Once the driver had left, Lachlan placed his cases on a

trolley, then picked up her overnight bag, but she quickly took it from him. 'I've got it.' They walked towards the terminal, through the small crowd of people outside, and Lucy could feel her neck itch. As they stepped inside, a glance at the screens told her she needed to check in at desk fifty – far away from the transatlantic flights.

'Are you sure you don't want me to wait with you?' Lachlan asked. His voice sounded strange. As though it had been stretched thin.

'I'm sure.' She took a deep breath, then gave him a smile. 'Thank you for a lovely weekend.'

'It was my pleasure.'

'Mine, too.'

Could this feel any more awkward? She did her best to ignore the little voice in her head, the one telling her this is why she shouldn't mix business with pleasure. Even if that voice spoke the truth.

She looked around the departure hall. It was teeming with people. 'I guess I'll speak to you soon. About the case.'

Lachlan was moving the trolley back and forth, like a mother rocking a baby to sleep. 'Yeah, sure.'

'Have a safe journey.' Should she kiss him? Maybe on the cheek. Anything else would feel strange.

Which was really messed up after the things they'd done this weekend.

Damn it, she leaned in and pressed her lips to his cheek. 'Goodbye, Lachlan,' she murmured.

He curled his warm palm around her neck, and moved his head, until his lips brushed against hers. 'Goodbye, Lucy.'

She stepped back, swinging her bag in one hand, raising the other in a goodbye salute. Then she turned and walked towards the check-in zone, refusing to look back and see if he was still there. They'd made a pact and she was determined to keep it, even if she was already missing him like crazy.

No tears, no recriminations, no promises. Just two adults spending a no-strings weekend in the city of love.

Maybe she wasn't as bad at this as she'd thought.

'Can I get you another drink, sir?'

Lachlan looked up from his laptop screen – and his IM conversation with Grant – to see the waiter standing next to his table. The business lounge was half empty – most of those travelling for Monday meetings had already left – and he'd found the silence useful for catching up on all those emails that had been piling up for the past few days.

'No thank you, I'm good.' He nodded at the waiter. 'Do you know if my flight's still on time?'

'Yes it is, sir,' the waiter told him. 'Boarding will begin in half an hour. I'll come and find you as soon as they announce it.'

As the waiter walked away, Lachlan glanced back at the screen. Grant had been busy in his absence.

You have five meetings tomorrow, plus a teleconference
with some investors, and your doctor wants to know why
you keep rescheduling your medicals. Did you know we've
had to cancel them four times already? You could be
dying of something and we wouldn't know.

Lachlan shook his head, suppressing a grin.

Try not to worry so much. You're my assistant,
not my wife.

186

Hey, if I was your wife, we'd be on our way
to the divorce courts already.

The door opened and a couple walked in – the man dressed in a tailored suit, the woman in a dress with matching jacket. Her blonde hair reminded him of Lucy, and for the tenth time that hour he found his thoughts wandering back to her.

Her flight had already left, and yet for some reason he couldn't stop thinking about her. He reached for his glass then remembered it was empty, his hand resting in mid-air for a moment. Strange how he'd half expected her to text message him before her plane departed, just to let him know she was okay. It wasn't as if they had that kind of relationship, was it?

Even stranger that he'd felt disappointed that she hadn't.

Pulling up his emails, he clicked on the red flag, his eyes skimming the urgent ones as he attempted to push her from his mind. But no matter how many times he read his messages, the only thing he could see was her.

Jesus, he needed to get a hold of himself. Just one weekend, that was all it was. Two stolen days with a beautiful woman – and that was supposed to be the end of it. They were grown-ups, they shared an attraction and they'd acted on it. That's as far as any personal relationship went.

It didn't matter that every time he closed his eyes he could see her standing on the top floor of the Eiffel Tower, the whole of Paris as her backdrop. That he could smell the floral scent of her shampoo as the breeze lifted her hair, revealing her slender neck. They'd had a weekend filled with mutual pleasure, and now they both had work to do.

It was time to get back to New York and get back to business.

And in the meantime, he would have another drink after all.

20

I must be cruel only to be kind

– Hamlet

'How is he?' Lucy asked, as she stopped at the reception desk to check in for the morning. 'Has he settled in yet?'

It had been over a week since she'd arrived back from Paris, and this trip down to see her father felt long overdue. The last time she'd seen him was the weekend they'd moved him into the home, and she wanted to make sure he was okay.

'He's doing fine,' the receptionist said. 'He's eating well, and he's doing his crossword every morning. He even joins some of the other residents to watch the television in the evening sometimes.' She smiled at Lucy. 'He's had a couple of episodes, which I'm sure the nurse will tell you about later, but overall he's very comfortable.'

'Episodes?' Lucy asked. 'What kind of episodes?'

'Nothing to be alarmed about, and completely normal for his condition. He sometimes gets confused, and that makes him agitated.' Another smile.

'Thank you.'

Lucy was directed to the day room, a large airy space with windows and glass doors that overlooked the main gardens. A television was on in the corner – though no sound came out – but most people weren't watching. Some were sitting in chairs just staring outside, others were reading. A thin, white-haired lady was dozing on the far side, occasionally letting out a loud snore.

She found her dad at one of the tables, the newspaper in front of him. Leaning forward, she pressed her lips against his papery cheek. 'Hi, Dad.'

He looked up at her through his pale blue eyes. 'Hello,' he said, his voice polite. Two furrows lined his brow.

'How are you doing?' She sat down in the chair opposite his, the table between them. 'Are you all settled in? Do you like it here?'

He took a slow look around the room. 'Yes, yes, it's very nice.'

'And you're eating well?' she prompted. 'Do you like the food?'

He blinked a couple of times, then picked up his pen, twisting it between his fingers. 'I think so, yes.' He pulled the lid off the biro then put it back on again. 'What's your name again?'

'It's Lucy, Dad.'

'I've got a daughter called Lucy.'

It was her turn to blink. 'I know you do. I'm your daughter.'

He shook his head. 'Don't be silly. Lucy's just a little girl.' He was still fiddling with the lid, pulling it off, pushing it back. 'You're a woman.'

She reached out for his hand, to stop him playing with the pen. 'Dad, it's me. Your daughter, Lucy.'

He pulled away as though she'd burned him. His bottom lip wobbled. 'You're playing tricks on me. I'd know my own daughter.'

189

She tried to bite down her tears. 'It's okay,' she said quietly. 'It doesn't matter.'

But it did. It really did.

Suddenly, her father reached across and grabbed her hand, yanking until she almost fell over the table. 'Where's Milly?' he asked, his voice raising an octave. 'Where is she? Where have you taken her?' He stared at her for a moment, then sat back. 'What did you say your name was?'

'It's okay.' Lucy tried to right herself, pulling her hand from his grasp. Over his shoulder she could see one of the nurses walking towards them. 'It's me, Lucy. Try not to panic.'

But she was the one who was panicking, her chest so tight she was finding it hard to breathe, her heart banging against her ribcage. Hot tears sprung to her eyes.

'Everything all right, Oliver?' the nurse asked, squatting down beside her father's chair. 'You a bit upset about something?' She shot a reassuring smile at Lucy.

'She's telling lies,' her dad replied.

'Ah, don't get yourself all upset. She just came to say hello.' The nurse turned her smile on him. 'I'm Grace, your nurse, remember?'

He gave the nurse a blank look.

'How about we go and get you a nice cup of tea?' Grace suggested. 'And maybe a biscuit, too. I know where they keep the good ones.' She offered her hand to him, and he took it. 'And then we'll come back and say hello to Lucy, okay?'

'Okay.' Oliver stood up, as compliant as a child.

'You all right here for a minute?' Grace shot a smile at Lucy. 'He's usually better after a walk and a drink.'

'I'm fine,' Lucy said, nodding rapidly. She watched the

190

nurse lead her father away, and then she sat as still as a statue, grabbing on to the edges of her chair with her hands.

She didn't know why she felt so shaken up. Maybe it was seeing his confusion first hand, or perhaps the strength he still had when he grabbed hold of her. His face had been taut with anger, as though for a moment he hated her with a passion.

She hated seeing him like this, hated knowing it would never get any better, only worse.

And though she had three sisters scattered across the globe, right then she felt completely alone.

'John Graves is here,' Grant told Lachlan, standing in the doorway of his New York office. 'And I sent those projections over to the finance team. They'll get back to you in a few days.'

'Can you keep on top of it?' Lachlan asked. 'Make sure it's their priority. I want to get back to Alistair with my initial thoughts next week.'

'Will do.' Grant glanced at his watch. 'And you have that videoconference with the Scottish attorneys in an hour. Do you want me to bring you and John a coffee?'

'Yeah, that would be great.' Lachlan smiled. 'And send John in.' It had been a few weeks since he'd seen his Chief Legal Advisor. He was looking forward to catching up with him, to finding out where the Glencarraig case was at.

And yes, maybe John might mention a certain Scottish attorney who Lachlan was doing his best not to think about.

He stood up, stretching his legs after a long morning at his desk, and turned to look out of the window, to the city that stretched out before him. It had been this view that had sold the office suites to him – the thought of being able to work high above one of the richest quarters in the world, to absorb the atmosphere of the financial district. To keep his finger on the pulse at all times.

But now, it all looked so crammed in. So grey. No rolling hills or mirrored blue lochs to be seen. Just a city full of people rushing from one place to the next, with no time to appreciate their environment. If it was even worth appreciating.

'Lachlan, it's good to see you.' John walked in, reaching his hand out. 'How was Scotland?'

'It was interesting.' Without thinking about it, Lachlan slid his hand in his pocket and felt the shiny paper of the photograph there. Two small boys wearing matching kilts. 'And wet. Very wet.'

John laughed. 'I spoke to Malcolm Dunvale, it sounds like his Scottish team have a handle on the case.'

'They're working out fine. We had an initial meeting with my brother and his solicitor while we were there. And then we went to visit the lodge.' He didn't mention Paris. Wasn't going to go there. 'They're confident we can see this thing through.'

'And then the real fun begins.'

'It does?' Lachlan frowned.

'Yeah, then you'll be in charge of this place thousands of miles away. You'll probably have to buy your own jet, the amount of travelling you'll be doing. First Miami, and now the Highlands of Scotland.'

'I wasn't planning on flying over there all the time,' Lachlan told him, gesturing at the conference table at the far side of his room. There was a television on the wall beside it, set up for videoconferences. 'I'll put somebody I trust in charge and let them do their thing.'

'The same way you do in Miami?' John raised his eyebrows.

'Miami's different. I have other reasons for visiting there.'

Why the hell did his thoughts immediately turn to the cool blonde with the hot body? 'Family reasons.'

'Of course you do. And how is your family?'

They spent the next five minutes on small talk, then moved seamlessly on to business. Grant interrupted them with a tray of coffee, then quietly left them to it. The next thing they knew he was interrupting them again, reminding them of the videoconference they were due to join.

'I've set up the conference bridge,' Grant was telling him. 'I need to switch on the monitor.' He walked over to the screen on the wall and turned it on, adjusting the camera above it to capture Lachlan and John. 'The microphone's off,' Grant told them. 'You can unmute it when you're ready to start.'

The monitor sprang to life, revealing a conference room with frosted-glass walls. A large oval oak table was in the middle of the screen, with an older man in a dark grey suit sitting there. Lachlan recognised him from his visit to Balfour and Robinson. Malcolm Dunvale – John's friend.

Malcolm leaned forward and pressed a button on the spider-shaped speaker in front of him. 'Ah, you're there. Good. We're just waiting on Lucy, she should be here in a minute.'

Lachlan ignored the way that made his pulse speed.

John leaned forward to unmute their own speaker, and spoke to Malcolm in a friendly voice. The two of them had known each other for years, Lachlan remembered, and they were reminiscing about old friends. From the gist of the conversation he realised that Malcolm – and Lucy, he assumed – were in London, not Edinburgh. Curiosity piqued him.

'Is Lucy's flight late?' Lachlan asked. 'Is that why she's not here yet?'

John shot him an interested look.

'No we travelled down last night,' Malcolm said. 'She just had some personal business to take care of this morning.'

Lachlan opened his mouth to ask what kind of business, then closed it again. It was none of his concern, was it?

He glanced at the clock next to the monitor, frowning. She was already ten minutes late.

'I do apologise for this,' Malcolm said. His accent sounded less broad than Alistair's, but it still made Lachlan think of that pub in Glencarraig and the warmth of the fire in the centre of the room. 'I'll just pop out and see if anybody has heard from her.'

Lachlan tried to ignore the way his stomach tightened. 'Yeah, that would be good.' Where the hell was she?

But as Malcolm went to stand up, the door behind him opened, and Lucy walked in. She was wearing a jacket and a scarf, which she unlooped and hung on a coat rack in the corner. 'My apologies for being late,' she said, glancing first at Malcolm and then at the screen. 'I hope I haven't kept you waiting too long.'

'Everything okay?' Malcolm's voice was low, but still audible on the speakers.

Lucy didn't say anything for a moment, but stood there, looking at her boss. Then she painted a smile on her face and walked over to join him at the conference table. 'Everything's fine,' she said, not quite meeting his eye.

'Hello, Lucy,' Lachlan said.

She looked up, and he felt the tightness in his stomach disappear. 'Lachlan.' Her voice betrayed nothing, and yet he could see there was a tenseness to her expression that wasn't there before. 'How are you?'

'I'm good. I didn't realise you were in London.' And he

didn't like it. He'd spent the last few days imagining her in Scotland, surrounded by misty rain and sandstone buildings.

She reached out for the glass of water in front of her. Was her hand shaking? 'Just for today. We fly back this evening. Malcolm had some business here, and I had something I needed to do.'

He bit down the urge to ask her what.

'You sound as busy as Lachlan,' John said. 'He's always on an airplane, too.'

Lucy looked up again, her eyes meeting his. Lachlan noticed a wariness that he hadn't seen before. 'Maybe that's why she gets me,' he said, smiling.

She didn't smile back. What was going on? Was she regretting their weekend in Paris? Lachlan didn't like the idea of that. Those days had been magical, sensual, and he wanted her to remember them that way.

'Lucy, maybe you could get the ball rolling with an update on where we currently are?' Malcolm prompted. He was looking confused too.

'Yes, of course.' Lucy leaned down for her bag, pulling her files out. When she sat back up, her expression was impassive. 'Shall we start with the most recent correspondence from Duncan MacLeish's solicitors?'

For the next twenty minutes they discussed the case, with Malcolm and John occasionally interjecting, and Lucy calmly answering their questions. They didn't seem to notice that she missed a beat a couple of times, nor that she answered a couple of their questions wrongly. They didn't notice an edge to her voice that wasn't usually there.

But Lachlan did. He had to grit his teeth every time she spoke.

As the meeting came to an end, and Malcolm and John were exchanging pleasantries, Lachlan found himself leaning in to the speaker. 'Lucy, can you stay behind for a moment?' he asked. 'There're a couple of things I want to go through with you. One on one.'

She picked up her glass and took a mouthful of water, her neck undulating as she swallowed it down. 'I'm not sure how long we have before we need to leave for the airport,' she said, glancing at Malcolm.

'You're fine. I have another meeting before we go. And this room is free for the rest of the afternoon.'

'Oh, okay.' Lucy nodded, but didn't look at the camera. Lachlan stared straight at her, as if willing her to look at him.

John stood, and stretched out his arms. 'Well, I need to head to another meeting, too. It was great to see you again, Malcolm, and you too, Lucy.' He turned to Lachlan. 'I'll call you later, okay?'

Lachlan nodded. 'Sure.'

As soon as the two older men left the room, Lucy looked at him. 'Once again, I apologise for my lateness. I hope I didn't cause any problems.'

'I don't care about your lateness,' Lachlan said.

'Oh. What was it you wanted to talk about then?' Her face remained impassive. 'Did you get the figures from Alistair for the renovations?'

'I don't want to talk about the lodge, Lucy.'

She said nothing.

He could feel himself tense up. 'I just wanted to check if you were all right.'

'I'm absolutely fine.'

'Bullshit.' Where was the woman she'd been in Paris? She'd opened up to him like a flower, slowly unfurling her petals one by one. But right now she was so tightly closed he couldn't see any colour at all.

She looked shocked at his outburst. Finally, a reaction. He wanted to shout hallelujah. 'I don't know what you're talking about,' she said firmly. 'Did I miss something? Are you unhappy with my work?'

'You know I'm not.'

'Then what's the problem?'

A flash of frustration washed through him. 'I'm not the one with a problem. You're the one who arrived late and then acted like a robot for the whole meeting. What's going on?'

'I thought you said you didn't care about my being late.'

'For fuck's sake, Lucy, what's wrong? You're acting weird. What kind of personal business were you attending to?'

She wasn't looking at him again. Damn, if they were in the same room he'd be tipping her chin with his finger until she couldn't avoid him. 'Lucy, what's wrong?' he asked, trying to keep his voice softer.

'It's . . . it's nothing.' She tried to smile, but her bottom lip trembled. 'Just family business.'

'What kind of family business?' He wanted to run his thumb along that lip, feel its softness.

'My father's not well. I went to visit him.'

'I didn't know your father was sick.' A mixture of sadness and relief washed over him. He hated seeing her upset, but was so goddamned pleased it wasn't him that had made her that way.

'We moved him into a care home a few weeks ago. I went to visit him this morning, to see how he's getting on.'

Lachlan quickly took a sip of water. 'And how is he?'

When she looked up, her eyes were shining. Christ, was she

crying? 'He . . . he didn't recognise me.' She covered her mouth with her hand, barely stifling a sob. For a moment she closed her eyes, and he could hear her inhale a deep breath. Without thinking, he reached out, then pulled his hand back again.

He didn't say anything for a minute, letting her collect herself. Finally she took her hand away, reaching for her water. 'I'm so sorry, this is really unprofessional.'

'I don't give a damn about being professional,' Lachlan told her. 'We're more than that, aren't we?'

Were they? There was that tightness again.

She tried to smile, and it looked genuine, in spite of the tears. 'Yeah, I guess we are.'

'Remember what we talked about in Paris?' he said gently. 'I just want you to be honest with me. Always.'

She took in another ragged breath. 'I am.'

'Good. And I'm so sorry about your father. Are you going to be okay?'

She gave a watery laugh. 'I will be once I've gone to the bathrooms and sorted out my make-up,' she said. 'Honestly, I'll be fine. It was a shock and I hated it, but it's just the way it is. He's only going to get worse, not better.'

Where had he heard that before? Lachlan scratched his jaw, then nodded at her. 'Okay, go wash your face, get your make-up on, and I'll talk to you soon.'

She looked straight into the camera. 'I will. Thank you, Lachlan.'

'You're welcome. And Lucy?'

'Yeah?'

'Even when you have eyes like a panda, you still look beautiful.'

21

I understand a fury in your words
– Othello

It was ten o'clock that night when she finally made it home. She was still wearing the suit she'd put on that morning, wheeling her small carry-on case behind her. Searching through her bag, she found her key and slid it into the lock, pushing the door open to walk inside.

Home sweet home. And it really did smell sweet. Elena had been – she could tell by the way everything looked neat and tidy, and the floral smell of the cleaning fluids she used. Lucy wheeled her suitcase in, then turned to close the door, but before she could the familiar flash of orange fur slid past her.

She tried to reach for the cat, but she was too quick, heading straight for the kitchen. Kicking the door closed, Lucy decided to worry about the intruder later. Maybe she'd even let her stay for a while, curl up on her lap. Goodness knew, a little bit of warmth and contact might do them both some good.

She slid off her shoes and placed them carefully in the hall closet, then shrugged off her jacket and hung it on a padded hanger, next to her other coats – some of them still in their dry-cleaning wrappers. As she turned to walk into the kitchen, she saw the huge bouquet of flowers in a large glass vase on the table. Reaching out to touch the petals, she saw a white card nestled in the bouquet.

The cat slinked around her legs, her silky-soft fur caressing her ankles, as Lucy opened up the card. Unfolding it, she saw a simple print-out stuck to the inside.

Thinking of you. Lachlan x

She traced the printed words with her finger, then looked back at the flowers. White calla lilies were mixed with the palest of pink roses, weaved in among blush orchids and a spray of heather. She breathed them in for a moment, then smiled a genuine smile for what felt like the first time in forever.

He was her client, and for a few days he'd been her lover, too. And right now, he was being a friend, and that touched her more deeply than she could say.

She grabbed her phone and walked into the living room, the cat following at her heels. When she sat down, the tabby jumped onto the sofa, then curled against her leg.

The call connected in less than twenty seconds. When he answered, his deep voice echoing down the line, her smile widened.

'Lachlan,' she said, reaching out to stroke the cat beside her. 'It's Lucy, I just called to thank you for the flowers.'

'What are you doing right now?' Lachlan leaned back in his leather chair, crossing his ankles on the desk. Outside his office window, the New York sky was beginning to darken, the early-evening sun slipping her anchor and sliding down towards the tops of the tall buildings.

'Is this a personal or a professional call?' Lucy asked. Her voice sounded like a laugh.

It had been a couple of weeks since she'd called to thank him for the bouquet of flowers, and somehow they'd drifted into the habit of talking in the evenings before she went to bed.

And yes, it was way beyond the normal client–lawyer relationship, but quite frankly he couldn't give a shit. He looked forward to these conversations all day.

'Does it matter?' he asked.

'Of course. If it's professional, I'll need to bill you. Plus, I'm already working on a contract for another client, so you'll have to call me back in the morning.'

'Are you teasing me?'

'Maybe.' She let the word stretch out.

'I don't like you working for anybody else,' Lachlan told her. 'You should be spending all your time on me. Why aren't I the Laird of Glencarraig yet?'

'The wheels of law turn slowly here. We're dealing with centuries of history, you know. Why are you in such a hurry?'

'Maybe I just want the estate,' he said. 'It impresses all the girls.'

'Oh, does it indeed?'

'It impressed you,' he said softly.

'Yes, it did.'

A knock at the door pulled his attention from the call. He looked up to see Grant walking in, carrying a steaming mug of coffee. Lachlan covered the mouthpiece. 'Thank you.'

'I'm heading out, we've got a pre-natal class. See you tomorrow?'

Lachlan nodded. 'See you then.'

'Everything okay?' Grant lingered, giving him a quizzical look.

'Everything's fine. I've just got to take this call.' Lachlan inclined his head towards his cellphone.

'Okay then. Have a good evening.'

'You, too.'

'And say hi to her from me.' With that, Grant left the room. Lachlan rolled his eyes at the closing door, lifting the phone back to his ear.

'Sorry about that. My assistant was just leaving.' He picked up the coffee, taking a sip. 'Now, where were we?'

'You were impressing me,' Lucy told him.

'That's right. Maybe I can impress you again some time.'

'Is that a euphemism?' she asked, her voice warm with humour. 'Am I supposed to tell you how impressive you are?'

'Feel free.' He grinned to himself.

'Haven't you got anything better to do than chat up somebody thousands of miles away? You know, like some work?'

'I'm working,' Lachlan protested, pulling his emails up on his laptop as if to make a point. 'I can multitask, you know.'

'What are you doing?'

'I've been reading my emails.' He wasn't sure why he was lying. To make a point? God knew which one.

'That's funny. I sent you an email five minutes ago, and got a delivery receipt straight away. Did you see it?'

'I saw it flash up, but I haven't checked it yet.'

'What a shame, it's a naked photo. I'll recall it,' she deadpanned. 'You're not reading your emails, are you? I haven't met a man yet who can multitask.'

'You're being very sexist, Miss Shakespeare. Assuming I can't multitask, and then thinking I'll be distracted by naked photos. What kind of man do you think I am?'

'Have you checked it yet?'

'Of course I have. It's a letter, not a photograph. And I'm disappointed now. I wanted naked Lucy.'

'You've had naked Lucy.'

And he wanted her again. It was driving him crazy. 'Come and see me this weekend. I'll arrange for a flight.'

'I can't just fly out at the drop of a hat,' she said. 'And anyway, I'm busy this weekend.'

He traced his lip. 'Then when can I see you?' he asked her.

'In court?'

He laughed. 'Is that a threat?'

'I was thinking it was more of a promise.' Her voice was softer. He glanced at the clock on his office wall. It was nearly seven p.m. in New York, which meant it was almost midnight in Edinburgh. Strange how he added five hours onto everything nowadays. When he arrived in the office, he automatically knew it was lunchtime in Edinburgh, and on the rare occasions he actually had time for lunch himself, he'd imagine Lucy walking home through the wet streets of Edinburgh, avoiding the huge puddles that gathered in the uneven pathways.

In short, he was obsessed, and he knew it, dammit. He just didn't know what the hell to do with that knowledge.

'You should get to bed,' he said, leaning back in his chair.

'And you should go home and eat something,' she replied, sounding tired. 'Before you waste away.'

'Good night, Lucy.'

'Good night.'

'Same time tomorrow?'

There was a smile in her voice when she replied. 'I'll be here.'

As far as he was concerned, it was a date.

*

'Try not to worry, we caught it early this time. I know it looks frightening, but she's in the best place.' The nurse turned to look at him as she adjusted the monitor above his mother's head. He didn't recognise her from last time his mother was here – maybe she was new.

Lachlan nodded, trying to ignore the way every muscle in his body seemed to ache. He should be used to this by now – the frantic phone calls, the rushed booking of airline tickets, the crazy dash to the airport.

In all the madness he'd missed his evening call with Lucy, and not being able to speak with her was making him edgy. Like the time he'd given up caffeine, and his whole body got the jitters. He'd lasted less than two days without it. He was pretty sure he'd last even less without speaking with her.

The nurse gave him a sympathetic smile. 'The night doctor will be around in half an hour. Why don't you go and grab a coffee? It's really not that bad for a hospital.'

Lachlan couldn't be bothered to disagree, even though he knew better.

It all felt so familiar – the walk to the café through the whitewashed corridors, the electric doors that seemed to open in a rush. The empty chairs, the barista leaning on the counter looking as bored as hell. Lachlan played his role, ordering the coffee, tapping his phone against the reader, carrying the Styrofoam cup over to the corner. He sipped it for a moment, not sure whether the extra shot he'd ordered made it taste worse or better.

He rested his head back on the wall, sighing, his eyes closing long enough for his breath to even out, his body relaxing into the chair. When he came back to reality with a start, half an hour had passed, and his coffee had gone cold. Stretching his arms, he walked back to the counter and ordered another one, this time determined to stay awake.

He pulled his phone from his pocket – turning it on for the first time since he'd arrived in Miami. Almost immediately her message flashed across the screen.

I missed you tonight. Hope everything's okay. Lucy x

When was the last time anybody had told him they missed him? She'd been the only person to notice he wasn't around. A few simple words, but they ignited a need in him that was impossible to ignore.

He pressed on her name, and then the green call button next to it, aware that it was either too early or too late to call. And yet he found himself lifting the phone to his ear, willing her to pick up, desperate to hear her voice.

He was as far away from professional as he'd ever been, but right then he couldn't give a damn.

'Hello?' Her voice was thick with sleep as she answered the call, her eyelids barely unsticking from each other. She could feel her heart racing – a side effect of the adrenalin rush that started with the shrill ring of her phone. She hadn't even bothered to check the caller ID – knowing it had to be about her dad.

'Lucy?'

She recognised his voice straight away. Deep, masculine, with the accent that made her body react even when half-asleep. 'Lachlan, is that you? Is everything okay?' She reached across to switch on her bedside light. 'What time is it there?'

There was a pause. She imagined him checking his expensive Rolex, the gold watch glistening against his skin. 'It's almost two a.m.'

'And you're still awake?' She sat up, rubbing her eyes with the heel of her hands. Slowly her eyes adjusted to the gloom. Shafts of light were invading her bedroom through the gaps in the curtains, though they were muted enough for her to tell it was early in the morning. She glanced at the clock beside her bed.

Six-forty a.m.

'I got your message,' he said. He sounded strange – as though his voice was echoing around the room. 'I'm sorry I missed our call last night. I had to catch a plane to Miami.'

'Is that where you are now? At the airport?'

'I'm at the hospital.'

Well, that woke her up. 'Why? Are you hurt?' A dozen different scenarios worked their way through her brain. And it was stupid, but she was starting to panic. The idea of something happening to him made her feel sick.

'There's nothing wrong with me. It's my mom.'

Her heart dropped. She knew that feeling well. She'd sat in too many hospitals too many times not to sympathise. 'Oh no. I'm sorry to hear that.' She paused for a moment, catching her breath. 'Has something happened to her?'

'She's been sick for a while. She has COPD.' His voice was soft, uncertain. It brought out every caring instinct she had.

'COPD?' she repeated. 'What's that?'

'Lung disease,' he told her. 'It's not cancer, but it's related to smoking. She's had it for years.'

'Can they cure it?' she asked. 'Will she get better?' All she could think about was that videoconference, when he'd talked

206

her down from her panic about her father. She should have guessed then that they had this in common too. That he knew exactly what it was like to have a sick parent.

'It's a chronic condition.' He kept his voice low. 'There's no cure. But it's not a killer either, at least not by itself. It just deprives your body of oxygen, makes you more susceptible to infections and heart failure. She has pneumonia right now.'

Lucy leaned back on the padded headrest, closing her eyes. She'd do anything to take away the pain – she knew how much it hurt. 'I'm so sorry to hear that.'

'Thank you.'

'It's hard to find an appropriate reply to that, isn't it? I find that with my dad. People tell me they're sorry but I never know what to say to them. *So you should be*? I'm not sure that works.'

For the first time he laughed. 'It's one way of shutting people up.'

'It's a horrible thing, watching your parents go through something like this. When my mum died, well it was fast. Dreadful, but quick. But when they start to waste away, it's excruciating. You feel so useless.'

'I imagine either way is pretty horrible.' He breathed deeply down the line. 'How's your dad?'

She shuffled in the bed. 'He's doing okay. No more incidents that I'm aware of. But he won't talk to me on the phone any more, says he doesn't like it.' She shook her head. 'It sucks, doesn't it?'

'Yeah, it does. I'm really sorry about your dad, Lucy.'

'So you should be.'

He laughed and it was like the sun coming out. She smiled, too, enjoying the lighter moment. She twisted beneath the bedcovers, stretching her legs out in front of her.

207

'Where are you right now?' she asked him. 'Are you allowed to make calls in the hospital? Doesn't it interfere with the equipment or something?'

'I'm in the café,' he said. 'The only equipment I'm going to interfere with is the coffee machine. And from the taste of this americano, that would be a blessing.'

She coughed out a chuckle.

'Where are you?' he asked. 'It must be morning there. Have you made it to the office yet?'

She considered lying to him. But somehow she found herself telling him the truth. 'I'm in bed,' she admitted softly.

Another pause. 'Alone?' His voice changed, and the thickness in it took her breath away.

'Yes.' Her heart was racing, and not from adrenalin this time.

'Describe what you're wearing.'

'What?'

'What are you wearing?' he asked again. 'Humour me, my mom's sick.'

'You're the sick one.' There was a smile in her voice. The abrupt change in the tone of their conversation had made her breathless. And yet she could sense how much he needed it, this brevity. And she wanted to give it to him.

She wanted to make him feel better.

'Touché. Now tell me what you've got on.' She could hear the smile in his tone, too. It sounded so much better than the sadness.

'Nothing.'

She heard a splutter, like he was choking on his coffee. 'Say what?'

'I'm lying naked in bed. I like to sleep with the heating cranked up, but last night it got crazy hot. I couldn't be bothered to get up and turn the thermostat down, so I stripped off.' Way, way too much information. 'So my pyjamas are in a pool on the floor, and I'm still under the covers.'

'Naked.' He said it as if it was a word of wonder. 'Do you talk naked with all your clients?'

'Only the ones that call me at stupid times of the day.'

'How many is that?'

'Just you, Lachlan.'

He gave a low whistle. Of appreciation? 'Glad to hear it.'

'I guess I should go,' she said, somehow unwilling to hang up on him. 'I need to get dressed and get to the office.'

'I should, too,' Lachlan replied, sounding as reluctant as she was.

'I'll be thinking of you and your mum. Let me know how she's getting on, okay?'

'Yeah, of course. Now go, get some clothes on before somebody sees you.'

'I'm hot, not an exhibitionist,' she pointed out.

'Yes you are.'

'An exhibitionist?'

'No, hot.'

'That sounds like a good way to end the call.'

'Goodbye, Lucy. I'll call you tonight.'

She was still smiling when she climbed out of bed and padded across the carpeted floor to her en suite bathroom. She could see herself in the large mirror opposite, her hair sticking out in strange directions, her face pale apart from the red spot on her cheek where she'd been resting on the pillow. And her pink and blue fleecy pyjamas, covered with images of sleeping sheep – a joke present from Cesca. She had a thing for cheesy nightwear.

It was only a white lie, wasn't it? He needed a distraction and she gave him one, even if her pyjamas were still fully fastened on her body, rather than in heap on her carpet.

The biggest problem was, she was getting distracted too.

22

*Young men's love then lies not truly in
their hearts, but in their eyes*
– Romeo and Juliet

'What?' Grant frowned, shaking his head as he looked at Lachlan. 'Are you serious? I've only just finished rearranging all your meetings after Miami, and now you want me to do it all over again? You're crazy.'

Lachlan's smile was wry. He couldn't blame Grant for looking at him the way he was. Because yes, he was definitely crazy, but he couldn't help it. He was like an addict, desperate for his next fix. And as much as he enjoyed his phone calls with Lucy, the need to see her in person was consuming him.

'It's only one day's worth of meetings you need to change,' Lachlan told him, trying to ignore the way Grant was shaking his head. 'Just clear my diary for Friday. I'll fly out in the morning, and I'll be back by Sunday night. You'll hardly notice I'm gone.'

He'd never seen Grant pout before, but damn if he wasn't pushing his lips out and frowning. It would have been funny if Lachlan wasn't serious about this. Grant gave a loud sigh, then clicked on his laptop. 'All right, I'll rearrange your Friday meetings but you need to start giving me more notice, okay? I'm trying to run a business here.'

'My business,' Lachlan reminded him.

Grant looked up from his laptop, taking a deep breath of air. 'You're right. Sorry, man. It's your call, of course it is.' He tapped his fingers on the keyboard, glancing back at the screen. 'I can get you on the first flight to London, then straight on a connection to Edinburgh. You should be there by Friday evening.'

'Sounds good.'

'You gonna tell me what this is all about?' Grant asked. 'Is it something to do with your inheritance?'

'Something like that.'

Lachlan wasn't ready to tell him the truth, no matter how close they were. What was there to tell, anyway? That he'd had sex with this woman a couple of times, and now he was calling her every night like a lovesick teenager, with no idea of how she felt about him? Grant would think he was even crazier than he already did.

'Okay, it's all booked,' Grant said. 'And I've changed the meeting times to next week. You're all set.'

'Thank you.'

Grant glanced at him warily. 'You're the boss. If you want to fly halfway around the world for some reason you're not telling me, then it's your call.' He pressed his lips together for a moment, as though trying to find the right words. 'But as your friend, and not your assistant, I have to tell you you're scaring the crap out of me. I'm worried about you, man.'

Lucy opened her refrigerator, feeling the breeze of cold air wash over her as she stared blankly at the contents. Salad, ready meals and two bottles of white wine were lining the shelves, but nothing took her fancy at all. She pushed it shut, running a hand over her tied-back hair, then walked back to the sofa and picked up her laptop, placing it on her crossed legs.

She was in a funk, plain and simple. Maybe it was the fact it was a Friday night and she had nothing to do. She'd come home, jumped in the shower, then tied her wet hair back, dressing herself in a pair of old pyjamas. And now it was eight o'clock, there was nothing on the television, and all she had to entertain her was work.

She really knew how to live it up, didn't she?

Twenty minutes later she was neck deep in writing up a deposition when her phone buzzed next to her. The sound almost made her jump out of her skin. A big smile broke out across her face when she saw who the caller was.

'Hi, Lachlan, you're early. It must be the middle of the afternoon there.' Not that she was complaining. In the past two weeks their phone calls had been the bright spot to her day. The one thing she looked forward to when she came home from work.

'Nope, it's definitely evening.'

She frowned, looking at her watch again. 'It's half past eight here, which makes it half past three where you are.' She heard the sound of a horn – though she couldn't quite place whether it was coming down the phone line or from outside her window. She moved her laptop onto the coffee table in front of her, straightening up her notes. A telephone call with Lachlan was worth ignoring her work for.

'It's half past eight here, too.'

'You're not in New York?' The strangest sensation came over her. 'Where are you?' But she knew the answer already.

She got up from the sofa and looked out of the large Georgian window to the street outside. It had been raining earlier, and though it was dry now, the puddles remained, the orange glow from the street lamps making them look strangely ethereal. But it wasn't the beauty of the light that drew her eye, it was the man standing at the front door to her townhouse, a small suitcase next to him, and a large takeout bag in his hand.

'Oh my God, you're there.' She put a hand to her chest to try to calm herself, but the thump of her heart was incessant. 'What are you doing here?'

'That's not quite the welcome I was hoping for.' He sounded amused rather than annoyed at her response.

'I'm ...' She had to take a breath to try to centre herself. 'I wasn't expecting company. I'm a mess. The apartment's a mess. Give me five minutes.' The thought of him seeing her like this, so unpolished and out of control, made her panic even more. Even in Paris – when they were both naked – she'd looked more sophisticated and elegant than this.

'You could never be a mess. And no need to tidy on my account. I've come to see you, not your apartment. I'm just glad you're home. I thought I might have to spend the night sitting on your doorstep, waiting for you to come back from a night out.'

'And how do you know I don't have a hot date up here with me?' She kept her voice light, flirting with him. Interested to hear his response.

'Because you weren't expecting company,' he said. And she thought she could see his grin from her window. 'Isn't that what you just told me?'

A car turned into the road, splashing water from the rain-soaked surface as it drove along. She could see a ghost of herself in the reflection of the glass. And yeah, she was a mess, but she was an excited mess.

'Don't go anywhere,' she said, letting the curtain fall closed. 'I'll just put something nicer on and I'll let you in.'

'I wanna see you messy,' he said. 'Don't make me wait. I've spent the past ten hours flying over to see you.'

Oh, to hell with it. She practically ran to the button by her door, pressing the buzzer to release the lock at the entrance way. Then she heard footsteps, and the banging of a case as it was being dragged up the flight of stairs. The next moment he was knocking at her door, and she was snatching it open, her grin wide, her mussed-up hair and pyjamas forgotten. Because he was there, on her front doorstep, and nothing else mattered.

She wasn't sure who closed the gap between them, but one moment they were looking at each other, the next he was running his hand down her neck, angling her head until his lips touched hers. Then she was kissing him back like crazy, weeks' worth of pent-up flirtation making her throw her arms around him, and meld her body to his without a single millimetre between them. She'd forgotten how well he could kiss, with that warm, demanding mouth, and those lips that made her whole body sing. She'd forgotten how he felt, his body thick and strong, his shoulders powerful enough to lift her up and carry her inside her apartment, as he kicked the door closed behind him.

And as it happened, it really didn't matter what she was wearing, because within five minutes their clothes were scattered over her living-room floor, in a trail of destruction that led to her bedroom.

He lay her on the bed, brushing kisses across her neck, her chest, her stomach, murmuring how much he'd missed her, how he'd been dreaming about her, how he needed to be inside her right then. When he finally slid inside, her thighs wrapped around his demanding hips, his arms cradling her as though she was something precious, all thoughts of being a mess had disappeared completely.

All she could think about was him. Right then, nothing else mattered.

They spent the weekend holed up in her bed, only emerging to make the odd cup of tea, or to head to the bathroom to freshen up. The first time they actually left her flat was on Sunday morning, when her milk had finally run out, and their mutual need for a coffee had overridden their need to stay naked and entwined. So they walked up to the Royal Mile, buying coffee-to-go from a small bakery on the corner, then carrying their Styrofoam cups up to the castle. The sun had come out in full force – as though she'd heard Lachlan was visiting and wanted to show him what she could do – and the blue sky did wonders for the city. It made Lucy smile so much her cheeks ached.

'Look at that,' Lachlan said, peering in the window of a gift shop. There was a mannequin wearing a blue T-shirt in the centre, with I LOVE SCOTLAND written across the chest. 'You think if I wear that shirt I might win the case?' He grinned at her, and just like that her whole body heated up.

'If you wear that,' she said, taking a sip of her coffee, 'I'll buy your brother off myself.'

He slid his hand into hers, tucking them both into the pocket of his jacket as they made it to the Portcullis Gate. Above the entrance, flags were dancing in the wind atop their poles. People flowed through the gate, stopping to buy their tickets. Lucy and Lachlan leaned against the stone bridge, watching them come and go, his arm wrapped around her waist.

'Come and visit me in New York,' he said, turning to brush his lips across her forehead.

'I can't.'

'Why not?' She felt him stiffening beside her.

She closed her eyes for a moment, wishing that perfect moment could come back. But instead a flood of thoughts washed through her, making her want to sigh. 'Because I'm your solicitor and you're my client. If I fly over to New York then I'm pretty much saying we're in a relationship, and I can't do that and represent you on the case.'

'You don't think we're in a relationship now?' he asked her. There was a mixture of amusement and confusion in his voice.

'I don't know,' she admitted. She'd not allowed herself to think about it. Fear had made her lock it away in a compartment deep inside of her. 'Probably.' She licked her lips, tasting the coffee on her tongue. 'I guess I could dismiss Glencarraig as a one-off, and maybe even Paris. But after this, I don't know.' She shook her head, trying to think it through. He'd flown all this way just to see her. Not for business reasons. They hadn't even mentioned his case once until now.

'Lucy, look at me.' His voice was strong. She turned her head, her face questioning. He reached out and cupped her cheek with his hand, the sweetest expression on his face. 'As far as I'm concerned this isn't a one-off, or a three-off or whatever you want to call it. I flew over because I wanted to see you, I wanted to spend time with you. And I want you to fly to New York to spend time with me.'

'But the case—'

'Fuck the case, I'll fire you from it if I have to.' He moved his hand back, fingers sliding through her hair. 'Glencarraig can wait, but I can't. I want you to visit me.'

'Let me speak to my boss tomorrow,' she said, her throat full of emotion. She couldn't believe she was considering this. Her career had always been the most important thing in her life – along with her family – and admitting to Malcolm Dunvale that she was in a relationship with a client wasn't going to win her any favours. 'I'll ask to be taken off the case.'

His eyes were soft as he stared at her. 'You'd do that for me?' He turned until they were face to face, still searching for her response.

She clenched her teeth together, trying to imagine what Malcolm would say in response. The thought of it made her feel sick. She'd spent her whole life working to get where she was now. Years of study, followed by years of working all the hours God sent to rise to the top. The thought of jeopardising it all scared her to death.

But the thought of not being able to see the man in front of her scared her even more. She couldn't put her finger on when she'd started to fall for him. Had it been that first night in Miami, when she'd felt a pull towards him in spite of herself? Or had it be in Glencarraig, when he'd lifted her so easily in his arms, and carried her to his bed to warm her frozen body.

All she knew was that every night she went to bed with a smile on her face, because he'd called. And now he was here, had flown all this way just to spend the weekend with her, and it felt as though everything she thought she knew about the world was wrong.

'Yes,' she said softly. 'I'd do that for you.'

23

Did my heart love till now? Forswear it, sight!
For I ne'er saw true beauty till this night

– Romeo and Juliet

She'd been putting this conversation off for hours. For as long as she'd been sitting in her office at Robinson and Balfour that morning, pretending to work on her laptop while she kept looking over at Malcolm's office, trying to work out the best time to go and speak to him.

The problem was, there wasn't a good time. She was about to admit she'd been completely unprofessional, and put the good name of the firm at risk. He'd be within his rights to have her disciplined for misconduct, and she couldn't blame him if he did. This firm had been around for longer than she'd been alive – about a hundred years longer, in fact – it was bigger than any one of them.

She dropped her head into her hands. How had she managed to get herself into this mess? Closing her eyes, for a moment she considered not telling him, but that wasn't possible. Even if there was nothing between her and Lachlan any more, she'd still stepped over the line too many times.

And the fact was, there was plenty between them. This

weekend had showed her that. As much as she felt sick at the thought of having to talk to Malcolm, the thought of not seeing Lachlan again hurt so much more.

She didn't really have a choice.

Lynn looked up from her desk as Lucy walked out of her office, giving her a big smile. 'Everything all right?' Lynn asked. 'Can I get you something?'

'I just need to speak to Malcolm.' Even saying it out loud made her chest ache. 'Do you know if he's free?'

'He is, but you'd better hurry. He's off for a lunch meeting in twenty minutes.'

It was now or never. Here went nothing.

'I don't quite know what to say.' Malcolm took off his glasses, rubbing the red patch on the bridge of his nose. 'I wouldn't have expected this from you of all people, Lucy. What on earth were you thinking?'

'I'm so sorry,' she said, looking down at her hands. 'I didn't mean for any of this to happen. And I know it must put you in a really awkward position. But I can't carry on with the case, it wouldn't be right.'

'Did he take advantage of you?' Malcolm asked her. 'Because if he did there are things we can do.'

Her eyes flew up to meet his. She felt horrified. 'No, no he didn't. Anything that happened was ... mutual.' Her face flushed with heat. This was mortifying. She could have stripped off and danced naked around the office and she would have felt better than she did now. 'I'm so sorry,' she said again, because really, what else was there to say?

He slid his glasses back on his nose, then leaned on his desk, his hands clasped together. 'What's done is done. I'll need to find out who has some space available to take the case over. And I'll expect you to make sure everything's shipshape before you hand it over.'

'Of course.'

'But I won't be able to stop the office gossip,' he warned her. 'People will speculate over why you've been removed from the case.'

She swallowed, her mouth dry. 'I understand that.'

'Either they'll guess right and realise you've been sleeping with a client or they'll assume it's too much for you. Either way you won't come out smelling of roses.' He shook his head slowly. She hated the way he looked so disappointed. She'd let him down, let the whole firm down, just because she couldn't control her emotions. What kind of person did that make her?

'I know.' She really did. She'd seen people ruin their careers for less than she'd done.

'Well, I suppose you've done the right thing in telling me.' He looked at his watch and sighed. 'I need to go to a meeting now, but I'll be back later, and I'll get to work on reassigning the case.' He looked at her through the thick lens of his glasses. 'I don't know what's going on with you and Mr MacLeish right now, but whatever it is, I hope he's worth it.'

So did Lucy. More than she could say.

'You're flying in to London?' Lucy spoke into her phone, looking away from the *Scottish Times* magazine she'd been reading. The cover showed Lachlan, leaning on the fireplace at Glencarraig, looking every inch the laird of the manor. In spite of the heated interview, Marina Simpson had gone surprisingly easy on him in her article, painting him in a very sympathetic light. There were only a few mentions of his father in there, and nothing about how his parents met, thank goodness.

Even if she was off the case, she was still desperate for him to win. For it to all work out okay. It felt as though her career depended on it.

'When are you arriving?' she asked her sister. 'How long will you be there?' It was a relief to be talking to Cesca, to hear her warm humour echoing down the line from LA. After the week she'd had, and the drama of telling Malcolm about her and Lachlan, her sister was like a breath of fresh air.

'It's a quick visit,' Cesca told her. 'Sam's sister is graduating next week, and he wants to put in an appearance. We'll only be in London for a few days. I'll drop in on Dad at some point while we're in town.'

'But I won't be there.' Lucy doodled a flower on the white lined paper, trying to swallow her disappointment. She so rarely saw her sisters, it hurt to miss this opportunity. 'I'm supposed to be in New York. I fly out tomorrow.' She felt torn. Desperate to see Lachlan, and yet needing to see her sister, too. It wasn't often they were all in the same country, after all.

'It's not a problem,' Cesca said. 'We'll miss you, of course, but you don't need to chaperone me. I can see Dad all on my own. And after that I might pop to the house, take a look at it before the clearance people arrive. When were you hoping to put it up for sale?'

'Early next month,' Lucy said. Two lines formed across her brow. 'Maybe I can change my trip, come down and see you. It's typical that the week I'm in the States, you'll be in London.'

'We're ships that pass in the night,' Cesca joked. 'But one day we'll all be on the same continent. The world won't know what's hit it when the Shakespeare sisters are all together again.'

A tiny smile formed on Lucy's lips, though it wasn't enough to push away the sense of sadness. 'Are you sure there's nothing we can do to meet up? Maybe I can push things back a few days.'

'Why are you flying over there anyway? Something to do with work?'

'Yeah, something like that.' For a moment she considered telling Cesca about Lachlan. Confiding in her sister about her fears. About almost ruining her career, about feeling out of control whenever her now-ex-client was in the vicinity. About how she thought she might be falling for him, and she had no idea how to deal with it.

She closed her mouth as quickly as she'd opened it. Better to go over to New York and see him before she started telling her family what was going on. They'd think she'd gone crazy if she told them the truth.

'Are you okay?' Cesca asked. 'Your voice sounds funny.'

'Funny? How?'

'You don't sound like you,' her sister told her. 'Is there a problem?'

'No, of course not. I just don't like disappearing for a week when Dad's unwell.'

'Well, now you can disappear without a care,' Cesca said. 'If there's any problem I'll be here. It's fate.'

'Yeah, I guess.'

'What's really up?' Cesca was insistent. 'It's not like you to be anxious about travelling. And Dad's not critical, he could last for years. I'm worried about you, Luce.'

Lucy lifted her eyes from her pad, and the intricate flower

she'd drawn. 'I don't know,' she admitted. 'Everything just seems a little crazy right now. Work is busy, I've got about a thousand cases to work on, and now I'm jetting off to New York. I don't know how to fit everything in.'

'Oh, is that why you're going to New York?' Cesca asked. 'Isn't that where the new laird lives? Or was it Miami, I can never remember?'

'He lives in both.' She should tell Cesca she was off the case. And yet there was that hesitance again, along with the fear she'd been carrying for days. She didn't want her sister thinking badly of her.

'So is it him you're going to see?' Cesca could be like a dog with a bone when she was interested in something. Lucy sensed she wasn't going to give up on this.

'Yes, among other things.' That was as much as she wanted to say.

'Other things?' Cesca's voice rose up. 'What other things? Don't tell me Lucy Shakespeare is interested in things other than work? Are you going to see a show? Or out for dinner? Don't tell me you're meeting up with a guy.'

'Of course not.' Lucy hardly recognised her own voice.

'Oh my God, you've got a guy, haven't you?' Cesca's words tumbled out in her excitement. 'Who is he? What's his name? Have you done the deed yet?'

'There's no guy,' she said firmly.

'Yes there is.' Cesca's certainty took Lucy's breath away. It was as if she had a truth antenna and was pointing it straight at Edinburgh. 'Wait, it's him, isn't it?'

'Who?' Lucy was playing for time now.

'The sexy laird. Are you combining business with pleasure? Jeez, Lucy, that's not like you.' Cesca sounded way too happy. 'You need to tell me all. How did this happen? Oh, this is fabulous.'

'Stop it.' She regretted even opening her mouth.

'Come on, give me something to work with. I'll put it in my next play.'

'So when are you planning to arrive in London?' Lucy asked.

'Stop trying to change the subject. Tell me about this guy.'

'Is that the time?' Lucy was determined to shut this down before Cesca got any closer to the truth. 'I've got a teleconference in five minutes. I'll speak to you when I'm back from New York, okay?'

'You can run but you can't hide, big sister.' Cesca was laughing now. 'And when you get back I expect to hear all the gory details.'

24

Affection is a coal that must be cool'd; else,
suffer'd, it will set the heart on fire

– Venus and Adonis

The moment Lucy stepped through the sliding doors and into the arrivals hall, she took his breath away. He was leaning on a pillar, trying to answer some emails as he scanned the crowd with half an eye, not giving either his full attention. But then she was there, her blonde hair curling around her shoulders, the New York sun streaming in through the glass wall of the airport, lighting her up like there was nobody else in the room.

And there wasn't. At least, not for him, and not right then. He wasn't sure what to do with that feeling, so he pushed it down the same way he pushed himself off the pillar, covering the distance between them in long strides, unable to get that smile off his face. When she spotted him fighting his way through the crowd, her eyes lit up, and the biggest, craziest grin formed on her lips.

He hadn't realised how tense he'd been until his muscles loosened, the tightness in his shoulders melting away. Hadn't realised he'd been holding his breath, either, until the air rushed out in one go.

'You're a sight for sore eyes,' he said when he was only a few feet away from her. She opened her mouth to reply, but then someone barged into the back of her, knocking her for six. She tumbled forward, loosening her hold on her suitcase just as it fell to the floor, and Lachlan reached out, catching her a second before her face joined her suitcase on the tiles. He scooped her up into his arms, frowning as he looked around to find the culprit, but there were way too many people, and they were swarming around them like ants.

'You okay?' he asked, staring down at her, taking her in. So much prettier than he remembered – if that was even possible.

'I'm fine.' She righted herself and grabbed hold of her case, staring up at him with those big, wide eyes. In the melee, her hair had fallen over her brow, and he gently brushed it off with his fingers, tucking the thick golden strands behind her ears. Once he'd touched her, he couldn't take his hand away. Instead, he ran his thumb across her cheek, her jaw, her full bottom lip. But that wasn't enough. He wanted to kiss her, taste her, to slide his tongue into her warm, velvet mouth. To do everything he'd thought about in the past two weeks.

As he brushed his lips against hers, she closed her eyes, letting go of her suitcase once again and looping her arms around his neck. Her body was pressed closely into his, enough that it was sending his senses crazy, at the feel of her, her soft fragrance, the way every time their lips parted she took a sharp mouthful of air.

'Christ, I've missed you.'

She opened her eyes, smiling up at him. 'I've missed you, too.' Her expression matched his – desire tinged with something deeper. Something he wasn't sure he could name even if he wanted to. Instead, he pressed his lips against hers again, the need for her pulsing through his body.

When they finally stopped kissing, he grabbed her case in one hand and put his other arm around her, not willing to have her pushed over again. They let themselves be carried along by the tide of people, spilling out onto the sidewalk, where the crowd finally dispersed. His car pulled up alongside them within a minute, and the driver climbed out and took her case, Lachlan opening the back door so that Lucy could sit inside.

'You have a driver?' she asked him, that cute grin on her face again. 'I always imagined you zipping around New York in a Ferrari.'

He laughed. 'It's impossible to zip around New York at all, whether you're in a Ferrari or an old wreck. And yeah, I have a driver during the week. It means I can work on my laptop while I'm travelling.'

The driver slowly eased the car into the middle lane, and Lucy looked around the interior of the Lincoln, taking in the cream leather upholstery, the spacious back seats, the monitor fixed to the back of the driver's seat. She glanced back at Lachlan. 'It's like an office away from the office.'

Damn if he didn't want to kiss her again. But this wasn't a limo, and the driver was only a breath away from them. And if he was being honest, he didn't want to embarrass her, knowing her the way he did. She was intensely private – even the kiss in the airport was out of character. He wasn't planning on pushing his luck.

He'd stretched it far enough already. He couldn't believe she was actually here with him, even less that she'd removed herself from his case. Her career was everything to her, and the fact she'd told her boss about their relationship had pretty much blown him away.

This thing between them may have started as a fling – or even worse, an itch he'd been desperate to scratch – but now it was so much more than that. Though the thought of something serious developing between him and Lucy scared him, the thought of it not happening scared him more. Just breathing the same air as her made his life so much better.

'Are you tired?' he asked, looking at her with soft eyes. 'Or hungry? We can stop off and get some food on the way back to the apartment if you like.'

'Don't you need to get back to work?' she asked, checking her watch. 'It's only the afternoon, I assumed you'd want to go straight to the office.'

'I was planning on taking you straight home,' he told her. And his tone didn't leave any space for guessing what he meant. Just because he could restrain himself while his driver was only a few feet away from them, didn't mean he didn't want to tear her clothes off and touch her all over.

'Oh.' She glanced at the driver from the corner of her eye. Lachlan mentally patted himself on the back for anticipating her response. He was getting to understand the way she thought – so different to him, and yet so very entrancing.

'And then tomorrow night I want to introduce you to some friends of mine,' he carried on. 'Though if you'd rather do some sightseeing, we can arrange that too.'

'I've already been to New York,' she told him, 'I don't need to go sightseeing. I came to see you.'

Christ, she knew exactly what to say to make his dried-up little heart beat faster.

'You'll definitely be seeing a lot of me,' he said, his voice low. She smiled, then bit on the corner of her lip, glancing down at her lap. She was driving him crazy with the coyness, the same way she drove him crazy no matter what she did. Would he ever get enough of her?

'That's the plan,' she said softly.

Nope. He could never get enough.

'You still want to take the bridge, Mr MacLeish?' the driver asked, flipping up the indicator to take the right exit. Lucy looked out of the window at the view ahead. The evening was creeping in, an orange glow cast across the island of Manhattan. The skyline rose and fell in geometric splendour, the tall buildings dark against the sky. It was breathtaking – a perfect blend of man and nature – so different to the ancient beauty of Edinburgh.

'This was my first ever view of Manhattan,' Lachlan said, leaning across her to point out the window. 'I was eight years old. My father was supposed to be arranging for me to be picked up from the airport, but when I walked into the arrivals hall, nobody was there.'

Lucy turned to look at him. 'They left you at the airport alone? In a strange city?'

He nodded, but he didn't look as upset as she felt. Lucy found herself taking his hand, wrapping her fingers around his palm as if she could save him.

'I found a payphone and called his office. He told me to jump in a cab and he'd pay for it at the other end.' He gave her a wry grin. 'None of them would take me, and in the end he had to send his driver out to collect me. I still don't know whether my father told him to take his time, or if he just felt sorry for me, but he took a slower route, just to let me see the sights. Told me the best view of Manhattan was from the Queensboro Bridge.'

'This bridge?' she asked, looking out at the old cantilevered construction. Set proudly on tall stone towers that rose out of the water, its iron trusses rose and fell in perfect symmetry.

'Yeah. He pulled up for a few minutes, ignored all the cars honking their horns behind him, and told me to take a good look. Told me that once upon a time there'd been nothing here, save for fields and rivers and animals. Said that somebody had stood here – the way we were stopped then – and decided they were going to build a city.' Lachlan smiled, his eyes misted with memories. 'That if man could make New York, then we could achieve anything. We just had to dream big enough.'

'He sounds nothing like any driver I've had in New York.'

Lachlan laughed, and the sound warmed her. 'He definitely was one of a kind. Though Frank,' he nodded his head at the driver, 'is pretty close.'

'I'm not stopping on the bridge,' Frank said, having clearly listened in. 'Not even for you, sir.'

Lachlan squeezed Lucy's hand tightly, amusement written on his face. His moment of vulnerability was gone, replaced by the easy confidence she was used to. She filed the memory away – another glimpse into the man beneath the hard skin and the cute smile. A reminder of what pulled her to him every time they spoke. They'd both had hard childhoods – in one way or another – and they were both the products of always wanting more than they could have. The need to succeed flowed in his veins the same way it flowed through hers. A way to prove to the world they mattered.

They were two people made from the same tough material, and it only made her want to know him more.

231

25

Good company, good wine, good welcome,
can make good people

– Henry VIII

'You never told me you had friends,' Lucy teased, as the bouncer lifted the rope and let them cut the line into the club. Behind them were at least a hundred people, dressed to the nines and ready to party. 'And there was me thinking you were brooding and aloof.'

'Have I spoilt my image?' Lachlan asked, his voice light. 'Should we go back home and pretend I'm some lonely billionaire?'

'You're not a billionaire.'

He held the door open for her, letting her brush past him and into the building. With his free hand he ran his finger lightly across her hip, feeling the fabric of her skirt hugging her skin.

'On paper I am. Or at least I have assets worth that much.'

'You also have debts,' she pointed out, grinning. 'But don't worry, once your empire comes tumbling down, I'll still like you.'

Resting his arm lightly on her shoulders, he led her over to the desk. The man standing behind it smiled broadly as they approached. 'Good evening, Mr MacLeish. We have your usual table reserved. Elise is working in the VIP area tonight; she'll show you to your seats.'

Lachlan slid his hand down Lucy's back, resting it in the curve between her hips. 'This way,' he murmured.

'You come here often, then,' Lucy said, her eyes wide as they approached the stairs leading to the VIP section.

'Occasionally.'

She turned to look at him. 'Enough for that guy to know your name.'

'He's paid to know my name,' Lachlan pointed out. 'He's good at what he does.'

A sudden realisation washed over her face. 'You own this place, don't you?'

'What makes you think that?' He was hedging his answer, trying to see what she was thinking. But she gave nothing away.

'The way we cut the line. Then the way that guy greeted you. Come on, admit it, you own it.'

He tipped his head to the side, his eyes crinkling. 'On paper.'

'I knew it.'

As soon as the hostess saw them enter the VIP area, she walked straight over, a huge smile on her face. 'Mr MacLeish, it's a pleasure to have you here.'

He leaned down to press a kiss to her cheek. Lucy tensed beside him, then wrapped her arm around his waist.

'Good evening, Elise. Are my guests here yet?'

'They just arrived,' Elise said, still smiling. 'I've put them in your usual booth. Can I bring you some drinks over while you get settled?'

'What do you want to drink, baby?' He looked down at Lucy.

'I don't know. Wine maybe?' She shrugged. 'Prosecco?'

'Bring a bottle. And four glasses. Plus some water, please.'

He could feel Lucy turning in his arms. 'Water?' she asked. 'Can't you take your alcohol?'

He laughed. 'Jenn's pregnant.'

'Jenn?'

'My friend's wife. She's married to Grant, my PA.'

Almost immediately her eyebrow raised up. 'Grant's your friend?'

'Yeah.' He wasn't quite sure where she was going with this.

'You have to *pay* people to be your friends.' Her grin widened. 'It gets better and better.'

'Are you going to emasculate me all night?' he asked her. 'Or are we going to go and have a good time?'

'I couldn't emasculate you if I tried,' she said. 'You're too damn alpha for that.'

'Thank you. I think.'

'You're welcome.'

He led her over to the booth in the corner, where the table afforded a view of the VIP area, and the floor below. As soon as they approached he saw Grant and Jenn turn their heads to look at Lucy. They stood up to greet him, Grant shaking his hand as Jenn kissed him on the cheek. 'Look at you,' he said, glancing down to see her small, yet obvious bump. 'You've grown since I last saw you.'

'Shut up.' Jenn slapped him on the arm. 'Introduce us to your friend.' She smiled at Lucy, who grinned right back.

'Lucy,' he said, taking her hand in his, 'this is Grant and Jenn. My *oldest* friends.' He was still smarting at her paying comment. 'Grant and I grew up next door to each other in Miami.'

'It's a pleasure to meet you.' Lucy shook first Jenn's hand, and then Grant's, before the four of them slid into the booth. Within moments, Elise brought over their drinks, popping the cork and pouring the frothing wine into tall, slender glasses.

'So, Grant tells me you're an attorney,' Jenn said, taking a sip of her water. 'That must be hard work.'

'Says the researcher who works all the hours God sends,' Grant said. 'And I didn't say she was *an* attorney. I said she was *Lachlan's* attorney.'

Lucy glanced at Lachlan, looking uncomfortable at Grant's response. Damn, he should have told him about her removing herself from his case. It just hadn't crossed his mind.

Lucy clearly wasn't impressed by his forgetfulness 'He's only one of my clients,' she told Jenn. 'And a very unimportant one, too.' She raised an eyebrow at him, as if in challenge. He couldn't help but grin.

Score one for the gorgeous attorney.

Jenn laughed. 'Oh, I like you already.' She tipped her head to the side. 'Where's that accent from? You sound British.'

'I'm from London originally.'

'But you're living in New York now?'

'She's based in Edinburgh.' Grant rolled his eyes. 'Seriously, I told you at least twice.'

Jenn shrugged. 'I'm pregnant. So sue me.' She looked at Lucy. 'Except don't. I can't afford it.'

'I'm not sure you can be sued for being pregnant,' Lucy said. She took a sip of her prosecco. 'Well, I've never heard of it anyway.'

'But you can get sued for inheriting a lordship, right?' Jenn leaned closer to her. 'Isn't that what's happening to Lachlan?'

Lucy glanced over at him questioningly. Yep, he really was bad at communicating with his friends. He smiled at her. 'It's okay. They know all the gory details.'

'It's not really what's happening. He's not being sued, exactly. They're contesting his claim to the title and the lands.'

'So if he loses, his brother gets it all?' Jenn asked.

Lachlan leaned back in his seat, watching as the girls talked, their heads close together so they could hear each other above the ambient noise. He took a sip of his wine, a smile tugging at the corner of his mouth. He hadn't realised he cared about Jenn's opinion so much, until she'd accepted Lucy with open arms.

But he did, he really did.

Lucy was laughing at something Jenn had said. Her eyes were crinkled at the edges, her pretty mouth open. Something about her expression made him want to bundle her up and sit her on his lap.

He was about to stand up and do it when Jenn leaned forward and whispered in Lucy's ear. She nodded in response, then the two of them stood up.

'Just going to the little girls' room,' Jenn told them.

'Together?' Grant asked. 'What are you, fifteen?'

'It's a club,' Jenn pointed out. 'There's safety in numbers. You never know what could happen when there's this much testosterone and alcohol.'

'It's my club,' Lachlan said. 'I don't let that happen here.'

'Okay, so you've got us. We want to talk about you. Happy?' Jenn rolled her eyes. 'You guys really need to learn to translate girl speak.'

As Lucy passed him, Lachlan reached out for her hand, running his thumb in a circle around the inside of her wrist. 'Hurry back.'

She blinked, as though she was looking into the sun, even though the light in the club was atmospheric at best.

As they left, Grant reached for the wine, topping up their glasses. 'Lucy seems nice.'

'Yes, she is.' Lachlan took a mouthful of prosecco. 'Jesus, this stuff is way too sweet. Shall we order something else?'

'Like beer?'

'I was thinking whisky.'

Grant grinned. 'Now you're talking.'

Lachlan motioned for Elise, who took their order with a smile. She brought their drinks back within a couple of minutes.

'So come on, spill. What's going on between you two? Is it serious?' Grant's voice rose up with his last question, as though he couldn't quite believe he was asking it.

Lachlan glanced over at the bathroom doors – no sign of the girls. 'Yeah, it's serious.' And maybe there was a little gravel in his voice when he said it. Not because he was nervous, exactly. More that this was important to him.

He wanted his best friend to see Lucy the way he did.

'Wow.' Grant shook his head, his eyes wide. 'I never thought I'd see the day.'

'What day?'

'The day you finally met your match.' Finally Grant grinned. 'Or maybe I'm being too kind to you, because, my friend, you're clearly hitting above your weight. What the hell does she see in you anyway?'

'The same thing Jenn sees in you, I expect.' Lachlan

swirled the ice around his glass, listening to the sound it made as it hit the sides.

Grant laughed. 'You're comparing her to Jenn? Oh man, this is even better than I thought.' He tipped his head to the side, listening as Lachlan swirled his ice around again. 'Are those wedding bells I can hear?'

Lachlan emptied his glass, motioning over to Elise to bring another. 'Leave the bottle,' he told Elise, as she finished filling their glasses. As soon as she left, he turned back to Grant. 'When did you turn into a such a gossip? Shouldn't we be talking about last night's game?'

There was a smile on Grant's face that looked as though it was never going away. 'Oh no, you don't get away that easily. Six years, that's how long you've been calling me pussy-whipped and domesticated. That's how long you've smirked every time I tell you Jenn and I are going shopping, or that I'm meeting her folks. You don't get to swat me away when we've been talking for less than six minutes.'

'I called you pussy-whipped?' Lachlan asked, appalled.

'Among other things.'

'Well, that was a dickish move. Sorry, man.' Lachlan wrinkled his nose.

'You're forgiven. As always.' Grant was still grinning. 'So tell me, when's she going home?'

'Lucy? On Sunday.'

'So she'll be here for the gala?'

Lachlan's already tense stomach tightened. 'Gala?'

'You know it's on Saturday, right? It's in your calendar.'

'Shit. I'd completely forgotten about it.' Lachlan rubbed his face, blinking. 'It's this Saturday?' It was the last thing he wanted to do – attend a gala for his dead father's favourite charity. The one time a year he had to see all his father's family in one place, Duncan included.

How many years had he sat there feeling excluded? Ignored by everybody as though he wasn't a true MacLeish. The thought of having Lucy there with him made his chest feel warm. He'd be somebody. He could face anything with her by his side.

'Yep, that's right. And lucky for you I already assumed you'd have a plus one, so there's room on the MacLeish Holdings table.' Grant grinned. 'I have to admit I hadn't been looking forward to going, but now I know Lucy will be there, maybe it won't be so bad after all.'

'Maybe it won't be,' Lachlan agreed, and it was strange how much truth was in those words. Even stranger how having her by his side made everything else seem so much less important, including this damn dispute with his brother. He glanced down at his now-empty glass, a smile curling at his lips.

When he looked up, Grant's own smile had doubled in size. 'You're in big, big trouble, my friend.'

Lucy ran her hands beneath the tap, feeling the cool water pouring over her flesh. The muted lighting inside the bathroom made her skin look warm, smooth. It was like staring at an airbrushed version of herself in the mirror. As she rubbed the fragrant soap into her palms, the door behind her clicked, and Jenn came out, taking the sink beside her.

'I swear I've got the bladder of an old lady,' Jenn told her, lathering up her hands. 'They say it gets much worse in the third trimester, but I can't see how it can. I already spend the majority of my life in the bathroom.'

Lucy smiled, shaking the water from her palms. 'My sister

had the same problem. She could rate the toilets of every restaurant and shop within a five-mile radius from her home.'

'You have a sister? Is she older than you?'

'I have three of them. I'm the eldest.' She reached for the towel – real, not paper, thank you, Lachlan. Rubbing it across her hands, she dropped it in the basket beneath the bank of sinks.

'Three? Wow. Your mom must have been a glutton for punishment.' Jenn rubbed her belly. 'I can't imagine going through this another three times.' She rifled through her purse, pulling out some gloss. She slicked it across her lips. 'So,' she said, glancing at Lucy from the corner of her eyes, 'you and Lachlan, huh?'

'Me and Lachlan.' Lucy liked the way they sounded. Just saying it sent a jolt of pleasure down her body.

'What's with you two?'

Lucy ran her fingers through her hair, pulling it out of her eyes. She'd spent a lifetime batting off her sisters' questions, but it felt harder with Jenn. As though she could see right through her. 'Um ... I don't know.'

'Seriously?' Jenn asked. 'Because I've only seen you two together for ten minutes, and even I can tell the chemistry's off the scale. The way you two look at each other ... ' She fanned her face. 'Smokin''

Lucy looked at Jenn in the mirror. She was petite, pretty. Her dark, glossy hair fell to her shoulders, the ends waving as they touched her back. She looked like a woman who didn't take no for an answer. 'If you say so.'

'Do you like him?'

'Yes?' Like felt too weak a word. 'I wouldn't be here if I didn't.' More importantly, she wouldn't have put her whole career on the line, not without this desperate need to be with him. The stakes couldn't be higher, but there was no way she was going to say that to Jenn.

'Well, he likes you.' Jenn's voice had an air of certainty to it.

'He does?' Lucy liked this change in direction. She'd be happy to hear more about the way Lachlan felt, and Jenn clearly knew him well.

'Of course he does. Didn't you hear him when we went to the bathroom, the man can't bear to be apart from you for more than a few minutes. His eyes followed you all the way in here. It's like you're his magnet.' Jenn leaned closer. 'But I guess you're right to be a little careful.'

'I am?' Lucy frowned, watching the lines form between her eyes in the mirror. 'Why?'

'It's not that I don't love Lachlan, because I do. He's like a brother to me and Grant. But he's not the best when it comes to women.'

Lucy swallowed. She really needed that prosecco now. 'What do you mean?'

Jenn sighed, turning from the mirror to look at her. 'I really like you, Lucy. And that's why I'd hate to see you get hurt. He's just ... I don't know ... ' She shook her head. 'He's his own worst enemy. I've seen it before. He gets close to people – women – but when they want something more he pushes them away. I blame his parents, that man has trust issues.' She tipped her head to the side. 'Just be a bit careful, okay? Guard your heart.'

Lucy stared at herself in the mirror, seeing the blonde-haired, creamy-skinned woman looking back at her. Though her expression was neutral, her emotions were anything but. She didn't know why Jenn's words had affected her so much. Maybe because Lucy had trust issues, too. But she'd thrown caution to the wind when it came to Lachlan.

'I'm so sorry, I shouldn't have said anything,' Jenn said, grimacing. 'I'd blame it on the pregnancy, but I always put my foot in my mouth. I'm an idiot.'

'It's okay.' Lucy shot her a smile. 'You don't need to apologise.'

'You should just ignore me,' Jenn said, still looking regretful. 'I'm a hormonal bitch, just ask Grant. As I said, Lachlan clearly likes you, which is more than I've seen with the other girls.'

'The other girls,' Lucy repeated. Three words that made her want to barf.

'Okay, I'm going to shut up now. I need to call the dentist to arrange to have my toes extracted from my throat.' Jenn looked like she wanted to cry.

'It's fine, it really is,' Lucy said, hoping her tone was reassuring. Hoping even more that Jenn was wrong.

She had to be, didn't she? Lucy's future depended on it.

As soon as they'd arrived back at Lachlan's building, and he'd sent his driver home for the night, the attraction between them had felt like a burning fire. He'd practically ravished her in the elevator to his apartment, and all but dragged her into his room in his haste to get them both naked. By the time he'd finished with her two hours later, she was wrung out and exhausted, falling asleep almost as soon as her head hit the pillow.

Lachlan lay next to her, watching her as she slept. Her body was curled up, her face relaxed, her lips slightly open as she inhaled regularly. She looked peaceful in slumber, as though any worries of the day had disappeared along with her consciousness, making her look younger, closer to twenty than thirty.

Curled up in his bed, her body soft and warm, she reminded

him of a cat. Difficult to win her affection, but once you did, she'd be fiercely loyal. He smiled, remembering the first time they met. Back then she'd shown him her tough side, she'd seemed hard, immovable. But only he knew that inside she was like candy – melting and delicious. He never wanted to stop tasting her.

Was this how it felt to finally win? He couldn't remember the last time he'd felt like this – maybe he never had. Having her in his bed made him feel afraid and exhilarated at the same time, like a free faller approaching the exit of an airplane. He was ready to step out, ready to fall, not knowing if he was going to survive the journey. Not even caring if he did, because the sensation was too good to miss.

She moaned softly in her sleep, turning over, nestling against him. Instinctively he found himself gathering her into his arms. She rested her head against his bare chest, her breath warm against his skin.

He closed his eyes, breathing her in, trying to commit this feeling to memory.

He was becoming addicted to her, and he wasn't sure he could ever go cold turkey again.

26

A heaven on earth I have won by wooing thee
– All's Well That Ends Well

'You doing okay?' Lachlan asked. Lucy was lying back in the bed, her blonde hair fanned out across the white pillow, her eyes open and staring at the ceiling. 'Can't you sleep?'

She moved her gaze to him. 'Not really. I've been wide awake for hours.' She wiggled down the mattress, resting her cheek on her hand. 'Sorry if I woke you up.'

Behind him, the red numbers on the clock told her it was just past four in the morning. 'You didn't wake me,' he said, though his voice still felt thick with sleep. 'I just turned over and saw you laying there.' He reached his hand out, stroking her face with the tips of his fingers. 'You think you can go back to sleep?'

'Even if I can't, you should. We don't both need to be awake at stupid o'clock in the morning.'

He grinned. 'I know a good way to make you tired.'

'Does it involve pills?' she asked him.

'No, but it does involve swallowing.'

She burst out laughing. Lachlan twisted in the bed, reaching out to stroke her cheek.

'Where did this come from?' she murmured, running her finger across the back of his hand, tracing a small, jagged line beneath his thumb.

He pulled his hand back, frowning. Lucy couldn't help but remember Jenn's warning. Lachlan didn't like it when you got too close. 'You don't have to tell me if you don't want to,' she whispered.

'It's not a big deal.' He slid his hand back to hers. 'Remember I told you about breaking my mom's vase? I got it then.'

She traced it again, leaning closer to see it in the half-light. The sun had risen, her early-morning rays pushing through the gauzy curtains. 'Did it hurt?'

'I don't remember. I was only six or seven.'

'But you said your mom was out. Did you have a babysitter?'

She felt him shake his head, the movement moving his chest where her head was resting. 'No, I was alone.'

'She left you on your own that young?' Lucy frowned, her fingers curling around his. Another reminder of how abandoned he'd been as a child. She ached to travel back to that time, to scoop that younger Lachlan up in her arms. Strange how such a strong, virile man could bring out her maternal instinct. 'Wasn't that illegal?'

He shrugged. 'She had a job to do. She could barely keep a roof over our heads, paying for a nanny was totally out of the question.'

'Couldn't she work when you were at school?'

His voice was soft. 'Nightclubs don't tend to keep school hours.'

Lucy's eyes widened. 'You were on your own all night? Jesus, what if something happened?' Her stomach dropped at the thought. 'I can't imagine how scary that must have been for a kid that age.'

He gave her a half-smile. 'I broke the vase when I was sleepwalking. The crash woke me up. I was so scared I tried to gather all the pieces together in my hand, that's when one of the edges cut me.' He swallowed, his Adam's apple bobbing. 'I hid those pieces for days, hoping she wouldn't notice. Until Grant's grandmother told me about Kintsugi.'

'I was surprised when you told me you lived next door to Grant as a child,' she said. 'I didn't realise that was how you met. I assumed you met at work.'

'I've known him ever since I can remember. We pretty much grew up together. Brought each other up, in a strange way. His parents worked all the time – in a restaurant in downtown Miami – so he knew how things were. He had his grandma, though. She lived with them too. But she pretty much left us both to our own devices.'

She closed her eyes, breathing in the scent of his skin. 'You had to grow up quickly.'

'We all did in that neighbourhood. It was dog eat dog, we learned how to defend ourselves. And that the best form of defence is to attack.' He flexed his hand beneath her touch, curling it into a fist.

'But what about your dad?' she asked. 'Didn't he help? Couldn't your mum sue him for alimony or something?'

'He sent money sometimes,' he told her. 'But Mom was never very good with it. I can remember coming home on the days he'd sent it – all the cupboards would be full of food, I'd have new clothes, she'd have a brand-new wardrobe. And then the following week it would be back to crumbs and working.' He smiled. 'New clothes don't do much for an empty stomach.'

'It must have been hard, though, knowing he had all this money and that you guys were going without.' She ran her finger up and down his inner arm, watching his tendons flex beneath her touch. She felt him press his lips against her head, breathing her in.

'I didn't like going to visit him,' Lachlan said, his voice muffled by her hair. 'Not because of the contrast – I think when you're a kid you don't question things like that. But because they were mean. His wife never liked me, and I can't really blame her for that. But when you're ten years old and they're flaunting wealth in front of you, it hurts like hell.' He ran his finger down her spine, following the curve where she was lying against him. 'And Duncan took things to a whole new level. Anything I did, he had to be better. If I mentioned I enjoyed football, the next day he'd get a season ticket and a new Dolphins top. On the rare occasion I was ever given something myself, it would end up disappearing or being ruined.'

Lucy blinked. 'Didn't your dad stop it?'

She could feel him shake his head, his lips moving against her hair. 'He wasn't there most of the time. He was a workaholic, in case you're wondering where I got it from. I think he liked the idea of having one big, happy family, but when it didn't work out, he just left us to it.'

Her tongue felt like sandpaper. 'They sound like a bunch of assholes.'

He laughed, his chest lifting beneath her cheek. 'That's as good a description as any.'

She lifted her head, looking straight into his deep blue eyes. 'But you showed them, right? You made something of yourself, you have your own business. You're a success.' He looked every inch of it, lying next to her. It was almost impossible to keep her hands off him.

The edge of his mouth lifted up. 'I guess.'

'What else is there to prove?'

'Nothing. And I think it's beyond proving anything to them. It's about me. About my success, about my drive. I want to be seen as someone other than my father's illegitimate son.' Wrapping his arms around her, he pulled her up until her body was resting on his. In his arms, everything felt right.

'You know, I'm really good with my hands. I could tickle them all to death if you want me to.' She grinned at him mischievously, running her fingers down his sides. He released his hold on her waist, reaching down to circle each of her wrists with his fingers like human handcuffs.

'I don't want you tickling anybody else,' he said.

'You don't even want me tickling you.'

'True story.' His grin widened. 'Anyway, you'll get to meet them in the flesh on Saturday.'

'Saturday?' she asked. 'What are we doing on Saturday?' She thought about the weekend – the fact she was flying home on the Sunday. Back to a country and a life that seemed more than half a world away.

'Going to a gala.' He rubbed his thumbs in small circles around her wrists. 'You, me, Duncan and half of New York.'

'Doesn't your brother live in Miami?'

Lachlan shrugged. 'They live all over the place. Like me, my brother has business dealings here, the same way our father always did. Plus the gala is for my father's favourite charity.'

'And you want us to go?' She felt uneasy at the thought. 'Why?'

'Because I want to show you off. I want to show them I'm

a winner, with a beautiful, intelligent woman by my side.' Releasing her wrists, he cupped her face in his hands, brushing the softest almost-kiss across her lips. 'Will you come to the ball, Cinderella?'

His eyes were blinding. She felt herself sinking into him, as though the two of them were made of molten iron. Tough, almost impossible to crack, and yet somehow becoming one.

She thought of the fact she'd be flying home on Sunday morning. About the fact his estranged family would be at the gala, staring at him, hating him, treating him like shit. Her whole body tensed up. Logically, she knew Lachlan MacLeish was more than capable of taking care of himself. The way his muscles flexed beneath her body was enough to prove that. And yet she felt a primal need to protect him – or at least the boy he'd once been. The same urge she felt with her sisters.

Looking up at him through her eyelashes, she nodded, swallowing to alleviate the dryness of her throat. Even still, her voice was croaky when she spoke. 'Of course I'll come with you.'

The smile she got back in return was blinding.

He wrapped her in his arms, her back to his front, his biceps strong against her sides. His legs pressed against hers, so that he was mirroring her position, the dessertspoon to her teaspoon. She could feel her chest tighten as the sensation of him holding her, his body almost like a shield to ward away evil.

She wasn't used to feeling protected. Wasn't used to being taken care of. But the sensation made her feel warm inside, as though he'd lit a fire inside her that wasn't ever going out.

She was falling in love with Lachlan MacLeish. She had seen through the persona he showed the world, broken down the skin he used to protect himself, and had glimpsed the man beneath.

Maybe Jenn was wrong. Maybe this time it was different. Because Lucy was in love with him and she had no idea what to do with that thought.

'Damn, we're out of coffee.' Lachlan slammed the cupboard door closed, the crockery inside rattling in protest at his vehemence. 'This is what happens when I give the housekeeper a week off. My life goes to hell.'

Lucy crossed her bare legs as she sat on his kitchen stool, leaning on the countertop. She was wearing only his white shirt and a pair of panties she'd found at the top of her case. 'Why did you give her the week off?'

He turned to look at her, his face heated. 'Because when I'm having sex with you against the back of the sofa, I prefer not to be interrupted.'

She stifled a laugh. 'I guess we'll have to go without coffee then.'

Lachlan shook his head. 'That's not an option. Without coffee I can't concentrate. And we have a lot to do today.'

She frowned, swinging her leg back and forth. 'I thought we were just going dress shopping?' Not her choice – but she had nothing suitable for the kind of event Saturday would turn out to be.

'We are,' he said, pulling his shoes on and grabbing his jacket. 'But we'll both need some sustenance. I have very specific tastes when it comes to clothing.'

'Me too,' she said, tipping her head to the side. 'This could be interesting.'

'Everything about you is interesting.' He pressed his lips to hers. 'Now get back to bed and I'll bring your coffee in there. We've got four hours until our appointment at Bergdorf's.'

'And we've got work to do, too.' She couldn't help but feel guilty at all those emails piling up in her inbox. Even though she was supposed to be on holiday, she still needed to keep things in check. Her career depended on it.

'It can wait.' He slid his keys from the counter, stuffing them in his jeans pocket. He looked every inch the rich, casual boyfriend. Hair still wet from the shower, jeans and shirt expensively tailored. He'd shaved the night before, but the smoothness of his jaw had been roughened by a shadow of beard growth. Sometimes she had to pinch herself to realise she wasn't watching some cologne advert whenever he was around.

But like an advertisement, their time together was all too brief. It was already Wednesday – and it felt as though she'd barely been here any time at all. It would be the weekend within a blink of an eye, and before she knew it she'd be flying back to Edinburgh. Like in *The Wizard of Oz*, she'd click her red heels to leave the beautiful colourful land to return to a black-and-white life.

Stop it, she told herself. It wasn't a dull existence. She'd worked hard to get everything she had – a beautiful apartment, a fabulous job, a family she loved more than life itself. And she'd still have Lachlan, just from afar for a while.

She swung down from her perch on the stool, her bare feet padding against the warm, polished wooden floor. She was almost at the bedroom when she heard the sharp trill of a phone.

Lachlan's phone.

Turning, she saw it lighting up on the counter, the case vibrating against the marble with every ring. He must have forgotten to take with him. Curiosity pulled her closer, until

251

she could read the name printed in black against the lit-up screen.

Grant.

Without thinking it through, she swiped to answer it, lifting the handset to her ear. 'Lachlan MacLeish's phone.'

'Er …' Grant seemed momentarily nonplussed by her answering. 'Lucy, is that you?'

'Hi, Grant. Lachlan went out for a minute. He forgot to take his phone. Can I take a message?'

Grant let out a loud sigh. 'Damn. Do you know when he'll be back?'

Alarmed at his tone, Lucy found herself standing up straighter. 'He won't be long. Is there a problem?'

'He's supposed to be in a meeting. These guys have flown over from Germany especially. I sent him an email last night reminding him.' Grant's anger was palpable. She felt goose-bumps rise up on her skin.

'I don't think he read them.'

'But he *always* reads his emails.' His voice rose up an octave.

'Okay.' She didn't want to argue with him. He was Lachlan's childhood friend, even if he was being a bit over the top. 'Well, I'll get him to call you as soon as he gets back.'

'Can't you go find him?'

'He's just out buying coffee.' She ran her finger in the figure of eight around the marble countertop. 'He'll be back soon.'

'Coffee?' He coughed loudly. 'Seriously?'

'He wouldn't have missed it on purpose. I'll make sure he calls you the minute he gets back.'

'I'm sorry, Lucy, I don't mean to be bitching at you. I just don't understand it. This company is everything to him, and I don't want him to mess it up.' Grant paused for a moment, then gave another long sigh. 'I'm sorry, I'm sure it will be fine. Just ignore me.'

'He wouldn't mess it up,' Lucy said, her voice certain. 'Success means everything to him.'

The same way it had to her. Or it had used to, before Glencarraig and that stolen night in his bedroom. After that, she'd been in a state, not knowing what was important any more.

And now look at her, staying here with an ex-client even though the gossips back at Robinson and Balfour must have been working overtime. Her heart started to beat faster, as though it was knocking on a door in her ribcage. They were doing the right thing.

Weren't they?

'I'll get him to call you back as soon as he's here,' she said, her voice low. Her eyes flicked up to the door, leading from the hallway. It remained stubbornly unmoving. Her stomach, however, was a different matter. It lurched inside her as though she was stepping off a roller coaster, her abdomen contracting as a sense of foreboding came over her.

Lachlan had been neglecting his work for weeks. She had, too, for that matter.

Reality was tapping on the door, and as much as she was trying to ignore the noise, it was only a matter of time before it burst its way into their lives.

27

When sorrows come, they come not single
spies, but in battalions

– Hamlet

With the floor-length dress bag in one hand, Lucy raised the other to hail a cab. The bright yellow car pulled up to the kerb, and she climbed inside, being careful not to wrinkle the dress. She'd barely fastened her seatbelt before the driver pulled away, weaving his way through the lunchtime traffic. As he took a turn down a side street, joining a line of cars who'd all had the same idea, Lucy stared out of the window at the shop displays. Almost immediately something caught her eye. She leaned closer, trying to see if it was what she thought it was.

'Hey, can you stay here for a minute?' she asked.

The driver looked at her warily, sliding his eyes to her newly purchased dress. 'If you leave that I will. And the meter stays on.'

'Okay then. I won't be long.'

Grabbing her purse she ran into the shop, seeking out an assistant as she looked at all the stock lining the shelves. A rapid conversation later, plus a hefty bill on her Visa card, she left carrying her delicate purchase in a cushioned box, climbing back into the cab and nodding for the driver to go on. 'Thanks for waiting,' she told him.

He muttered something unintelligible and put his foot on the gas.

They were only a few minutes away from Lachlan's apartment when her phone rang. She couldn't hide her smile when she saw his name on her screen. 'Hello?'

'How's the shopping going?' he asked her.

'It's done. I found the right dress.' She glanced at the long black dress bag; emblazoned with the signature Bergdorf logo. Zipped inside was a strapless gold floor-length gown, ruched at the bust, tight on the waist and then flowing like champagne down to the ground. As soon as she'd tried it on she'd just known it was the one. From the coos of the assistant, he'd thought so too.

'What's it like?' Lachlan asked, his voice distracted. 'Can you send me a photo?'

'No. You don't get to see it until the night. It's bad luck.'

He laughed. 'I think you'll find that's a wedding dress.' His voice became muffled, as though he was covering the mouthpiece. 'Grant, can you book a table for four at Barouche? We'll eat at seven.'

While Lachlan carried on his conversation with Grant, Lucy watched the world pass by, enjoying the view. She'd come here by subway – in spite of Lachlan's disapproval – wanting to see if it was just like in the movies. But there was no way she wanted to carry this pretty dress into the depths of the tunnels.

'Did I tell you how happy I am that you're coming to the gala?' he asked her, his conversation with Grant clearly over.

'You did.' She smiled at his excitement, remembering how he'd looked at her when she'd said yes. Like a child opening his Christmas presents.

'It means a lot to me,' he said softly. 'Thank you.'

'You're welcome. And what are your plans for the afternoon?'

'I'll be in meetings all afternoon,' Lachlan said. 'And then we have dinner with my German customers.'

'We do?'

'Yes, we do. I won't make it home before then, but I'll arrange for a car to pick you up at six thirty.'

'I don't need a car. I'll get there myself, just text me the address.'

'I'm not having you walk the streets in a sexy dress and heels.'

'Who said I'm wearing a sexy dress and heels?' She smiled, toying with him.

'I did.'

'I can't wait to see your face when I turn up in jeans and a sweater.' An ambulance weaved past, sirens blazing. 'Sorry. I didn't hear what you said.'

'I said my face will look perfectly normal if you turn up in jeans and a sweater. You look beautiful in anything.'

She opened her mouth to reply, but the words remained stubbornly silent. Sometimes he could take her breath away with just a sentence.

'That sounds like a good place to end the conversation,' she said, grinning widely. 'I don't think you can top that.'

He laughed. 'I can try. What are your plans for this afternoon? You want me to organise anything?'

She still wasn't sure whether to feel annoyed or flattered at

256

the way he always offered to do things for her. It was taking some getting used to.

'I'm going to do some work,' she said firmly. 'If I want a job to go back to that is.'

'Maybe you shouldn't,' he said, his voice light. 'That way I can keep you here for ever.'

'As tempting as that may sound, I'm not the type to be a kept woman.' Though the thought of staying with him made her feel warm. She didn't even want to think about how she'd feel getting on that plane on Sunday. Instead, she tucked it away deep inside her. Something to think about another day.

'Well, don't work too hard,' he told her. 'And if you get bored, call Grant, and he can arrange for a car to take you anywhere.'

'I can take care of myself.'

'I know you can, but I like to take care of you.' His voice was as soft as velvet. She closed her eyes, remembering the previous night, how safe she'd felt in his arms. She could almost feel his hard biceps wrapped around her and his lips feathering the sensitive spot between her neck and her shoulder as she gently drifted to sleep.

God, I love you.

It took her a moment to realise she'd said the words out loud. They hung in the air like a stale odour. Lachlan cleared his throat, but said nothing.

Lucy waited a moment, unsure of what to do. Should she laugh, take it back? The cab pulled up at a stop light, the engine idling as the red light diffused over them, matching the blush on her cheeks.

She was such an idiot.

'I've got to go to a meeting,' Lachlan said, sounding awkward as hell. 'Don't forget the car at six thirty. I'll see you at dinner.'

'Okay,' she replied, still kicking herself for saying those damn words out loud. 'I'll see you then.'

Lachlan slid his phone into his pocket, his jaw tight. Did she really just say she loved him? He could feel his heart hammering against his chest, the way it did after he'd finished a ten-mile run. Yes, she'd said it.

So why hadn't he said it back? As soon as the words slipped out of her mouth he'd been like a scared kid, frozen in place. He hadn't known what to say at all.

Grant popped his head around the door. 'Your visitors are back from lunch. I've put them in the boardroom. Marcus should be joining you soon.'

Lachlan nodded. 'I'll be there in five minutes.' Finishing his half-empty mug of coffee, he looked out of the window, staring down at the city below.

She was out there and she loved him. And he cared deeply about her, too. He might not have been able to say the words yet – even the thought of it panicked him – but maybe he could show her. And tonight, when they were back at his apartment, he planned to do exactly that.

She wasn't sure she recognised the girl staring back at her. Her hair was wet, hanging in a damp curtain past her shoulders. Her face was freshly scrubbed, glowing from the shower. She looked healthy, she looked happy.

She looked like somebody she used to know.

Behind her, the steam was still drifting in the air, a leftover effect of her over-long stay in the shower. Her skin could still feel the heated blades of water that had crashed down from the rainfall showerhead, her cells tingling with the tactile memory. She looked around the room – at the expensive ceramic wear, the perfectly laid marble tiles, the beautifully fragrant toiletries that Lachlan had bought for her to use.

Wrapping a towel around her hair and tucking it in, she grabbed a bathrobe and slid her arms inside, blushing when she knotted the belt around her waist. That night in Paris when he'd used a very similar belt to tie her to the bed didn't seem so long ago. And yet it seemed like forever, too.

She was walking back into the bedroom when her phone rang, buzzing on the dressing table where she'd left it. Smiling, she walked towards it, expecting to see Lachlan's name flashing on the screen.

But instead, it was her sister, Cesca.

Something made her hand freeze in the air as she reached for it. A sense of foreboding, maybe? Whatever it was, her fingers trembled as she finally picked it up, the cellphone almost slipping out of her grasp.

'Cesca, is everything okay?'

A second's silence was followed by a sob.

'Cesca?' she said again, her chest tightening at her sister's cries. 'Are you still in London?' Just hearing her sister's gasping breaths was enough to send a shot of ice-cold panic through her veins. 'Are you with dad? Is he all right?'

'He said . . . he said . . . ' Another hitched gasp. 'It's not true, is it?'

'What?' Lucy asked. 'What's happened?'

'He thought I was Mum. Started shouting at me, telling me not to leave him, then told Sam to . . . to . . . eff off.' She sniffed.

'The nurse tried to calm him down, but he started trying to grab Sam. He was so confused, he started crying and wailing. Begged me to stop my affair before I hurt our girls. Except it wasn't me he was talking to.' Her voice was drowned by another sob. 'He was talking to Mum.'

So her father knew about the affair after all. A fresh surge of panic made Lucy's legs weak. 'He's talking nonsense, you know that. He doesn't know what he's saying.' Her breathing was rapid, as though she'd been running for miles.

'He doesn't make things up,' Cesca's voice was low and raspy. 'He just remembers old things. That's what the doctor said.'

Lucy sat down on the edge of the bed, lowering her face into her hand, her fingertips digging into her wet hair. *Think, Lucy.* She just needed to find the right words, and it would all be fine. The way it always was. 'It was all so long ago, Cesca, it's not important.' She shook her head. 'He's sick, that's all.'

'Did you know?' Cesca asked, then coughed out another cry. 'You did, didn't you? You don't sound surprised at all.'

Lucy's stomach lurched, and she tasted the pasta salad she'd eaten for lunch all over again. 'I didn't ...' She searched her brain, trying to find the words. 'I just ...'

'You knew, didn't you?' Cesca said again. 'Oh my God, you knew about this. You lied to me, to us.' She was talking quickly, her voice loud over the connection. 'Who else knows?' she demanded. 'Who else is lying? Does Juliet know?'

'No,' Lucy said, squeezing her eyes shut. 'Just me. I didn't tell anybody at all. It didn't mean anything.'

'Of course it means something.' Cesca's tone became angry. 'It means everything I thought about my family was wrong. I wrote a bloody play based on Mum, or who I thought she was. You must have been laughing at me all along.'

'No, Cess, I promise I wasn't.' Lucy shook her head. 'It's not like that.'

'What is it like then?' Cesca demanded. 'You seem to know everything that's going on. Tell me what it's all about.'

'It doesn't matter,' Lucy said, leaning against the dressing table, her body feeling leaden and achy.

'Of course it matters,' Cesca wailed. 'Everything I thought I knew is a lie.'

Lucy covered her mouth to stifle her own sob. Her chest hitched, feeling painfully constricted when she tried to inhale some air. She felt dizzy, as though everything in the room was slanted – only to realise it was her that was half-falling to the floor.

'No, honey, no. That's not true.' She closed her eyes, seeing her mother's face, the moment before she crashed into that van.

'Why should I believe a word you say?' Cesca asked her, her voice still wavering. 'You've been lying to us for years. What else have you been hiding, Lucy? What else have you been telling lies about?'

'Nothing.' Her breath came out in shallow bursts. 'I promise, that's all there is. I didn't want you to be hurt.'

'So you lied instead?'

'I just didn't tell you about it.' She rubbed her palm over her face, feeling the wetness of her tears against her skin. 'Please, Cesca, let me explain.' Shaking her head, Lucy bit her lip, trying to calm herself down. She felt jittery and high, as though she couldn't quite hold on to her thoughts. They were racing around her brain like it was an Indy 500 track.

'No, I don't want to hear it. I don't believe a bloody word you say. I don't want to talk to you.'

'Please don't hang up!' Lucy begged. 'Cesca, listen, it's not like—'

But the connection was gone. Lucy looked down at the white robe she was wearing, and at the thousand-count bed sheet she was sitting on. What the hell was happening? She dialled her sister back, but the phone just kept ringing.

With shaking hands she scrolled through her contacts, calling up Juliet's number. Almost immediately it clicked through to voicemail. Either her phone was turned off or Cesca was calling her right now. Both filled Lucy with a sense of foreboding.

'Juliet, can you call me when you get this?' That was all she managed to get out before she choked back another sob. God, she needed to get a grip. Still holding her phone she thought about calling Kitty in LA, asking her not to speak to any of their sisters until Lucy had a chance for damage control. But she knew Kitty too well – she was as curious as the rest of them. She'd be phoning Cesca and Juliet like a shot.

Lucy lay back on the bed, her hair dampening the sheets, staining them a darker shade. Staring at the whitewashed ceiling, she shook her head, trying to get things straight in her mind. But nothing was making sense. She couldn't even remember why she'd lied to them for so long – how the hell could she explain it when she didn't even understand it herself?

Frowning, she sat up, tucking her knees beneath her chin. *Think, Lucy, think.* She took a deep breath in, as much to calm her racing heart as anything else. But the memory of Cesca's cries, her accusations, were like little jabs of adrenalin, sending her pulse racing as she recalled her sister's rejection.

I don't want to talk to you.

But she had to, didn't she? Cesca couldn't ignore her for ever. Somehow Lucy had to make her understand. She'd tried to protect them, to keep the family together, to make sure they still had a father, a home, a life together.

She lied because she loved them.

With her arms wrapped around her knees, she rocked back and forward in a soothing movement. Everything was going to be okay. She'd make it all okay – she'd done it before, after all, and she could do it again. They were family, and that was all that mattered.

Lachlan plastered a fake smile on his face and called the waiter over, trying to ignore the empty chair beside him. Jurgen and Klaus were already in good spirits, half a bottle in to the fine wine they'd ordered, and neither of them noticed the way he kept sliding his gaze to the restaurant door.

Where the hell was she?

'Yes, sir?' the waiter asked. 'Would you like to wait for your guest, or are you ready to order?'

'We'll order now,' he said, nodding at Jurgen and Klaus. 'That's if you two are ready, of course.'

'Sure.' Jurgen grinned, his face flushed from a glass of wine on an empty stomach. Combined with jet lag it was lethal. He started to go through the menu with the waiter, as Lachlan tuned his voice out, checking his phone under the table to see if she'd returned his message.

Nothing.

He wasn't sure whether he was annoyed or worried. It wasn't like Lucy to be late for anything.

'I need to make a quick phone call,' he told Jurgen and Klaus after the three of them had ordered. 'Will you excuse me for a minute?'

'No problem,' Klaus said, nodding as Lachlan stood up.

As soon as he was in the lobby, Lachlan called her number. Straight to voicemail, damn it. Then he called the apartment phone, but it kept ringing until the dial tone made his head ache. Biting down his frustration, he called the front desk.

'Mr MacLeish, what can we do for you?' The concierge answered straight away.

'Do you know if Miss Shakespeare has left the apartment?' he asked. 'Did the car arrive okay?'

'He waited for twenty minutes, but she didn't come down,' the concierge replied. 'I did call up a number of times but we got no response.'

Lachlan leaned against the brick wall of the restaurant, the phone still glued to his ear. 'Have you seen her at all?' he asked, trying to hide the note of alarm in his voice.

'Not since she arrived back this afternoon. I've been sitting here since, and I haven't set eyes on her.'

'I've called her phone and she's not answering. Can you send someone up to check on her?'

'Of course.' The concierge was reassuring. 'I'll ask John to go up.'

'And call me straight back when you're done.'

'No problem.'

As he waited for the phone call, Lachlan stood outside the restaurant, checking in on Jurgen and Klaus through the plate-glass window. The two of them seemed happy enough, laughing and drinking from the second bottle of wine. Still, he knew they'd eventually notice he was taking too long.

Not that he really cared.

As soon as his phone rang he picked it up.

'Mr MacLeish?' The concierge again.

'Yes? Is she there?'

'John spoke to her through the intercom. She's feeling unwell, said she was in bed, and she'd speak to you later.'

'She's sick?' he asked. 'Should we send for a doctor?' His relief at her being in his apartment was quickly replaced by an anxiety at her illness.

'John offered, but she refused.'

None of it made sense. If she was sick, why hadn't she called him? 'Thanks for checking on her.'

'No problem, Mr MacLeish. Just call if you need anything else.'

He hung up and slid the phone into his pocket, a frown pulling at his lips. Then he walked in to give Jurgen and Klaus his excuses, before calling a car to pick him up.

It was time to go home and look after his girl.

28

A heavy heart bears not a nimble tongue

– Love's Labour's Lost

She'd been so self-centred. She could see it all clearly now, as she zipped up her case and pulled it off the bed, rolling it out to the hallway. She left it next to the door, with her documents resting on top, waiting for the taxi that she'd already called.

The gift she'd bought for Lachlan was still in the hall, too, where she'd left it when she first walked in. She looked at it, twisting her fingers together, wondering what on earth she should do with the thing now.

It didn't seem like the right time for gifts.

It didn't seem like the right time for anything, other than to get home and do what she should have done all along. Make sure her family was okay, that it didn't fall apart. That it wasn't as fractured as the Kintsugi vase that dominated Lachlan's hallway.

She checked her phone to see if the taxi had arrived yet, but there was no notification. Just some texts from Lachlan and some missed voicemails. Ones she planned to return just as soon as she was in the cab.

After her futile attempts to return Cesca's call, her problem-solving skills had kicked into overdrive. Within thirty minutes she'd booked herself on the next plane to London, packed her bags and ordered a cab. Checking the taxi app, she saw her car was still ten minutes away. She shook her head. This was all her fault. She'd taken her eye off the ball, had thrown every piece of herself into this thing with Lachlan. She'd neglected her family and her career, the two things that had always meant everything to her.

For a moment she thought of that dress still hanging in its black bag, hooked on the back of his bedroom door. Thought of how she would have looked in his arms, the pale lace and silk champagne contrasting against his black dinner jacket. But it was all fake, wasn't it?

A daydream she'd allowed herself to indulge in – one where he felt as deeply about her as she did about him. But he didn't. That much was clear from their telephone conversation. She'd blurted out that she loved him and he hadn't said a word. If she stayed and went to the gala – like one of his 'girls', as Jenn had described them – she was putting this thing between them above her family. And she couldn't do that.

She'd been as selfish as her mother had been. It needed to stop. She needed to go back home and be Lucy Shakespeare, the woman who had everything under control. Maybe then everything would go back to normal.

It had begun to rain by the time the car pulled up at his apartment block, and the doorman appeared with an umbrella, shading Lachlan from the dampness. 'Good evening, Mr MacLeish.'

'Hi, John. Thanks for checking on Lucy for me.'

'No problem,' John said, matching Lachlan step for step as they walked towards the lobby. 'Whatever she's got must have come on very quickly. She was fine earlier.'

Lachlan frowned, walking through the door John held open for him. The doorman remained outside, shaking the dampness from his umbrella. Nodding at the concierge, Lachlan made his way to the elevator. It arrived almost straight away.

As soon as he unlocked the door to his apartment, something seemed off. He stepped into the entrance hall, taking in the pale walls, the polished floor, the table with the large Kintsugi vase. It all looked the same.

But there was another addition – well, two if he was counting. Her case was by the table, along with a big blue box. Resting on top were all her documents.

'Lucy?' he called, taking another glance at her luggage. 'Are you okay?' He could feel his chest tightening, like somebody had tied a rope around it and pulled hard. 'Where are you?'

'I'm in here.'

He spotted her as soon as he walked into the living room. She was wearing a pair of tight jeans and a cream cashmere sweater – the soft wool somehow complementing her complexion. But when he brought his gaze up he saw the redness of her eyes, the paleness of her face, her milky skin covered with livid blotches.

'You look awful,' he said, reaching for her. But she pulled away from his outstretched hand.

'Thanks,' she said, rolling her lips between her teeth. 'I'm not feeling the best.'

'Can I get you something? Some Advil? Are you sick or in pain?'

'I'm fine,' she said, looking anything but. 'I just need to get home.'

'What?' He blinked, trying to let the words sink in. 'But you are home.'

'No.' She shook her head, wincing as if in pain. 'I mean, I'm going back to London.'

'You're flying on Sunday, not today.' She was making no sense. 'You can't leave when you're ill, that's crazy. Get to bed and we'll see how you are in the morning. I'll call my doctor if you're no better.'

'My flight leaves in four hours,' she said, ignoring his suggestion. 'I've got a cab coming. It should be here in five minutes.' Her face was shiny beneath the glow of his chandelier. As he came closer her could see her skin looked raw, as though she'd been scrubbing away her make-up with a brush instead of a cloth.

He shook his head. 'I don't understand. If you're sick then you shouldn't leave. Let me take care of you.' This time when he touched her, she flinched. 'Lucy?' he said, still not comprehending what was happening.

'I'm not sick.' Her voice was dull. 'I have to go home. My sister needs me.'

'Which sister? What's happened to her?'

Slowly Lucy brought her gaze to meet his. Her eyes were bloodshot and yet somehow dull, as if a screen had been pulled down over them. 'Cesca. She found out . . .' She trailed off, pulling her lips together in a thin line. When she blinked a tear escaped.

'Found out what?' He hated the way the air between them felt solid. Like an invisible barrier.

'She found out about my mum. About her affair. She said I'm a liar, she hates me.'

'Why would she hate you?'

Lucy stifled a sob. 'She thinks it's all my fault. She won't talk to me.'

He stroked her arm. It was freezing cold. 'It's just a shock for her, that's all. It would be for anybody. You should have told them about your mom years ago.'

'Do you think this is all my doing?' she asked him. 'You think this is my fault, too?' She pulled her arm away and held it by her side. Her body was as tightly wound as her words. At that moment she looked impenetrable.

He frowned, reaching around in his brain, trying to find the right answer. 'No, that's not what I'm saying. But you couldn't keep this a secret for ever.'

She blinked her tears away. 'My sisters need me, they've always needed me, and I'm not there. I'm here, doing God knows what.'

'You're here with me.'

He could feel her start to shiver beneath his touch, in spite of the warmth in the room. 'But I shouldn't be. I should be at home. Everything's always okay when I'm there. As soon as Cesca told me she was coming to London I knew I should have stayed. But instead I ignored that little voice in my head and got on a plane anyway. And now everything's gone wrong and I have to make it right.' She was hysterical, her voice thin and edgy. There was no softness in her face at all. It was like brittle glass, hard yet breakable – threatening to cut him with every touch.

He could feel the panic rising in him. 'So one phone call from your sister and you're leaving?'

It was as if she didn't hear him. 'I can't believe I've been so stupid. I don't know what I was thinking coming over here.'

270

She shook her head, staring into space. 'I risked everything for what? A fling?'

Her words were like a kick to the gut. 'What?'

Of course it wasn't a fling. She knew that, didn't she? Hadn't she meant it when she said she loved him?

He thought of all the other people who were supposed to love him, too. His mother – disappearing every night – his father – who didn't seem to love anybody but himself. And now Lucy was leaving him, too. The way everybody did.

Not this time.

'I'll come with you,' he said, his voice firm. 'Let me call Grant, he can get me on the flight.'

Lucy looked at the phone she was clutching tightly. 'I'm leaving any minute now. The cab's just around the corner.'

'Then I'll catch you up.'

She looked up at him. 'No.' Her tone was vehement. 'Don't do that.'

'Why not?'

'Because I don't want you there.'

If her earlier words had felt like a kick to the gut, this time they were like a body blow. 'You don't want me?'

'Don't you see? We're not good for each other. I've messed everything up. My sister hates me, my job is hanging in the balance. Even Grant told me that you were neglecting the business. And for what?' Her telephone beeped and she swiped it silent. 'That's my cab, I need to go.'

'And the gala?' he asked her. 'What about that?' He was doing everything he could to keep his cool, but all he could see was red. 'What about the dress you bought?'

'I'll transfer some money to you,' she said. 'As soon as I'm back in London.'

'Don't bother,' he spat, the anger finally rising to the surface. 'Consider it payment for services rendered.' He turned his back on her, unable to look at her, squeezing his fingers tightly into a fist.

'I'm sorry, I . . .' She trailed off. 'I need to go. I'll call you when I get to London.'

'If you walk out that door now, don't bother coming back.' As soon as he said it, he wanted to take the words back, wanted to spin around and look at her. Wanted to beg her to stay. But pride made him a statue, his back still firmly turned on her.

Lucy didn't say another word. But the soft click of the door closing as she left told him all he needed to know.

With his lips pressed together into a thin, bleached line, he walked back into the bedroom. The closet door was closed, but he knew without needing to look that her clothes were no longer hanging there.

His eyes were drawn to a long, black dress carrier, with Bergdorf Goodman's insignia printed on the front. He walked towards it, unzipping the plastic to reveal the dress hanging inside.

A champagne-coloured silk bodice was covered with lace, the boning of the corset clearly visible where it hung. It was tight by the looks of it, down to the waist, where it flared out to become full and flowing.

He stared at it without blinking. Could almost picture how beautiful it would look against her warm curves, her golden hair pinned up to reveal her creamy shoulders. Next to his dark colouring, and even darker suit, they would have made a glamorous couple. The kind that people stopped and stared at on the red carpet.

The kind that would have showed everybody he was a winner.

Reaching out, he took the dress in his hands, feeling the layers of silk and lace between his fingers.

A wave of fury washed through him. Taking the bodice in both hands he ripped at it, until the fabric began to protest at his roughness. His bicep muscles contracted, his hands tightening their hold on the dress, as he yanked at the delicate fabric until it tore apart beneath his grasp.

Damn her for making him feel the way she did. For making him feel like he might just be worthy of care and love.

Damn her for giving with one hand and taking with the other.

Damn her for not wearing this beautiful dress as she glided into the gala on his arm.

Damn her to hell. Which was exactly where he was headed, too.

29

*You told a lie, an odious damned lie; Upon
my soul, a lie, a wicked lie*

– Othello

'Would you like me to take that for you?' the flight attendant
asked her as she stepped onto the plane, raising his eyebrows at
the large box she'd carried on to the flight. She was cradling it
like it was something precious. She supposed it was. For some
reason she felt very protective of it.

'It's very fragile,' Lucy told him, not quite willing to let it
go. 'I don't want it to be broken.'

'We'll take good care of it, ma'am,' he promised her, taking
the dark blue box from her grasp. 'I'll give it back to you when
we land.'

She nodded, her arms still outstretched even though the
box was gone. 'Thank you,' she whispered quietly.

By the time she made it into her seat the plane was almost
full. Businessmen already dressed for meetings in London the
following morning mingled with families with small children
who were fussing with their seatbelts. She sat down heavily,
letting her head fall against the rest behind her and closed her
eyes for a moment. They felt swollen from her tears, the skin

274

around them red and tender. She reached up to touch it with her fingertips.

'Ladies and gentlemen, welcome to flight five seven two to London Heathrow, due to land at eight a.m. local time. We're fully boarded, and once everybody's in their seats we'll be getting ready for take-off.' The announcement continued as the flight attendant introduced the captain, the staff, and explained that everybody should watch the safety demonstration. It sounded like white noise to Lucy. Her mind was too full of dark thoughts to process anything else.

Was it only a few hours ago that she was trying on dresses for the gala? She'd felt like a princess when she was wearing that beautiful gown, or maybe more like Cinderella. For the first time in her life, she would go to the ball.

No, she wouldn't think of that. Nor would she think of the way Lachlan had looked at her when she told him she was flying home. There'd been a darkness to his eyes she'd never noticed before, almost as though he hated her. She breathed in a ragged mouthful of air, trying to get the image of his expression out of her mind. If she thought about it too much, it might kill her.

'Would you like a drink before take-off?' the flight attendant asked her.

She shook her head. 'No, thank you. I just want to sleep.'

The attendant frowned. 'Are you feeling okay? You look a little unwell.'

Lucy attempted a smile, but fell short of the mark. 'I just need to get some rest. It's been a long day.' Or maybe a long few months. Everything had been out of kilter since the day she'd stepped off that plane in Miami.

The attendant didn't look so certain. 'Okay, but if you

need anything, just press the button.' He pointed at the plastic above her. 'Once we're in flight, I'll come and help you set up the bed.'

A few minutes later the cabin crew did their usual check of the plane before taking their seats, and the captain taxied the plane to the runway. As the plane lifted into the air, Lucy let her eyes close once again, knowing that for eight hours, at least, she could disappear into sweet, soft oblivion. A kind of limbo between the maelstrom she'd left behind her in New York, and the mess she was heading into in London. The calm at the eye of the storm.

Suddenly, eight hours didn't feel like nearly long enough.

'Where to, love?' The taxi driver glanced over his shoulder at her through the glass partition. One hand was on the steering wheel, the other resting lightly on the back of the chair next to him.

If she squinted her eyes she could be back in New York, with her dress lying next to her as she clutched an oversized box from a local gallery.

The dress was gone. So was New York, but the box remained in her hands, the base resting lightly on her thighs. For its size, it weighed hardly anything, in spite of the big dent it had made in her credit card.

What wouldn't she give to be back in that yellow taxi again? Make everything that happened afterwards melt away?

She leaned forward to give her father's address. Except it wasn't his address any more, was it? Just the empty shell of a family home, echoing with the memories of the four sisters who used to live there. If she closed her eyes she could hear Juliet laughing on the telephone to a boyfriend, while Kitty turned up the volume of the television to drown out her flirtatious conversation. Cesca was usually in the corner, notepad in front of her, a pen tapping against her teeth.

As for Lucy? She wasn't sure where she'd been. Worrying, mostly, or making sure everything was organised. Writing letters to her sisters' schools, making up packed lunches for the next day. Going through her dad's chequebook to make sure there was enough money to pay all the bills.

And then making sure the bills actually got paid.

Her face screwed up in misery as she thought about those days. They'd all been a little broken back then, trying to live in a world where their mum no longer existed. It was like the solar system without the sun, their sense of gravity had completely disappeared.

'Been on holiday?' the driver asked, pulling out of the airport complex. Ah, he was one of those. Lucy wasn't sure whether to be happy or sad that she couldn't be left alone with her gloom.

'Just visiting a friend.'

'Did you go anywhere nice?'

'To New York.' She held on tightly to her box as he put his foot down to beat the lights.

'Ah, lovely. Took the missis there once, for our anniversary. Did the whole shebang. Statue of Liberty, Empire State Building. Even ate oysters in Grand Central Station. Disgusting little things. Taste like snot.'

She smiled in spite of herself. 'I managed to avoid the oysters.'

'It's a great city, though, isn't it?' he continued. 'One of those places you can visit again and again. I must ask the missis if she wants to go back.' He steered right, filtering onto the motorway.

'Yeah, it's great.' She stared out of the window at the fields as they drove past them. Patches of green and yellow, with tall hedges dividing them. So different from the concrete jungle she'd just left.

'Will *you* go back, do you think?'

If you walk out that door now, don't bother coming back. His final words echoed in her mind. 'I'm . . . ' Frowning, she looked down at the box in her hands. A gift ungiven. 'I'm not sure.'

Around an hour later he pulled up outside her father's old house. She took in the imposing red-brick façade, the white criss-cross Georgian windows, the three chimneys jutting proudly from the roof. It looked the same but different. Where once the front path was lined with pretty flowers and hedges, now there were weeds. The paint on the front door was peeling, the glossy black giving way to dull grey wood. But more than that it looked wan and lonely. As empty as she felt.

As he pulled her case out of the back, she checked her phone. No messages. Not from Lachlan, not from her sisters, not even from Lynn at work. It was as though for the hours she was in the air she had ceased to exist. She couldn't remember the last time somebody didn't want *something* from her. Whether it was a sandwich to take to school or a deposition for the court. There was always something she was having to respond to, from the earliest age.

And now. Nothing.

Thanking the driver, she pulled her case up the pathway, ignoring the dirt ingrained in the Victorian tiles. In her right hand she still held that box, gently placing it on the top step as she rooted for her keys to open the door.

She hesitated for a moment, as metal slid into metal, not quite willing to make the turn that would unleash all those emotions again. Standing on that porch, she felt heavy, like a ton of weight was pressing down on her shoulders. The same weight she'd managed to forget about when she was in New York with Lachlan.

She was about to turn the key when the door was wrenched open. Standing on the other side of the threshold was her sister. Cesca looked smaller than Lucy remembered, more delicate, too. Like a tropical flower you needed to protect from the cold, harsh winter.

'Hey.' Lucy gave her sister a half-smile. 'I'm home.'

Cesca stared at her, saying nothing. Her tongue peeked out to moisten her lips. Lucy watched as she inhaled, breathing in through her nose, then slowly breathing out, her mouth pursed.

'I'm sorry,' Lucy whispered. 'I'm so sorry.'

'I'll make us a cup of tea.' Cesca turned on her heel and walked back up the hallway to the kitchen, leaving Lucy to follow with her case and her box. She left them at the bottom of the stairs, before kicking off her shoes, and padding back to her sister in her sock-covered feet.

'Have you had something to eat?' Cesca asked. 'I'm pretty sure Sam bought some food yesterday. I haven't eaten anything, I'm not very hungry.'

Lucy shook her head. She came to a stop next to the old kitchen table, and curled her hands around the top of one of the chairs. 'I'm not hungry either.' She traced a crack in the wood with the pad of her thumb. 'I wasn't sure you'd still be here.'

Cesca filled the old, metal kettle, then put it on the hob, lighting up one of the gas burners. 'We fly back to LA tomorrow,' she said, pulling her hand away quickly when a flame flickered up. 'I don't know why Dad couldn't just have an electric kettle like everybody else.'

'I don't suppose it matters now,' Lucy said. 'It's not like he's coming back. We don't have to worry about him burning the house down any more.'

Cesca sniffed, then turned her back to Lucy, reaching up in the cupboard for some mugs. When she spun back round, her eyes were glinting in the early-morning sun. 'Why didn't you tell us?'

Lucy opened her mouth to speak, but none of the usual excuses appeared. She'd had half a day to think of all her reasons, but every time she tried to pin them down they seemed to disappear like smoke into the air. 'I don't know,' she finally said, pulling the chair out and sitting in it. She rested her elbows on the table, dropping her forehead into her hands. 'It just seemed like the right thing to do. I don't know how much you remember, Cess, but things were crazy back then.'

'It's no excuse. You've had years to tell the truth. And yet you've kept it from us for all that time. You were supposed to be our sister. We were supposed to be a family.'

'We *are* a family,' Lucy said firmly, looking up from the palm of her hands. 'And it got harder as time went on. When would have been a good time to get you all together and announce, "Mum was having an affair, and I found out just before she died"? At Juliet's wedding? Before Kitty moved to LA? Or maybe I should have done it at your premiere? There was no good time.' She sighed, knowing how ineffective her words were. They sounded stupid even to her own ears. 'Please sit down, Cess. Let me make the tea.'

'It's done.' Cesca's voice was thick and throaty, as though she'd been crying all night. 'There you go.' She slid one mug across the table to Lucy, cradling the other in her hands as she sat down opposite her.

280

They stared at each other for a moment, older and younger sister, with matching red eyes and blonde hair. Lucy frowned, feeling the skin above her eyebrows pucker, as she still searched for the words to make everything right.

But maybe they didn't exist. Maybe there was no right to be made here. Just one woman, doing her best, making mistakes. Breaking her sisters' hearts the way hers was broken.

'I really am so sorry.' Lucy looked down at her tea, seeing the faintest of reflections in the murky brown liquid. 'I never wanted you to find out like this.'

'You never wanted us to find out at all, did you?'

She brought her gaze up. 'No, I didn't.'

'Why not?'

Lucy took a sip of her tea, feeling the hot liquid scald her tongue. It felt like a good kind of pain. 'Because I didn't want to hurt you any more than you were already hurting. You'd just lost your mum, I didn't want to take her from you all over again.'

'Our mum. She was *our* mum.'

Lucy nodded, confused. 'Yes.'

'She wasn't just my mum. She was *your* mum.' Cesca's voice was vehement, as though she was trying to make an important point. 'You lost her twice, too.'

Everything in that kitchen felt filled with emotion. Like a heavy rain cloud, reaching saturation point. Lucy could almost feel the downpour waiting to start.

And once it began, she wasn't sure she'd be able to stop it.

'But I was the eldest. It was my job to protect you.'

Cesca shook her head. 'We should protect each other. It doesn't all have to fall on you. You're our sister, not our mother.'

'It does. It always has. It felt like all my fault.'

'No. No it wasn't.' Cesca shook her head vehemently. 'You got hurt, too. And I hate to think of you being all alone with this knowledge for all these years. You must have felt so lonely.'

A fresh flood of tears pooled in Lucy's eyes. She lifted her hand, wiping at them with her fingers. 'I'm sorry, I'm not usually a crybaby like this.'

'Maybe you should be,' Cesca said, tipping her head to the side. 'You can't always be the strong one. Everybody needs carrying sometimes.'

For a moment Lucy's thoughts were full of Lachlan, and the way he'd lifted her out of that bed in Glencarraig. He'd carried her as though she was as light as a feather-filled cushion, his strong arms flexing as he laid her down on his bed.

And for a few moments it had felt so good to be held.

She smiled weakly, tasting her tears as they moistened her lips. 'I never wanted any of you to hurt the way I did. I wanted to take the pain for all of us.'

'It doesn't work that way. I should know, I tried to shelter myself from pain for long enough. But if you wrap someone in cotton wool you stop them from working out how to deal with the hurt. It's like a child learning to walk – you know they're going to stumble and scrape their legs, but you have to let them learn by their own mistakes. You can't shield them from the tears and the blood, you can just be there to mop them up afterwards.'

Lucy sighed. 'When did you get so clever?' she asked, feeling a flush of pride for the woman her sister had turned out to be. 'You're so good with words. You should be a writer or something.'

Cesca laughed, and the kitchen suddenly seemed warmer. Lucy felt the muscles in her shoulders relax. 'Will you tell

282

me about Mum?' Cesca asked. 'I want to know exactly what happened.'

Lucy nodded. 'Of course I will. But I need to try and get it all straight in my head.' Was it strange that she felt some sort of relief at finally being able to talk things through with her sister? 'And I'd like to tell Kitty and Juliet at the same time, if that's okay? That's if they're willing to talk to me.'

'They'll talk to you. I spoke with Juliet earlier, she was worried about you. We all were. And Kitty wanted to jump on a plane to New York to give you a hug. It was me being all emotional and angry, and I shouldn't have been.' She shook her head. 'I can't believe you came straight back here.'

'Can't you? You're my sister and you were hurt. I couldn't stand to hear you cry and not be able to hug you.'

'A hug sounds perfect just about now.'

Lucy was on her feet before Cesca finished her sentence. Her younger sister wrapped her arms around her, the two of them hugging the breath out of each other.

'I can't believe you left the sexy laird,' Cesca whispered against Lucy's shoulder, clearly remembering their conversation. 'I hope he's not too angry at me.'

'He's not angry at you at all.' Not a lie, but not the truth either. But she wasn't quite ready to share that story with them. Yet.

She'd tell her sisters about it after she told them about her mum. And maybe it would even be a relief to share her pain, the same way it was a relief to finally share the truth about that cold, wet day all those years ago.

The day they all lost a mother and somehow Lucy took on the role herself.

30

That I have shot mine arrow o'er the
house and hurt my brother

– Hamlet

The office was like a ghost town – not a big surprise, since it was a Saturday. When he'd walked through the frosted-glass doors that led to MacLeish Holdings, Lachlan had been greeted by sleeping computers and dim security lights. The movement sensors detected him as he made his way to the oak doors leading to his office, causing the lights to flash above him as he moved, like a strange upside-down homage to *Saturday Night Fever*. Not that he intended on dancing.

He put his Styrofoam mug of coffee on his desk, flicking on his computer as he leaned forward on his elbows, his palms cradling his stubbled jaw. It had seemed like a good idea to come here – anything to avoid his memory-laden apartment – but now it just felt sad.

Maybe he should have gone for a run instead. Or called Grant and seen if he wanted a pre-gala drink or two. What was it that normal people did on Saturdays anyway? For the past few weeks, he'd spent most of his time talking with Lucy. Or looking at Lucy. Or sleeping with Lucy.

Dammit, he didn't need to think about that right now.

He pulled his emails up, quickly deleting the ones that meant nothing, flagging those he wanted to read. Some were easy wins – forwarded to the appropriate department, or to Grant to set up meetings. The others would wait until Monday. Nobody was hanging around at the weekend just to hear from him.

Then he saw the email from Alistair. *Your Official Invitation to the MacLeish Gathering.* When he clicked on it, the email opened, revealing a photograph of Glencarraig, the lodge nestled in its highland surroundings, the loch as perfectly clear as he remembered it. And of course there was the MacLeish tartan, forming a border around the invitation.

Lachlan MacLeish,
Laird of Glencarraig. Plus one.

His first thought was to forward it to Lucy, but why the hell would she care?

She'd gone, and he'd pushed her away with every piece of strength he had. All those words, said in the heat of the moment, came back to him with a force that made him wince.

If you walk out that door now, don't bother coming back. He shook his head, squeezing his eyes shut to erase the memory.

The fact he called the dress payment for services rendered. Christ, what a dick he was. No wonder she walked away. He'd all but bundled her out of the door himself. The pain of it was like a blunt spoon digging at his heart. He'd lost her and it was all his own damn fault.

The urge to call her was almost impossible to ignore. Only the need to curl up and lick his wounds stopped him from grabbing his phone and hitting her number.

Shaking his head, he turned off the screen. There was little point in doing any work when he could barely concentrate for more than five minutes at a time. It was almost four in the afternoon – only another three hours to kill before he needed to get ready for the gala.

He was pretty sure they were going to be the longest three hours of his life.

Lachlan stood at the entrance to the hotel, smoothing his dinner jacket as he waited for the people in front of him to make their way up the red carpet. Camera flashes were coming from both sides, as photographers and reporters in the press area shouted out directions and questions, and the guests stopped to pose in front of the sponsors' banners.

'Mr MacLeish, we're so pleased you could join us tonight.' The host walked forward to shake his hand. 'I can't tell you how much we appreciate your generosity.'

'It was a cause close to my father's heart,' he murmured, watching as a beautiful couple walked past him, the man placing his palm in the small of the woman's back. She was wearing a backless dress – a cream silk that rippled to the ground. His heart lurched as he remembered the torn dress hanging in his closet at home.

'Mr MacLeish, will you be sitting at a table with your brother tonight?'

Lachlan turned, recognising the society reporter from the *Post*. 'I don't think so, no.' His smile was wide and completely false. 'MacLeish Holdings have their own table at the gala. I wouldn't want to appear cheap.'

'And who's accompanying you tonight?' The reporter looked around expectantly.

'I'm here alone.'

Her face dropped. 'You are?' She looked as though he'd just told her the world was flat.

After a few more questions he was ushered into the lobby, crossing from the red carpet to the marble floor tiles. The table he'd bought for an extortionate price was half-full. He saw a few friends and clients filling the seats, and he smiled when Grant and Jenn waved at him from their position at the far side. He made his way around the table, shaking hands and kissing cheeks, having to speak loudly to be heard over the orchestra. By the time he made it to Grant, his friend had already secured him a drink.

'I thought you might need this,' he said, passing a glass of champagne to Lachlan. 'You made it through the wolves okay?'

'The same old, same old.' Lachlan lowered his voice. 'Is he here yet?'

Grant tipped his head towards the other side of the ballroom. 'Yep.' Lachlan followed Grant's gaze, at the table right next to the stage. A man was sitting at the head – a little shorter than Lachlan, a little stockier, too, but with the same dark hair and strong nose.

For a moment their eyes met, before Duncan looked away, turning to talk to the person next to him. Lachlan waited for the familiar feelings of hatred to fill him, but instead he felt nothing at all. He didn't feel any need to go over to talk to the man he shared blood with. Didn't feel the need to do anything to him. At the end of the day, what did any of it matter?

'Lachlan.' Jenn stood, offering her cheek to him. He brushed his lips against her warm skin, smiling as she pulled him in for a hug.

'Jenn, you look beautiful as always.'

'You know what they say, you can put lipstick on a pig, but it's still a pig wearing lipstick.'

He burst out laughing. 'Are you comparing yourself with a pig? Jesus, you look all glowing and gorgeous. Stop putting yourself down.'

She patted his arm. 'And that's why I like you, Mr Charm.' Her voice dropped, enough that he had to lean in to hear her. 'I'm so sorry about Lucy. Grant told me.'

Lachlan looked over at his friend. Grant shrugged, in a don't-blame-me kind of way. 'Oh did he?'

'I can't help but feel some of this is my fault,' Jenn said, rubbing her neck with her palm. 'I hope I didn't drive her away.'

Lachlan frowned. 'Why would this be your fault?'

She bit her lip, not quite meeting his gaze. 'I kind of said something about your other girls.'

'What other girls?' He shook his head. She wasn't making sense. 'I don't have any other girls.'

'And I told her you had trust issues.'

He blinked. 'What?'

'You're not making it much better, babe,' Grant warned.

'I'm so sorry. I really liked her, Lachlan.'

'Jenn ...' His voice was a warning. 'What did you say to her?'

'Remember, it's illegal to hit a pregnant lady, okay?' She stepped back, as though bracing herself. 'I told her you pushed women away when they got too close.'

This time, Lachlan was the one frowning. 'Why did you tell her that?'

'I'm sorry.' Jenn grabbed his arm again, her fingers circling around his bicep. 'She's so lovely. I was worried you were going to treat her the way you treat all the others. But then Grant told me how much you're in love with her, and I realised I messed everything up. You have to forgive me, okay, otherwise you're not going to be godfather to this baby.' She was out of breath, and still clinging to him.

'Calm down.' Lachlan patted her hand. He was worried she was going into premature labour. 'You weren't that wrong. I did push her away. And what's all this about me being in love with her?' He turned to Grant, who was conveniently looking away.

'He told me about you missing that meeting. And the way you tried to cancel another one in Paris. And about all the late-night phone calls you didn't think he could hear you making.'

'You don't work late at night.' Lachlan looked in Grant's direction.

'Lucy's late night, not yours,' Grant pointed out. 'I thought you'd turned into the fashion police or something. You were always asking her what she was wearing.'

Lachlan wasn't sure whether to be amused or appalled.

'We had to talk business,' he protested. 'It's hard to time transatlantic conversations right. It was the only spot we both had free every evening.'

'You don't even talk to your own attorneys every evening, so why would you need to talk to her? Face it, you've fallen in love with the girl.' Grant shrugged. 'Not that I ever thought I'd see the day.'

Lachlan opened his mouth to argue, but closed it swiftly. What was there to argue with? His phone calls definitely hadn't been about business. Anything between him and Lucy had ceased to be about the Glencarraig inheritance a long time ago.

He slid his hand in his pocket, feeling the paper he'd shoved in there before he left for the hotel. Soft, shiny, and a little bit battered.

'It doesn't matter anyway,' he said, lifting his hand and grabbing another glass of champagne from a passing waiter. 'It's over. She's gone.' The expression on his face left them in no doubt he didn't want to talk about it any more. What else was there to say?

He'd lost her, and at some point he'd have to accept it. And for now, he'd just bluster his way through.

He made it through the evening without bumping into his brother. He'd been deliberately avoiding that whole side of his family, sticking to his own table, the bar, and the occasional foray to speak to friends. But still, at least he'd be able to leave the gala without any fuss.

Inside the ballroom, the party was still in full swing: the low beat of the music, the constant stream of chatter reverberating through the doors, which opened regularly as people made their way to the bathroom. Lachlan nodded at the hatcheck man, sliding a ten into the bowl even though he hadn't brought a coat. Glancing at his phone, he checked to see if his car was here yet.

Five minutes away, that wasn't so bad. He decided to wait outside – the New York spring was slowly giving way to summer, and the evening was feeling warm. He loosened his tie as he walked out through the exit, and unfastened his top button.

He'd barely stepped onto the sidewalk before he came to an abrupt stop. In front of him was a man who shared the same hair and the same nose as him, though very little else.

'Duncan.' Lachlan nodded at him.

'Lachlan.' Duncan looked him up and down. 'Are you leaving already?'

How long had it been since the two of them had exchanged more than a nod? Since they'd grown into men, the two of them had barely spoken. There was too much bad blood – and too many bad years – between them.

'I have somewhere else to be.'

There was a twitch in Duncan's jaw, as though he was clenching his teeth too tightly. 'Well, thank you for coming anyway. Dad would have been pleased.'

It was strange the way those words made Lachlan feel. A mixture of pride alongside a dash of resentment that Duncan would know what their father would have felt.

Because Lachlan had absolutely no idea at all.

His thoughts turned to Lucy again, and her choice to always put her family first. It was hard to imagine ever feeling that way if his brother needed him. Not that Duncan ever did.

'It was a good evening,' Lachlan said. 'I'm sure you'll raise lots of money.' He glanced at his watch. Where the hell was his car?

'I was hoping we'd get to talk tonight.' Duncan looked uneasy. 'I wanted to speak with you about this court thing. I wanted to explain.'

Lachlan shrugged, trying to look nonchalant. 'Nothing to explain. It's business.' And quite frankly he couldn't give a flying damn about the inheritance. It didn't matter, not any more.

'No, it isn't.' Duncan took a step forward. 'I didn't want to take it to court. There's nothing more distasteful than family suing family. I just don't have a choice.'

Lachlan looked up at him, frowning. 'What do you mean?'

'It's really important to Mom that I keep that part of our father with me. I promised her I wouldn't give up.' Duncan

291

inhaled deeply, his shoulders lifting up. 'I don't want to fight you for it, but I don't know what else to do.'

For a moment, Lachlan thought of Duncan's mother – his father's wife, even when Lachlan was conceived. She'd been a shadowy presence whenever he'd visited. Stoic, but clearly upset by his being there. And no wonder, Lachlan was a walking, breathing reminder of her husband's infidelities.

He squeezed his eyes shut for a moment, remembering the way Lucy had tried to hide her own secret for so long. How many years were the children expected to pay for the sins of their parents? Would they ever be able to shake off the shackles of their past.

'My mother felt the same,' Lachlan said when he opened his eyes. But he was really questioning himself. What his mother – and Duncan's mother – wanted was irrelevant. Even their father's wishes weren't written in stone. It was up to them to decide how to deal with things, they were the ones in control here.

For the first time he saw himself and Duncan as they really were: puppets who were taking roles in somebody else's play. As children, they'd obeyed their mothers, become their proxies in this crazy fight for their father's love and attention, the same father who showed no interest in them. And he had sympathy for the boys they'd been then. They were only kids, after all.

But they weren't kids any more. And the two of them had the power to change things.

'Can I show you something?' he asked, having to raise his voice as a police car flew past, sirens screaming.

'Sure.'

Lachlan pulled the piece of paper out of his pocket, turning it over so Duncan could see the photograph. He passed it to his brother, who lifted it close to his eyes, his lips pulling down as he looked at it. 'What's this?'

'I was given it at Glencarraig. I can't even remember it being taken.' Lachlan shrugged. 'According to the estate manager we were both a pair of thugs. He didn't know what to do with us.'

'It's hard to look like a thug when you're wearing a kilt,' Duncan murmured. His frown had gone, but the look of confusion hadn't. 'What the hell were they thinking, dressing us up like that?'

'I think it's the only time we wore the same clothes.'

'Like twins.' Duncan's eyes met Lachlan's, and for a moment neither of them said a word. They simply looked at each other.

'I wanted to tell you about Glencarraig,' Lachlan finally said, as a crowd of partygoers walked past them. 'Are you staying in New York next week?' he asked. 'We could meet to talk.'

'Sure.' Duncan nodded. 'I'll get my lawyer to call yours.'

Lachlan shook his head. 'No, no lawyers. Just us two for now.'

'Okay then, just us.'

From the corner of his eye, Lachlan saw his car pull up to the kerb. The driver climbed out, and opened the door for him. 'That's my ride. I'll speak to you next week.'

It was Duncan who put his hand out first. Lachlan looked at it for a moment, staring at his half-brother's outstretched arm as though it was an alien object. It took him that long to realise that he was offering him a handshake.

Feeling the blood flooding his face, Lachlan reached out his own hand, clasping Duncan's palm in his. The contact lasted for only a few seconds, before Duncan stepped back, offering his brother the smallest of smiles.

'Good night, Lachlan.'

'Good night.' Lachlan gave him a final glance before climbing into the car. The driver closed the door behind him, and Lachlan leaned his head back on the leather seat, letting a mouthful of air escape his open lips.

'Are you going back to your apartment, Mr MacLeish?' the driver asked, turning around from his position in the front seat.

'Yes, please,' Lachlan said, running his hand through his hair. He wanted to jump in the shower, pull on some sweatpants and climb into bed, resting his head on the pillow that still smelled of her.

Maybe tomorrow would be a better day.

31

Let us not burden our remembrance
with a heaviness that's gone

– The Tempest

At first it was a relief to walk back into her flat in Edinburgh. Even the cat's sneaky – and successful – attempt to run inside didn't ruin Lucy's sense of calm. But as soon as she looked at the breakfast bar and remembered how they'd shared dinner there the day he'd flown into Edinburgh, it felt less like a sanctuary and more like a prison. She couldn't look at the kitchen without remembering cooking with him, or glance at the sofa without remembering making love with him there. Everything held memories of the man who had touched her everywhere.

From the corner of her eye she caught a glimpse of tabby fur, as the cat stole her way into Lucy's bedroom. Picking up her box again, Lucy walked into the kitchen, laying it gently down on the breakfast bar. As she pulled the lid off, she felt her throat get congested. The flight attendant had been right – it had come to no harm as they'd crossed the Atlantic Ocean. It had survived the journey from London to Edinburgh, too, as Lucy had placed it on the seat next to her on the train, guarding it as though it was something precious.

Maybe because it was.

Holding her breath, she took hold of the delicate object, lifting it gently from the foam packaging that had kept it safe. She placed it on the counter, running her fingers across the smooth porcelain, taking in every inch of it.

It was a black plate – much bigger than one you'd use for dinner. The curator in the gallery had explained that it had probably been part of a larger set at one point, from the Edo period in the early nineteenth century. But it wasn't the provenance that enchanted her – it was the beautiful gold repairs that criss-crossed the china, turning something banal and workmanlike into a work of art.

As soon as she saw it, she'd known she wanted to buy it for Lachlan. A thank-you gift for having her stay with him. But for some reason she'd taken it with her when she left New York, unable to give it to him without an adequate explanation.

He wouldn't have wanted it anyway.

She ran her fingers across the china, tracing the gold lines as they crossed the centre of the plate. Closing her eyes, she remembered the way they'd traced each other's scars, fingers soft, words softer, as he whispered that sometimes being broken could make you stronger.

A screech from her left brought her attention back into the room, as the cat hared from the bedroom and into the kitchen, running as though she was being chased. She jumped onto the counter, bumping against Lucy's arm as she rushed for the closed door.

It happened as though it were all in slow motion. Lucy lurched to the left at the impact, her hold on the plate precarious. Then her elbow banged against the worktop, pain shooting up her arm, as the plate crashed onto the wooden floor. Bending over, she grasped for the black china, fingers outstretched as it made impact with the ground. She watched as it broke into pieces, the splintering sound echoing through her kitchen, the sharp china gouging into the soft wood of her floorboards. Almost immediately she fell to her knees, her mouth falling open as she saw the broken plate lying there.

She could feel her chest hitch as she picked up the largest piece, running her finger along the jagged edge. It was sharp as a knife, almost cutting her, and the sensation brought tears to her eyes.

Or maybe it wasn't the sensation. Maybe it was the realisation that she'd broken something beautiful all over again. In spite of the gold lacquer repairs, and the foam packaging, the plate was still fragile enough to fall apart at a single impact. As hard as she'd tried to protect it, just a simple fall was enough to make it shatter.

And as she held that piece in her hands, she felt the tears start to pour down her cheeks.

It had taken three days for them all to be available at the same time. By that point, Cesca and Sam were back in LA, and had invited Kitty and Adam over for lunch. Lucy couldn't help but smile softly as the four of them huddled around the laptop, Adam towering above Kitty as she sat, his hands resting lightly on her shoulders. Sam was sat next to Cesca, his arm resting lightly on the back of her chair. It made Lucy's heart ache in a good way to see her sisters so happy, so taken care of. It was everything she'd ever wanted for them.

But then she looked at the corner of the screen that showed Juliet. Like Lucy, she was alone. But unlike Lucy, she had a husband who should have been there, too. Taking care of her, holding her, telling her everything was going to be okay.

Damn Thomas. He was more absent than he was present.

'Where's Poppy?' Kitty asked. Like Lucy, she'd noticed the emptiness in Juliet's kitchen.

'She's at a friend's house for the afternoon,' Juliet said quietly. 'I thought it'd be for the best.'

The second of the four sisters, Juliet was by far the most classically beautiful. And yet even that wasn't enough to cover up the shadows beneath her eyes, nor the pinched expression on her face.

'Are you okay, honey?' Lucy asked gently. 'Is Thomas there?'

Juliet shook her head but said nothing. Lucy wasn't sure whether she was answering the first or the second question – or perhaps both.

'Yeah, you don't look very well,' Cesca piped in, her face a picture of concern. 'Is there anything you need?'

Juliet licked her bottom lip. 'I'm just tired, that's all.'

That wasn't all, but Lucy wasn't sure whether now was the right time to get into it. She hated the way Juliet looked more beaten down every time they talked.

'I'll be okay,' Juliet said, attempting a smile. 'More importantly, how are you?'

'Me?' Lucy raised her eyebrows. 'I'm fine, as always.'

'Bullshit.' Cesca coughed the words into her hands. 'Come on, Lucy. You don't have to be the strong one all the time.' She turned to Kitty, who was sitting beside her. 'Can you believe these two? They're supposed to be older and wiser than us.'

Kitty grinned. 'Well, they're definitely older.'

'Uh, do you want to shut up now?' Lucy retorted, feeling a warmth flooding through her. There was something about having her sisters close – even if it was only on a screen – that made everything feel better. 'You need to respect your elders.'

'Not falling for that one again,' Kitty replied, a smile still playing at her lips. 'That was always your excuse for everything.'

'How about you all hush up for a minute and let me talk?' Lucy said. 'I swear I can never get a word in edgeways with you lot.'

'Must run in the family,' Sam muttered.

'I heard that,' Lucy told him.

'I think you were supposed to,' Cesca said, grinning.

Lucy shook her head, smiling to herself. After the past few days it felt good to be surrounded by the ones she loved again. Even if seeing Sam hook his arm around Cesca's shoulders made her feel wistful.

'Look, do you want to hear what I have to say or not?' Lucy asked. 'Because there are a thousand better things I could be doing right now.'

'Like what?' It was Adam's turn to grin at her, as he gently poked fun at her.

'I used to like you, Adam,' Lucy said. 'Now I'm not so sure.'

It was a lie. She loved Adam the same way she loved Sam – because they made her younger sisters happy. It had been one of the greatest gifts of her life to watch her sisters blossom and fall in love. And as she looked at Juliet, all alone in spite of being married and having a family, she couldn't help but wish that her third sister had experienced the same.

'Okay, I'm going to call this videoconference to order,' Lucy said, realising that if she didn't, the six of them would carry on like this for ever. And as much as part of her would like that, she'd been honest when she said she had other things to do. Like a whole pile of work she'd been neglecting for weeks. 'Are you all right with me just getting everything out there?' she asked them. 'Or do you want to ask me questions?'

Five faces looked back at her through the screen. 'Just get it out there,' Cesca said. The others nodded.

Okay then. Lucy grabbed her glass of water, swallowing a mouthful to moisten her tongue. She'd done nothing but think about this for the past few days – well, this and the mess she'd left behind in New York – and somehow it felt good to be finally talking about it.

'I guess the first thing to remember was we were all so young back then,' Lucy said, putting her glass down on the counter beside the laptop. 'I know we thought we were old, and the bee's knees, and that we knew everything. But really, we were still kids. And in those days I saw everything in black and white. The girls at school were either my friends or my enemies – though that could change on a daily basis. And as far as we were all concerned, our mum was a beautiful angel who took care of us all.'

Across the Atlantic, her sisters were nodding at her words. She could see that their eyes were already glassy. Thinking back to those days was stirring up emotions in them all.

'And I don't want what I have to say to make you change your opinion of her, or of Dad. They were just human like the rest of us, that's all.'

She took another swallow of her water. She wasn't sure whether it was all the talking that was making her mouth dry, or the memories. 'It was one of the last days of term – I remember that because it was Sports Day, and I really didn't want to take part. So when I actually felt sick, I thought all my Christmases had come at once. I spent a morning in the school nurse's office throwing up, while they tried to call Mum to pick me up. They

300

even tried to call Dad, but he was in a meeting at college, so in the end they told me to make my own way home.'

She closed her eyes for a moment, remembering that day. The memory was so vivid she could almost feel the way her stomach had griped all the way home, and how she'd clasped her hand across her mouth to stop herself from being sick on the pavement. 'There was a strange car on our driveway when I got home, but I didn't think anything of it. I don't know if you remember but we were always having workmen come in – a house like that was under constant repair. But as soon as I put my key in the lock and opened the door, I was greeted by silence, not the banging or drilling I usually heard.'

She could hear her voice start to wobble. All this detail she was giving them was more of a way to put off the inevitable than anything else. And it was making things worse – she could almost be standing there in that hallway, waiting for her world to cave in.

'I called out but there was no answer. Nobody in the kitchen when I walked past it. By that point I thought there was nobody in the house, and decided to go and sleep whatever bug I had off.' Her chest tightened as she continued to speak. 'I was walking past Mum and Dad's room when I heard a noise. And for a second everything made sense. I thought Mum must be ill, too – maybe she had the same bug as me. So I pushed the door open to tell her I was home.'

She had to bite her lip not to cry out, the same way she had when she'd walked into that bedroom. The carpet had been soft beneath her feet. Across the room a window was open, the curtains dancing in the breeze, but that wasn't what had drawn her attention.

'I saw her in bed with a man. It was only later that I

recognised who he was. He was her co-star from the play she was in. Dan Simons was his name. But he really didn't look the same with his clothes off.'

'Oh, Jesus.' Cesca shook her head, covering her mouth with her hand. 'You saw them.'

'Only for a second, and then I ran out. I barely made it to the bathroom before I was being sick all over again.'

'Were they . . . ?' Juliet trailed off, though her question was clear.

'No, thank God.' Lucy wrinkled her nose, not wanting to think about that. 'But they were lying together on her bed. On Dad's bed.' She could feel the anger take over her, the same fury she'd felt as a teenager. Her mother's betrayal had felt like a slap to every one of them.

'It was a few minutes later that she came into my room. We had an almighty row. I told her I was going to tell Dad, I was going to tell all of you, too. I said she was a bitch and I hated her.'

She could see her sisters were crying, and felt a tear roll down her own cheek. She wiped it away impatiently. 'That was the night before she died.'

'And did you tell him?' Juliet asked. 'Did you tell Dad about them?'

Lucy shook her head. 'I wasn't brave enough. I wanted to, but I was scared. I couldn't stand the thought of them divorcing, and him leaving us all. I thought it would all be my fault that our family would be broken.'

'You're wrong, it was never your fault.' Kitty's voice was soft. 'None of this was your fault.' Behind her, Adam hooked his arms around Kitty, pulling her closer to him. She rested her head against his abdomen. Seeing the tenderness between them made Lucy's heart clench.

'The rest all seems a bit messed up in my head,' Lucy told

them. 'Of course I remember going to school the next day, and Mum picking me up. I wasn't expecting her, she obviously decided to have a chat with me, to tell me that it was nothing, just a fling. That's when I lost it with her, and we were both screaming at each other, making all kinds of accusations. She was driving too fast, and it was raining too hard. As soon as she lost control of the car it was all over.'

'And she wasn't wearing a seatbelt,' Cesca said.

'That's right. But I was.' And that was all it took – the difference between life and death. A thick strip of fabric and some moulded metal. 'And she died because of me.'

A loud sob escaped from Juliet's mouth, echoing over the connection. 'She didn't die because of you,' she said, her voice thin. 'None of this was your fault.'

Lucy paused to take in a lungful of air, feeling the oxygen course through her like a bolt of adrenalin. She couldn't stop now, not when it was almost over. She owed them the rest of the truth. 'As soon as I came home from hospital I tried to talk to Dad about it, to tell him what had happened. But he blanked me. He'd hole up in his office for hours, he'd forget about meals and the fact he had four daughters. He was in his own world of pain and it was like he couldn't be reached.'

'But you told him eventually, right?' Cesca asked.

Lucy shook her head. 'I never told him, he wouldn't let me. I kept it all inside. I felt as though you'd all hate me. We'd already lost our mum, and our dad was hiding away from us. I couldn't bear to lose my sisters as well.'

'Oh sweetie.' Juliet reached her hand out to the screen, as if to touch her. Lucy lifted her fingers, pressing them against the image of her sister's hand. 'It wasn't your fault. You'll never lose us.'

'Does Dad know you know?' Kitty asked.

'About the affair?' Lucy shrugged. 'I don't know, and it's too late to ask now. It was only when he started to become ill that I wondered if he knew something. He started saying some strange things.'

'Like he did with me,' Cesca said.

'Exactly. And I'd have given anything for you not to have found out like that. It must have been horrible.'

Sam squeezed Cesca's shoulder. 'It was pretty bad,' he said. 'You should tell them,' he urged her.

'Now?' Cesca grimaced. 'It doesn't seem very appropriate.'

Sam leaned towards her, running his finger across her soft lips. 'I can't think of anything more appropriate. All of you are here together, what better time is there?'

Kitty turned to look at Cesca. 'What's he talking about?'

Cesca blinked a couple of times and looked down at her lap. 'We went to see Dad because Sam wanted to ask him something.' She shifted in her seat.

'What?' Lucy asked, not sure whether to be concerned or not. 'What did you ask him?'

Finally Cesca brought her gaze back to the laptop. Sam pulled her closer to him, until her body was crushed against his. 'Sam's asked me to marry him,' she told them, a small smile playing at her lips. 'That's what he wanted to ask Dad, but then Dad got all upset, thinking I was Mum and I was marrying somebody else.'

'You're engaged?' Kitty's face exploded into a smile. 'That's wonderful.' She leaned forward, hugging Cesca tight. Lucy could feel her biceps flex, as she wished she were there to hold her sister, too. For a moment their connection exploded with congratulations, as all the sisters talked at once, and none of them listened to anybody.

'Have you set a date yet?' Juliet asked, when the others finally quietened down. In the middle of the melee, Sam had sat down on the chair, with Cesca perched on his lap. The two of them looked the picture of happiness.

'Not yet,' Cesca told them. 'We need to talk to some wedding planners. And obviously we want to keep things under wraps as much as we can.'

'Once the press find out, we'll have to go into hiding,' Sam agreed. 'So we're keeping things on the down low for now.' He leaned forward to kiss Cesca's cheek.

'Fat chance of that,' Cesca said. 'Those guys can sniff out a white dress like a vampire smelling blood.'

'I'm so happy for you both,' Lucy said, her heart feeling full. 'It's the most wonderful news. Especially after the week you've both had.'

'It is, isn't it?' Cesca grinned. 'And I'm sorry I didn't tell you when I was in London. I wanted to save it until we were all together.'

'I can hardly tell you off for keeping secrets, can I?' Lucy smiled. 'And anyway, it's the best kind of secret, and one I don't mind keeping at all.' She looked at them, her three sisters, her family, feeling an immense surge of pride rushing through her. She'd never really been able to fit into her mother's shoes after her death, but she'd kept things stable until all three of them were ready to face the world. Maybe she could be proud of herself for that at least. 'Look at you all, growing up and settling down.' She licked her lips, to try to take away the dryness. 'You know if Mum was still alive, she'd be proud of all of you right now.' And if her dad were still able to focus, he would be too.

'She'd be proud of you, too,' Juliet pointed out. 'And thankful that you took care of us all when she couldn't.'

'And when are you planning on settling down, too?' Kitty asked. 'Cesca told me you might have been visiting a certain laird in New York last week.'

'Yeah, well, don't hold your breath,' Lucy said, feeling that familiar ache in her chest. 'I messed that up the way I do everything else.' God, was she crying again? When did it ever stop?

'Oh honey, what happened?' Cesca touched her fingers to the screen. 'Is everything okay?'

Lucy shook her head, wiping her tears with the heel of her hand. 'No, it isn't,' she answered truthfully. 'We had a terrible argument before I left, and now it's over.' Her sobs got louder. 'I ruined everything.'

'Do you love him?' Kitty asked. Like Cesca, she was touching the screen.

Lucy looked up at them, her eyes shining. 'Yes, I'm in love with him. But he hates me and there's nothing I can do.' She squeezed her lids closed to stem the flow of tears, but they just pooled up and spilled over anyway.

'Oh sweetie,' Cesca said, tipping her head to the side in sympathy. 'Of course there has to be something you can do. Love doesn't just disappear because you've had an argument. Why don't you tell us what happened, and we can try to figure things out.'

For the second time in the video call, Lucy found herself telling her sisters her story of woe, listening as they commiserated with her. And it felt good to not be hiding everything, to have it all out in the open with them. They were her family, after all. At least she'd always have that.

32

Justice always whirls in equal measure
– Love's Labour's Lost

Warmer weather had finally arrived in Edinburgh while she'd been away. Blossom had fallen from the trees, creating a pale-pink and white blanket of petals in Prince's Park, and the early snowdrops and bluebells had been replaced by a riot of yellow daffodils, their trumpets heralding new beginnings. A shaft of yellow sunlight shone through Lucy's office window, reflecting on her laptop screen. She angled it, trying to read the contract she had up on there, highlighting the parts she wanted to change.

'Lucy, do you have a minute?'

She looked up to see Malcolm Dunvale standing in her office doorway. She clicked save on her document then pulled the screen down. 'Of course. Do you want me to come to your office?' Please God, don't let it be bad news. She'd had enough of that to last her a lifetime.

'Yes please.' She followed him to the glass-walled room, walking in as he pulled the door shut and sat on the corner of his desk. 'I just wanted to let you know the Glencarraig thing is over.'

'It's over? How?' A sense of panic washed over her. 'I thought you were waiting for a court date to be confirmed.'

Malcolm shrugged. 'All I know is that the two parties have come to some kind of agreement and the case is off.' He gave her a tight smile. 'I thought you'd be pleased. Hopefully now we can forget all about it and just get on with our work.'

She didn't feel pleased, though. She felt as though the final corner of the rug was being pulled out from under her, and she was tumbling downwards. Even though she'd been taken off the case, Lachlan's inheritance was still one of the last things tying him to Edinburgh.

And maybe tying him to her.

'What kind of agreement have they come to?' she asked.

'I've no idea. Apparently Dewey and Clarke are taking care of that, and John Graves will sign off on the other end. As far as Robinson and Balfour are concerned, the case is officially closed.'

'Oh.' It was hard to ignore the look of relief on Malcolm's face. As her boss, she knew she'd put him in an awkward position, and he was clearly pleased to be free of it. She should be pleased, too, shouldn't she?

'Do you know if Mr MacLeish is keeping the title and the lodge?' she asked. For a moment she could see Glencarraig in all its glory, against the backdrop of mountains and hills. Had he given it all up just so he never had to see her again?

'Which Mr MacLeish?' Malcolm asked her.

'Lachlan. The client.' She swallowed hard.

'I've no idea. He was vague about the details, just said there was nothing for us to worry about. And asked for me to pass on his thanks for the hard work, of course.' He frowned for a second. 'Am I right in assuming that you haven't spoken to him?'

'That's right.'

He looked at her for a long minute, and she could almost guess what he was thinking. Why had she put them all in such a tight position, only to pull away from Lachlan? He didn't voice the question, though, just stood and stretched his arms, his action all but dismissing her. 'Right, well, that was all really.' He paused before nodding at her. 'This is a good thing, Lucy. You can get on with your work and not worry about how this affects your career any more.'

She nodded, and attempted a smile, whispering a thank-you as she left the room. As soon as she was back at her desk, she lowered her head into her hands, covering her face with her palms.

It was as though she'd gone from treading water to being washed away by a tidal wave. There was an emptiness inside her, a profound feeling of loss. As though the final tie that bound her to Lachlan had unravelled.

You don't have to worry how this affects your career any more.

But right now her career was the last thing on her mind.

Her fingers hovered over the dial pad of her telephone, as she stared at the black plastic handset. Next to the phone her full cup of coffee had cooled to a barely tepid mess, her stomach too churned up to be able to drink from the mug that Lynn had brought her. Lucy rolled her bottom lip between her teeth, tasting the metallic tang of the soft flesh inside her mouth.

She reached out to pick up the handset, then pulled her arm back again, as though she'd just been burned. God, she couldn't remember the last time she'd been so indecisive. That kind of behaviour just wasn't in her genes. She was Lucy Shakespeare, the girl who took charge. The woman who made decisions and stuck by them.

Or at least, that was who she used to be.

Before she could bring herself to lift the receiver to her ear, the telephone started to buzz. She looked out of her office window to see Lynn gesturing at her.

'Hello?'

'I have Mr Tanaka on the line for you.' Lynn shot her a smile through the glass.

'Mr Tanaka?' Lucy repeated. 'Okay, put him through.'

Within a moment she heard a click. 'Grant?'

'Lucy. How are you?'

'A bit confused. Is Lachlan there?' she asked.

'He's travelling.' Grant's tone held a note of regret. 'I just wanted to bring you up to speed on the Glencarraig situation.'

'Is Lachlan okay?' she asked. 'I really need to talk to him.' She should have spoken to him days ago, she knew that now. But every time she picked up the phone she couldn't find the right words. Maybe they didn't exist.

'He's on his way to Miami. He needs to explain some things to his mom.' She could hear Grant shifting something on his desk.

'Oh. Of course.' Family came first, always. Wasn't she the one who told him that? 'So what happened? My boss just told me the case is closed.'

'That's right. Lachlan and Duncan have been talking. They've come to an agreement.'

'He's been talking with his brother?' She sat up straight. 'When did that happen?'

'At the gala you missed.'

His words hit her like a rebuke. She recoiled at their impact. 'Oh.'

'I'm sorry. I didn't mean to sound like that.'

'It's okay.' Her voice was soft. 'He's your friend, of course you're going to stand up for him.' She couldn't help but taste the regret on her tongue. 'How is he?'

The silence lasted for long enough that she began to wonder if the connection was lost. She shook the handset to see if there was something wrong with it.

'He's not been great,' Grant finally said. 'You messed with his mind, Lucy. He thought you liked him. Hell, the guy fell in love with you. You broke him.'

His words felt like a dagger scraping against her heart. 'No,' she whispered, as much as herself as to Grant. 'I'm the broken one.'

Grant gave a little laugh. 'Well, you know what they say: broken attracts broken.'

'And hurt people hurt people,' she said, her heart still stuck in her throat. She tried to inhale, the air catching in her mouth. 'But I really didn't mean to hurt him.'

'He didn't mean to hurt you, either.' Grant sounded genuine. 'But you left him when he needed you. Do you understand how that made him feel? Nobody has ever stayed with him. Not his father, not his mother. Hell, even I'm moving away. He thought you were different and you ...' Grant sighed. 'You left.'

'I had to take care of my family,' Lucy told him. 'He must understand that. They have to come first.'

'You have a very narrow definition of family,' Grant pointed out. 'It doesn't just mean blood ties. Look at Lachlan and me. We're from different families, heck we're from different races. And yet I love that man like a brother. And it doesn't matter where either of us end up, if he needs me, I'll be there.'

'He's very lucky to have you.' She couldn't hide the tears in her voice.

'The feeling is pretty mutual,' Grant said. 'He's a good guy, Lucy. Beneath all that bravado and that alpha male shit, he's just a guy. Someone who deserves to be loved.'

She closed her eyes to stem the flow of tears. How many had she cried these past few weeks? There had to be a water shortage somewhere because of her. But even her mind was against her, her dark eyelids providing a screen for a replay of her memories. Of her first glance of Lachlan when he walked into that Miami restaurant, commanding the room as soon as he stepped inside. Of him walking into her bedroom in Glencarraig, lifting her as easily as if she was a blanket, his body warm and hard against hers.

Of the way he opened up to her, laying himself bare as he told her the story of his childhood.

And then she'd left him, and broken both their hearts.

'I didn't know what to do,' she whispered, her eyes still tightly shut. 'I had to see my sister, I had to leave ...' She shook her head, trying to make sense of it all. 'Everything was so out of control.'

'What happened, Lucy? You could have called him when you got home. Instead, he got days of silence.'

'I was waiting for him to make the first move. I didn't want to make things worse.' God, it sounded so stupid now. Why the hell hadn't she called him? 'I was afraid,' she admitted.

'Of Lachlan?' Grant sounded surprised. 'Why were you afraid of him?'

It was all making sense. Saying it out loud was like a light bulb sparking up in her head. For the weeks she and Lachlan had been together, there was always a part of her waiting for it to end. The way things always ended with somebody she loved.

Love? The word was enough to send a chill down her spine, and yet warm her at the same time. Because love made you vulnerable, it opened you up to hurt. Love meant losing control.

'It wasn't him I was afraid of,' she said, more to herself than Grant. 'It was me. I was afraid I was falling for him. I was afraid he'd hurt me. So I left before he could.'

'You're as bad as each other.' Grant gave out a little huff. 'I've never met two people who are so successful professionally, and yet have no idea what they're doing with their personal lives. If I didn't know any different I'd say you were made for one another.'

Was it wrong that his words felt like a bouquet of hope blooming inside her?

'Maybe we are,' she said. 'And maybe we're both too blind to see it.'

'If you just talked occasionally, it would help. And I don't mean telling him what clothes you're wearing whenever he calls.'

Her cheeks pinked up. Grant knew about that?

'Seriously, call him. Stop dancing around each other, it's getting you nowhere. He misses you, he wants you, but he's scared. Since he was a kid he's been determined to pull himself out of the life he was born into. Determined to prove himself to his dad and his brother and God knows who else. He's still learning that life isn't just about winning, but about enjoying the journey.'

'I could help him.'

'You already started. But you got interrupted mid-project.'

'I'll call him,' she said, her mind made up. 'But what if he doesn't answer?'

313

'You tell me. Will that be enough for you to give up? Are you that afraid of being rejected?'

She was. But maybe she could stop letting the fear guide her. Maybe she could make herself vulnerable, open herself up, and see where the breeze took her. Yes, it was going to be as scary as hell, and yes she'd stumble on the way. But the alternative – to lose him – was even more painful.

'Grant?'

'Yes?' he said patiently.

'What agreement did he come to with his brother?'

'How about you ask him that?' Grant suggested. 'All I can say is he seems happy with the situation.'

She nodded, still clutching the phone to her ear. 'Yes, I'll ask him.'

'That's good.'

It was, wasn't it? Even if her whole body was shaking at the thought. They said their goodbyes and she gently replaced the phone on the receiver, tapping the plastic casing with her fingers, deep in thought.

She couldn't help but remember the way he'd flown to Edinburgh that Friday night, giving her the shock of her life in the most exquisite way. He'd made a grand gesture, made her feel wanted, cherished, taken care of. Opened his heart to her when he told her he wanted more.

Maybe it was her turn to make a grand gesture right back.

33

But if the while I think on thee, dear friend, all
losses are restor'd and sorrows end

– Sonnet 30

'What did you say?' His mom leaned forward, her mouth pinched tightly together. She was so much better than the last time he'd seen her, her breathing regular thanks to the tubes in her nose. She was on the ball, too, her eyes glistening as she waited for his answer. So much healthier now she was back in her care home.

'I said Duncan and I have come to an agreement.'

'Did you lose the case?' She frowned, shaking her head. 'We should appeal. Was it that solicitor you had? Maybe you should get a different one.'

He swallowed away the taste of Lucy's memory. 'It wasn't the solicitor's fault. The case didn't even make it to court. Duncan and I have been talking.'

She winced at the mention of his half-brother's name. 'You have? Why?' She looked confused. 'I thought you were going to fight and win.'

'Just because I didn't fight, doesn't mean I lost,' Lachlan pointed out. 'I'm more than happy with the agreement we came to.'

She was silent for a moment, taking in his words. It was impossible not to see the expression of disappointment on her face. 'But you wanted your father's inheritance. We talked about this the last time you were here. You were going to show them all exactly who you were. That you were the rightful heir to everything they wanted.'

'I realised something along the way,' he told her, his voice soft. 'A prize is only worth fighting for if you want it. I've never really wanted anything my father had. All I wanted was his love, and that was something I could never get.' And all the titles in the world weren't going to get him what he never had.

'But it will make you legitimate,' she protested.

He shook his head. 'Nothing would make me legitimate. And it doesn't change any of their minds about me. It's only made things worse. I don't have anything to prove to them, not any more.' Maybe he never did. From the moment he was conceived, he never really stood a chance in the MacLeish family. And no wonder. He represented his father's weakness, his betrayal. They would much rather have ignored his existence than acknowledge him as part of the family.

His mother reached out to stroke his cheek. 'But they hurt you, over and over again. They deserve to feel the pain, too.'

'Because of my father's mistakes?' Lachlan asked. 'No, I don't agree. Duncan didn't ask to have an illegitimate brother, any more than I asked to be born. And his mother didn't ask to be cheated on either.'

She winced. 'We were in love . . . '

'No, *you* were in love.' Lachlan could see it clearly now. 'He took you for a ride then pushed you out of the car. And for years I think you hoped he'd fall in love with me, and that would make him love you, too. But that's not the way love works, Mom. You can't make somebody love you if they're not ready to do it.' His voice cracked, his emotions shining through the gap. 'And getting a pointless title isn't going to change any of that.'

'So that's it. You've given up?'

'No.' It didn't feel like giving up. It felt like he'd been wasting so much energy chasing something he was never going to get. 'I've decided to concentrate on things that are more important to me.'

'Like what?'

He shrugged. 'My work, my health. Happiness. Maybe even settle down with my own family eventually.'

'Your own family?' Her expression softened. 'Have you met somebody?'

He blew out a mouthful of air. It still hurt to talk about it. Hurt to think about it, even. And yet that was nothing compared to the pain of *not* thinking about her. She was in everything he did.

'I met her and I lost her,' he said.

He felt his mom slip her fingers between his, squeezing his hand tightly. She was surprisingly strong for a sick woman. 'You had your heart broken?' she whispered.

'Something like that.' Lachlan's attempt at a smile slid into a grimace.

She stared at him, her lips pursed together in sympathy. 'Who is she?' she finally asked.

'Her name is Lucy,' Lachlan told her. Just saying it was like another stab to the heart. 'She's beautiful, she's funny, and she's everything I never knew I wanted.'

His mom frowned. 'So what happened?'

'I let her slip through my fingers because I couldn't give her what she needed. And she left me.' Shit, was his voice breaking? He coughed, to try to even it out.

'She must have been very special for you to fall in love with her.'

He looked up, into her unblinking blue eyes. Like his, they were as vivid as the ocean. 'I didn't say I loved her.'

'You didn't have to.'

No he didn't. He felt it through his entire body, every time he thought about her smile, her voice, the way she would curl into him in the middle of the night. He could almost feel her there now, could almost smell the floral fragrance of her shampoo, hear her soft laughter.

Yes, he was in love with her. In love with Lucy Shakespeare, the most beautiful, funny and aggravating woman he'd ever met. No wonder he couldn't stop thinking about her.

'I do love her,' he whispered, to himself more than his mother.

His mom laughed. 'Don't sound so unhappy about it.'

He shook his head, still trying to think straight. 'I said some messed-up things to her . . .'

She listened as he told her the whole story, occasionally interrupting to ask him a question. He couldn't remember the last time he'd been so honest with his mom, or the last time he'd been this emotional about anything.

'It doesn't sound irretrievable,' she finally said, her hand still squeezing his. 'It just sounds like you're both as stubborn as hell. You've finally found your match, darling.'

For the first time he laughed, and it felt good. 'You're not wrong. She's like a wild animal, almost impossible to tame.'

'I know you, Lachlan. If you want something badly enough,

you don't give up until you have it.' She licked her lips – the oxygen was always making them dry. 'You didn't want your father's title badly enough, I get that.' There was still a note of disappointment in her voice. 'But this girl, if you want her, you'll have to fight until you get her. You've never shied away from a fight before.'

But maybe the stakes had never been so high before, either. He'd lost her once, the thought of losing her for the second time was devastating. There was part of him – the old Lachlan – that wanted to slink off and lick his wounds, to soothe them with meaningless liaisons and his usual workaholism.

But that was the coward's way out. He'd been doing those things for long enough – for years, according to Jenn – and they'd done nothing but dull the pain.

Lucy was the biggest prize he'd ever fought for and lost. Was he brave enough to throw himself into the ring for a second round?

The hotel bar was half-empty. He'd spent most of the evening catching up with the work he'd missed during his visit to his mom, writing emails and making calls, and asking Grant to rearrange his diary just one more time. Ever stoic, his friend and assistant had patiently moved meetings around and changed some into videoconferences, while muttering to himself that Lachlan had finally lost it.

And maybe he had. But somehow he felt like he was gaining something, too. A peace of mind he'd never felt before.

'I promise this is the last time,' Lachlan told Grant down the phone, taking a sip of the ice-cold beer the waitress had slid onto the table.

'I'll believe that when I see it,' Grant said, his voice warm with humour. 'Anyway, I can get you on the red eye into Heathrow on Monday night. That will give you enough time to meet with your British investors before taking the train up to Edinburgh. Does that work?'

'Yeah, sure.'

'When do you want to fly back? Should I book it to New York?'

Lachlan didn't have an answer to that one. The fact was, it all depended on *her*. On whether she'd give him the time of day, or whether she'd had enough of him already. 'I don't know,' he said. Some of the condensation from his cold beer glass had dripped on to the wooden table. He reached out with his finger, tracing patterns into the water. 'I need to visit with Alistair too, bring him up to speed with the situation. Let's leave it flexible.'

'Sure.' Grant still sounded amused.

'Burger and fries?' The waitress was smiling when he looked up at her. She slid the plate in front of him,

He breathed in the aroma – meaty and hot. 'I didn't order any food.' It smelled good, though, enough to send a grumble through his stomach.

'I thought you looked hungry.' Another woman appeared behind the waitress. One with blonde hair, a heart-shaped face and eyes that kept him awake at night.

'Lucy?' He stood, his chair scraping the wooden floor behind him. It took him a moment to become aware he was still holding his cellphone against his ear, Grant's voice asking him what the heck was going on.

'You're going to need to cancel that flight,' Lachlan said into the mouthpiece, still unable to take his eyes from her. 'I'll call you back later.'

Grant didn't protest at the sudden change in conversational direction. Instead, he said goodbye, hanging up straight away.

The waitress walked away, leaving only Lucy and Lachlan, plus the five feet of space between them. It seemed too much and not enough. His skin felt like it was on fire.

'You're here.'

She nodded, her chest rising and falling with her breaths. 'The last time you flew in to see me you brought food. I'm just repaying the debt.'

'You are?' He was still having problems forming full sentences. She'd stolen those, too.

'Yeah.' She was nervous, he could tell by the way she was wringing her fingers together. 'And the way I see it, apologies always go down better with food.'

His hands clenched and unclenched by his side. He wanted to reach out, to see if she was real. To feel the softness of her skin against his rough fingers, to feel her warmth melting into his own.

'It's not much fun eating alone,' he said. 'Will you join me?' He pointed at the seat opposite his.

'I only ordered one meal.'

'I can share.'

Her hand shook as she reached for the chair, pulling it out so she could slide onto it. He sat back down, the table between them, and pushed the plate until it was in the middle, close enough for them both to reach. 'Eat,' he said.

She took a fry, but didn't lift it to her mouth. He did the same, still staring at her. He'd forgotten how beautiful she was. How her skin looked like porcelain, the red discs on her cheeks as though they'd been painted by an artist. He knew every plane of that face; the way her eyes crinkled when she smiled, the way her sharp cheekbones gave way to the smooth dips below. And then there were her lips – pink, swollen, always so goddamned kissable.

'I'm not really hungry,' she confessed, still holding the fry.

'Why not?' He frowned.

'I lost my appetite somewhere across the Atlantic.'

'You flew in today?'

'I arrived an hour ago.'

His chest felt full. She managed to ignite every tender emotion it was possible to feel. He wanted to pull her against him, tell her it was going to be okay. He wanted to take care of her, the same way she took care of everybody else. 'Lucy—'

She lifted her hand up. The fry was still between her fingers. 'No, please just listen to me for a minute. If I don't say this now, I might lose my courage.'

He smiled, but said nothing. It was on the tip of his tongue to tell her she was the bravest person he knew.

'I've been an idiot,' she said, letting out a mouthful of air after her words, as if relieved at finally admitting it. 'I thought that if I could just keep everything under wraps then my family would be okay. But I was wrong. You told me as much yourself. It wasn't my job to hide secrets from my sisters, and all I did was make things so much worse.'

He bit down hard on the inside flesh of his lip to stop himself from protesting. He was too curious to hear what she had to say to stop her from talking now.

'And by trying to clear things up, I ended up making things even harder for myself. If I'd have just taken a while to think things through instead of jumping on the first plane home, then I wouldn't have ended up hurting you,' she blinked, her long eyelashes sweeping down, 'and hurting myself at the same time.' The French fry was still clasped between her fingers. She twisted it, pulling it apart, revealing the fluffy white interior. 'I fell for you. And I was so scared you didn't feel the same way that I ran back to London. And then instead of calling you or messaging you straight away, I panicked. I wanted you to be the first one to make a move even though I was the one who walked away.'

'That's not true.' His voice was raspy. 'I pushed you away. I was the one who told you to leave and never come back.' He shook his head at his own words. 'I was a fucking fool, and I'm so sorry. I didn't mean a word of it.'

He thought of that airplane ticket that Grant was cancelling as they spoke. She was so close to the truth – he was planning to make the first move. Even if it had taken him too long to do it.

Her eyes were soft. 'I'm sorry, too. For hurting you. I'm sorry for promising to be by your side at the gala and then walking out on you. I'm sorry for hiding and being too scared and too proud to call you when I should have done it straight away.' She abandoned the fry, wiping her fingers on the napkin, before lifting it to dab at her eyes. 'And you have no reason to forgive me. God knows, you've dealt with enough people letting you down in your life, there's no reason to have one more.'

'I forgave you before you even left the airport,' he told her, his throat tight. 'It's me I'm finding it hard to forgive.'

Wrinkling her nose at the now-cooling plate of food, she glanced up at him. 'Are you at all hungry?'

He shook his head, still silent.

'In that case, will you come to my room?'

A rumble of laughter rolled up through his abdomen,

escaping his lips in a deep chuckle. 'Are you trying to pick me up?' he asked her.

Her eyes widened. 'Oh God, no. I just wanted to show you something.' The pink on her cheeks deepened to a vivid red.

He was still grinning. Her words had created a lightness inside him that felt impossible to hide. As though somebody had inflated a balloon in his chest, lifting him until only the tips of his toes were still in contact with the ground. 'I don't think I've ever been picked up in my own hotel before,' he said. 'It's a first for me.'

She swallowed. 'For me, too.'

For some reason he liked the sound of that. 'In that case,' he said, sweeping his arm towards the exit, 'let's go.'

34

They do not love that do not show their love

— The Two Gentlemen of Verona

Lucy slid her keycard into the lock, only too aware of Lachlan standing directly behind her, his body casting a long shadow on the painted door. She could feel him too, sense the warmth radiating from him, and could hear his soft breaths as he waited for her to open up. Their mutual apologies had made her feel as light as air. As if she could conquer the world if she wanted to.

As soon as they were inside her hotel room she could feel her face start to flush. It felt intimate, having him in here, even if she had protested that she had no ulterior motive.

'Would you like a drink?' she asked him.

'I'm good,' he replied, looking around the room. 'If you'd told me you were coming I could have gotten you an upgrade. I know the owner.' There was that smile again, all dimples and warm lips.

'I was scared that if I told you I was coming you'd say not to bother.'

He tipped his head to the side, still staring at her. 'Why would you think that?'

'Because I was wrong. I should never have left you like that. I shouldn't have left at all. If I'd just let things be and seen what happened I could have gone home after the gala.'

He winced, the smile temporarily disappearing from his face. 'I really wanted you there.'

'I know you did.' Her voice was soft. 'And I should have been there. For you.' She took a step forward, trying to ignore the way her whole body felt on edge. 'I'm so sorry I left you to go alone.'

She wasn't the only one who needed to apologise. 'I'm sorry I ruined your dress.'

'What are you talking about?' She looked at him in confusion.

'I was so angry I tore your dress up.' He had the good grace to look embarrassed. 'I thought it would make me feel better.'

'Did it?'

'Nope.'

It was her turn to wince. She could just picture him standing in front of that dress, taking all his anger out on the silk. 'It was a beautiful dress,' she said wistfully. 'I'm sorry I pushed you to that.'

'We both did a lot of stupid things that day. I should never have shouted at you, or given you an ultimatum. It's killed me not to call you and tell you how much I miss you.' His expression softened. 'It's been a special kind of torture not being able to speak to you.'

'I kept hoping you'd call or email me,' she told him. 'When you didn't I thought maybe you didn't care any more.'

'I cared,' he told her, taking another step to close the gap between them. 'I cared a lot. Too much. I just didn't want to make a fool out of myself.'

She looked up at him, taking in that familiar face. The hard angles and the soft skin. Everything about him made her feel warm inside, and yet more afraid than she ever had. 'You could never make a fool out of yourself. You always win, remember?'

'I haven't feel much like a winner. I haven't felt much of anything.' He reached out for her, running the tips of his fingers along her cheek. 'It took everything I had not to fly over and demand you explain yourself.'

'Why didn't you?'

'Because I needed you to come to me. Or to call me at least.' He laughed, but the humour didn't reach his eyes. 'I guess I wanted you to tell me you were wrong.'

'I *was* wrong,' she whispered. His finger traced down from her cheek to the corner of her lip. Her skin felt as though it was on fire. 'I shouldn't have left like that.' She looked down, not quite able to meet his gaze. 'I thought everybody needed me, that if I let go of control it would all come tumbling down. But it turns out that my sisters don't need me like that any more. They're all grown up and in charge of their own lives.'

'So where does that leave you?' he asked her, running the pad of his finger along her bottom lip.

'Here with you. If you'll have me.'

He looked at her, unblinking. 'Of course I'll have you.' He leaned forward. His face was only inches away from hers. She wondered if he was going to kiss her. 'I know I said I was trying to wait, but I was just getting Grant to arrange my flights to London before you arrived. It turns out I'm not as patient as I thought.'

She smiled at him. 'That's one of the things I love about you,' she said.

He looked gratified at her words, closing the gap between

327

their lips, kissing her deeply. He curled his hand around the back of her neck, angling her head so he could kiss her harder, deepening it with a slide of his tongue against hers.

She looped her arms around his neck, arching herself into him, all thoughts of apologies and torn dresses disappearing from her mind. His other hand pressed into the dip of her lower back, his fingers burrowing under her shirt until they were pressed against her flesh, and she felt herself shiver beneath his touch.

'What was it you wanted to show me?' he murmured, brushing his lips down her jaw and then kissing at her neck.

'Hmm?'

He moved his fingers up her spine, making her shiver, his lips still worshipping at her throat. 'You asked to show me something,' he said, his words muffled by her skin. 'Or was that just an excuse?'

Briefly, her thoughts were pulled to the box, placed carefully on the table on the far end of her bedroom, but then he moved his hands to the buttons of her blouse, deftly unfastening them until it gaped open, and he kissed his way down her chest to the swell of her breast.

'It doesn't matter,' she gasped, as he moved his face down until his lips were tugging at the lace of her bra, sucking at her nipple through the delicate fabric. She felt her skin harden, her body reacting to his warm, wet mouth.

She could feel him harden in the same way.

'It doesn't?' he clarified, moving his lips to her other breast. She loved the way he always played fair.

'Nuh uh.'

Looping his arms around her back, he unhooked her bra, sliding it down her arms along with her blouse, until they were both pooled on the floor.

'Well, I've got something to show you,' he told her, unbuttoning his own shirt, and shrugging out of it.

'You have?'

'Yep.' He reached down, unzipping her skirt and pushing it down her hips with his warm hands. 'Now get on that bed and close your eyes.'

'You're as bossy as ever.'

'Always.'

'And what if I want to be in control?' she asked.

He looked up for a moment, a curious smile playing at his lips. 'Do you?' he asked.

She stared back at him. 'No, not really. Not this time, anyway.'

'Then do as you're told and get on the bed.'

'Yes, sir.'

'You want me to get a bathrobe?' he asked her, his voice teasing. 'It would make a good gag if nothing else.'

'You've forgotten we're in the cheap rooms,' she pointed out. 'No complimentary bathrobes in here.'

'Then I'll have to find another way to keep you quiet,' he said, dipping his lips to hers once again.

'You could try,' she murmured, closing her eyes as she felt him lift her up, and carry her over to the bed.

'Yeah, I could,' he said, laying her down onto the mattress, her hair spreading out on the pillow. 'But I have a feeling I might fail, and we don't want that.'

'You said you didn't care about winning any more,' she pointed out, letting out a little gasp as he ran his fingers lightly down her stomach, past her hips, hooking them into the waistband of her panties.

'Lucy?'

'Yes?'

'Will you shut up and let me make love to you?' he asked her, tugging her panties down, making her lift her hips to aid the movement.

She wasn't sure what she loved the most, the way he looked at her like she was the most beautiful girl he'd ever seen, or the way he ran his fingers down her thighs, leaving a trail of fire on her flesh. Either way, right now seemed like a good time to be quiet.

For a few minutes, at least.

He was the first to wake in the morning, his eyes blinking rapidly as reality seeped in to his blurred dreams. She was still lying beside him, her blonde hair fanned out against the white pillowcase, her face flushed and crumpled from where she'd been lying on it.

Her suitcase was still by the door, unzipped where she'd hurriedly found her washbag at some point in the night. Next to it was a large box, similar to the one she'd left his apartment with in such a hurry.

No, not similar. It looked exactly the same.

He couldn't help but wonder what was inside.

It was another twenty minutes before she opened her eyes. He watched as she focused on him, then pulled her lip between her teeth, as memories of last night made them both heat up.

'Good morning.' He reached out to trace the scar on her forehead, made visible by the way her hair was falling. 'Did you sleep well?'

'When you finally stopped molesting me,' she said, grinning.

'I was wondering, what's in that box?' he asked her, inclining his head to where her luggage lay. 'It looks interesting.'

It was as though a light had turned on behind her eyes. 'Oh God, I'd forgotten about that.' She covered her mouth for a moment, as though embarrassed. 'That's what I wanted to show you.' Her fingers muffled the sound.

'When?'

She sat up, curling her legs beneath her. 'When I asked you to come up to my room last night, remember? I said I wanted to show you something.'

'I remember.' He tried to keep his amusement down. 'And I think you showed me, all night long.'

She shook her head. 'You have a dirty mind, do you know that?' She scooted off the bed. She was naked as she walked across the beige carpet, and he couldn't help but admire the way her hips swung, her ass high and toned as she walked.

God, she was enticing.

She grabbed a T-shirt and sleep shorts from her case, pulling them on before lifting the box. Padding back to the bed, she laid it on the mattress, picking off the tape that fastened it shut.

'There's a good story to this,' she told him, lifting the cardboard flaps to reveal the packing foam. 'I bought it on the way back from Bergdorf's that day. I saw it and thought of you.' Gently, she took the foam out, to reveal an oversize black plate nestled into the box. It was old, the chips on the side of the rim were enough to tell him that, but that wasn't what made it beautiful. It was the criss-cross of gold lacquer, metallic jagged lines that glued the pieces together, that made it stand out.

'It's exquisite,' he told her. Reaching out, he touched the surface of the plate, feeling the smooth porcelain give way to thick glue. Each line told a story, of something broken but not irreparably. Of beauty rising from pain.

331

'I brought it home with me,' she told him. 'I didn't want to give it to you after our argument. And then as soon as I took it out in my apartment, it got broken.'

'It did?'

She nodded. 'My neighbour's cat pretty much jumped all over it. It smashed to pieces on my kitchen floor. It looked as though it could never be mended.' She touched the chip on the edge, where his finger had just been. 'I couldn't even find this piece.'

'It must have been tiny,' he said, watching her finger move back and forth over the jagged hole. 'But it doesn't matter. It's still beautiful.'

She looked up from the plate, and into his eyes. 'It reminded me of us. I think that's why I was so upset when I broke the damn thing. It felt as though I'd messed everything up, and it was irreparable. But then I called a woman in London who specialises in Kintsugi. She offered to take a look at it to see what she could do.'

'She did an amazing job. It's hard to tell what's old and what's new.' He felt a lump growing in his throat. The way she was touching the plate reminded him of the way she touched him. Softly, reverently, as though he was something worth taking care of.

'It's silly,' she said, 'but I always pictured it in the entrance hall of the lodge at Glencarraig. It would have looked beautiful on the table beneath the mirror.' Her eyes dropped, as though she was embarrassed. 'I guess that won't happen now that your brother has it.'

He reached out for her chin, lifting her face up until her gaze met his again. 'My brother doesn't have it. I didn't give him the lodge.'

'What?' She blinked, not understanding. 'I assumed you agreed to give it up.'

'Didn't Grant explain what happened?' Lachlan asked. He tipped his head to the side.

'No, he didn't explain. We got into a bit of a discussion about you, and that was that.'

'Do I want to know what you were discussing?' No, he probably didn't. Best not to go down that road.

'Stop changing the subject. I want to know what this agreement was. One that wasn't condoned by your ex-legal representative, I might add.' She wrinkled her nose.

He grinned. 'You're very sexy when you're angry.'

'It always comes down to sex, doesn't it?'

'I can't think of much else when you're half naked in my bed.'

'I think you'll find it's my bed,' she pointed out. 'This is my room, I'm paying for it.'

'And I own it.'

'On paper, which in this case means you've probably got a huge debt on it. And anyway, what makes you think I'm impressed by your properties?'

'You were impressed by my lodge.' He wiggled his eyebrows, and she couldn't help but laugh.

'So tell me how it's still yours.'

Lachlan sat up, pulling her with him, until they were both resting against the headboard. 'It's not quite mine, but it's not Duncan's either.'

She let out a strangled groan. 'Stop stringing it out. I'm on the edge of my seat here.'

He swallowed a chuckle. 'Okay, so I saw my brother at the gala and we had a talk.'

She looked guilty at his mention of the gala. 'I'm sorry I wasn't there. How did your talk go?'

'Surprisingly okay. There were no shots fired, no blood spilled, so I counted that as a win.' He reached out and stroked her shoulder, her chest, the swell of her breast. 'And then we met again the following week to discuss the case, just the two of us. No advisers, no lawyers, just two brothers.'

She stayed silent. As though she knew this was his story, and he needed to tell it.

'And I told him about the lodge, about Alistair and the clan website. It seemed crazy that here we were, two American businessmen, fighting over a title and a castle in a country that isn't ours.'

'So what did you agree to do?'

He carried on as if he hadn't heard her. 'I'd always wondered why my father left it to me. He hadn't shown any interest in me when he was alive. I asked Duncan about it, and he had no clue either, except that Dad always liked to fuck people over. I'm guessing he's been laughing in his grave over this one. It was literally a no-win situation.'

Lucy sighed. 'He sounds like a bastard.'

'He was. Pure and simple. He was an asshole to Duncan's mom, and he was an asshole to mine. He didn't treat either of us much better. And from what I can tell he had no interest in Glencarraig or his title. He never went to the clan meetings, hardly went to the village. He was an absentee landlord, and the place has suffered because of it. It needs investment and someone with a vision.'

Lucy blinked. 'Wait a minute, you're not thinking of moving there full time, are you?'

'No.'

334

'Then what? How are you going to avoid your dad's mistakes if you're the laird?'

'Because I'm not the laird. Or I won't be.'

She stared at him. 'What does that mean? Duncan's moving there?'

'He won't be the laird either.'

'Then who?'

'It will all become clear, I promise. But right now I can't say any more. My lawyer insists on it.' He winked at her.

'I can't believe you're not going to tell me,' she said, her mouth dropping open.

A smile danced around his lips. 'Can't you just be happy that Glencarraig will flourish?'

'It's important to you, isn't it?' she asked softly.

'Yes, it is. It impressed this girl I once knew. I watched her fall in love with it, and when I saw it through her eyes, I fell for it too.'

'She sounds like a fool,' she whispered, her voice tight.

'The most beautiful kind of fool,' he said, curling his hand around the back of her neck. 'The kind of fool you'd move mountains for. The kind of fool that keeps me awake at night, longing to talk to her, to touch her, to see her smile. The kind of fool I can't stop thinking about.'

She swallowed. 'She sounds fascinating, maybe I should meet her.'

'I like to keep her for myself.' He leaned forward, barely brushing his lips against hers. 'She's special.' He breathed against her skin, making her shiver. 'She's clever, she's funny, she drives me batshit crazy, but I'm already having a hard time imagining life without her.'

'It's a shame she lives so far away.'

He slowly shook his head. 'I'm giving us a year, and then we'll sort that, too. I like planes, but I like waking up with my girl more. And she *is* my girl.'

'It sounds as though you've got it all worked out.'

'I nearly lost her once, I don't intend to do it again.'

'She nearly lost you, too.'

The thought made his stomach twist. Being here with her felt so natural, he couldn't believe they'd almost thrown it away. In the few hours they'd been back together, he'd become used to her voice, her words, her touch; to be without it would be painful.

'And then she found me.' He kissed the tip of her nose. 'And everything was right with the world.'

She exhaled slowly. 'If you keep talking like that, I might just fall for you.'

'That's good. I've already fallen, so I'll be down there waiting to catch you.' The moment was right, so right, and yet he hesitated. The words were on the tip of his tongue, demanding to be let out.

He looked at her, eyes closed, face relaxed. She was already his, he just needed to say it.

'I love you.' His voice was raspy, his throat like sandpaper.

She opened her eyes, meeting his deep-blue stare. 'Do you know what you do to me when you say things like that?'

The band on his chest loosened. 'The same thing you do to me.' He smiled. 'Let's never stop doing it.'

'That sounds good to me.' She licked her lips. 'And just in case you didn't know, I love you too.'

'Oh, I know.' He winked.

'You're still a cocky bastard sometimes. aren't you?'

He shrugged, the relief still making him grin. 'Just sometimes?'

Slowly she nodded. 'Yep. And don't tell anybody,' she lowered her voice to a whisper. 'But I kind of like it.'

'Does it make you want to tear off your clothes and throw yourself at me?' he asked her.

'Pretty much.'

He pressed his lips to hers, more firmly this time. Threading his fingers through her hair, he kissed her until her body started to vibrate against him.

'Then be my guest,' he murmured.

35

*Come, gentlemen, I hope we shall drink
down all unkindness*

– The Merry Wives of Windsor

'I'm so glad you guys have worked things out.' Jenn sat down on the sunlounger next to Lucy's, huffing as she held her bump and swung her legs on to the chair. She and Grant had arrived in Miami the previous evening, having spent a few days looking for apartments near her new job at the University of Florida. While he and Lachlan spent the morning working in the business suite of the Greyson Hotel, Lucy had decided to take advantage of the warm sun, and had made her home next to the sparkling pool, overlooking the hotel's private beach.

'So am I,' Lucy agreed, pulling her sunglasses over her eyes to block out the sun. 'It was touch-and-go there for a while.'

'Can I bring you ladies a drink?' The waiter stopped beside them, clad in white shorts and a grey polo, a small insignia of the hotel stitched into the pocket.

'Yes please. Can I have a daiquiri?' Lucy smiled at him.

'Sure.'

'Very retro,' Jenn teased. 'And I'll have a water, please. Notice how that almost rhymes with martyr? Which is exactly what I've been for the past six months.'

'But it'll all be worth it,' Lucy said, watching as the waiter headed over to the pool bar. A shack, topped by what looked like a thatched roof, it had the 1980s cocktail scene written all over it.

'So they tell me,' Jenn said, her smile belying her dry tone. 'Though it's amazing how slowly the months have passed. It seems like forever since I last saw you.'

The waiter arrived, passing a tall glass of water to Jenn, then placing Lucy's cocktail on the table beside her lounger. It was a deep red, topped with a strawberry and a straw, and of course there was an orange paper umbrella propped against the side of the glass. It looked deliciously kitsch.

'So anyway, back to you and Lachlan,' Jenn said, as Lucy sipped at her drink. 'He's a great guy, and you're really good for him. Grant said he hasn't seen him this happy in years. He says he has this goofy grin on his face in their meetings.'

Lucy couldn't help but feel herself lighting up at Jenn's words. He made her deliriously happy, too. Every time he walked into a room it felt as though the world started to make sense. Without him, she felt off-kilter.

'Oh my God, you're grinning, just like Lachlan.' Jenn spluttered out the water she was drinking. 'Man, you both have it bad.'

'Yep,' Lucy agreed. And she couldn't find anything wrong with that.

'Who has it bad?' A shadow fell across them. Lucy looked up to see Lachlan standing at the end of her lounger, with Grant beside him. Both men were wearing suits, practical for business, completely impractical in the already-hot Miami sunshine. It was pushing eighty degrees, hot enough for Lucy's body to take on a sheen of perspiration as she lay there. She watched as Lachlan's gaze flickered to her, taking in the black and white bikini she was wearing, and the skin it revealed.

'We do,' Lucy said, her voice deadpan. 'Lying here doing nothing is hard work.'

He sat down on the end of her lounger, lifting her feet onto his lap. His hands stroked her skin, caressing, touching. She giggled when he found a sensitive spot on her instep.

'You know, you guys could have changed out of your suits,' Jenn pointed out. 'You look like sugar daddies or something.'

Lachlan caught Lucy's eye. He smiled warmly at her, and she found herself grinning back. Was it always going to be like this? The intense attraction, coupled with the way she felt like she was the only woman he could see, was making her temperature rise more than the blazing sun. 'Sugar daddies,' he repeated, his eyes crinkling. 'What does that make you ladies then?'

Lucy shrugged, still looking into his eyes. Behind him, there were a line of palm trees, separating the pool area from the beach. Beyond the stretch of pale golden sand, she could see the ocean, as vividly blue as his irises. 'Maybe it makes us sensible.'

'Which is a lot better than whores, which is where I think he was going,' Jenn pointed out. 'And anyway, we're professional women, we make our own money. We don't need you guys.' She clocked Grant's mock-wounded expression. 'But luckily for you we want you anyway.'

Lachlan moved his hands from Lucy's feet, caressing her ankles with slow circles of his thumb. As much as she and Jenn were making fun of their suits, somehow he managed to fit in with the Miami vibe. Maybe it was the sunglasses slung casually in his suit pocket, or the way he'd taken off his tie and unbuttoned his crisp, white shirt. 'You're like a chameleon,' she said to him, wiggling her feet with pleasure as he continued to massage her. 'You fit in wherever you go. In New York you look all polished and businesslike, and here you look like a sexy lounge lizard. How do you do that?'

He tipped his head to the side. 'How do I look when I'm in Scotland?' he asked.

'Cold,' she said, trying to bite down a laugh.

'You're the one who gets cold,' he pointed out. 'Remember how you practically begged me to take you to my room? "Oh, Lachlan, I need your body heat."' His voice went up an octave, as he attempted a particularly bad impression of her.

She played with her lip between her teeth, studying him. 'You're the king of bullshit,' she said, kicking him lightly in the side. 'You've completely rewritten history. I was happy to freeze in my bed, you're the one who carried me into your room.'

'But you liked it.'

Yeah, she did. Even back then, when there was little more between them than a professional relationship, she'd felt drawn to him. As though there was an invisible cord between them, pulling them together. And now it felt stronger, more like iron than cotton. Unbreakable.

'You two should really get a room,' Jenn said, blocking out the sun with her hand over her eyes. 'All this dopamine is making me feel crazy. It's not fair to old married couples like us.'

'We have a room,' Lachlan said, his eyes never leaving Lucy's. 'In fact, we have two hundred.'

341

'Well, could you use one of them?' Jenn asked. 'I love you guys, I really do, but this baby is precious.' She rubbed her dome-like stomach. 'I feel like I'm exposing him to porn.'

Lucy burst out laughing. The thought of climbing into the soft, cosy bed in their air-conditioned room really did sound attractive right then. But with Lachlan around, everything sounded attractive.

'Are you going to be like that when we have kids?' Lachlan asked. The words had barely escaped his lips when Jenn threw one of her sandals at him. She had a surprisingly good aim. Lachlan had to dodge to the side to avoid the flying shoe, catching it in his right hand before it sailed into the swimming pool.

But Lucy didn't pay attention to any of that. She was too busy thinking about his words. *When we have kids.* They should scare her to death, make her want to run far far away. But instead she was lying there, her legs stretched out across the lap of the suited man in front of her, the man she'd come to realise she was falling crazy in love with.

Was it possible to have it all? For the first time, she really thought it might be.

This care home wasn't so different from the one her father lived in, though the buildings were more suitable to the Floridian surroundings than a damp, grey London suburb. It had a different name, too – Assisted Living – where the emphasis was put on what the residents could do, rather than the round-the-clock medical care they also offered. Still, the staff wore uniforms, and as soon as they signed in at the desk they escorted them both to the air-conditioned day room, where Lachlan's mother was sitting overlooking the gardens. It was filled with towering palm trees and flowering azaleas surrounding a sparkling blue lake. As they walked over to join her, Lucy was taken by the atmosphere in the room. People were laughing, playing chess and listening to music; there was a sense of life here that didn't seem to exist in her father's home. Maybe you really did get what you paid for.

Lachlan's mother looked nothing like Lucy had expected. For a woman suffering from a chronic illness, she seemed remarkably alert, her hair perfectly arranged into a French knot, her make-up artfully applied to highlight her cheekbones and vivid blue eyes. Just like her son's. Even the oxygen tank next to her, and the tubes looped around her face couldn't disguise the beauty she'd once been.

'You must be Lucy.' She reached her hand up, taking Lucy's and shaking it. Her voice was hoarse. 'It's a pleasure to meet you.'

'It's a pleasure to meet you too, Mrs—' Oh God, what on earth should she call her? She'd never been a MacLeish after all, even if that was the name she'd given her son. And Lucy hadn't thought to ask Lachlan what his mom's surname was.

'Please call me Lori.' She gestured at the seats opposite. 'Do sit down. Would either of you like a drink?'

Her accent sounded nothing like Lucy had expected, either. Her words were perfectly pronounced. If she closed her eyes, they could be sitting outside on the veranda of an old plantation house, drinking iced tea and gossiping about the local goings-on.

After their drinks arrived – waiter service, no less – Lucy found herself drinking the cool water and looking between mother and son. Though they had the same eyes, there was very little about Lachlan that spoke of his mother. He'd inherited most of his dark looks from the MacLeish side of the family.

As Lori gave them the run-down on her current condition, explaining the tests she'd had earlier in the week, Lucy watched the two of them interact, Lachlan's expression soft, his voice gentle, and she found herself falling for him a little bit more.

There was something very sexy about a man who took care of his mother. Maybe it was the hope he'd take care of her, too. Or maybe it was just seeing yet another side to him that warmed her. Her chameleon man with many faces.

'Lachlan tells me you're a lawyer,' Lori said, turning to her.

'That's right,' Lucy said, placing her glass down on the table beside her. 'I work for a small firm in Edinburgh.' She noticed her fingers were shaking as she released her glass. What the hell was wrong with her?

'Do you enjoy it?'

She nodded. 'I do, for the most part. It's hard work, but what good job isn't? Plus I studied a long time to get where I am, so I'm trying to enjoy it.'

'Do you think you'll always live in Scotland?' his mother asked. Lucy looked up at Lachlan, alarmed. She could see he was biting back a smile.

'Mom,' Lachlan said, as though he'd let Lucy suffer for long enough, 'what kind of question is that?'

His mother shrugged, her shoulders thin beneath the silk fabric of her blouse. 'I'm just interested. You're not getting any younger, Lachlan. I want to know if you intend to settle down over here or over there.'

It was his turn to look uncomfortable. Lucy probably would have enjoyed his awkwardness more if she didn't feel the same way herself. When was the last time she'd been taken home to meet the parents? She could barely remember.

'What Lucy and I decide to do, and where we decide to live, is our business.' His voice remained indulgent. 'And when we do decide, you'll be the first to know.'

He looked up from his mother, and over at Lucy. His eyes were warm, enough to calm Lucy's nerves. Every time their eyes met she found herself wanting to touch him, to feel him. Not very appropriate when they were visiting his mother.

There was something about the way he said 'we' that made her feel all gooey inside – and she liked it a little too much. It reflected the way she felt about him, that it was the two of them, separated from the world by an invisible barrier. And whatever they decided, they'd decide together.

'I suppose I'm not allowed to ask if she wants babies, either?'

'Shall we talk about something else?' Lachlan suggested. 'Maybe we can discuss world politics, or the economy, or something less contentious like that?'

Lucy felt the corner of her lip twitch. There was that baby question again.

It was strange how it already seemed less frightening, as though exposure to it was lessening the shock. And deep inside her – in the part of her she was still barely acknowledging – the thought of making anything with this gorgeous, funny, strong man sent a delicious shiver through her body.

For her whole life, she'd been looking for control. Funny how the moment she let go of it, good things had started to happen.

An hour later, they were walking through the parking lot, her hand neatly tucked into his. He was half a step ahead of her as they weaved past the cars, ducking and dodging the wing mirrors as they made their way from the home. Though it was late afternoon, the heat of the day was still clinging on, warming up the wool of his suit jacket, and making the tiny hairs stick to the back of his neck.

'You're still here,' he said, as they reached his car. For a moment he savoured the minor miracle.

'Where else would I be?' She tipped her head to the side, her face curious.

'I thought my mom might have scared you.' He tugged at her hand, pulling her closer until the front of her body was only inches from his. 'All that talk of settling down and having babies, I thought it might send you heading for the hills.'

Though his tone was teasing, he could feel his body hesitating. Waiting for her response. She'd run from him before – from New York and from Glencarraig – he wasn't sure he'd survive a third time.

'I'm not afraid of you,' she murmured, reaching out to trace circles across his shirt-clad chest. 'Why would I run from you?'

But it was never him she'd run from. He knew that now. It was herself.

It had been the right thing to do, not to chase her. And though it had led to two excruciating weeks without her, she'd come running right back.

Thank God.

'Love me, love my mom. Isn't that what they say?' He circled his arm around her waist, pulling her closer. 'Doesn't that scare you?'

She lifted her head to look at him. 'Should it?' she asked. Two tiny lines formed between her brows as she thought the words through. 'I'd be more worried if you weren't close to your mother. I liked watching the two of you together.' She smiled

346

wickedly, looping her arms around his neck. 'And anyway, my family is bigger than yours, so I figure you'll have more to deal with than I do.'

'Three more like you,' he whispered, brushing his lips against her cheek. 'I'm not sure if that sounds like heaven or hell.'

'It all depends on the day,' she said, her voice full of humour. 'When we're good, we're great. And when we're bad . . . '

'It's time to head for the hills.'

'Stop it.' She was laughing, her arms still clasped around his neck. This close he could see a line of freckles across her nose, teased out by the hot Miami sun. He could see how beautiful she was, too, with her supple skin and blue eyes. Her hair almost glistened beneath the afternoon rays, falling in soft waves down to her shoulders.

She was gorgeous, in that perfect English-rose way. But her beauty went more than skin deep, he knew that now. It was in her humour and her sadness, in her bravery and her fears. It was in the way she always gave as good as she got, and yet somehow made him feel like he'd won.

Leaning his head towards hers, he kissed the tip of her nose, moving lower, capturing her lips against his. He pressed his palms firmly into the small of her back, feeling her warmth through the thin fabric of her summer dress. She arched against him, opening her mouth to let him, her body pliant, yet demanding more. And as they kissed, their tongues teasing and sliding in a way that made them both breathless, he realised that you can't mend a plate with gold-filled lacquer until it's broken, and you can't have beautiful scars without being wounded first.

They'd stumble and fall, and they'd scramble back up, dust themselves off and start all over again. But this time they'd do it together, which sounded pretty damn perfect to him.

Epilogue

Their lips were four red roses on a stalk, which in
their summer beauty kiss'd each other

– Richard III

'Well, this all seems in order,' Alistair's solicitor said, passing the document to him. Thick pages of black type had been scrutinised and annotated, each one initialled at the bottom. 'I'm happy for you to sign it.'

'Are you sure you want to do this?' Alistair asked, looking over at Lachlan. 'It's not too late to back out.'

'I'm certain,' Lachlan agreed. 'Everything's as it should be. You just need to sign and transfer the money.'

'Very well.' Alistair pulled a pen from his shirt pocket, twisting it until the nib came out. He turned the pages, then signed the last one with a flourish, dating it, then passing it back to his solicitor.

'And the payment?'

'Here you are.' Alistair walked across the room, placing a Scottish bank note in Lachlan's hands. He looked at the blue note, seeing the rolling Cairngorms mountains printed across the thick paper. 'Five pounds, as we agreed.'

The solicitor brought the contract over to Lachlan. 'It just needs your signature now.'

Lachlan took out his own pen and signed quickly, dating it then passing it back. 'So that's that.'

'Pretty much. Some "i"s to dot and some "t"s to cross, but everything else is done.'

Lachlan looked at Alistair. 'Are you ready?'

'As I'll ever be.'

'Then let's go.'

The two of them stood, leaving the library and walking out through the kitchen door to the land beyond. A stage had been set up opposite the loch, with audio equipment and lights on the rigging. They made their way across the grass, skirting around the crowd that had gathered in front of it. Locals mingled with MacLeishes from across the world, creating a sea of blue and green tartan.

As soon as they reached the microphone, Lachlan tapped it, a dull 'boom' echoing across the grounds. He cleared his throat, his eyes scanning the crowd, but he couldn't see her.

Where was she?

'Good evening,' he said, leaning in so his mouth was closer to the microphone. 'First of all I'd like to welcome you all to the annual MacLeish gathering. It's a pleasure to have so many of you here, from near and far.'

A loud cheer went up.

'As you know, my father, the Laird of Glencarraig, died a few months ago. In his will, he left the estate and his title to me. And though I was very flattered, and fell in love with this estate as soon as I saw it, I realised something.'

He took a breath, scanning again. He could see Duncan near the front, along with his wife. And in the corner he could see Lucy's family – Cesca and Sam, Kitty and Adam. But no sign of the woman herself.

'The thing I realised was that I didn't deserve this place.' He waved his arm. 'Or rather, it didn't deserve me.' He glanced at Alistair, standing stoically beside him. 'An estate like Glencarraig doesn't need an absentee landlord, or just to become another bland corporate retreat. It needs love and dedication, somebody who not only understands the land but its heritage. In short, it deserves Alistair MacLeish.'

A hum of conversation rippled across the crowd. People were craning their heads to look at Alistair.

'Like so many of you, Alistair's connection to Glencarraig stretches back generations. And like you, he's part of our blood line. And I'm delighted to announce that he has purchased fifty-one per cent of the Glencarraig estate, which makes him Laird of Glencarraig, and leader of the MacLeish clan.'

A roar of approval followed his announcement, and for a minute Lachlan couldn't be heard over the cheers. As the noise died down, he leaned into the microphone a final time. 'Ladies and gentlemen, I'm delighted to introduce to you Alistair MacLeish, the Laird of Glencarraig.'

A movement at the back of the stage caught his attention. He saw her from the corner of his eye, his Hitchcock blonde with the steel determination.

'It's all yours,' he whispered to Alistair, backing off as the new laird addressed the crowd. He walked over to the corner where she was waiting for him, a huge smile on her face.

He stood and looked at her for a moment, taking in her golden hair, swept up at the back of her head, a few tendrils hanging down. At her elegant neck and soft shoulders, leading down to her dress.

That dress.

It had taken him more than a few phone calls to find the right person to work on it. And the cost of repair had been more than the dress itself. Yet it had been important to him – to them both – to mend it, and to make it even more beautiful than when she'd first bought it.

When he'd presented it to her this morning, Lucy had called it a 'Kintsugi dress'. Though the repairs were almost invisible, they both knew they were still there. They weren't embarrassed about their scars, they weren't embarrassed about their pasts. Today was a celebration of everything they were, and everything they hoped to be. Beautiful scars and all.

'I couldn't see you,' he said, pulling her towards him and wrapping his arms around her back. 'I started to worry.'

'I was back here all along,' she said, lifting her face for a kiss. 'I didn't want to interrupt. And you were wonderful, by the way.' She glanced down, smiling. 'And the only man I've ever met who can make a kilt look sexy.'

Lachlan grinned, following her gaze down to his legs. 'Let's not go too far now.'

She reached for his arm, curling her hands around his wrist. 'Are you sure you're okay?' she asked. 'It must be difficult giving this place up.'

He looked around them, at the lodge and the loch, and at Alistair standing in front of a crowd of MacLeishes and Glencarraig residents. He was talking about his plans for the future, for the lodge and the estate, and the crowd were lapping it up.

'I'm not giving it up,' Lachlan said. 'I still own forty-nine per cent of the place. Plus I'm investing in it, too. I'm just putting the right man in charge.' He reached out, tracing his finger along her jaw. 'We'll still come here to visit whenever we want to, and I promised Alistair we'd always come to the gatherings. But look at them, they're delighted. Nobody could be laird as well as Alistair could.'

Her lips broke out into a smile that lit up her face. 'Then I'm happy too. Even if you are losing all your connection to Scotland.'

'I don't think so. My girlfriend still lives here.' He traced her lips, curving up to her cheeks. 'For now, at least.'

She laughed. 'Lachlan, I thought we talked about this.'

'We did. When are you moving to New York?'

'When are you moving to Edinburgh?' She arched an eyebrow.

'Touché. I guess I'm going to have to make an honest woman out of you before you'll obey me.'

'I'll never obey you.' Her voice was light. 'You know that.'

'Not even if I use the belts again?' He pushed his fingers into her hair, angling her head up until his lips met hers.'

'Maybe then,' she murmured, her words vibrating against his lips.

He'd settle for that. Not that she left him much choice.

If she'd thought Glencarraig Lodge was beautiful in the early spring, in late summer it was positively glowing. Lucy stood back, her glass of champagne in her hand, and admired the castle, taking in the rounded tower and the leafy green trees that surrounded it on three sides. Behind it, in the distance, rose the craggy hills of the Scottish Highlands. Dusk was falling, causing the thousands of tiny lights strung throughout the trees to twinkle on, making the lodge seem like the setting of a fairytale.

'It's beautiful.' Cesca's voice came from behind her. Lucy turned to see her walking alongside Kitty, the two of them resplendent in long, summer dresses, their hair curled, their eyes sparkling. Like Lucy, the two of them were carrying a glass of champagne each – taken from one of the waiters, no doubt.

'And so are you,' Kitty said, coming to a stop beside her. 'I love your dress.'

Lucy smiled and ran her hands down the sides of her bodice. Had anybody ever given her such a thoughtful present as Lachlan? She didn't think so.

The three of them stood together, looking up at the castle. The speeches were over, and the gathering had begun. Waiters were weaving among the crowd, passing out drinks and canapés.

'So what are your plans now?' Cesca asked. 'Have you and Lachlan decided what you're going to do?'

'What do you mean?' Lucy took a glass from a passing waiter, lifting it to her lips.

'You can't keep doing this transatlantic thing all the time,' Cesca said. 'You must be exhausted.'

'That'll explain why she and Lachlan spend so much time in bed,' Kitty said, laughing.

'I told you, we're going to be throwing ourselves at each other in arrival halls when we're using Zimmer frames,' Lucy said. 'We both have careers to think about.'

Lachlan walked up behind them and leaned down to kiss Lucy's bare shoulder. 'Don't listen to her. We're working it out. I can move some work over here, Lucy can shuffle some things to New York. We'll be okay.'

She turned to look at him, an eyebrow raised up. 'Is that right?'

Another kiss to her shoulder. 'Yes it is. I don't want our kids being brought up with parents on separate continents.'

Every time he said something like that he made her heart clatter against her ribcage. It wasn't fear, though, it was anticipation, and the knowledge that this gorgeous man really wanted her. He'd touched her scars and he thought them beautiful – even the invisible ones.

'Our kids?' she repeated, unable to take the smile off her face. 'We're having children?'

'Right after we get married.'

'I love the way you've got it all worked out.' She rolled her eyes at her sisters, but the two of them were grinning back at her. Kitty pretended to do a mock-swoon. It felt so good to have her sisters near her. All except one.

'Are you okay?' Lachlan asked her, sliding his arm around her slender waist. He must have noticed her change in expression.

'I was just thinking about Juliet,' she told him. 'How I wish she could be here, too.'

'She's so upset she couldn't make it,' Cesca agreed, her expression as downcast as Lucy's. 'But right now she can't do anything to rile Thomas up, not until their divorce is settled.'

In the past few months, things between Juliet and Thomas had become irreconcilable. The sisters had spent long hours on the telephone or computer, talking about her options, and how he was using their daughter, Poppy, as a pawn to control Juliet. Lucy had wanted to fly over to Maryland to beat her brother-in-law up; not only had he broken Juliet's heart, but he was breaking her spirit, too.

'I wish she'd let us help,' Cesca said, her voice quiet. 'That place she's renting is tiny, and needs so much work doing on it. But she won't accept a penny.'

'Look who's talking,' Kitty said. 'You're the one who refused any help when you were hopping from apartment to apartment in London.'

'And you're the one who refused any help from me or Sam when you were looking for an internship in LA,' Cesca pointed out.

'I think we can agree we're all as stubborn as mules,' Lucy said.

'Yep, I can agree with that.' Lachlan winked, and she rolled her eyes at him. 'But that's the way I like you all. Strong willed and full of pride. That's the Shakespeare sisters all over.'

He meant it as a compliment, Lucy knew that much. He'd told her enough times it was one of the things he loved about her. The way she never let things bring her down, the way she tackled life head-on. She was a fighter, she didn't give up, no matter what twists and turns she encountered.

'Hopefully things will be sorted with Juliet soon,' Kitty said.

'They will,' Lucy said firmly.

From the corner of her eye, she could see Sam and Adam walking towards them, both holding a pint of beer in their hands.

Sam walked up behind Cesca and slid his arm around her. 'Everything okay?' he asked.

'It is,' Cesca said, her face lighting up as soon as she heard his voice. 'I was just wondering if we could get married here. It feels like the perfect place.'

Lucy felt the excitement grip her. 'Would you want to?' she asked. 'There's a gorgeous little chapel in the village, and the lodge is perfect for a reception. Or it will be, just as soon as they get the renovations done. And it's remote, too. Lots of privacy.'

'When will they be done?' Sam asked.

'It's going to take at least six months,' Lachlan said. 'Why don't we talk to Alistair in the morning?'

Cesca turned in Sam's arm. 'Do you think you could wait?' she asked him. 'It would be easy to keep the paparazzi away if we did it here. Between Lucy and Lachlan, they'd pretty much scare them off.'

Lucy laughed. 'Don't be rude.'

'I can wait if you can,' Sam whispered, caressing Cesca's face with his fingers. 'Whatever makes you happy, baby.'

'Maybe by that point Juliet's divorce will be final, too,' Lucy said, 'and she and Poppy could be here for the wedding.'

'That would be wonderful,' Kitty agreed. 'It would be so nice to have all of us together for once. Video calls just aren't as good.'

'When was the last time you were all in the same place?' Lachlan asked her.

'It was at my wrap party,' Kitty said. 'The day Adam asked me to move in with him.'

'I don't think we've all been together since,' Cesca agreed. 'I mean, we've all visited each other, but not at the same time. Like tonight, there always seems to be someone missing.'

The old Lucy would have felt panic at that thought. She'd have been planning to somehow corral them all together. But letting go meant accepting that right now their lives wouldn't allow them all to be in one place. For now, video calls would have to be enough.

'The four Shakespeare sisters together is a sight to be seen,' Adam said. 'The world may never be the same if it happens again.'

'Good job nothing scares you, baby,' Kitty said, grinning.

She tucked her hand into Adam's, leaning her blonde head on his shoulder.

'And it's not just the four of us any more,' Lucy said. 'We have Poppy, too.' She smiled. 'Not to mention you guys.' She looked at Adam, Sam and Lachlan. Three such different men, yet they fitted into the family perfectly. The pieces of the puzzle none of them realised they were missing.

They were the gold lacquer to the sisters' broken pieces of china. Or maybe it was the other way around. All Lucy knew was that together, they were more than the sum of their parts.

They made broken look beautiful.

The fireworks began just after ten that night, the sky exploding into a rainbow of colours that reflected on the faces of the guests. The loud bangs were interspersed with the oohs and aahs of the crowd, as everybody inclined their heads to watch the spectacle above them.

Lachlan was the only one not watching the fiery flowers bloom above them, as the peonies and chrysanthemums unfurled into a cornucopia of blazing stars. He was too busy watching Lucy, taking in the way her bare shoulders glowed in the reflected light, the way her eyes were wide, her mouth slightly agape as she looked up into the sky.

How the hell did he get so lucky? It was a question he asked himself all the time. It was as though every time he looked at her he saw something new, and it made him want to never take his eyes from her.

He walked up behind her, looping his arms around her waist, the silk and lace bodice of her dress beneath his palms. He pressed a kiss to her neck, breathing her in, smelling her floral fragrance, her skin warm in spite of the evening air. She leaned her head back on his chest, her blonde hair a contrast to the black of his jacket. For a moment they could have been anywhere – a girl and a boy at the end of prom, making out in the open air.

'Things always make sense when we're together,' he whispered in her ear.

'That's because we're meant to be.' Her words were simple, but they tugged at his heart. He'd spent a lifetime being rejected by the family he'd wanted so badly. To step into this ready-made one felt like a gift. He wanted to be worthy of it.

'Do you think you can be happy with me, wherever we end up living?' he asked her. 'I don't want you to end up resenting me.'

She twisted in his arms, until her front was pressed against his. Lifting her hand, she gently stroked his jaw. 'I know I keep joking about us being old and grey and still living in different countries,' she tipped her head, 'but I'm as determined as you to work it out. Look at Cesca and Kitty – they manage, and I know we will too.' She looked over his shoulder, smiling. 'It doesn't matter where we are, as long as we're together.'

Was it possible for a heart to melt? He wasn't used to feeling these emotions, but he embraced them anyway. 'Together,' he said, his voice soft. 'I like the sound of that.'

He looked over his shoulder, following her gaze to the imposing lodge behind them. It was strange how pivotal it had become in their relationship. It was the thing that had brought them together, and it was the place where he'd first held her in his arms. And even if he hadn't realised it at the time, it was where he'd first started to fall in love with Lucy Shakespeare.

And now it had provided them with the means to be together. It was more than a lodge, it was a home.

'I'd like our children to visit here often,' he murmured, turning back to look at her. Her head was inclined, but it was him she was looking at, not the fiesta exploding overhead. 'I'd like them to know what it's like to have a real history, a real family. I'd like them to understand where they've come from, because without that, they'll never know where they're going to.'

Were those tears he saw forming in her eyes? It was hard to tell beneath the glow of the fireworks. 'I'd like that, too,' she told him, twisting her arms around his neck as he pulled her in tight.

As the fireworks reached a crescendo, a rapid series of bangs drowning out all but the loudest of voices, he lowered his lips to capture hers. Their kiss was familiar yet new, demanding yet giving, and it set him on fire inside the same way the sky was blazing.

He'd lost so many things in his life, but winning the heart of this determined girl felt like the biggest prize of all.

Acknowledgements

As ever, huge thanks to Anna Boatman and all the team at Piatkus for being so lovely and hard-working. Making Lucy's story shine was a big team effort, and I'm very grateful for your wise counsel.

Meire Dias at the Bookcase Agency isn't just an agent, but a friend. Thank you for your never-ending support and kindness. Thanks also to Flavia and Jackie at the Bookcase Agency for everything you do.

To my family – the lovely Ash, Ella and Oliver – thank you guys for always being there. Your encouragement and love is everything.

Finally thank you to all of you who have read and supported my books. Whether you're a reader, a blogger, or a reviewer, I truly appreciate it. There is a whole world of books out there, and the fact you took the time to read mine is an honour.